DARK CORPORATION

Max Sargent Corporate Espionage Mystery Thriller 1

BEN COLT

Max Sargent Corporate Espionage Mystery Thrillers
currently available in the series by the author BEN COLT

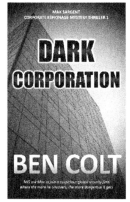  

1

John Lyttleton went over the fourth-floor railing of the Dark Corporation's executive suites. Adrenalin instantly fuelled his demand to survive, but to no avail. He knew there was no way of taking back the inevitable fall. Time slowed down as his brain raced to take in so much information in milliseconds. He looked back up at the balustrade he'd gone over and then consciously turned his head to look down on the rapidly approaching atrium. He could see his fall path and realising he was going to crash into the edge of the large marble reception unit, had just enough time for two thoughts. His contempt for Frank Dark, and 'this is really gonna hurt!'.

Max Sargent paced up and down the living room of his London home then paused at the window to look out over Clapham common. 'What an idiot I've been, I can't believe I was so stupid to have done something like that,' he fretted. Max was worried and didn't really know what was going to happen to him now.

Max Sargent was one of the top UK based Chief Procurement Officers with twenty years' experience leading Buying departments for some of the world's largest companies. Before this at just nineteen, he'd served very briefly with the Royal Marine Commandos, where after his first deployment involving a harrowing incident, he'd opted for a civilian career away from the military front line.

He was forty, six-foot-tall, slim, dark hair and a discerningly handsome face. He wore snappy dark suits and inspired by Steve McQueen and Roger Moore, sported a non-date Rolex Submariner watch. He grew up with his parents in Twickenham south-west London, where his father had run a plastics moulding business churning out specialist stampings mainly for the car manufacturing industry. His father had named him Max after a couple of his favourite movie stars, Maximilian Schell and Max von Sydow.

Max went to the local state schools where he quickly became known for his righteous beliefs, logic and communication skills. He would often eloquently and politely pick up a teacher's mistake or inaccuracy in class, much to their silent envy. However, they understood that's what you get with a plain-speaking, honest and reliable student. Max could be trusted and had utter contempt for the bullies of the school. He was neither part of the cool crowd nor was he ever bullied himself because he simply wouldn't stand for it.

When once cornered by three large boys in the playground he plainly stated to the largest thug, "I promise you, whatever you do to me, I'll do back to you twice as hard." One of the other boys then shoved him back so Max immediately launched at the big boy pushing him back even harder. His reaction was to kick out at Max and catch him a glancing blow on the thigh. Max then managed an even harder kick at the boy's stomach sending him reeling. Max knew this escalation tactic could go badly wrong, but it worked as the larger bully gathered himself up and with a tirade of angry swear words retreated with his two accomplices. They never tangled with Max again, bullies don't like it when people stand up to them.

When Max saw anyone else being picked on he was always the one to step in and calm things down by persuading the nasty boys to leave off, or he'd pretend a teacher was about to come over or distract them in some other way with his articulate persuasiveness. His reasonableness and integrity won him the Head of school position which was voted for by students and teachers.

He started to help out at his father's small factory and quickly homed in on the way raw materials, equipment and sundries were being bought. Realising how important the costs of a business were to its success, he started calling up the suppliers asking them for better prices and using his negotiation and communication skills. Even as a teenager, he began agreeing price reductions and better terms which made a tangible improvement to his father's company profitability.

By the time he'd done his A-levels he knew he didn't want another four years at university and was torn between following his father into business, or utilising his tougher, athletic abilities while he was still at his physical peak, for something more challenging.

One of his best friends Peter had always been destined for an elite military club, either the Special Air Services or the Royal Marine Commandos. He'd chosen the Marines and set about persuading Max to enrol with him. After the medicals and a four-day Potential Royal Marines Assessment, they embarked on the thirty-two-week training and assessment course at the Commando Training Centre Royal Marines, Lympstone near Exmouth. With a high level of fitness, unwavering determination, mind over matter and the ability to follow orders unquestioningly, they both excelled there. They handled the rope climbs, the nine miler, twelve-mile night yomp and thirty-mile speed marches, fireman's carry, endurance and Tarzan jungle assault courses, firing range and attention to drilling and kit layout, endured team punishments, learned weaponry and honed their range firing. They hadn't hit their twentieth birthdays when they both won their green berets, Commando knives and insignias. They were both assigned to Four-Two Commando Royal Marines based at Bickleigh Barracks just north of Plymouth in Devon. This was a subordinate unit within the Royal Marines 3 Commando Brigade, the principal Commando formation, under the Operational Command of the Fleet Commander, who were often deployed outside of the UK.

Within nine months, in May 2000, they were deployed off to Sierra Leone in West Africa, to retrieve officials and deal with an advancing revolutionary force, hell-bent on murder, power and a takeover of the country. That's where it all went wrong for Max and Peter, more so for Peter. The events that transpired forced Max to request a discharge which given what he'd done, was honourably granted along with being one of the youngest servicemen to receive the Military Cross.

Max was just twenty years old when he felt compelled to turn his back on the Royal Marines and retreat into civilian life. The baptism by fire had taken its toll on him and without his friend by his side, despite the loyal comradery in his squad, he felt alone. He opted to spend a year as his father's Buyer and do a proper job of sorting out the company's costs, suppliers, contracts and spends. This gave him the new start he needed and put the first business career notch on his CV, which had no mention of his Navy service. He could then go on to bigger and better Buying roles for larger companies and in no time, Max was leading his first Procurement department for a large Cash and Carry wholesale chain. After several more jobs, each with larger teams, larger spends and much larger salaries and benefits, he joined one of the UK's biggest media companies, where his team of forty staff looked after a spend of almost £1 billion across all parts of the business with around 2,000 suppliers.

After just twenty years, Max was now at the top of his game. He had won the coveted individual Procurement award from the Chartered Institute of Purchasing and Supply and was well known across his profession having covered both the UK and global businesses. He'd sometimes check the Procurement salary reviews often published by industry consultant and recruitment firms, and was always satisfied that his package was well over the market bands for his role.

Max had several long-term relationships but never felt he'd found the right woman to settle down with and marry, though he was ready to do that. So as a relatively well-off bachelor, his lifestyle was a good one. He liked his holidays to Europe, the Caribbean and North America, whether they were with a girlfriend or mates. He'd decided to find a home on the up-and-coming Clapham Common and had patiently waited for the right opportunity to come along. Eventually, a wealthy Frenchman's house sale fell through, who needed the money for a business commitment within the next two weeks. Max deployed his persuasive negotiation skills to buy the house at a hugely reduced price, moving heaven and earth to organise the sale process within the brief allotted time frame. He had a large mortgage on the new house and a temporary bridging loan on his previous home, both of which he managed to clear quickly with the help of his package bonuses and some share option windfalls.

The prestigious detached house lay on the west side of Clapham common just off a small semiprivate road which effectively served as the private driveway for a row of six houses. Each house had an electric gated parking area with steps leading up to the front door of the three-story homes. They had relatively large rear gardens, at least for the middle of South West London where space was at a premium. One of the other houses had sacrificed its entire underground floor and installed an amazing indoor swimming pool area. Max was able to indulge in his love of fancy sports cars having installed into the spacious single garage and up and over underground car lift system, whereby one car can be parked into the lower lift then at the press of a button it slowly disappears into the pit where another car can be parked on the ramp above it. He'd had over the years a long list of sports cars including Ferraris, Lamborghinis, Porsches and a few American muscle cars.

The first car residing on the lower part of the lift was a rare and unusual Vector W8. Made by the American Vector Aeromotive Corporation loosely based on a jet fighter plane with a sharp sweeping wedge front, scissor doors, LED dash display and a gear lever resembling a fighter pilot's throttle, with a six-litre twin-turbo engine. Only twenty-two cars were ever made and when Max managed to buy his Vector at auction for just £90,000 he knew the laws of supply and demand would one day increase the value of this extraordinary supercar. The car was now valued at £600,000.

Similarly, the car on the upper part of the lift was one of just 1,300 of the iconic Ferrari F40's in beautiful Rosso Corsa red with its instantly distinguishable huge rear curved aerofoil. Once again Max read the astonishing rise in the value of classic sought-after Ferraris and having bought the car for £260,000 it was now worth almost four times that value. Out on the small driveway sat a comparatively simple little VW Golf GTI he'd use for getting around town and doing the station run.

Max had recently met one of his old bosses Luke for dinner. They had always had a great relationship and Max's mentor had supported and looked after him when they worked together at their previous company. They had both then moved on to separate media companies and were now effectively each working for competitors. At the dinner, without any ill-intentioned inference, Luke had told Max about the problems they were encountering trying to set up a particular app interface for a more effective way to charge on-demand programs and movies. At the time Max hadn't thought anything of it other than he knew his company had cracked this piece of customer interface and were already using it.

It had been so nice to spend the evening with Luke again, reminiscing about the fun and achievements they'd had together at their previous company, so Max wanted to help out his old boss. As Chief Procurement Officer he and his team were the keyholders to the company's supplier contracts database where all the deals were electronically stored. The on-demand charging app was one of the few projects procurement wasn't involved with as it was heavily technology and IT-based, however, Max had just been logged in to the contracts database to check another supplier deal, out of curiosity he quickly brought up the supplier contract for the charging app. It had the usual 30 or so pages of the main terms and conditions then there at the back in the many appendices' documents Max could see a single page summarizing the core programming for this particular product. Without thinking he took a download of the document before logging out.

He only wanted to do something to help his old boss Luke and had assumed this charging app program would soon be in the public domain anyway and completely bypassing his usual high integrity radar, that evening from home emailed a copy of the document to Luke.

The following morning when Max went into the office all hell had broken loose. He walked in to find five consultants from the Price Waterhouse Coopers fraud team at his desk and searching through everything in his office. Max's world fell in on him.

Max had himself installed an alerting system into the supplier contracts database so that for certain highly sensitive contracts, he would be informed when they were viewed or downloaded and by whom. The Technology Director had rightly put this same tag on his precious charging app contract and late yesterday had received the automated email stating that Max had downloaded a copy. Whilst he thought Max was a brilliant CPO he had no choice but to advise the Chief Executive, who agreed that to be safe the only thing they could do was get PWC involved.

Max was immediately transparent with the investigative team and told them everything that had happened before they even asked for access to his home computers as well. Max just wanted to make a speedy retreat away from the embarrassing situation in the office and following his full disclosure demanded to quickly see his Chief Executive. Max speedily summarised again to him what had happened and apologised profusely. The Chief Exec was shocked by the whole incident, but he did like Max who had in his view earned a considerable credit bank of goodwill with him, so until he could get his head around the whole thing and speak with PWC, he suggested suspending Max pending further investigation and told Max to go home and wait to be called. Max had left immediately and here he was now pacing up and down his living room a few days on, wondering what on earth was going to happen to him next.

2

As John Lyttleton disappeared over and beyond the shiny bronze railing, Frank Dark's heart missed a beat at the surprising and shocking incident unfolding before him. As he edged backwards away from the horrible scene, he heard the sickening thud and crunch of his colleague's body smashing into the edge of the hard, unforgiving marble reception desk and floor. There was an ear-piercing scream from the poor unsuspecting receptionist sitting at her desk about to answer an incoming call, only to be greeted by a person slamming onto the desktop right in front of her and then onto the floor. There was no warning, John Lyttleton hadn't made a sound during his brief and fateful fall. He was resigned to it and fell in silence.

Simultaneously there were several other gasps and shrieks from people either sitting in or passing through the reception area with one uttering "Oh my God!", and another "Jesus Christ, what the…!"

More people in the open areas of floors one, two and three who were anywhere near the large open atrium and staircases, also rushed over to their balustrades to see what the commotion was about. They were greeted with the sight of a delirious receptionist falling back over her chair with what appeared to be a crumpled, deformed body in a suit lying on the marble floor in front of the reception desk, which had a splattering of red on its corner. A small pool of blood was slowly becoming larger from underneath the body, edging its way across the cream white marble floor.

As Frank Dark continued to move backwards, he felt overwhelming pity for his Chief Financial Officer. He was a good kind man who had served him for some years, perhaps in some ways too good, with integrity standards far higher than his own and that was what started to cause conflict between the two of them. Whilst he now felt huge remorse for the man he also, somewhat surprisingly, felt a slight tingle of nervous excitement. His thoughts were interrupted, as backing up he bumped into the door frame of his own office and was brought back to the reality of here and now. But before he attended to the awful scene unfolding below and the welfare of his staff, he had one thing to quickly sort out over and above anything else.

He turned and rushed across his large office suite, skirting round the equally oversized desk and sat in his black leather cushioned chair. He focused his attention on the keyboard and screen in front of him.

"Mr Dark, Mr Dark," hurried in his fussy and alarmed personal assistant Sheila, an older and dignified woman, appearing from her interconnecting office next door. "What on earth is going on out there, everyone's screaming and…"

"Not now Sheila," interjected Frank rather harshly. Sheila was a little taken back as her boss Frank Dark was always very polite and professional with her, even though she was well aware of his tougher less compromising demeanour with others. "I'm sorry Sheila, but there's been an awful incident." He quickly gathered his thoughts to decide how best to put his next words which he was already acutely aware would be innocently relayed to the police by Sheila. "I'm very sad to say that John Lyttleton has taken his own life by jumping into the reception area."

Sheila staggered backwards with her arm out feeling for the office wall to steady herself with. "Oh my God, you're kidding, that can't be, not John, John Lyttleton, surely not?"

"I'm afraid so Sheila, why don't you call for the police and an ambulance immediately," he instructed as Sheila started to make for the main door of his office to have a look for herself at the commotion below. "Sheila, I really don't think it's a good idea for you to go and have a look, it's not a pretty sight, indeed it's most distressing and upsetting," warned Frank.

Sheila started to protest. "But Mr Dark I must see what I can do to help, they…"

"No. Sheila, please do as I ask and go back to your office and call the police, that's the most important thing you can do right now," said Frank in a less calming voice. Sheila got the message this time, paused, then turned and bustled back into her office to call 999. The door closed behind her giving Frank the privacy he now needed.

He quickly tapped the mouse button waking his PC screen from sleep, hurriedly typed in his login password, then raised his gaze to the large screen in front of him as his Outlook email program appeared. His heart was pounding as he clicked on the Inbox file revealing a long list of email senders and topics summarised for him. He moved his head slightly nearer the screen and his eyes narrowed as he searched the last few emails for one particular name. John Lyttleton.

'Shit!' he thought immediately seeing that the third email from the top was from his Chief Financial Officer entitled 'Resignation'. Looking at his gold Rolex Daytona then back at the screen he could see the email was sent barely 5 minutes ago just before his discussion, or rather argument with John Lyttleton. 'Damn, damn, damn it!' he raged to himself.

He clicked on the email headline and a box sprung open to reveal the whole email. To his immediate horror, he noticed his name was not the only recipient listed at the top. Whilst 'Frank Dark' rested alongside the 'To' label, unfortunately, there were more names listed by the 'CC' tag. He read them out in his mind, they were 'John Dawlish' his Chief Technology Officer, 'Brett Harding' his head of Special Operations, 'Cindy Ramar' his Human Resources director and finally 'Sir Kieran Sinclair' his company chairman.

'Bloody hell!' he thought, 'this isn't good, what's he going to say in the email?'. As his eyes wandered down the page the gravity of the situation and what John Lyttleton had deemed necessary to put in writing below became very apparent. As he started to read through the email, he was worried, and not much worried Frank Dark.

'Resignation.

Dear Frank, It is with a heavy heart that I feel forced to tender my resignation to you from my role as Chief Financial Officer of the Dark Corporation with immediate effect. I have always endeavoured to act honourably but I feel my position with your company has now been made entirely untenable by the overwhelming and unethical constant requests and expectations you and some of your colleagues have made on me.

As a long-serving and highly qualified Chartered Certified Accountant, I should abide by my financial code of ethics; objectivity, integrity, professional competence and confidentiality. I fear your actions and your expectations of me are now compromising these standards and I, therefore, cannot and will not continue in this role.

I respectfully request your understanding and acceptance of my resignation and trust that you will grant me garden leave for my 12 months notice period. In view of my invaluable services to you and the Dark Corporation, I'd ask that you take a positive view on granting my full £2 million bonus for this financial year and allow me to exercise all the share options I have been granted to date within my garden leave period.

Yours most sincerely, John Lyttleton – CFO Dark Corporation.'

Frank Dark stared into the screen focusing on the text in front of him and then gazed beyond the words that were so damning of him and his empire. Everything could come crashing down on him like a ton of bricks. 'Was this it, was this really how it would all end'.

His thoughts were abruptly interrupted as his office door swung open and his trusted Chief Technology Officer John Dawlish burst in, rushing up to Frank's desk exclaiming, "Frank, John's jumped down to the reception area. He's dead Frank, what the hell happened, what are we going to do!"

"Calm down John, just calm down, yes it's awful," giving himself time to gather his thoughts. He trusted John Dawlish with his life and Frank knew he needed his help on this. He beckoned John to come round to his side of the desk and pointing at the screen said, "Look John, right now we've got a major problem, read this resignation email sent to us just now by John Lyttleton. I need you to do something for me. For us."

John Dawlish read the email. At the end he was speechless, panting lightly as the gravity of the contents sank in. He looked at Frank, paused again, then pleading said, "What are we going to do? Tell me what you want."

Frank replied, "Right, I've got to get down to reception to start sorting this out as soon as possible, but first we've got to somehow delete this email and completely eradicate it. Can that be done? Look, he's copied Cindy and Sir Kieran as well!"

John sighed and concentrated for a moment. Marshalling his many thoughts, options and desired outcomes as only a hugely experienced and adept computer programmer could, he carefully relayed to Frank what they needed to do.

"Okay, firstly you and I need to simply delete this email then delete it again from the 'Deleted items' file." He quickly twice deleted the email on Frank's screen. "I will then make sure they're also scrubbed from our main network 'pst' file, that's the Personal Storage Table which holds a record of all email activity, and hopefully it won't show up on any mobile devices they also have synced to their emails, unless they are actually looking at their mobile right now." Frank let out a sigh of relief as the email disappeared from sight. He felt reassured that his computer genius friend and colleague might be able to make this problem go away.

"I'll do the same on my PC as soon as I get back to my office," said John. "Just checking Frank, but does anyone else have access to your emails, what about Sheila?"

"No, no one, Sheila only has access to my calendar and diary invites but not my emails," nodded Frank as if reassuring himself just as much as John.

"Right, next I will call Brett, that's another easy one as he's with us on everything, and simply tell him to go straight to his laptop and do the same. Sorted."

John and Frank then both stared at the remaining two names copied on the email.

"How the hell do we deal with these two," asked Frank, "these are the ones we've absolutely got to ensure they don't get to see this email. They've no idea what's going on. They can't get to read this email."

John Dawlish allowed himself a few more moments to recheck his thoughts, then despite the awful circumstances they were in, somewhat proudly announced to Frank, "I think I've got it. Sir Kieran hardly ever uses his laptop let alone mobile phone, he hates them. He's an old-fashioned city gent. So we'll have to rely on him not checking his emails until probably this evening or tomorrow morning, that's when he seems to login and usually sends out any email replies. I will get one of my London based IT guys to immediately contact Sir Kieran and retrieve his laptop from him. We'll tell him we're doing an upgrade, or better still giving him a much better new laptop. He'll like that, he does like to be looked after with all the latest gear even though he barely uses it. I'll have his old laptop brought to me, delete the email then reconfigure his new PC myself."

Frank Dark was impressed, John Dawlish could certainly think through a problem quickly and come out with a clear set of steps and actions to reach a successful outcome. "Brilliant. Now what about Cindy, she's only downstairs on the floor below, how on earth are we going to get to her PC, she doesn't use a laptop, she still uses the desktop PC in her office?"

Without hesitation, John Dawlish had already come up with the simplest and most direct course of action. "Well, I'm assuming with all the fuss going on in reception Cindy won't be quietly sat at her desk in her office, she'll be downstairs in the midst of it trying to help sort things out and reassure staff. I'm going to walk straight into her office now and quickly delete the email myself. It's a bit of a risk but it's now or never, hopefully, no one will notice me going in and out, and even if they do it's not unusual for people to see me fiddling about on someone else's PC fixing and checking things."

Without waiting for any further agreement from his boss, John Dawlish walked out of the office and made his way down the stairway to Cindy Raymar's office which was indeed empty, to sort the email deletion. He'd then quickly go back up to his own office, call Brett Harding in Beverly Hills to get him doing his own email deletion on his laptop, then he'd get one of his guys to pick up Sir Kieran's laptop and finally he would sort out the 'pst' file himself from his desk.

Frank Dark stood behind his office door before exiting and took a few moments to gather himself, adjust his tie and clear his throat. He knew the moment he passed through this door all eyes would be on him. He was used to charming, persuading and instructing people every day, but for the next few days, he was going to have to put on the Oscar-winning performance of his life. He took one last deep breath then exited through the door and out onto the fourth-floor open area in front of the several plush offices of his top executives and their personal assistants. Fortunately, most of the offices on the floor were empty. Brett Harding's office was as usual empty as he was at his main office base in Beverly Hills. The office provided for chairman Sir Kieran Sinclair was almost always empty, but he'd insisted on an office in the corporate base. The company secretary and general counsel were nowhere to be seen, and of course, John Lyttleton's empty office served as a bleak reminder of what had just transpired. The relatively sparse executive floor was just how Frank Dark liked it. He knew what was best for his company and didn't need lots of other directors popping in and out with their keen, well-intentioned advice, with him having to give them time when he was busy, politely push back on their uninformed ideas and even worse pass the time of day with idle chitchat. Only John Dawlish was there, walking back to his office from the top of the stairs having just come from Cindy's office below.

Although there were perfectly good lifts Frank Dark always preferred to use the stairs, on the basis of providing at least some token exercise for him each day. As he started on the top of the stairway, the reception area below came into vision and even though he knew what was waiting for him, the sight of John Lyttleton's body lying there lifeless surrounded by shocked, fussing office staff, still gave him quite a shock. He hastened his pace down the several flights of stairway as people started to notice his arrival on the scene, some calling out to him, others exchanging their glances between him and the body waiting to see how he would react, wondering what he'd do and what he'd say. He finally got to the bottom of what felt like a never-ending staircase and immediately started taking control from Cindy Raymar who had admirably held the fort until his arrival. The next hour for Frank Dark was a surreal blur of regaining order with confident, sympathetic assurance to everyone there. He immediately asked a couple of women to look after the receptionist who was now uncontrollably sobbing and shaking with shock. They carefully escorted her away.

Telling everyone not to go near or touch the body, he asked one of the guys to quickly find some kind of cloth from the canteen and carefully place it over John Lyttleton's body. Turning to Cindy he suggested she walked through the offices telling all staff except the essential people, that once the police had taken names if they would like to go home for the rest of the day then that was quite understandable. Also to tell the staff that he would give them an update in the next few days once things had become clearer. Cindy nodded in agreement and set about communicating this throughout the whole office.

Frank then waited in the atrium area for the police and ambulance to arrive, greeting them outside as soon as they pulled into the car park. He quickly explained to the first police officer approaching him what had happened and took them and the ambulance crew through the entrance to where John Lyttleton lay. After a brief check by the paramedics, they confirmed to the police officers and Frank that the man was dead. Given this was clearly a suicide and there was no further evidence to be collected in the atrium, they all agreed to remove the body as quickly as possible so as not to continue causing stress to those people still in the office or passing through. Cindy returned and alongside Frank provided all the necessary details the police requested of them including the names of everyone the slightest bit involved, both before and after the unfortunate incident.

Frank Dark reassured the police as they left. "The Dark Corporation will provide full and transparent assistance with all enquiries relating to our colleague's terrible death. We've nothing to hide here."

3

Sir Kieran Sinclair sat back in the large brown leather high backed chair just in time for one of the Boodle's staff to arrive with the Financial Times' distinguishable pink coloured paper and a black coffee served in a delicate but large China cup with saucer. No spoon, it should already be as he liked it. He leant forward and took a sip of the coffee to check it had precisely the right amount of his favourite Martell XO cognac added in. Perfect.

Sir Kieran was a member of various private clubs but Boodle's gentlemen's club in St James London was probably the one he felt most at home in. He knew most of the other members, he had his favourite comfy lounge chair and his favourite corner table in the restaurant which allowed him to view all other tables and clients dining. The manager of the establishment was a dear old friend of his and almost all the staff there knew him well, what he liked and also what he didn't like. The club was a long-standing establishment founded in 1762 by the soon-to-be British Prime Minister Lord Shelburn, otherwise known as William Petty. Boodle's is one of the most prestigious gentlemen's clubs in London getting its name from its original head waiter Edward Boodle, with a fabulous food and wine menu, strict discerning rules and regulations and an admittance system strictly overseen through a nomination process by its distinguished and wealthy members.

Sir Kieran had spent his whole, long career in the world of banking, working his way up through several high street banks to then get into financial insurance, private equity and investment banking. His final years were spent on the board of directors for the Bank of England where he had more of an advisory role and added to the board's experience, expertise, and integrity count. The well-earned knighthood was always a door opener for him and he never hesitated in using it, after all, he deserved everything he had. He was well thought of in the city and apart from a questionable incident with a call girl some 20 years ago which was conveniently suppressed by his company at great expense by their 'PR fixer', his record was more or less impeccable.

Sir Kieran first met Frank Dark at one of his salubrious dinner functions at the historic and prestigious Vintners Hall in Upper Thames Street London about 10 years ago. The Vintners livery company of which he was a member, were hosting the dinner for new up-and-coming captains of industry in the city. At that time the meteoric rise of Frank's security-focused Dark Corporation was well known across industry and banking. By complete coincidence, the seating plan put Sir Kieran next to Frank Dark and with their shared love of fine wines, money and business acumen they enjoyed a wonderful, happy evening. Then a few years ago when Sir Kieran retired from the Bank of England he took on several light non-executive directorships. Not because he needed the money as the pay was never that good, but more just to keep his hand in and continue the many fringe benefits one gets in such roles and maintain his networking across the city he loved.

Frank then approached him out of the blue and took him for an unforgettable seven-course taster menu dinner at The Square restaurant in Mayfair. Sir Kieran still remembers the rare and very expensive wines Frank had the Master of Wine sommelier select for them to pair with each of the courses. Notably, including a delectable Burgundy Domaine de la Romanee-Conti from a tiny four-acre vineyard in the Cote d'Or priced at, he later found out, £33,000 for the bottle.

By the fifth course of the meal when Frank asked Sir Kieran if he would consider taking up the position of non-executive Chairman of the Dark Corporation, his brief, slightly intoxicated and hearty response to Frank was simply "I'd be absolutely delighted to dear boy, when do I start." The £2 million salary with share options was probably one of the highest Chairman's non-Exec salaries in the city and Frank said he need only attend as many of the monthly board meetings as he could and do a few speeches.

Over the last couple of years in the role, Sir Kieran had come to realise that Frank Dark had probably set out to capture a knight of the realm as a figurehead and sign of integrity at the top of his company. But he was happy to overlook this given their strong, fun relationship and the latitude Frank gave him in exercising his expected chairmanship duties. He was also acutely aware that Frank had another side to him which he'd occasionally seen at board meetings involving the wider leadership team, where he could be quite overbearing, bordering on outright harassment and bullying. However, whenever he'd dare to pick Frank up on it outside of the boardroom, Frank was always contrite and apologetic. Well, no-one's perfect, overall he thought Frank seemed like a nice chap.

One of the longer serving Boodle's staff gracefully approached Sir Kieran and quietly hovered waiting for a nod of acceptance from the Knight. He then relayed, "Sir Kieran, I'm sorry to trouble you but the young visitor you're expecting is waiting in reception for you."

Sir Kieran replied "Ah yes my good man, I know it's a little unorthodox to have non-members come into the lounge but I honestly don't want to have to get up and drag my way across the club to meet this fellow. Would you be good enough to escort him through to me, I only need to see him for a few moments?" Less experienced staff members could have taken this as a question, but this particular man knew full well this was not a request but an instruction and giving what appeared to be a small bow quickly slid away to fetch the visitor.

George was a senior but young manager within John Dawlish's group IT Department and had recently picked up a call from his boss asking him to immediately go to the Boodle's club and retrieve Sir Kieran's laptop from him to be replaced with a new upgraded version. He momentarily thought it was a little odd when John Dawlish added that under no circumstances could he let Sir Kieran open and use his laptop when he was collecting it. But John was the boss and knew what he was doing so George merely assumed the old city gent had probably gone and picked up some dodgy computer bug which needed fixing.

George was collected by the staff member and closely escorted through the club to the lounge area where Sir Kieran was waiting.

"Good morning my young fellow," greeted Sir Kieran, "there's a good lad, close your mouth now, you're looking like a blithering idiot standing there gawking at everything." George was indeed in awe of his surroundings and had already spotted several gentlemen he'd recognised as politicians from TV programs or on the news.

He immediately complied and closed his mouth. "Sir Kieran, I do apologise, what a lovely club you have here." George realised how pathetic that sounded as soon as he'd finished saying it.

"Now what's all this about young man? You told reception that John Dawlish had sent you on an urgent mission and needed to collect my computer, what's this all about?" enquired Sir Kieran.

George replied, "Indeed that is correct Sir Kieran. Something about a computer virus I imagine, in any case, the good news Sir is that you'll be getting a brand new and much better laptop in exchange. I gather John will see to it himself and transfer any files and information you have on the old PC across to the new one." George was now more pleased with his performance.

"Well this is all very inconvenient old chap, swapping computers, transferring files, what a bore. However, John is the techie bod and I'm sure he knows what he's doing," said Sir Kieran as he leaned over the arm of his large chair and pulled out his laptop from a small leather briefcase. He placed the laptop on his knees and was about to open it up when George quickly interjected.

"Er Sir Kieran, you're not to open the laptop please in case it does have a virus waiting to be activated." George had endeavoured to be courteous and polite but realised the urgency of his demand may have come across a little bit heavy. One of the other nearby members looked up from behind their Times newspaper with raised eyebrows.

Sir Kieran stopped opening the laptop, paused and turned to

look George in the eyes. George frowned, and gulped. "Look here my young fellow, before this computer gets whipped away, I would like to just quickly check my emails to make sure there's nothing urgent I need to attend to. Is that all right with you?" Although Sir Kieran had already understood it was advised not to open the laptop in case of a virus, he didn't like being told what to do, especially by this young whippersnapper. The poor boy in front of him was speechless and wasn't going to argue with him. Sir Kieran waited a few moments to firmly put the lad in his place, he then quietly and slowly closed the part open screen lid of the laptop. "But there again I don't want to lose all my emails if this wretched machine has some damn virus in it. Here you are, take it and make sure John gets me my new one delivered to my home this evening."

George nodded and took the laptop gratefully, thanked Sir Kieran and looked over to the staff member prompting he was ready for a hasty withdrawal from the lounge and the club. Outside George paused on the club step and allowed himself a deep sigh of relief. He took out his mobile phone and quickly called his boss John Dawlish to report that he had collected Sir Kieran's laptop unopened.

John Dawlish put the phone down from George after the call and gently nodded his head satisfyingly allowing himself a smile. He then popped into Frank's office doorway and simply gave a thumb's up sign, then left.

Frank Dark allowed himself a wry smile.

4

Frank Dark sat behind the large desk in his office, finished off another email, then allowed himself to recline back in his chair and take a deep breath. A few days had passed since the terrible incident with John Lyttleton and things were now getting back to normal in the offices. Despite the tragic and dramatic event the aftermath of which was seen by many staff down in the reception area, it had only taken several days for the hushed gossips and chatter to die down and people to get back to their normal jobs and lives. Life goes on, despite such a tragedy, very quickly.

He and Cindy had also held a brief town hall meeting, with them both standing on the first-floor staircase overlooking all the staff in the offices gathered below in the large entrance atrium, ironically where John Lyttleton had fallen. They had covered the terrible incident carefully, passed on their condolences and thoughts to John's family and close colleagues and offered counselling services to any staff feeling they wanted to talk to someone professional. Following a brief eulogy praising John's work, in particular at the Dark Corporation, Frank had asked for a minute's silence to remember the man. As the staff dispersed at the end Frank remained standing above them closely scanning faces, demeanours and body language. Just to satisfy himself he'd done everything required to put the matter to bed and square everything off with the good staff who worked there. As the last people left the atrium, he was happy the matter was now behind him.

The police had got onto the case very quickly and professionally and having taken a long list of everyone's names on the day. They had come back to him and Cindy requesting all the named staff be in the office on a given date for them to quickly meet with and interview individually in the boardroom. Frank had got the impression that the police were rightly doing this so quickly because it was an open and shut suicide case and being so busy probably just wanted to wrap it up as quickly as possible.

Frank realised that he was the only person to witness the poor man disappearing over the top floor's balustrade and the night before the police interviews were due, had started to lose faith in the competence of any interrogating officers likely to turn up. So felt he perhaps needed a little bit of extra backup. Early the next morning he'd gone into John Dawlish's office closing the door behind him and had explained to John everything that happened that fateful day and that he wanted to avoid any spotlight being turned on him or the Corporation.

Thankfully his trusted friend had agreed to also say that he had seen from his office John Lyttleton climb over the railing and fall to his death. Frank could tell John wasn't entirely happy doing this but knew he could rely on him. Frank was certainly indebted to him for what he managed to do with the email and now this. When the time was right he would make sure to reward him well, whether that would be with shares, bonus or something else, he knew it would be worth millions to the man.

But this whole inconvenient blip regarding the death of his CFO was nothing compared to the bigger plans he had with the help of his ally John Dawlish. Frank had come up with a highly valuable use for his genius programmer's skills. He'd been negotiating to sell something for a huge payoff. Something that had a massive destructive capability, but that's why he could sell it for a lot of money. Enough money to disappear and never want for anything again. His foreign investor, or rather buyer, for the services he was planning to sell, would no doubt get to hear about the unfortunate death in the office and would want reassurance. Frank would call him later and with charm and confidence, ensure his big deal was still on track.

Frank Dark struck an imposing figure, he was well over six-foot-tall, athletic build, brown eyes and thick, strong, wavy brown hair. His face was calm and reassuring, with a strong jawline and cheekbones. But this impressive combination when required could also portray a determined, unwavering resolve not to be trifled with, complemented by his assertive military toned voice. When he was about to enter a meeting room, everyone inside would stop talking and sit up ready. He had gravitas.

Brought up in a well-off middle-class family in the Sussex countryside, his father had a distinguished career in both the Royal Air Force as a Squadron Leader and then the Royal Navy. Being a doctor, he'd served on the Royal Yacht Britannia as Chief Medical Officer accompanying the Queen and Queen Mother on many trips around the world. The latter part of his career was then spent as a sought-after doctor in Harley Street London attending to the rich and famous. Both his father and mother were caring, loving parents to him and as a result of being an only child he was well looked after, indeed rather spoilt, and due to the fact neither parent liked conflict or argument, as the years went by Frank realised he could get his own way more and more.

Dr and Mrs Dark sent their son Frank off to boarding school at the age of eight, he never forgot them dropping him off in the courtyard with his tuck box and trunk and leaving him there. The strict Headmaster's rule of law and expectation of utter discipline from all the boys immediately clashed with Frank's defiant and arrogant manner. Throughout the five years at prep school, he lost count of the number of times he was beaten with a slipper or gym shoe. On one occasion when he was the last in his class to get to grips with a certain Latin noun's recitation, the Headmaster sent Frank himself to the gym lockers to pick out the gym shoe he'd then be beaten with. Frank had spent ages testing each shoe to find the softest one he could, angrily throwing all the rejected ones across the gym. He exacted his revenge several days later one night by pouring an ink bottle over the Headmaster's chair up on the gym stage for him to discover the following morning at school assembly in front of everyone. He made the school sit there in silence for twenty minutes demanding that the perpetrator confess and be punished. Frank sat there quietly, unmoving, enjoying the rewarding satisfaction of the chaos he'd caused.

He was regularly being awarded, not commendations, but 'black marks' for minor infringements, which when added up in the week led to being put on report if academic, otherwise attending evening playground litter clear up duty, stacking chairs for events and other general grotty duties. However, whilst Frank got by with his studies, he excelled at sports, tennis, rugby, cricket, football, billiards, table tennis, anything really involving a ball he was ahead of his peers. It was this combination of sporting prowess, good looks, arrogance and defiance of the system that made Frank one of the 'top dogs' at school. Unfortunately, he had little time for the less able and allowed himself to assert his authority by often taunting, picking on or outright bullying other boys. As with all bullies he had his team of close followers, some friends, some who had failed to get the top position so now stayed close to their leader, some just grateful to support the bully rather than be in the firing line themselves.

He then went off to the prestigious 'public school' Harrow, which is an unchecked British irony, as it's very much an elite private school. The old-fashioned uniforms, traditions, foibles and discipline continued and so did Frank's popularity as a top sportsman and bully, almost always able to stay one step ahead of any real scrutiny or challenge by teachers. Just a few years before capital punishment at schools was banned, the cane was still used for exceptional misdemeanours. Frank managed on several occasions to be up in front of the Headmaster to receive 'education' from this nasty whippy stick. It hurt like hell, but Frank would still force a smile at the Head when he left the room afterwards.

One particular major incident occurred when Frank was a Prefect and he along with a colleague were getting some backchat from a younger boy up in their study. One thing led to another and ended up with Frank and his friend holding the poor lad's legs, pushing him out their window and dangling him one floor up in mid-air. The frightened and panicked boy started kicking and thrashing causing the older boys to lose their grip and the unfortunate youngster fell fifteen feet onto the grass below breaking his wrist which swelled up like a balloon.

The injured boy's parents threatened to sue Harrow and Frank's father had to intervene with the help of a lawyer, who managed to persuade the angry parents to settle for a 'damages' payment to make the matter go away. As Frank and friend were soon to sit their final 'A' level exams the lawyer also persuaded Harrow not to expel them, after all, any publicity of bullying in such a prestigious school would not be good, but rather send them home to only return to sit their exams. This big ask was also helped along with another donation to the school. By the time all this blew over Frank had had enough of 'school' and rather than going to University as he was expected to, he decided to forge his way in the big wide world, much to his parent's surprise.

After a few years of lowly jobs in a couple of banks, Frank met up with one of his old Harrovian chums, a capable half Asian lad called Simon. They rekindled their close friendship with Frank keeping half an eye on a potential prize, being that Simon came from a wealthy Malaysian family. Very wealthy. Simon was only twenty-one but was living in his own house in Kensington, driving a new Aston Martin, had an unlimited allowance and was now searching for some new project to put his time into.

Frank had read an interesting article late eighties about the newly formed Cisco technology company based at San Jose in so-called Silicon Valley California and how they applied for hundreds of design and software patents each year. This not only protected ideas from being used by competitors, at least not unless they paid Cisco a licence or royalty, but was also swept up protecting the many attempts to forge new technologies on the basis many will fail or never come to fruition. But of the few that are successful, they were really successful and would be worth the risk taken on the others that became worthless. Effectively they were trying to corner the market on innovative technologies, hardware and software.

Frank presented the concept to Simon of buying up batches of expired patents then sitting on them, keeping the patent live, and waiting to see if any of them were then required by large conglomerates for their new product's capabilities. Once a patent expires it's a good sign the creator and owner have lost interest in their once 'save the world' idea. Frank and Simon would approach the registered albeit expired owner and offer to buy their patent. The owner would then revive their patent and once live again could then legitimately sell and transfer the patent to a new owner.

This all required a patent lawyer on a standby retainer, money to buy the patents, money to set up a limited company to manage it all through and money to pay for the patent's office fees. Frank had charmingly persuaded his friend and 'banker' to agree to a sixty-forty split in Simon's favour to fund the operation. They would both work on everything including selecting target patents to add to their portfolio. Frank was entirely satisfied with his forty per cent share given he'd put in no money, just the idea and drive, and indeed Simon was overjoyed that he could report back to his wealthy parents he'd started a technology patents brokerage, everyone was happy.

They had a few minor successes with patents they'd taken over, one for a part that contributed towards a new cyclone suction technology for vacuum cleaners and another for a new cable fastening implement in the building trade. But then they hit the jackpot, having bought a batch of patents from an individual who was clearly a serial patent creator using his knowledge of semiconductors and microchips. This person had let many of his patents expire and with the firm belief they would never be required, was happy to take the offers the boys made to him to take over some of the registrations. After a year, the boys read of the same man's success in selling a few of his ideas and patents to large companies for tens of millions of pounds. When he came back to the boys offering to buy back some of the patents he'd sold to them, Frank and Simon realised they could be onto something amongst the patents they'd acquired from him.

They patiently waited and sure enough, a consortium of mobile phone manufacturers approached them through a large attorney's office in San Francisco to buy one particular microchip encryption technology patent. Negotiations went back-and-forth for almost a year, with both parties at one point almost pulling out as is often the case with contract discussions. There's a fine line between signing it and throwing it in the bin. However, the need to now incorporate this tiny piece of inbuilt encryption and security into their mobile phones grew ever more pressing. Frank and Simon finally concluded the sale and transfer of their patent for the princely sum of £200 million. Frank's share of this was £80 million. The celebrations and spending spree went on for a straight six months before Frank then gracefully bowed out of the partnership with Simon who continued the patent brokerage, leaving Frank free to look for his next entrepreneurial opportunity.

Having been touched by the power of the technology industry and more so by the reliance on its security measures, he came across a small struggling virus checker software company called Guardian Angel founded and run by a certain John Dawlish. The fast-rising market for anti-malware software products was being dominated by such firms as McAfee and Norton who had the funds to spend money on product placement, complimentary hardware partnerships and advertising. John Dawlish had a good product which he had developed and written himself, but he simply didn't have a backer willing to take a risk and fund what was still a relatively new and untried offering. Frank stepped in and bought a majority share of the company from sole owner John, but more importantly then became the financial and selling drive Guardian Angel desperately needed to fight its way to the top table alongside the big firms.

As the years went by their virus checker went from strength to strength almost globally, except for controlled markets such as Russia and China who had their own monitored security systems. Frank sharpened up the brand name by dropping the 'Guardian' label and relaunching the product as just Angel. This simple tweaking of brand clarity gave the product another boost and whilst they had been left behind by the bigger brands, Angel virus checker software had established its place in the huge anti-malware market.

Leaving John to manage Angel, Frank went on buying up every alarm, man guarding, security delivery firm he could get his hands on. First in the UK, then Europe, a few small deals in North America and finally parts of Asia and the Far East.

This was when he was courted by an imposing Chinese businessman, who offered to help broker and fund some of his acquisitions in the region. Doors were opened, with surprising ease, and deals were done. Whilst Frank expanded his empire, he couldn't help feel he'd gotten into bed with the devil who one day would call upon him wanting some kind of dreadful payback. He was right. Preparations were now underway to square off the deal. He'd get a huge payoff and though the price was high, he didn't have a choice.

Over the decades Frank's huge collection of security businesses were incorporated into his new conglomerate, the Dark Corporation. His PR and media consultants advised against the unfortunate negative connotation of using the company name Dark, but Frank was quite determined that he had earned the right to call his company after his own name and so prevailed.

The Dark Corporation now employed almost 20,000 staff worldwide and had a turnover of £1.5 billion. It incorporated the original Angel software company which started in the UK, then briefly moved out to Israel, a leading centre of excellence for encryption companies, then the main development offices had been moved to Barbados. The man guarding business was run out of each region using the same umbrella formula of uniformed security guards under the Dark Corporation banner, as was the security van service for cash and valuables collection and delivery. Frank had also managed to part acquire a CCTV manufacturer in China and another firm in Hong Kong making security alarm products, which he then absorbed into the China location under one brand and one set of management. The alarms and CCTV were then sold almost globally by the rest of the Dark sales teams. He'd also acquired an unusual business in India that had managed to win a license from the Indian government's Ministry of Finance to act as a contingency backup rupee notes money printer, in case of any disasters affecting the approved money printer suppliers.

Finally, Frank had a special operations division headed up by Brett Harding based in Beverly Hills California, who in addition to acting as the Corporation's police force, investigators and enforcers, also provided specialist bodyguard services to the wealthy, elite and politicians.

With the Corporation's growth and success, it had been frequently suggested to Frank that he took the Corporation public to raise yet further funding and increase again the value of the company and indeed himself. Frank was certainly attracted to the prospect of increasing his personal fortune, but every time one of the top financial consulting firms came in and started to take him through the detail of the implications of taking your firm public, he'd always gone cold on the idea. He hated the thought of handing over so much control of his own company, the company he'd built, to other people he'd have to listen to and in a worst-case scenario could even end up taking his company away from him.

Frank was worth about £800 million on paper and had enough cash in the bank, not the business's bank but his own personal banks, to pretty much buy anything he could desire. He had a love of exotic sports cars and owned beautiful houses in Surrey, Nice, Beverly Hills and Barbados.

He'd been married twice to beautiful women, neither of whom could or would align themselves to his endless drive for perfection through a selfish and uncompromising character. He loved them both and certainly looked after each of them at the time of their divorces, with multi-million-pound settlements. He was now single again and for the time being felt that was the most uncomplicated way to continue concentrating on the business, whilst he was able to have brief, fun relationships on his terms.

He had big plans and before the unfortunate John Lyttleton matter, he had already started to confidentially headhunt for a replacement Chief Finance Officer just in case John wouldn't fall into line. He had planned to have that discussion with him about differing views on how the company should be run and therefore perhaps John should consider his position going forwards. Of course, he'd put such an attractive leaving package on the table John would have been mad not to graciously retire a wealthy man. But none of that was needed now, John had taken matters into his own hands and ended their relationship with his suicide.

He now needed to fill the vacancy of CFO quickly and having privately met with a number of candidates under strict confidentiality agreements, was sure he'd found just the right person to be his new Chief Finance Officer. One Doreen Leader.

5

Simon Lawson sat down at his desk in one of the MI5 buildings in London and nodded through the glass partition at his number two Vince, waiting expectantly outside. He immediately came in and sat in the visitor's chair across the desk from his boss Si, as he liked to be called.

"What have we got on our list today Vince?"

"Well the most important thing is preparing for our quarterly presentation to the Deputy Director General in a few weeks, so per our briefing to the team the other day they're already drafting out the information and slides to give you a first look in a couple of days." Si nodded approvingly and Vince continued. "You've got a new staff member interview this morning and you have all the information you need for the weekly cross teams briefing this afternoon."

"Great, thanks Vince, anything else?" asked Si.

"Just one thing Si, you remember that call you put onto me from the finance chap at the Dark Corporation who wanted to come in and see us. Well, I had him booked in for a quick meeting with me here for late afternoon yesterday."

"Yes, I remember, what did he want then?"

Vince continued, "I've no idea, he never turned up. Do you want me to follow it up? He did sound a little stressed when I spoke to him."

"Absolutely Vince, if someone has got to the point where they call the UK's Cyber Counter Espionage Unit at MI5 then we have to take it seriously, you know that Vince," reminded Si.

Vince shifted slightly in his chair, he knew that would be the response but just wanted to add the topic onto his morning touch base with his boss, more so to advise him, not really to ask what to do. "No problem I'll put in a call to him, diplomatically as always." He was well versed in communicating carefully with members of the public or potential whistle-blowers to ensure neither his nor their cover was blown or compromised. He retreated from his boss's office and immediately looked up the telephone number for the Dark Corporation's head offices in Guildford Surrey.

He called and asked the receptionist if he could speak to John Lyttleton and when asked, said he was an old friend just trying to get in touch. To Vince's surprise, he was then told that Mr Lyttleton had sadly taken his own life a couple of days ago. He thanked the girl for her time and apologised for bothering her at this sad time.

Vince then logged straight into the police intranet network he had access to and searched for John Lyttleton's name under the Surrey Constabulary. The file summary immediately appeared and Vince quickly scanned through the description which concluded 'Suicide - no suspicious circumstances'. Excited at the prospect of a new case to be explored he darted back into Si's office without waiting to be invited in and sat back in the spare chair. Si looked up from his paperwork inquisitively.

"I think we might have something here boss," Vince relayed hurriedly, "the John Lyttleton chap from Dark, well in between calling us wanting to report something and then not turning up for the meeting last night, he's died." Si sat up more interested now. "Apparently he committed suicide."

Si's eyes narrowed as he quickly took in the information. "You don't contact a division in MI5, book a meeting to see us and then before the meeting takes place go and kill yourself. Nah, that's not normal. Vince, just park everything for the rest of this morning and do some digging on this Dark company, then let's aim for you to give me a roundup after lunch. Then we can decide what to do." Vince nodded and went back to his desk.

Si Lawson had found his calling at MI5, he loved his job, he loved the routine work but also you never knew what each day would bring, and whilst he didn't show it to his staff, a new possibly dubious case excited him just as much as Vince. It was like finding a treasure trove and then sifting through it in more detail to see what you really had.

Si started in the Met police where he worked his way up steadily through the ranks specialising in the Fraud squad then in particular corporate financial fraud, working closely with many of the large consulting firms who had their own so-called fraud teams and were often the first point of call when company fraud was suspected. Boards of directors still felt more comfortable getting expensive consultants in rather than immediately involving the police, which did at least in theory have the consultants sift through the case before escalating it to someone like him in the Met. Once they had established that a criminal act had 'allegedly' been committed then his team would be called in to investigate and handle any prosecutions including the high-profile arrests often surprising the perpetrator in their offices in front of all their staff. On one occasion they'd met a corrupt property director at the airport and arrested him in front of his family on their return from holiday.

Then the lure of more money from Ernst & Young to head up their global fraud team was too irresistible to refuse, so he jumped from his Met role and generous pension prospects into the corporate consulting world. The pay was much, much better. After many good years there he simply grew tired of the constant demands upon him to suddenly be in New York, then off to a client in Dubai, then again with no warning he's told to come back to Paris because a Chief Executive wants to see the boss before considering taking action against another potential corrupt director. He was being pulled in too many directions and with the generous pay and rewards of being a partner, was expected to just drop everything when required and immediately go to the next case, whenever, wherever. It was simply not worth it to him, so when a contact recommended him to the MI5 Cyber Espionage unit, he jumped at the opportunity to be UK based again as one of several team leaders with ten staff, but with more control, power and access to more information than he'd ever before had access to.

Military Intelligence Section 5 better known as MI5 are the UK's security and counterintelligence agency working alongside the Government Communication Headquarters, the Defence Intelligence and its sister agency MI6 the Secret Intelligence Service, which is the one better-known by its fictional star spy James Bond. MI5 often called 'Box 500' within the organisation after its wartime Post Office box number, is directed by the Joint Intelligence Committee and ultimately falls under the Cabinet Home Secretary to protect British economic interests, Parliamentary democracy, and act as the lead counter-espionage and terrorism unit. Originally there were around ten Military Intelligence Sections which have over the years been absorbed into just MI5 and MI6. The work and operations that are now undertaken by them mainly consists of intelligence gathering, analysis and investigation. However, the word Military in their titles serves as a clear reminder of the other strands of more action-orientated work they handle in the front-line battle against terrorism and espionage. They either have within their ranks or can call upon at any time from a huge wealth of specialist military, police, tactical, ordnance, transport, equipment and field operatives.

MI5 has around four thousand staff under the Director General, who then has three main divisions working alongside a legal advisory team. There is a Director General of Strategy, a Director General of Capability involving technical operations, analysis and surveillance. Then lastly the number two of the organisation, the Deputy Director General heads up International Counter-Terrorism, Northern Ireland Counter-Terrorism and the division that Si's teamwork in being Cyber and Counter Espionage.

MI6 Secret Intelligence Service is based in the now well-recognised sandstone and green building on the River Thames by Vauxhall Bridge, as seen in several spy-related movies. Most people assume this building houses all of the Intelligence Services, but in fact MI5 are based a short distance up the river on the other side, in a huge building called Thames House between the Tate Modern

Gallery and the Houses of Parliament.

Thames House is a monumental eight-floor building in Millbank built in 1930 just by Lambeth Bridge. It was previously used as the offices for the huge corporation ICI Imperial Chemical Industries along with a number of government offices, until late 1994 when it was taken over by MI5.

The main original entrance archway which was part infilled to allow greater access through the building, has the high up statues of St George and Britannia looking down on visitors and passers-by. Anyone trying to trespass and enter the building without the rigorous authorisations in place are committing a criminal offence and can be arrested under Section 128 of the Serious Organised Crime and Police Act 2005. Security is tight and every road and access to the building is covered by uniformed police officer's day and night.

Si was just finishing off the last of his cheese and ham sandwich when Vince reappeared through the doorway clutching his iPad onto which he'd summarised the information he wanted to take his boss through.

"Ah yes about this Dark thing, tell me what you found?" asked Si.

Vince sat opposite him across the desk and placed his tablet in front of Si and started pointing and swiping as he spoke.

"Well overall it all looks legit, but I have to say from looking through everything for the last few hours you can't help but feel there might be something going on there." Si nodded then pointed to the tablet for Vince to continue.

"Top-level, the Dark Corporation was founded by a Frank Dark, no record with us, he's built up this huge security firm over past decades with CCTV, alarms, man guarding, security vans, an anti-virus checker and somewhat oddly a Government approved rupee notes printer in India."

"Money printing, yes a bit strange, but as you say, must all be legit, I guess," added Si.

Vince continued. "Turnover about £1.5 billion, 20,000 staff globally, quite a big deal, I've seen their brand around on a few products. Surprisingly they're still a private limited company with the vast majority of shares held by the owner and CEO Frank Dark, with a long list of smaller shareholders including directors, a Chinese businessman and likely previous owners of the many companies he's taken over and swallowed up into his group. I've also watched a few corporate videos on YouTube of Frank Dark, quite the professional CEO, bit of a charmer I'd say."

"Okay so what's our hook to take more time on this," asked Si, who had already made his mind up.

"Honestly boss I feel we should get into this quickly, if for no other reason than this poor finance chap topping himself for no apparent reason when he's due to come in and see us. He must have had something," concluded Vince.

Si concurred. "I agree. As we've not got anything concrete, we can't go blundering in, we don't know what the hell we'd be looking for, no, we need to get someone in there."

"Agree boss, I'll see what senior roles they're recruiting for over the next few weeks then cross-check it with our EP list to see if we have any possible contenders." Vince left Si's office to officially open up a new case file to be entitled 'Dark Corporation'. He'd leave the sub-title blank for now until they knew exactly what the potential corruption was.

The EP list held the names and case files of all 'Executives Pending' investigation or prosecution. Across the UK, company staff, directors, owners, consultants and interims were committing fraud, trying to swindle their companies or employers out of money and value. Occasionally blackmail came into play, often it was financial corruption and accounting dupes. Sometimes corporate espionage, passing on secrets, insider trading, or intellectual property disclosure for competitors. Other times the roving execs such as consultants or short-term interim placements would come across some nugget of information, a process, a recipe or takeover plans. The temptation for a quick buck could sometimes be too hard to resist, despite the confidentiality and non-disclosure agreements they had inevitably signed.

At any one time, MI5's EP list had around 1,600 people on it either having been reported, pending investigation, waiting or under prosecution. Most of these executives would be dealt with by their companies, some with police involvement, a few would come to the attention of MI5 and Si's team, but they had visibility of all cases.

If they were lucky, somewhere in the upper echelons of the Dark Corporation there might be a vacancy coming up. If they were really lucky, they may find a matching, malleable EP on their list whom they could get into the company, to find out what was really happening there and why their Chief Finance Officer wanted to see MI5.

6

The doorbell rang and the video intercom inside sprang into life showing a picture of a suited man standing strongly upright in the front porch waiting for an answer. Though Doreen Leader was expecting the man she would always double-check over the intercom.

"Yes?" she inquired.

"Good morning Ma'am, Alan your driver here to take you into the Dark head offices," stated the man.

"Wonderful," she replied, "I'll be right there."

She grabbed her suit jacket, keys, handbag and small briefcase with its carefully prepared contents and exited the medium-sized terraced house on the Kings Road, Chelsea London. Alan the driver had retreated to the pavement and was already standing beside the black Range Rover with the rear door open and waiting. He tried to conceal an admiring smile as he watched the beautiful woman in front of him glide towards the car, but she noticed, she always did. She knew she was highly attractive to almost all men and indeed many women. She placed her two bags and jacket carefully on the rear seat then started to make her way around the back of the car saying, "I'll sit in the front thank you, there's more room and I can't stand sitting in the back staring at the front headrest." She knew what she wanted and would always say so.

As Alan tried to hastily catch up with her to open the door she was already settling into the seat and making herself as comfortable as possible pushing down the armrest to her right. Alan skirted around the front of the Range Rover and climbed in simultaneously pressing the 'start engine' button as he sat down, putting on his safety belt and engaging drive in a well-finessed routine.

He professionally announced, "If it's alright with you I'll take us over Wandsworth Bridge then straight down the A3 to the offices, should only take us about half an hour traffic permitting." Years of experience as a chauffeur had taught Alan to always quickly run through the route so the client knew what to expect and if they wanted to suggest any alternative route then now is the time to hear it from them. He used to hate it when halfway to a destination someone would angrily pipe up demanding why they weren't on a certain road. The stunning lady next to him gave a slight smile in agreement then settled back focusing her gaze forward. Alan gave her a smile and a nod and tried desperately not to linger his gaze on her for any longer than he could help it.

Doreen Leader was indeed an unusually beautiful Chief Finance Officer at forty-three. At about five foot nine with curves in all the right places, perfectly groomed, expensive latest-fashion clothing and high heels, she struck an impressive figure. Her clear silky skin had a small amount of carefully and subtly applied makeup on, mainly accentuating her blue-green eyes which were another of her strong points, they were quite enchanting. Her light hair was professionally enhanced towards a blended light golden off-blonde colour and though it was beyond shoulder length, it was neatly wrapped up around her head with a few tantalising hair strands left at the whim of the air and breeze around her.

She liked the good things in life, including enjoying the best kind of food and wines either at home or in one of her preferred restaurants around the world. She'd also had one of the double bedrooms in her house converted into a large walk-in dressing room where her love of buying beautiful, expensive and eye-catching clothes, suits, skirts, dresses, jackets and fabulous shoes were on full display, like a mini-museum, for her to select from each morning or evening.

One of the other things she realised over the years she liked, was women, well one in particular. Tired of many complicated relationships with possessive men wanting her as a trophy, she'd strayed to the other side when she met her now partner Maureen with whom she shared her lovely King's Road home with. They were true to one another, each had the space for their respective careers, Maureen was a top London homes designer for the wealthy, and they both loved one another and the setup they'd now carved out for themselves. Doreen had often had to let down flirting male admirers with an 'I'm not into men' put-off only to watch their utter shock and then disappointment. Unfortunately once, one of her peers went on to say "What a waste" to her face in front of some colleagues. She admonished him so savagely that the poor man came in the following day, profusely apologised to her, then promptly resigned from the embarrassment of the whole situation.

In the centre of her dressing room was a jewellery island with a large array of fabulous looking necklaces, bracelets, rings, broaches and earrings. Each item had its own compartment and were neatly organised into colours and sizes. Mostly the items were bought for the way they looked and their perceived quality, but mixed in among the less expensive chattels were a few far more impressive and very expensive pieces of jewellery. She knew which items they were, few others would know the difference at first glance but when she needed something with unquestionably rare taste and quality she had them. There was no accompanying collection of watches as you'd expect. She'd previously had a couple of Rolex ladies 'Datejust's' and a Cartier but had long since settled for a trusty and eye-catching steel and gold Rolex Yachtmaster.

Doreen Leader was a Chartered Certified accountant and had quickly worked her way up through a number of smaller corporate finance departments in London and the Home Counties. She was still quite young when she got her first Finance Director role with a large food manufacturing company. From there she took up a similar but far weightier role for one of the biggest high street retailers which provided the perfect stepping stone to then move up to a Chief Finance Officer position with one of the large drug and pharmaceutical global firms based in London. There she oversaw around 1,800 finance, administration, analytics and back-office staff around the world and had intended for this to be her final long-term appointment. But then an intriguing call from one of the boutique head hunters had caught her interest, not just because of the company, but mainly because of the extraordinary package that might be on offer for the right person.

After several conversations with the head-hunter, she had met Frank Dark CEO and John Dawlish CTO of the Dark security corporation for a long evening of interview-dinner. They'd gone to Michel Roux's Le Gavroche in Mayfair where they had a rarely used small private dining room just off the main underground restaurant and had talked and dined from six pm through to the early hours, way past their normal closing time but Frank knew the owner so that wasn't a problem.

She understood the 'interview' was speculative as the existing CFO was still in post, hence the tight confidentiality. It was sadly often the case in the corporate world that an unsuspecting executive would be going about their duties, completely unbeknown to them that their boss was actually recruiting to kick them out and replace them as soon as the right candidate was found. Sometimes a recruiting agency would bungle things and a drafted ad for the role might get accidentally released, causing the uncomfortable situation of a director storming into their boss demanding to know why *their* job was being advertised. This would then prompt the inevitable 'leave today' outcome, which simply cost the firm more to quickly wrap up the now badly needed compromise agreement so there were no comebacks, tribunals or adverse publicity.

The evening with Frank and John had gone well, they were charming, especially Frank, engaging, open, professional and asked a lot of questions. That was expected, but Doreen felt they were incredibly thorough in their albeit polite but intense examination of her career, life, friends, education, beliefs, character, achievements, everything was laid bare. Then at the end of a satisfying evening's performance she felt, having just excused herself for a moment, she returned for Frank to advise her they had enjoyed meeting her and indeed she would be one of several candidates they were now considering.

'One of several candidates' she'd reflected. This annoyed her afterwards, surely after that seven-hour interview for which she deserved an Oscar, she was the *only* candidate for the job. Nevertheless, she continued to express her interest, after all, there was no decision to be made until one gets offered the job... then the power would start to shift in her favour.

She'd kept a close eye following the Dark Corporation, news updates, group announcements and past results as well as briefly looking up the incumbent CFO a John Lyttleton, after all it was his job up for grabs. He seemed like a typical top corporate finance guy, professional, hard-working, perhaps a bit dull, definitely not a front-line man but they had that in Frank. Then came the shocking announcement a short while ago, that John Lyttleton had sadly taken his own life, nothing suspicious. She had put it down to personal problems likely exacerbated by the stress of such a high-powered job. She understood the pressures, deadlines and expectations of the role and though awful, accepted it at face value.

Soon afterwards the head-hunter had booked her an evening call with Frank. She could tell from his even more charming tone he was about to offer her the role. Indeed after quite a lot of pre-amble extolling the virtues of the role and company, the role was now hers to lose. The overall package he offered with basic, bonus, golden greeting, shares and benefits totalled around £4 million, double what she was on in the drug firm. She managed to contain her excitement and voice tone, and calmly pushed back. 'One of several candidates indeed' she still thought, 'now we'll see'.

Frank clearly wasn't wanting to be pushed believing his generous offer was exceptional, so by the end of the call when she'd managed to persuade him up to £5 million she felt redeemed and ecstatic at the result. Frank wanted her to start as soon as she could extract herself from the current role, which she did with considerable charm, professionalism and a little pleading thrown in for good measure. Fortunately, her boss was most understanding though disappointed to lose her.

From getting to know Frank Dark she believed that half her huge salary package was indeed for her to do a great job as CFO, but the other half was more than likely Frank's way of ensuring, or buying her complete loyalty, something she clearly understood from their discussions was very important to him. Fine either way, it was £5 million per annum.

Doreen Leader would have been practically perfect, that is if it wasn't for just one small vice she had, which she loathed and loved in equal measures. She liked to gamble. Not in the sense that she wanted to constantly bet on things every day, but when she did go for a fun evening at the casino, the sums of money involved always escalated into large five-figure numbers. Her one weakness, which unbeknown to her, the new boss she was about to start working for had stumbled across through one of his many London club owner pals.

The Range Rover pulled off the A3 adjacent to Guildford and along the slip road into the business park alongside the dual carriageway and immediately turned into the large car park of the impressive Dark Corporation black one-way glass-fronted buildings. Alan pulled up in front of the main reception entrance, got out and gathered her bags and jacket from the rear seat. He ventured an "I hope your first day goes well Ma'am," handed them over as she then swept up the steps. He watched her admiringly until she disappeared through the doors.

Doreen unknowingly stood exactly where her predecessor's body landed as she introduced herself to the receptionist. Moments later both Frank and John came down the stairs to welcome her on board, show her around, make the first of many introductions around the offices, then eventually take her up to the fourth-floor executive offices and her own empty large office.

After the initial tour, John peeled off leaving Frank to take Doreen to his office.

Sheila his PA appeared to offer drinks but was dismissed rather harshly by Frank, "Nothing for now thank you Sheila, and absolutely no interruptions from anyone please, I want to give our new CFO my full attention."

Doreen felt for the hapless secretary, guessing Frank's macho show was put on for her benefit, though it didn't impress her at all.

"I'm so glad you're on board with us Doreen," said Frank enthusiastically, and began his welcoming speech, or rather 'rules of engagement' with his new CFO.

After about twenty minutes of conversation about how both of them like to work and what Frank expected of his new Director, Sheila cautiously popped her head around the interjoining door, waiting for Frank to acknowledge her.

Frank stopped mid-sentence and huffed. "Sheila, I said absolutely no interruptions whatsoever!"

Sheila frowned but pressed on. "Frank. It's him!"

Frank was still caught up in the moment and enjoying trying to impress Doreen. "Who is *him*? I can't be disturbed, tell them to call back later," he demanded.

Sheila sighed and started to show signs of being irritated. "You know. The one person you've always said to put through no matter what you're doing. Mister Xiaoping!"

Frank's whole alpha façade instantly regressed, much to Doreen's surprise.

"Ahh," said Frank standing. "You should have said Sheila, I'm sorry." He gesticulated his hand to Doreen for her to leave the office quickly. "Sorry Doreen, let's catch up later, I need to take this call. Sorry."

Sheila shrugged apologetically to Doreen, who gathered her things up and with some puzzlement edged back out of Frank's office, somewhat put out that after all the talk of not being interrupted, she was now being booted out for this special caller. Sheila disappeared back into her own office, "I'll put him through at once Frank." Doreen exited and the door closed behind her. She could just make out Frank greeting the important caller with even more enthusiasm and some deference. 'How bizarre' she thought. 'Who on earth has that kind of sway over the famous Frank Dark?'

She spent the next few days cramming in more meetings and calls to introduce herself to her finance staff and teams worldwide, understand the workings of the company, get across any urgent projects and deadlines needing immediate attention and had a long handover briefing from Frank and her deputy on just about everything and everyone. She was already impressing staff and indeed Frank, and to be fair Doreen was equally in admiration of this man who has founded and built such a large global security company within his own lifetime. He certainly was a charmer, but that would be wasted on her.

Doreen found herself in Sheila's small office sorting out some regular diary update meetings for her and Frank. Frank was out so she ventured, "That was a little odd the other day Sheila, that thing with the caller interrupting my first meeting with Frank?" Doreen realised this would be a test of Sheila's loyalty to see how she reacted to the topic.

Sheila initially gave her a questioning look. She was indeed very loyal to Frank. Many years working for him and the huge salary, for a PA, helped. But then swayed by just the two girls together in this male-dominated environment, softened to Doreen's understandable question.

"Yes, usually when Frank says no interruptions, that's it. But this particular gentleman is very special."

"How so?"

"Well, he's a wealthy businessman and has helped Frank buy some of the firms across the corporation, and investing, that sort of thing I guess."

"Oh I see," said Doreen not wanting to push her luck anymore. "Yes, he must be special."

"I think they're working on some very big deal. Don't know what. Frank won't even tell me anything about it which is unusual," said Sheila. "But now you're CFO I'm sure you'll get to hear all about it."

"Hmm, yes, I'd assume so," replied Doreen smiling, and wondering. She thought to herself it was clearly something very big, and very sensitive, so she would wait for Frank to raise it rather than ask anything herself.

Doreen had a number of corporate functions under her and one of the non-finance departments she controlled was Procurement. This team were responsible for ensuring the firm found and used the best suppliers, obtained value for money and handled the deals and contracts for all goods and services the company spent money on. John Lyttleton had lost his previous Chief Procurement Officer and was just about to start recruiting for a replacement when his unfortunate incident halted proceedings.

Doreen wanted to get the ball rolling quickly for this key position and called her favourite recruitment agency to get onto finding someone. They felt they could get her CV's in a few days from trawling their database. She pondered, then told them she wanted a single ad for the CPO vacancy in that week's executive jobs section of the Financial Times paper, with a similar ad in their online recruitment pages for one week only. 'That should get me someone special' she thought.

7

Max Sargent had been waiting to hear from someone about his corporate indiscretion and noticed a car nearing his Clapham Common home's entrance.

'Well this looks interesting,' he thought as a new looking black BMW 5 series pulled into his gate approach. He watched as a smartly dressed older man got out and pressed the buzzer. Max dispensed with the usual 'who are you' via the intercom and pressed the button to open the gates. The visitor pulled in just missing the gates which were still opening.

Max greeted the man at the door who pulled out an ID card saying, "Si Lawson MI5. And you must be Max Sargent, may I come in please?"

Si knew the mere mention of MI5 scared the living daylights out of people and got their full attention at once.

"MI5!" Max repeated in shock as he'd been expecting one of the fraud chaps from PWC to drop in and probably start mediating some kind of leaving settlement on behalf of the company. "Yes of course, come in," as he led Si into the living room to be seated.

They sat down and Si continued, "Please don't be alarmed by the MI5 bit, I'm actually here to help you. I gather you're in a spot of trouble with your firm after committing corporate espionage." Si knew from experience to go in quite hard to start with, they had to understand who was calling the shots from the beginning.

"Corporate espionage!" Max was starting to sound like a parrot repeating everything. "That's hardly what happened."

"Well stealing sensitive company intellectual property and passing it onto a competitor, is the most perfect definition of corporate espionage I've ever read anywhere. You should look it up," countered Si triumphantly.

Max paused to gather his thoughts. It felt a lot more serious when the term was being said out loud. "Okay, you mentioned something about being here to help, and where's PWC in all this?"

"Forget Price Waterhouse Coopers, I've spoken to them and your firm and I now have the casting vote on how this matter proceeds. Privileges of pulling rank you might say, and rest assured my rank is way above theirs." Si studied Max and continued, "From time to time we do ask members of the public to assist us with on-going investigations into things like corporate cyber corruption, financial deception, fraud and company espionage. We have a particular opportunity to utilise someone with your profile, experience and CV, inside a Company we simply want to know more about."

Max wasn't at all happy about this, "Sounds very risky, dangerous," then with his negotiator's hat on continued, "something that demanding would take a big commitment on my part, what's in it for me then?"

Si had discovered the records of Max's brief but distinguished stint in the Royal Marines and had also picked up that this interesting executive had clearly chosen to eradicate the events some two decades ago from his business profiles and CV. He decided for now not to mention it in the context of Max not needing to be worried about anything dangerous in the 'civi' environment. He smiled and closed in for the win. "There's no danger, we're talking pencil pushers and board room swindlers, you just observe and report." He then paused for effect. "And in return for maybe 2 to 6 months of your time, on full pay for your job anyway, I will expunge your criminal charges and give you a clean bill of health to continue your successful career. This dirty little matter will disappear." Si beamed broadly at Max, who had just one more question.

"And if I don't want to do this little job for you, what then?"

Si's smile fell away turning to an expression of pain and regret. He sighed, "Then my friend, you will be charged by the police for breach of confidence, misuse of confidential information and breach of the Data Protection Act resulting in possible imprisonment and or a hefty fine, not to mention the end of your career!"

Max was stunned, "Jees, don't hold back why don't you. Hmm. Don't really have much choice here do I."

"Well you do have a choice, but I know which one I'd choose, it's up to you," said Si.

"I'd like to know more about it all before I commit."

"Excellent," said Si, "Then I suggest you pop into my offices tomorrow, here's my card, sort out a time with my deputy Vince. Then you can meet some of my guys and we'll give you all the details you need on the case we'll work on together." Rising to make for the door, "Until then Max, take care. Oh and no need to have any more contact with PWC nor your old firm, I'll sort the leaver's package for you once we get started."

Max showed him out and reopened the gate for him to drive off. He watched him disappear. 'Bloody hell,' thought Max, 'MI5!'

8

Max had dutifully called Vince and agreed an appointment for him to come in and find out more about what they had in mind for him. He set off from home walking to the other side of Clapham Common to the underground station there and then took the Northern line 5 stops on to Waterloo station, the largest and busiest of its kind in Britain. He walked through the huge, covered complex, under the famous hanging clocks in the middle, which served as the popular meeting point for many people over the decades, and out of the main Waterloo station entrance down the steps and off towards Westminster Bridge.

Walking towards this iconic bridge opened in 1750, to his left was St Thomas's Hospital and the Marriot hotel was on his right. As he neared the bridge he was greeted by the large white stoned lion on the right, which was bizarrely also known as the Red Lion because it was painted red in the 50s and 60s.

As Max walked across Westminster Bridge over the murky River Thames past County Hall and the impressive London Eye, looking across the bridge he was greeted with one of the most iconic sites in the world. Westminster Palace, the Houses of Parliament and Big Ben, named after its largest great bell. This hallowed and historic place began as a Royal residence and Palace in 1050, with its first government officials in situ around 1220 and the first record of a Parliamentary sitting was 1259. For well over 750 years this had been the constitutional democratic seat of governing power for the United Kingdom. The age and history of this and so many other buildings and monuments around the city simply had to impress all onlookers. Max loved being in London amongst it all.

As he reached the end of the bridge, opposite Big Ben on the right stood the bronze chariot statue of Boadicea and her daughters, celebrating this famous Briton who led the uprising against the incumbent and unwelcome Romans. Approaching Parliament Square Max turned left opposite the statue of Sir Winston Churchill looking down on him and passing tourists disapprovingly. He walked along the heavily protected Houses of Parliament with high spiked iron railings, gates, crash barriers and police presence, past Oliver Cromwell's statue. On his right was the smaller St Margaret's Church, which then behind it was overlooked and dwarfed by the massive Westminster Abbey, where many kings and queens had been crowned, married and buried.

He continued down Abingdon Street past the Palace of Westminster and alongside the leafy Victoria Tower Gardens. Lambeth Bridge was ahead of him with its distinctive red paintwork, the same colour as the red leather benches in the House of Lords, the two obelisks straddled its entrance by the Millbank roundabout. As he crossed over the junction the huge building that was Thames House loomed above him on the right, directly overlooking the River Thames. Max started to feel a little nervous with the sight of this imposing building of power and mystique, as he reached the large entrance arch, smiling and nodding at two police officers standing outside. He entered the building through one of the three doorways.

Reception were expecting Max and asked him to complete a short visitor's form on an iPad, show proof of his identity, took his photo, finally handing over an encapsulated visitor's ID badge with the clear instruction, "Please wear this and ensure it is visible at all times." The cameras throughout the building were extremely high-definition quality and in the event someone needed to be identified quickly, the ID badge could quickly be zoomed in on to ascertain who anyone was.

Vince came downstairs and warmly greeted Max, then took him to an upper floor where the Cyber team's offices were. It was a large space with about twelve open plan desks each separated with low-level partitions, every desk occupied with industrious but calm team members. There were a number of large whiteboards around the office walls with lots of scribbled notes, spider-grams, pictures of individuals and post-it notes, tracking various operations Max surmised. To one side there were several glass meeting rooms and a single enclosed office which Vince was leading them towards.

Si Lawson stood up from behind his desk as they entered his office and came over to greet Max. "Max, it's good to see you again, and thank you for agreeing to help us with this little piece of work."

"Well yes I'm here, but I don't actually know what it is you have in mind for me yet, so am reserving judgement for now," stated Max a little defensively.

Si gestured to the doorway, "Let's go into the meeting room and meet a couple of the guys that will be working with you and tell you all about it."

Si, Vince and Max settled down around the table in one of the glass meeting rooms and were joined by a couple of the team, Josh and Ellie who brought in with them tea, coffee, water and of course biscuits. Vince had prepared a clear well thought through PowerPoint presentation, which he took Max through with Si interjecting where more clarity or reassurance was required.

The first ten slides were skipped through fairly quickly, being the standard MI5 Cyber presentation telling Max all about the organisation, its remit and then more detail about Si's team, its staff and what it does. Vince then started pulling up slides introducing the Dark Corporation.

Max interjected immediately. "Dark. Is this the company you want me involved in?"

The team were surprised at his reaction to the first slide about this company. Vince responded. "Yes Max, it's the Dark Corporation we need your help looking into, is there a problem?"

Max's eyes glanced amongst the onlookers. "No problem. It's just that I read about their Finance Officer committing suicide recently. Awful."

"It was terrible and that's why we want to find out more about what's going on there Max. John Lyttleton their CFO was concerned about something and was due to come in here to tell us, but he died before that happened," said Si.

"Was it really suicide?" asked Max bluntly.

"Apparently so," replied Vince. He continued with the slides.

The reality of the 'mission' abruptly came to life for Max once more when a slide flashed up with a picture of John Lyttleton.

Si took over from Vince at this point. "This is a picture of John Lyttleton who is, or rather was the Chief Finance Officer of the large security-focused Dark Corporation with their global head office based in Surrey."

Max stared at the picture in a trance. The team in the room realised the man's death had clearly disconcerted the young executive they were asking to get involved. As if reading his mind Si reassuringly continued.

"Now there's nothing to worry about, the poor man took his own life, nothing suspicious. I'm afraid it's another case of too much stress in the job and possibly other problems he was having to deal with." Max looked momentarily unconvinced. Si continued. "However, the reason we are interested to find out more about the Dark Corporation, is that right before his passing he had just spoken to Vince here asking to come in and see us as he was unhappy with some of the things going on there. As Vince mentioned earlier."

Max found himself stating the obvious out loud, "That's a bit odd to book in a meeting with you guys and then go and commit suicide."

"Indeed," agreed Si. "Vince, why don't you take us through what you have on the Dark Corporation."

Vince then went through a number of slides giving a summary of all the publicly available information on the Dark Corporation including financials, business types, geographies, ownership, history and concluding with the people. He gave a roundup of the top executive team, then covered the non-executive board directors including the chairman Sir Kieran Sinclair, building up to the shortlist of the few main board directors. He summarised a quick bio for pictures of John Dawlish, Doreen Leader, Brett Harding and finally he spent a little longer talking through the impressive career of Frank Dark, whose picture he left upon the screen while they continued talking.

Si led again. "The reason we need your help Max is that we have to get somebody into the senior management levels of this Dark Corporation. We can't just go piling in there as we don't yet know what the problem is. But John Lyttleton their ex-CFO wasn't happy about something and we assume it must have been pretty important for him to want to come in and see us. So important in fact and perhaps intimidating, that he changed his mind and felt he couldn't carry the burden any longer."

"And how on earth do you expect me to suddenly start working for this company," asked Max.

Si looked over at Vince who triumphantly placed a copy of the Financial Times on the table amongst them, flipped through to the executive jobs pages and turning the paper round to face Max, pointed to the ad circled with a thick black pen.

Max read the heading out loud. "Chief Procurement Officer for leading global security firm, Surrey-based, highly attractive package to suit an exceptional candidate." He then quietly scanned the rest of the ad with the others in the room patiently waiting, then allowed himself a grin and nodded. Max loved the hunt and chase of winning a new high-powered job, beating other strong candidates and reminding himself how good he was at what he did. There was nothing in the job description that worried him.

"Okay, I see where you're coming from now," said Max, as Vince intuitively moved the PowerPoint back a couple of slides to the picture of Doreen Leader. "And this is the new CFO recruiting the Chief Procurement Officer vacancy," noted Max.

"At least we know she's clean as she only just started in her new role there, so can't be involved in anything dodgy going on," said Si.

"Wow, quite a looker isn't she," observed Max.

"Of course this all relies on you actually being offered the CPO job Max," continued Si. "What we need you to do is immediately apply for the role through their nominated recruitment agency as soon as you get home, as the short deadline finishes at the end of this week. Assuming you're as good as you appear to be and win this job, we have a few more things to take you through before you go if that's all right."

Vince added, "So Max, you've been careful not to commit yet, but we need to know now if you're willing to work with, or rather for us on this assignment?"

Max took a deep breath taking everything in, clicked the slides back to the poor unfortunate ex CFO, and nodded. "I'm up for it. For him."

"Just one quick thing before we get started, can I please ask you, Max, to let Ellie have your iPhone, we just need to make a few adjustments for you, how we communicate and things like that. We'll have it back to you before you leave?" Si asked. Trustingly Max pushed his mobile phone across the desk to Ellie who gave it a cursory inspection then quickly left the room with it. Max gave her the unlock code as she passed by him.

The team then spent the next several hours briefing Max on the objectives, what to be looking for, covering a multitude of scenarios and some role-playing, and patiently fielding the many questions and concerns Max raised. Si and his team exuded confidence and had won Max's faith and trust, they had run operations like this many times before and were well versed at this onboarding routine with a new EP assignment.

As they were starting to wrap things up with Max, Ellie came back into the room closely followed by a young-looking man with very short hair wearing jeans and T-shirt, contrasting to everyone else in the room wearing suits.

"This is Alan from Technology who'll take you through a couple of things on your phone Max," introduced Ellie.

Alan ambled in awkwardly and asked Vince if he could kindly move and let him sit in the chair next to Max. He placed the iPhone on the table to explain what he'd done.

Alan was your typical geeky technology and gadget obsessive and worked in the large ordnance and equipment department. He didn't have anything to do with the weapons and armoury section which was handled by much more experienced and older people than him. However, as part of the Technology team which mainly involved online analysis, tracking and interventions, occasionally he would be allowed to utilise his real passion of computer-based or technological gadgets and innovations. What he'd done for Max's phone had been a rather mundane and easy task, but he was grateful to be taken away from his usual day's activities for just an hour or so.

"I've just made a couple of minor adjustments to your mobile." Alan then noticed Max's steel Rolex Submariner watch. "Ah, nice watch, same as the one Roger Moore has in Live and Let Die. You know the one with the high-powered magnet and the spinning bezel cutter." No one in the room said anything but at least the comment brought on a few smiles.

Alan continued. "For you to call into Si and the team here I've installed a high-end quad encryption speech and data channel for you, can't be tracked or hacked into, so your calls with Si will be completely confidential. Obviously, you have to keep your voice down, that can still be overheard." Alan's attempt at light humour failed again, but still elicited a smile from Max.

Alan went on. "In order to make a call to Si don't use the usual phone app, calls from that show in the history. Instead, go to the 'Notes' app that comes with all iPhones as standard, and let's face it never gets used by anyone. Then once you're in Notes simply type in 'c a l l 2 2' and it will immediately dial Si's mobile number."

"Why the 22?" asked Max.

Alan shrugged, "No reason, just a random number I thought of, doesn't mean anything. By the way, if you need to send over a picture or file whilst your talking, just clearly say 'Add File' and the screen will switch into your files then just select what you want to be sent over to Si whilst you're speaking. Just a little thing I added myself, not yet available in the shops folks," Alan proudly beamed at his audience.

This time Vince piped up with a "Nice one Alan" in praise

of the lad's ingenuity. Alan waited briefly for anyone else's comments, then looking a little disappointed carried on.

"You have to say 'Add File' again though if you want to send more than one across, I'm still working on making that a bit slicker. Now the next gizmo is a bit more interesting, I've replaced the standard microphone on your phone with a highly sensitive directional one, which will allow you to record conversations from some way off." Alan pointed at the tiny pinhole where the mic was at the top of the iPhone and continued. "Simply go back into your 'Notes' app and this time type in 'l i s t e n 2 2' then point the mic as accurately as you can at the person or people you want to pick up. You can't listen to what they're saying real-time but as soon as you have typed in the command it will start recording what it hears into a sound file. You can then listen to the sound file once you finished recording by pressing the 'Home' button."

Max eagerly picked up his phone, "Wow, that's pretty cool, can I quickly try it out?" Alan nodded and Max carefully typed in the first command, moments later Si's mobile in his pocket started ringing. Max then went out into the main open office, typed in the 'listen22' command and then pointed his phone at the two people on the far side of the office having a conversation. After a few moments, he came back into the meeting room and quickly brought up the sound file that had just been recorded. He pressed 'Play' and they were all treated to an almost crystal-clear recording of the two people's conversation about when they would go to the canteen for lunch. Everyone seemed most impressed with Alan's efforts and Si made a point of thanking him for his time and help. Alan left feeling very pleased with himself and the team dispersed leaving just Si and Max.

"Before you go Max," ventured Si pausing, "I've seen your records, not your career ones, your military records." Max continued to look down at the table. "Less than two years as a green beret Commando. Seeing your friend killed in Sierra Leone. Honourably discharged with a Military Cross and still only twenty years old. Quite extraordinary Max. Anything you want to tell me about it all that maybe I need to know?"

Max took in a deep breath and slowly sighed. "It's as it says in the reports, but the words on paper don't tell you how awful that day was. It was two decades ago anyway. I prefer to forget about it."

"Quite understandable Max, I can't imagine what that must have been like. I guess what I'm trying to say is that you don't have to take on this assignment? You've earned the right for a free pass, if that's what you want. I should be able to swing it for you. I just had to check, hear it from you, that you're up for this thing with Dark?"

Max pondered, briefly remembering that day back in 2000. He'd put the whole thing in a tightly shut box and buried it in the back of his mind. He wasn't a soldier now, he was an executive, with twenty years of working his way up the corporate ladder. After what he'd been through in the Marines, he couldn't imagine anything the corporate world threw at him would phase him.

"I'm fine. Let's go ahead with the Dark company," Max said. There was a pause as he struggled to find more words, but they eluded him just for now.

"Well I think that's everything we have for you Max, let's call it a day there, good luck with the interview application, make sure you keep me posted all the way," concluded Si.

Once Max had left Vince came back into Si's office. "Si, are you sure Max is up to this job? I detected some reticence."

Si sat back in his chair, subtly nodding to himself. "Strictly in confidence Vince. Our young Max was a Marine Commando. A long, long time ago mind you."

Vince was as much surprised as he was impressed. "Really?"

Si continued. "Sent into a war zone at nineteen. Saw some bad things. Killed a lot of people. Left the outfit before he'd even served two years. Oh yes Vince, Max is up to it alright, he's a bloody hero. Military Cross. Don't judge a book by its cover eh. Max was a hard arse, whether he wanted to be is another story. I suspect not though."

Vince felt stupid that he'd questioned Max's form and ability for the assignment. It was just a bit of corporate intelligence gathering after all.

Max pondered the whole situation whilst walking back to Waterloo Station. This all felt a bit strange, but he certainly wasn't going to risk charges being brought against him for his little slip-up. He resigned himself to getting on and tackling this assignment as he always did, damn well. As he boarded the Tube back to Clapham Common he couldn't help but wonder, with a tinge of excitement, what the Dark Corporation held in store for him. 'Probably just snoop around, copy a few documents and job done', he thought to himself. But it would be so much more than that.

9

Max always kept his CV up to date even when he was happy in the job he had. Years of fighting his way to the top and being ready to jump on opportunities that came his way from recommendations or head hunters had taught him that in the corporate world you're never indispensable and always have to be primed for the next big role.

He'd studied the CPO ad in the FT and after compiling an introductory letter on Word, emailed it with his CV attached to a Paul Jones at Regency, the recruiting agency the Dark Corporation had employed to handle applications.

Max had only had to apply cold for a couple of his early career jobs when he was unknown and had to rely on his CV to get him through to a first interview. After that most of his jobs came from either recommendation from people in his network, his own efforts writing directly to Chief Executives, or friendly head hunters suggesting it would be worth their while giving this 'exceptional CPO' half an hour for a chat.

At such meetings with the top executive of each firm Max would turn on the charm, engage and relax his audience with eloquent, measured professionalism extolling his experience and expertise. He'd once gone to meet a rather grumpy Chief Exec who had been told he had to see him and who sat there for the first ten minutes with his arms folded huffing and puffing at everything Max said. But gradually as Max worked his magic the man unfolded his arms, then started to smile, lean forward onto the tabletop engaging Max with more interest and finally after half an hour was talking to Max about start dates and the package. Whilst Max had performed impeccably from start to finish he was not impressed with the senior director's demeanour and attitude, so as soon as he got into his car after the interview he called the agency to say he didn't want the job there. The Chief Exec called Max later to apologise and try to persuade him to join but to no avail. It served as a good reminder for him that interviews are not just all about the candidate having to impress the potential employer, they are very much a two-way process and as Max understood when he was the interviewing manager for vacancies, you still had to impress the candidate and sell the job and the company.

Unfortunately with this faceless application process through the Regency recruitment firm Max was worried that this Paul Jones 'consultant' as they liked to call themselves, would end up with a huge pile of applications and CVs and be expected to sift through them very quickly given the short deadline for the applications. Max quickly looked the man up on LinkedIn then picked up the phone and dialled Paul's number.

A mildly harassed Paul Jones answered, "Jones here, senior consultant at Regency, how may I help you?"

Max couldn't help but muse at the man's vain pride in stating he was a *senior* consultant. He also deliberately ignored the use of his surname. "Paul, good morning, Max Sargent here, I hope you don't mind me giving you a quick call, I just wanted to make sure you'd received my application for the Dark Corporation CPO role?" The commanding and complete opening sentence quickly gave Paul Jones everything he needed to avoid time-wasting chitchat, after all, he was a busy senior consultant.

"Oh, right, good morning, Max Sargent was it, let's have a look. When did you send it across to me?" replied Paul as he opened up the Excel spreadsheet he'd painstakingly prepared to log all the applications.

Max responded. "Well actually just a few minutes ago so if you're in front of your PC perhaps you could check that it's at the top of your Inbox?"

Paul had no time to think about telling this caller he was too busy and would get back to him and found himself being swept along by the caller's charming and precise words. He opened his inbox to see Max's application email at the top.

"Max Sargent, yes here it is, I've got it," then momentarily gathering himself managed to say, "I'll have a look at it later and log it in with the others, thank you for your application."

Max wasn't going to let that ride. "Before you go, Paul, would you be so kind as to open the email and check my CV pdf file opens up okay, you know how these different formats can mess things up sometimes?"

Max deliberately wanted to get Paul to open his email and CV to visually connect his application with the call they'd had. He knew that almost no other candidate would bother to speak to this chap to introduce themselves and make an albeit small connection with him. One that would hopefully make his application more interesting and personal over the other faceless letters and CV's he'd be looking through.

Paul dutifully scanned the email then opening the CV also had a quick look through, already picking up in his mind some of the key sentences and previous jobs Max had put on the document. The bond was starting.

Paul reported, "Yes it's opened up fine. I can see from your CV you have significant experience as a CPO, so thank you again for applying, will be in touch once I have discussed the applications with the recruiting director at the Dark Corporation."

Max quickly came back with his final play. "I noticed on your LinkedIn profile Paul that you're a black belt in martial arts, that's amazing, I've also got a first Dan, in Choi Kwang Do, which style did you do?" Max really had done four years of training and gone through eighteen gradings to get his cherished Il Dan black belt.

Paul had almost been about to put the phone down thinking the call had ended but with this new topic was now fully re-engaged and flattered that Max had both taken the time to introduce himself and also bothered to look him up on the business people's website.

"Why thank you, yes it took me five long years of hard training to get that. I did Taekwondo."

Max finished, "That's great Paul, people simply don't understand the huge commitment and effort we go through to get that treasured black belt. Anyway, I mustn't keep you, I know how busy you are so I look forward to hearing from you on this vacancy, it's a role I'm confident I can make a success of. Take care and thanks again." Paul said goodbye though would have happily struck up a longer conversation about their shared martial arts achievements, 'what a nice guy' he thought to himself.

Max put the phone down quietly confident that Paul Jones of Regency recruitment would put his application amongst his highly recommended suggestions for an interview with hopefully Doreen Leader and not via some uninterested and unqualified HR executive. He called Si to report that his application was in, received and that he'd be shocked if he wasn't invited in for an interview.

Sure enough, a few days later Max received a formal looking email from Paul Jones stating that following a thorough review of all applications and discussions with the client, a shortlist of candidates had been invited for interview with the recruiting manager Doreen Leader, Chief Finance Officer of the Dark Corporation and would Max please confirm his availability to attend at the said time and date at the head office address in Guildford. Max congratulated himself that his simple two-minute call with Paul Jones had paid off apart from the fact that he was probably the best man for the job anyway, sometimes these things needed a little help along the way.

Although Max had benefited from the MI5 briefing from Vince telling him all about the Dark Corporation, Max had another day before the interview to do some more research on the company. He'd always believed that anyone turning up for an interview who didn't have a fairly good knowledge and understanding of the company they were applying to were simply wasting everyone's time. He spent the afternoon trawling through the corporation's website, accounts, presentations, videos then googled the company and some of the main directors. He scanned everything he saw sifting through in his mind a few key pieces of information that he could draw upon in the interview to demonstrate his in-depth knowledge and reading of the firm.

The next day suited and booted he climbed into his VW Golf and made his way straight down the A3 past Wimbledon and Putney then out into the Surrey countryside, over the M25 London orbital and on towards Guildford. The journey only took about 40 minutes which Max thought would be a most satisfactory commute if he got the job, as many Londoners have to be content with at least an hour travelling to and from work. Sitting in the comfort of his own car, even if he had the odd traffic jam, was always far better than squashing into a Tube train with four other people all invading his personal space coughing, yawning and sighing, oblivious of containing themselves in such a cramped space. Max smiled as he thought of the various commuters on a train he witnessed carry on with sensitive and private conversations. They'd completely forget they were sitting in a confined carriage with 30 other people, all carefully listening to every word they were saying. He remembered one particular lady speaking on the phone telling someone how she apparently gave her boss a right talking to, then after a flaming row with him told him where he could shove the job. By the end of the call, she got quite worked up about relaying the story and as she put the phone down, looked up to see almost everyone in the carriage staring at her. Then as the embarrassed lady began meeting their stares everyone quickly looked back down to their newspapers or mobile screens.

Max turned off the A3 and approached the two large smoked glass buildings of the Dark Corporation offices, parked up and went in. Having checked in with reception he took a seat and waited. The building, one of two, was impressive with four floors circling the central reception atrium which towered right up to the top of the building. On the walls hung carefully framed posters of many of the company's security products and advertising campaigns along with various industry commendations and certifications of compliance. There were also several pictures on the far side of reception of the man himself, Frank Dark, accepting various awards from distinguished celebrities or government officials. Max wondered if this man was vain, or arrogant, or there again just dutifully and professionally proud of the company he had built.

As a buyer, Max rarely had to wait in reception to be seen, as it was always the suppliers that would come to his office to meet him. Sitting in this grand atrium reminded him of the importance of making a good and perhaps slightly intimidating first impression on visitors to any corporation. It was only now whilst patiently waiting there that Max felt that first nervous knot in his stomach and remembered that unlike usual jobs he went for, where if he didn't get the role it wasn't the end of the world, he really did need to get this particular appointment given the arrangement he'd made with Si Lawson. He had to win this one. His attention drifted towards the unfortunate death of their ex-CFO John Lyttleton, where he'd read that he'd fallen to his death here in this very atrium. Max studied the marble floor imagining the scene there recently when the terrible incident occurred.

His gaze was caught by the receptionist smiling at him and nodding towards the staircase. He looked round to be greeted by the sight of a stunningly attractive woman carefully making her way down the staircase. He recognised her from Vince's presentation to be Doreen Leader his potential new boss and quickly concluded her photo didn't do her the justice she deserved. Doreen's concentration coming down the steps was not due to the pressures of work nor nervousness about interviewing another candidate, it was merely to make an impressive entrance whilst battling against the tight black pencil skirt she was wearing and four-inch-high stiletto heels. As always she managed the task admirably.

She greeted Max confidently with a firm handshake whilst introducing herself and thanking him for coming in to meet her. Max was immediately impressed by this lady who led him to the lift to go back up to the fourth floor, where she gestured towards the boardroom for their interview. Doreen placed herself at the head of the table and Max obligingly sat in one of the chairs immediately next to her, slightly turning himself to face her directly.

Doreen had already conducted several interviews for this role so now had the usual introduction about herself, the company and the CPO job down to a fine art, which she took the first 10 minutes explaining to Max. She then handed over to him with a number of open discussion-style questions such as "So tell me about yourself Max?" and "why do you think I should pick you over other candidates for this role?" Such questions gave the candidate plenty of latitude to either impress her with clear, relevant and concise answers. Or for those less equipped people it provided an opening for awkward, disjointed and badly thought through answers completely missing the opportunity to impress and ending up doing the exact opposite. Max, however, was in his forte, his answers were measured, well thought through, he had a wealth of good examples and facts to drop in, he was professional and charming. Doreen felt herself giving way on several topics to his logical and highly persuasive arguments. She was beginning to think that Max Sargent just might be the CPO she was looking for, although the last candidate a Liam Summers had also been pretty impressive and had already met Frank Dark who seemed to like him a lot.

"So how would your colleagues describe you, Max, in just a few adjectives?" she asked.

Max replied without hesitation as this was often a question he would ask. "Professional, loyal, reasonable, excellent communication skills, high integrity and reliably goal focused." After several decades in business dealing with lots of people, these were the attributes that defined Max and also what he hoped for in other people. Acting professionally embodied everything you do and the way you do it. All bosses want staff to be loyal to them and put them first, reasonableness was rarely mentioned by candidates to Max but was an important attribute in dealing with both people and negotiating with suppliers. Given that most things in life are all about people, then communication skills are a prerequisite to succeeding with almost anything. Integrity was a vital component of any senior managerial post and especially in procurement where you are being trusted to handle and agree huge spend numbers, and finally, every boss wants someone they know will just get on and ensure the job is done.

Doreen smiled approvingly and allowed herself to openly admit to Max, "That's probably the best answer I've ever heard to that simple question, thank you Max." She went on to the next question.

"Let's say you get the job, what are the first things you'd do during your initial month?"

Because Max had had a number of these jobs, he was well versed in getting to grips with a new role in a new organisation during that critical first four weeks when everyone was watching you. "Firstly Doreen I'd sit down with you to understand what your priorities were, whether you had any critical deadlines or urgent things needing sorting, then I would prioritise meeting staff across the procurement community in the UK and other regions via FaceTime calls. Next, I'd get round management and stakeholders, you can't leave it too long before getting in front of everyone important before they start thinking you've ignored them or don't realise how senior they are. At the same time, I would be asking staff to pull together summaries of all spends, major supplier terms, savings, present and planned activities so I had a good overall view of where procurement sits across the organisation and what the immediate opportunities and priorities are for me to get onto."

Doreen held up her hand stopping Max from needing to continue with his answer, "No need for any more, I can see you know exactly the right things that need to be done." They spent another 20 minutes talking as the conversation turned away from testing interrogatory style questions and more towards getting to know one another, their characters and the way they liked to work, would they be a fit. Max knew at this point that Doreen was starting to think more about how well they could work together rather than if he had the skills to do the job. They seemed to click well and as the conversation came to a natural end Doreen wanted to get on with the process of hiring Max so excused herself from the room to go and find Frank Dark to see if he could pop in and meet Max for himself. She knew that Frank wanted to be involved in such a senior appointment so she may as well try to get him in here now whilst

Max was there rather than have to rebook another date. She went straight into Frank's office and as he looked up from his screen, she explained to him excitedly she thought she might have their new CPO sat in the boardroom and would like him to meet this Max Sargent right away.

Frank Dark confidently strode into his boardroom exuding presence, authority and power. Max immediately stood to greet him and again smiled at Doreen as they both entered. This time it was Frank who sat at the head of the table and Doreen and Max sat in the chairs either side of him. Doreen introduced Frank with a brief bio and summary of his founding and Chief Exec role of the Dark Corporation. Max was acutely conscious of this successful, wealthy man closely studying him as he listened to Doreen, gently smiling and occasionally meeting Frank's strong gaze.

"Well Max it seems you've made a good impression with my new CFO Doreen, how do you feel your interview went?" Frank opened.

Another open question thought Max. "I very much enjoyed talking with Doreen, we seemed to have a lot in common and I hope I managed to convince her that my experience and expertise would put me in a good position to do some great things for you in the CPO role. It sounds very exciting here at your impressive corporation Mr Dark." Max had endeavoured to balance his answer with the right amount of confidence, humility and praise of his new interviewer. He noticed Frank's head ever so slightly betray a small nod of approval.

The boardroom door opened and John Dawlish the CTO slid in with an apologetic nod to Frank Dark for being a little late. As Frank had made his way to meet Max he'd asked his personal assistant Sheila to see if John could also join them in the boardroom for his view on another CPO candidate. John shuffled down the side of the boardroom table, quickly introducing himself to Max and took a seat several places away from the three of them at the top of the table. He gestured to Frank as if to say, 'You carry on, don't mind me.'

Frank then touched briefly on a few procurement-related technical questions before then focusing more on Max's character and beliefs. He also threw in a few more personal probing scenario questions.

"What annoys you at work Max?" wanting to see if this candidate might have a fiery temper. He wouldn't want any prima donna's.

"I wouldn't say anything *annoys* me at work, I'm not one to get angry at anything, perhaps just a little impatient or frustrated when I can't get things done as fast as I'd like to." Max fielded the question knowing what it was fishing for.

"How do you know when you've got a good deal?" asked Frank.

"There are a number of ways one can get an indication of whether they might have a good deal, clearly they will have gone through a tender process which allows lots of suppliers responses to be compared and benchmarked like-for-like. Using extensive market or product research including trends, seeing what the competition is doing with a similar product or pricing and undertaking a full cost breakdown enables you to determine what the supplier's costs and therefore margin might be. Also, perhaps the willingness a supplier has when you're pushing them to walk away from the deal is usually another indicator you've probably got them to their limit."

Frank paused with an expression that looked like he was dumbstruck by the comprehensive answer. He was just taking in each part for his own knowledge embellishment, whilst studying the young man sitting in front of him. Satisfied he continued.

"Let's say you're in a meeting with a supplier, you've spent a lot of time putting a deal together and you're just at the point where you're going to close the agreement. I come in and interrupt the meeting and ask you to pop out with me as I have something urgent that needs your attention." He paused for effect and to again study Max's face. "How do you feel about that?"

Max imagined the scenario he'd just been put in and was

already onto the trap neatly set for him to fall into. He knew that most people envisaging themselves in that situation of being about to close a big deal wouldn't want any interruptions and would probably find themselves blurting out disappointment or even outrage. He answered calmly and concisely.

"I'd ask the people in the room if I could please be excused, apologise and thank them in advance for waiting to continue until I returned, but that my Chief Exec needed me for an urgent matter and I was sure they'd understand."

Frank now allowed himself to nod and smile openly, turning to Doreen saying, "I like him." Back to Max, "A pleasure to meet you Max, Doreen's probably explained that we have a few other candidates to consider so we'll be in touch very shortly with whether we wish to progress or not."

John Dawlish who had been quietly watching and listening to the proceedings but hadn't said anything, rose from his seat and followed Frank out of the boardroom closing the door behind him. Doreen thanked Max again for his time and explained she had one other candidate to see then she would discuss everything with Frank and John and hopefully be in touch one way or the other in the next few days. As she escorted Max to the lift she quietly hinted that she hoped Frank would share her view on him but that there was another candidate they'd seen that Frank also seemed to like so she would be fighting Max's corner for him. As Max got into the lift, Doreen felt drawn to watching him closely, there was something about him she liked. Max turned around as the lift doors closed and Doreen quickly turned on her high heels and walked away. Max watched her impressive figure closely as it swayed off.

Max returned to his car, opened up his Notes app and called Si Lawson to update him on his interview performance with Doreen Leader and that he'd also met Frank Dark and John Dawlish. Si was interested to know what Max thought of them, especially Frank, but Max explained at this stage they all seemed very professional and that Frank was certainly the big Boss man with a discerning view of others.

"There was just one thing you should know," Max advised, "I'm pretty sure Doreen has me as her number one choice but on the way out she did mention to me that there was another candidate that Frank Dark might prefer. I've done everything I can to win this job Si but there's no accounting for taste, so it sounds like it's going to be a close call on who they choose."

Si asked Max, "I don't suppose she mentioned who this other candidate was did she?"

"I'm afraid not."

Si thought for a moment. "We've got to ensure you get this job otherwise I've got no other way right now of finding out what's going on there. Hmm, it's a little unorthodox but I'll ask Alan the techie guy here if he's got any ideas on how we might be able to help the situation. Regency wasn't it, the recruiting agency?"

"Yes," confirmed Max, "and the guy there I spoke to was called Paul Jones."

"Okay leave it with me and tell me if you hear anything in the meantime?" said Si leaving the call.

After showing Max to the lift Doreen had gone straight back to Frank's office to discuss the candidates.

"Frank, I know I've still got one more interview booked in but honestly I think Max Sargent is the one I want to offer the CPO role to, what do you think?" pitched Doreen confidently.

Frank tore himself away from his screen and keyboard and reclined back in his comfortable executive chair, pondering for a moment, it was a big decision.

"I know you want to get on with it, but shouldn't you at least see the last candidate before we make a choice?"

"Max is my choice so why waste any more time, let me make him an offer along the lines of the parameters we discussed reference package?"

Frank countered. "I thought Max was very good, great answers, looks the part, but there was just something about him I can't quite put my finger on that I'm not sure about. He was very assured."

"But we want someone who is confident and assured, it's a big role and we need someone who can get straight into the big savings we know there are," said Doreen playing to Frank's monetary side.

Frank still wasn't convinced. "No, my view is the candidate we saw yesterday, Liam Summers, he's the one for the job. Granted he's not quite up to Max Sargent's level but we want someone we can mould into the team quickly, perhaps a little more compliant. Being part of the team is really important to me Doreen, you know that."

Doreen could feel she was starting to lose this battle and continued with growing visible frustration. "Come on Frank, I'm the one this role reports into, I'll be managing him day-to-day, not you. I hear your view on both of them and I'm sure we can as you say mould Max into whatever you want, I believe he is a very loyal person. Let me offer him the role?"

Frank listened and carefully watched Doreen's usual cool momentarily fade as she wasn't getting what she wanted. "Enough of this now, I've made my decision, offer the role to Liam Summers and I'd ask you to now please get behind that decision," bringing the discussion to a swift close.

He didn't like to disagree with his new CFO and as Doreen nodded her compliance and turned to leave the office, he said, "I tell you what, if the Summers bloke pushes back on the package or it falls through for some other reason, then I'm entirely happy for you to offer the job to Max Sargent."

Doreen Leader's frown instantly became a knowing smile as she exited Frank's office.

Back at Thames House Si Lawson had asked Alan the young technology guy who'd sorted out Max's iPhone to pop up to his office. It wasn't often Alan got a call from such a senior MI5 manager and team leader and on the way up was desperately trying to think what he might have done wrong. Perhaps the installs he'd put into that Max Sargent's phone might have failed. He nervously went into Mr Lawson's office and could see immediately from the look on his face that he was probably in the clear.

Si briefly explained to Alan that Max was being considered for the role he needed him to get but that there was one other candidate also in the frame.

"Is there anything we can do, or rather you, to help Max gets offered the job," asked Si. Alan looked a little puzzled with a tiny shrug of his shoulders.

Si elaborated more clearly this time. "How about this then. The employer will likely ask the recruitment agency to do a basic vetting on the two candidates. Perhaps there's something you can dig up, with your analytics and research hat on, that shall we say might not look too good for the other candidate?"

The penny dropped and Alan looked up, eyebrows raised with a big grin. He closed his eyes for a moment and quickly thought through some options then as another lightbulb went off proudly announced, "Firstly I need to find out the name of this other candidate which I assume you don't have otherwise you would have already told me. To do that I need to hack into the recruitment agencies back-office, just their emails, then I should be able to pick out who this other person is."

Si nodded and smiled for Alan to continue, he was on a roll now.

"Once I have a name I can then do a vetting process myself to see if the person has any skeletons in their cyber closets, exams, schools, records, and of course the motherload of all negative information I'm likely to find on him," shaking his head in disapproval of it he added, "his social media trail, both live and deleted."

"That's brilliant," congratulated Si. "But I now need you to get onto this immediately, and I mean as soon as you leave this office, do it now. We don't know when these guys will be vetted by the recruitment agency, by the way, they're called Regency and the guy dealing with Max was a Paul Jones. Keep me updated, no one else to know please, and it goes without saying, don't leave any footprints yourself when you go into their system."

Alan practically ran out of the office and couldn't wait to get back to his computers to tackle this exciting assignment.

Paul Jones at Regency recruitment put the phone down from speaking with Doreen Leader the CFO at the Dark Corporation who had just given him her first and second choices for their CPO role. He was sorry that the nice chap he spoke to recently had got the second-choice position but as requested by Doreen would carry out the standard vetting process on both candidates. Paul was impressed at how quickly Doreen had got on with the task of briefing him, approving the ad, conducting the interviews and now was ready to make an offer. It seemed the Dark Corporation paid way over the market norm and he was very keen to wrap this up quickly as his commission on this particular assignment would be one of the largest he'd ever earned. He had a busy day ahead of him so would leave the vetting until later this afternoon to do with a nice cup of tea.

Meanwhile, Alan had managed to find his way into the Regency recruitment firm's back-office servers by searching round the rather basic coding on their website which had a very lightly protected link into their systems to enable their consultants to update online jobs and announcements from their individual PCs. Alan was always amused at how easy some companies were to hack through their business websites. Once inside their system, he'd been able to look at a mirror image of Paul Jones's Outlook files and individual emails. After a few minutes of searching through, he found the email exchange between him and Doreen Leader giving the two leading candidates names as Liam Summers and Max Sargent.

Next, Alan trawled all his usual online directories, registers and of course Google to see if anything untoward appeared for Mr Summers. Nothing stood out so he moved on to the far more interesting areas of social media to look through and could see that the man had infrequently used accounts with LinkedIn, Facebook,

Google, Pinterest and a dating agency, but the one Mr Summers was using on a very regular basis was Instagram.

Alan spent the next hour looking through every picture and posting Mr Summers had made or commented on during the last nine years, he was an early adopter of the app, but couldn't find anything negative. He had one last avenue to explore which for him was always the most exciting when snooping around someone's past activities and that was the deleted postings. One of the privileges of working at MI5's Cyber division was their unpublicised access to all those postings and pictures that the public thought they'd permanently deleted never to be seen again.

Alan pulled up the various codes and programming procedures to get into the right system, then as access appeared against Mr Summers' account he shuffled his chair forward so he was closer to the screen and started to scroll through the man's deleted pictures. Given these were the photographs that had been posted when it seemed like a good idea at the time and then in the light of day had clearly been inappropriate and quickly deleted, it didn't take long for Alan to find one particular posting that would work a treat.

Paul Jones retreated to his desk with a nice cup of tea and made himself comfortable to go through the vetting of the two Dark CPO candidates. Such reviews rarely pulled up anything of interest, these were top executives with long careers who surely had been vetted many times over before today. However, this was a big role with big commission, so he may as well go through the usual checks.

Many professional recruitment agencies use vetting companies to do a proper job of going through the backgrounds of potential candidates, but Regency had always felt subscribing to one of these firms to do what their staff were quite capable of doing themselves was a waste of money. Paul went through his list of around 10 things to check on Max Sargent and everything looked just fine. Having looked through Max's career and spoken to him recently Paul briefly wondered why he hadn't got the job over Liam

Summers, he felt Max was the better candidate.

Paul now worked his way down the list of items to check for Mr Summers and ninth on the list was merely written 'Check social media for inappropriate postings'. He found little activity against the man's Facebook account and then logged into Instagram to finally look through this then he was done. His eyes focused in on the fourth posting from the top just visible at the bottom of the first screen view and he sat bolt upright spilling hot tea onto his desk. 'Bloody hell' he thought as he re-examined the screen.

The posting was time-tagged earlier that day and in his shock, he didn't notice it as odd that this senior executive would now put up such an inappropriate photo. It showed an old picture of a younger-looking Liam Summers on a beach somewhere at night-time with a bunch of mates. They were all clearly smoking something undesirable, most had hand-rolled spliffs, with one of the lads also bending over a large stone about to take in a line of white powder. "Oh my God, I don't believe it, geez, that's it for you Mr Summers, you've blown it."

Minutes later Doreen put the phone down from a very excitable and apologetic Paul Jones at Regency. She sat back in her chair and smiled. She'd pick her moment to mention it to Frank, perhaps when he was busy and preoccupied with other matters. She'd be offering the CPO role to her choice, Max Sargent.

10

Max was in his VW golf back on the A3 driving down to Guildford for his first day as Chief Procurement Officer with the Dark Corporation. Doreen Leader had called him shortly after they'd met with the news that despite tough competition and another very strong application, she'd persuaded Frank Dark that he was the best man for the job and hoped he could start immediately. Max had already worked out that Doreen was a highly astute woman but on this occasion her apparent excitement to tell him he'd got the job had pushed to one side what should usually be the first exploratory discussion. That of the package. Max smiled to himself, for as soon as it was clear Doreen wanted him and didn't have another option, all the chips fell in his favour going into the salary and benefits negotiation. He knew Doreen would likely have been given an upper limit by Frank Dark and after a fair bit of back-and-forth on the call he was happy he pushed Doreen to the top of her band, after all, neither of them wanted Frank to have to be involved again, it could have allowed him to change his mind.

From his two decades in the business, Max knew the average large company procurement directors could get a total package of between £50,000 to £130,000 and CPO's were probably earning totals of anywhere from £130,000 up to £400,000. For the last couple of jobs, Max had been in excess of this upper level and was delighted to have secured a package from Doreen more than double his previous salary at just under £1 million. From talking to Doreen this felt like the upper number Frank had given her. This included his basic salary, a discretionary annual bonus that Frank and Doreen would award against his achievement of goals and key performance indicators. There was a small golden handshake payment rarely offered these days as a sign-on bonus. Also short-term and long-term incentive plans offering share options and finally all the usual fringe benefits like a cash car allowance, private health insurance and help with mortgages, loans and moving house.

As Max peeled off the A3 and approached the two large black buildings he knew it was unlikely he would be at the Dark Corporation much longer than 3 to 6 months given this was not a long-term career move but a one-off investigative job for Si Lawson. He wondered if maybe he might discover the information Si needed in his first few weeks and then be free to get on with his life and career. At least he'd be able to use his latest remuneration package as leverage for any future jobs.

Max entered the building and so began those first few critical weeks of absorbing and learning tons of information, numbers, product details, and meeting, impressing and assessing lots of people. Trying to work out who was important, relevant, political, good and as always, those who were utterly useless in their jobs. Max's father had always told him, "You'll always find someone that does half the amount of work you do but gets paid twice as much, don't worry about it, it's a fact of life."

Max never forgot listening to the opening introduction from a previous managing director on his first day addressing the senior staff in front of him. He said at the end whilst closely eyeing the senior executives and to everyone's surprise, "Now I know that every company has an arsehole somewhere near the top, a highly political, troublemaking corporate terrorist if you will. You're in here somewhere so fair warning to you, when I find out who you are, you're straight out the door! Right everyone, thank you for your time, let's get to work." Probably not something you'd get away with in today's times and political correctness, but it certainly made an impression on Max as he wondered who the difficult person was going to be at the Dark company.

Max worked long days to start with, not just because everyone was watching him and his staff were taking their lead from him, but simply because he wanted to get up to speed as quickly as possible. He hated being in a position where other people knew more about what was going on than he did. That lack of information, contacts and relationships always frustrated him at the beginning, as it prevented him from making decisions and improvements and getting on with the job in hand.

He had a relatively small procurement team with around 12 staff with him at the HQ sitting in open-plan outside Max's office on the third floor, and another 10 buyers dotted around the world in key countries being the States, France, Germany, South Africa, Italy, Dubai, India, Australia, Hong Kong and China. On the whole, his team seemed pretty good and whilst he started concluding there may be a handful of them who were not effective or best placed in their roles, he knew it was unlikely he'd be around long enough to have to deal with them. The priority for Max right now was to keep asking questions, investigate everything going on across the corporation. Under the guise of his CPO role, no spends or any part of the business should be off-limits to him, he'd try to find out what the ex-CFO had a problem with that was so important to tell MI5 about.

Once Max had settled in and got his feet under his desk the most important task was to gain a complete understanding of all the company's external spends with suppliers, that was his battlefield and where he'd be able to start reviewing contracts and making significant savings to impress Doreen and Frank with. He asked all his procurement staff to gather together into spreadsheets every single supplier spend for the last 12 months each labelled into product and service categories and tagged with the country and part of the business they supplied. If they didn't already have this information he told them to get it immediately from their financial systems or accounts payable departments. Information was power for procurement and they had to have a clear start point of understanding every spend and supplier across the whole business.

Max was looking through never-ending reports in his glass-walled office on the third floor and noticed Doreen Leader gliding through his team outside coming towards him. Because they were both relatively new starters at the company, they had already built an affinity for one another and felt like the new team on the block.

"Hi Max, how's it all going, I've got another date for your diary and it's an important one," said Doreen not waiting for an answer and continuing. "Frank's got his big quarterly review meeting with the top team in a week and you and I need to start showing them all how wonderful we are. I'll be covering finance across the organisation, we have far too many people and I've got quite a few big change recommendations I'll be making. You need to put together your first views and recommendations of global procurement with a full playback of everything we are currently doing on suppliers and spends."

Max responded, "Sounds good to me Doreen, I've already got the team working on exactly that, so I'll be ready to take you through some draft slides in a few days."

"Fabulous Max, I kinda suspected you would already have that in hand, just pop in as soon as you've got your draft presentation ready." Doreen walked out smiling thinking again she'd definitely picked the right person for the role. Max couldn't help but watch her as she walked back past his team with the male and some of the female staff watching her intently whilst pretending to be getting on with work.

During a number of conversations with members of his team, Max was conscious of them often referring to his predecessor in the CPO role being an independent individual who liked to do things his own way and perhaps pushed his remit too far. One of his guys had told Max, now that his old boss had gone, "James was a bit odd, not really a team player, certainly not with us and I don't think he won over too many people up at Frank's level either. Probably his downfall, we never quite knew why he left so suddenly, of course, he came and told us he'd got another big job to go to but I think he must have fallen out with either John Lyttleton or maybe even Frank Dark."

Max had afterwards asked someone in IT if he could have access to his predecessor's emails given he was never able to have a handover from this James chap. His emails would contain important information and documents that Max would need to have possession of and understand. Shortly after he spoke to the person in IT John Dawlish came to see Max.

John said somewhat sensitively, "One of my guys tells me you want to see the old CPO's emails, how come?"

Max sensed John's interrogatory manner and was careful not to react to it. "Not having met the guy, this James, I'm just concerned that I might be missing something important he was working on or perhaps needing to be across some of his last communications with key suppliers on deals and activities."

John wasn't budging. "Well you can get all of that from your team can't you, they should have been across anything James was doing?"

"I don't think James would have shared all of his work and emails with his staff do you? If it's a problem, John, then no worries, but don't lay it on me if I miss something important if it's not shared with me. I don't know what I don't know." Max hoped he hadn't gone too far.

John Dawlish was slightly taken aback then abruptly said, "James was obviously in a mood before he left and deleted most of his email files before he went, one of my staff had a look after he handed over his laptop." Max couldn't help wonder why John hadn't mentioned this at the beginning. John concluded whilst turning to walk back out, "I shouldn't worry about it Max and I'll cover you if anything does bite you in the arse from what James might have been working on."

Max politely smiled at John and watched him leave, but he wasn't at all satisfied. Whenever someone told him not to bother looking at a spend or that they already had a great deal so no need to look at it, Max's interest in it would always be sparked. Invariably he'd later find something that could be improved or some underlying hidden discrepancy. Max had also learned that John ran a tight ship there in IT, judging by how fast he got to hear about his initial conversation with his staff member about the ex CPO. 'What was he hiding,' Max thought.

During his first few weeks, Max had to go through the usual

IT setup processes and have help with various computer niggles and logins. Each time he'd been visited in his office by a young and highly efficient girl from John Dawlish's IT Department called Sian Reeves. She was an attractive curvaceous girl in her 30s with bleached hair and a couple of tattoos on her arms only occasionally on display when she wore shorter-sleeved blouses or tops. She'd always come bouncing into Max's office greeting him with a "Hi Max what have you gone and done now," joking with him about the next thing she'd need to fix that he'd gone and messed up on his PC. The two of them got on really well, not in the sense they'd ever have a relationship, they just clicked together and always had a bit of a laugh whenever their paths crossed.

From the way she referred to the rest of the IT department, Max deduced that despite her bubbly personality she was probably a bit of a loner amongst the usual IT geeks in her department. She didn't sound as though her loyalties lay too close to her line manager or ultimate boss John Dawlish.

During one of Sian's visits up to Max's office, she needed to get him logged into HR's online training tools which all staff had to go through and verify that they understood the company's policy on such dull items as health and safety, Internet security and staff training, ensuring your workstation and seating position were ergonomically correct. Max had been building up to asking her about access to his predecessor's emails ever since his conversation with John Dawlish and felt that today was the day he needed to broach the subject with her.

"Sian, you've helped so much with my bloomin' computer I really appreciate it and was wondering if you might be able to help me with something else?" Max opened.

"Of course Max, what have you gone and done now?" joshed Sian.

"I need to have a look at my predecessor's emails before he left, just to check I'm not missing any important deadlines he might have been working on for the old CFO or Frank Dark."

"That shouldn't be a problem, I can just get you his email

password and you should be able to login as him and see his email files," said Sian, pleased to be able to help Max once again.

"There's a couple of problems though," said Max. "Firstly I gather James deleted most of his email files before he left and presumably would have known not to just leave them in the Deleted folder." Sian's happy smile dropped and her top lip curled up. "And secondly I'd rather not bother John Dawlish with this, he might not like me looking through an ex-employee's emails, you know data protection and all that." He looked up at Sian standing alongside him at his desk to gauge her reaction.

"Crikey Max that's asking a lot."

Max thought he'd blown it, but Sian then continued.

"I'm not too bothered about the data protection thing nor to be honest my boss finding out, but once emails have been deleted from the Deleted folder they're kind of gone," explained Sian.

Max's many years of negotiating and listening out for the slightest hint of flexibility or unspoken nugget of information betrayed by a look or a word, immediately tuned him into a possible chink of opportunity.

"When you say the deleted emails are 'kind of gone' what did you mean by that Sian," he asked.

Sian thought for a moment. "Well I wouldn't call myself a computer programmer by any stretch of the imagination, but I do know that once something is typed and emailed, texted, saved or posted, it's never really, truly deleted. It's always out there somewhere if you know where to look."

"Where would that be, for example regarding James's emails?" checked Max carefully.

"Everything gets saved, recorded or mirrored somewhere, in the back office, on mainframe servers, networks, caches and drives. They don't just give anyone in IT access to those kinds of sensitive, confidential systems, it's probably all sitting with the supplier's servers somewhere else." She continued thinking then added, "I imagine here at Dark they must have a terminal somewhere in IT that enables them to login to these systems for routine maintenance, upgrades and troubleshooting."

"Look Sian I don't want to get you into any trouble but is there any way you might be able to find out where such a terminal might be in the office and how you'd get access to it?" Max asked.

"That should be a breeze," Sian replied. "Most of the nerdy guys I work with have the hots for me. I'm sure I can find one unsuspecting sap who'll know. Let me get back to you on that, sounds like a nice challenge for me."

Max had a good response from his team around the world in collating all the spend information he'd requested and had already amalgamated the many spreadsheets into one huge master showing pretty much every supplier, spend type and value by country across the whole group. He'd then summarised this onto charts for the main regions and products and services applying the 80-20 rule where the majority of the spends came from a relatively small number of the bigger suppliers.

He'd also drafted a number of slides using either bullets or nicely laid out boxes with his findings on the procurement organisation, split between Present, Goals then leading onto his Recommendations. Towards the end of the deck he'd covered off the all-important potential savings and benefits he would be expected to deliver. He was pretty satisfied with what he managed to pull together in just a few weeks. Max was always amazed when coming into an organisation which already had a procurement function, at the lack of basic information and progress he'd have expected his predecessor to have already made. This was one of the attractions to Max of working in procurement, it was very rare to find a function that had got everything sorted and was running perfectly. Procurement was an infinite process and there were always benefits and savings to be found, each deal was only the best deal on the day it was done and would quickly be taken over by improving technologies, more competitive suppliers and cost bases and improving supply market trends and choices. Max had sat in front of Chief Execs in the past outlining to them what perfect blue-sky procurement functions looked like, safe in the knowledge the Chief Exec's own procurement department couldn't possibly be doing everything he was mentioning.

He gathered his slides and went off to see Doreen. Sitting down with her to the side of her desk they went through the information and discussed it all in detail, it was as much a learning exercise for her as it was for Max. As they talked and went through the slides, he found himself being drawn into her eyes. He was sure there was nothing in it, sexually, they were just so enchanting to look into.

"How are you finding working with Frank and John," Max casually asked Doreen.

"They're both great, I don't have that much to do with John and his IT staff but I'm in and out of Frank's office every day. I guess I'm still in that honeymoon period and as he builds his trust in me he's giving me more of a reign to get on and do things myself without me constantly checking with him," said Doreen.

"As the newbies in the team it does feel like we are yet to earn our wings and to be fully accepted, but I guess these guys have worked together for decades building up 'their baby', it's understandable," added Max.

The door then suddenly opened and Frank Dark popped his head in seeing the two of them at the desk. "What are you two chatting about then? Doreen, have you got a moment?"

Doreen quickly answered. "Max was just taking me through his draft slides for your quarterly review, they're looking good, we've got lots of information to share with you and some big ideas."

"Great, I'll look forward to it, but I'll be the judge of whether they're big ideas or not," and with that, he disappeared again back to his office.

"I'd better go and see what he wants. Let's knock their socks off at this presentation next week and show them how we can help improve their company to everyone's benefit," said Doreen.

As Max walked out of Doreen's office he felt he had a good ally in his new boss and was desperate to share with her the task he had been given by Si Lawson at MI5. But that would be way too foolish of him at least at this stage, to assume she wouldn't report him to Frank and blow his cover. Max felt quite alone all of a sudden, reminded again why he was here and what he had to do.

Max later came across Sian at one of the coffee machines and she seemed keen to take him to one side and quietly update him.

"You owe me Max, I think I've had a bit of a breakthrough on that email thing you asked me about. I found one of the lads who seemed to know all about it, but as part of coaxing the information out of him I had to agree to him buying me lunch in the canteen one day," relayed Sian.

"That doesn't sound so bad, what's the problem?" asked Max.

"You haven't seen him," joked Sian, "he's not the prettiest boy in the bunch." They both chuckled then she continued. "As I suspected, there is one terminal inside the air-conditioned server room which has access to the system areas we'd need to get into to view your bloke's deleted emails."

"What do you mean *we*?" asked Max. "I thought you could just copy them or print them out for me?"

Sian shook her head. "No bloody way Max, I'm not going in there by myself. Anyway, you need to be there to have a look for whatever it is you think you need to see, I don't know what you're after and I'm not doing any copying or printing thank you very much."

"Okay, okay, I get it, so how do we do this," conceded Max.

"My lot in IT tend to work quite late but they don't usually start coming into the office in the morning until about nine-ish. I know John Dawlish is at some meeting in town tomorrow so why don't you pop down to IT and see me around 7:30 AM?" said Sian.

Max agreed and conscious that a couple of Sian's IT lads were waiting to get coffee and probably starting to wonder if the pair of them had something going on, they went their separate ways.

The next day Max was in at his usual time of just after 7:15

and as he walked over to the lift he had a quick lookup to the fourth floor and was relieved to see all was quiet at this early hour. He exited the lift and walked along a corridor which passed unseen one of the sales and HR offices and went into the IT area. As he entered the large open office he was thankful to see it appeared empty apart from Sian dutifully sitting at her desk on the far side. As he came into full view of the office he saw a couple of youngsters in the corner behind him already working at their desks. 'Damn it' he thought as he proceeded over to Sian.

"What about those two over there?" he asked Sian as he flicked his head towards them over his shoulder.

"And good morning to you too Max," she greeted him. "Don't worry about those two, they're just a couple of temporary interns, not the slightest bit interested in what we're doing." Max thought Sian was taking this all much more in her stride than he was, there again she probably had less to lose and wasn't that bothered about their little exercise.

Sian picked up a post-it note with some scribblings on it and led Max along the back of the office and through another smaller office to a door at the end.

"This is our main server room, it'll be a bit cold in there but the terminal should be inside." With that, she opened the door and a blast of cool air hit them both in the face as they walked in. The medium-sized room was full of aisles with shelving stacked high with flashing, buzzing equipment, servers and computers the likes of which Max couldn't recognise one from the next. They walked the length of the first aisle and then spotted a desk with a PC terminal hidden away in the far corner.

"This must be the access terminal," said Sian triumphantly. She sat down. "Just give me a few moments to figure out how to get in from what my friend told me."

Max stood there nervously out of his comfort zone watching Sian refer back-and-forth between the post-it note and the keyboard and screen. There seemed to be a lot of gateways and logins to go through but finally, Sian let out a gratifying "Yesss!"

"I'm in. Wow, I've never seen this before, it really does keep a trail of everything everyone does with their computers." She familiarised herself with the various menus then as a quick test or maybe just curiosity searched her own name, a new menu appeared. "Oh my God, they can view my live emails, deleted emails, the intranet pages I've viewed and all of my Internet browsing history, even though I always delete it. Do you want to sit here and have a look for your procurement man's stuff?"

She slipped out of the seat and Max sat down. He looked blankly at the screen then back at Sian. She exited the current menu then said, "Just type your guy's name in the search field and you should get what you're looking for."

Max typed in his name 'James Montague' and after hitting Enter was shown a menu of the various areas he now had access to. He selected Email and was then taken to a slightly user-unfriendly list of hundreds of email titles which had to be clicked on to expand them into the full email showing recipients, text and any attachments.

Max started to browse through some of the emails finding a few interesting ones to read through but only covering business, supplier or staff-related matters. His heart rate started to increase as he thought if he could bring himself to dare to look into Frank Dark's emails or would there be some alarm tag waiting to catch him out as soon as he typed in Frank's name. No, it was too risky, and frankly, he was scared of the consequences if he got caught. He had another idea.

Turning to Sian he said, "I just need another minute on this, can you pop out and check down the corridor that no one's likely to walk in on us?"

Sian complied and walked back down the aisle between the servers and out the door.

Max turned his attention back to the screen and bringing up the main search field again slowly and deliberately typed in a new name. 'John Lyttleton'.

He took a deep breath as the menu options appeared and

waited a few moments expecting the computer to start flashing with alarm bells ringing and warning signs on the screen. But the computer sat there quietly and patiently waiting for him to select from the choices in front of him. Max hit Email and immediately the same huge list of emails appeared including those that had been supposedly permanently deleted, denoted with a tiny Asterix next to each. Max could feel his heart practically jumping out of his chest at this point as he quickly looked down the list from the top.

Behind him, he could hear quick footsteps coming down the corridor which he assumed to be Sian spooked by someone approaching. He concentrated back on the email list in front of him and then spotted one email title he believed it was worth taking a few extra valuable seconds to open. The subject of the email read 'Resignation'.

Sian burst through the server room door as Max opened up the email which could be seen on the screen from start to finish. He quickly grabbed his phone and took a picture of the screen just as Sian appeared beside him hurriedly saying, "Some of the guys in the office have arrived early. We need to get outta here right now!"

As she was speaking Max exited the email and menu screens back to the empty search box. He quickly stood up saying, "Here, log out or shut it down, whatever you need to do then let's go."

Sian didn't bother sitting and lent over to the keyboard, logged out and closed down the terminal. As they both quickly walked down the aisle Max suggested to Sian, "If anyone asks us you were just showing me around as the new boy." Sian nodded as they exited the door and moved across the smaller office towards the corridor. As they entered it they could see down into the main open IT office where people were starting to gather and one particular manager looked up and saw them.

As he started to make his way towards them, Max suddenly remembered something. Looking at Sian he whispered, "You did pick up your piece of paper didn't you?"

Sian frowned and without saying a word turned around and ran back through the small office and into the server room. She'd left her post-it note with the passwords on the terminal desktop.

The IT manager was now coming down the corridor and walking deliberately towards Max, looking slightly suspicious and curious. Max gathered himself and calmly went to greet him saying, "Good morning, I'm Max Sargent the new Chief Procurement Officer," knowing that he had to explain who he was quickly and perhaps throwing in the big title would help. He continued, "I was having a chat with Sian the other day and couldn't believe when she told me how cold the server room was and when I bumped into her this morning as we arrived I asked if I could see for myself." Max had had to think very quickly but was pleased with his explanation which from the relaxing demeanour of the IT manager may have done the trick.

The IT man looked over Max's shoulder to see where Sian had gone. "Ah, okay Mr Sargent, I guess that's okay, although you're not meant to go into the server room without authorised access, there's a lot of precious kit in there. I should just notify Mr Dawlish anyway, he likes to know who comes and goes," said the man. Max's heart missed a beat. Before he could speak the IT man looked behind Max again then asked, "Where's Sian anyway?"

Max was about to start another blag but was saved by Sian appearing behind him and concurring to the IT man, "Oh hi Martin, bit silly of me, I was just showing Mr Sargent our new CPO how cold the server room needs to be kept, he didn't believe me when I told him." She gave him a big girly cheeky smile and made her way past him beckoning to Max. "Come on Mr Sargent, before Martin thinks we are having some odd office affair or something."

Max smiled at Martin as he passed him who seemed placated by their reasons for being there and was now feeling a little awkward about the notion he might have walked in on some office romance. Leaving him behind and as they made their way into the main open IT office Max whispered to Sian, "Was that such a good idea to joke around with him like that? He said he'd have to tell Dawlish!"

Sian lent over and whispered back, "Martin's a nice guy and if he thought for a moment something was going on between you and me, there's no way he'd dream of snitching on us and getting us into trouble. We can't have him mentioning that he saw us both down here to John Dawlish, so let's leave him with the thought we're having a fling and hope he doesn't tell anyone." She separated away back to her desk as Max exited the IT area, thinking for a moment that a fling with Sian wouldn't be such a bad thing.

Martin came back into the main office and watched Max leaving thinking to himself, 'Bloody senior executives, come down here and get off with one of our best birds, bloody liberty'. Accepting the two of them were indeed having an office liaison, and albeit jealous, Martin certainly had no intention of mentioning this to anyone else, especially not his boss.

"What on earth are you doing down here with my IT lot?" asked John Dawlish curiously, almost bumping into Max leaving.

Max jumped, "Jees, John, you gave me a start!"

"Yes, I can see. Well?"

Max quickly regrouped. "Oh, I was just thanking one of your staff for sorting out a problem on my pc!" He smiled and quickly continued on his way, leaving John surveying him closely. 'Oh my God that was close!' thought Max to himself, not looking back.

That evening when Max was at home, he pulled out his iPhone and for the first time that day opened up the photo of that email on the screen he'd taken earlier. He'd been dying to see what it said all day but was too afraid to have a look at it in the office in case someone walked in on him. He scrolled down the picture as he read the email to himself under his breath, imagining its writer John Lyttleton composing it and typing it out on his keyboard in a state of high stress and anger. He read it out loud.

"Subject; Resignation. Dear Frank, It is with a heavy heart that I feel forced to tender my resignation to you from my role as Chief Financial Officer... ...Yours most sincerely, John Lyttleton," Max lingered on the name, then ended, "CFO Dark Corporation."

Max felt sorry for John Lyttleton and whatever he'd got caught up with for Frank Dark and wondered what had really happened to him. Did he actually jump? No way. Accidentally fall?

Unlikely. Pushed? He could feel the anger swelling inside him, no-one deserved to die for some lousy business deal or a Director on the take. He opened up his Notes app and called through to Si Lawson who picked up after a couple of rings. He explained to Si what he'd been up to and the whole IT server office investigation and whilst talking sent over the picture of the email. Si told him to give him a moment to read it.

"That's great work Max, well done, this email at least gives me proof that something is definitely going on in the Dark Corporation that shouldn't be, and the fact that Frank Dark deemed it necessary to suppress this email from publication effectively withholding evidence certainly implicates him. John Lyttleton must have sent this at the same time as speaking to Vince about wanting to come in here and tell us all about it," Si concluded.

Max eagerly chipped in. "Does this mean I can finish up here and hand this all back to you and your guys to sort out?"

"I'm sorry Max but we're not done here by a long shot. All this email confirms to me is what we already suspected, that something is going on, but unfortunately, we still don't know what it is. We would have if John Lyttleton had lived long enough to keep his appointment with us, but it seems something happened after he sent this email that caused him to take his own life. Max, I'm afraid I need you to keep going with this, keep digging and for God's sake be more careful, that IT office thing was a close one."

"Tell me about it, I was the one there not you. I practically had a heart attack when I thought I was going to be caught. I've still got to see if the IT guy has told John Dawlish or not. I'll keep going for now Si, speak to you soon."

Max ended the call and was disappointed that the email wasn't enough for him to pull out of this job. He felt a bit more vulnerable now he'd seen for himself that something was going on in the corporation and as with everything else of any importance happening in this company, it meant that one particular man was involved and not in a good way. Frank Dark.

11

Frank Dark loved his quarterly senior management review meetings. Occasionally he'd hold them in one of the regional offices such as Paris, New York or Hong Kong, but usually, he would get everyone from around the world to fly into London and attend the meetings at his Guildford head office. It was his opportunity to have all of his key management personnel in one room from Group, the regions and the product divisions to get a thorough briefing on everything that was happening and planned and ensure things were on track and targets would be met. It was also his stage and he loved the performance and drama involved. He could watch debates, sometimes arguments, then interject with his views and decisions and occasionally if one of his senior directors got too opinionated he could throw his weight around. Staff don't fear a good consistent and reasonable boss, they do fear someone who can be unpredictable and react differently to what is expected, especially if one minute they are charming and the next angry and shouting.

His top team would be gathered around the boardroom table on the fourth floor and each, in turn, would present their updates and would bring in as part of their presentation any of their senior staff to also present more specific topics.

On this occasion Doreen Leader would lead the finance update and presentation and would be accompanied just for her time slot by several of her senior staff including Risk and Audit, Treasury, Operations Finance and finally Max would lead the Group Procurement section.

Max was well accustomed to such Chief Exec reviews from previous companies and was comfortable with the format and what was expected of him. They provided an opportunity that couldn't be flounced to show everyone how good his procurement function was performing, wave the flag and show off a little. Equally however he knew such review meetings also magnified any poor performing managers, bad communicators or indiscretions. You had to ensure when you turned up for these shows you'd achieved or exceeded everything you promised to do or had some damn good reasons if anything fell short. You also had to stand your ground as you had the top 10 to 15 highest-paid executives in the company all in one room vying for attention, kudos and often trying to score points off one another. Max's philosophy of strong logic, calmness and courtesy would usually prevail. There wasn't much about procurement anyone could ask him that he wouldn't have a good answer to and on the rare occasion a curveball did fly in he would promise to get the answer immediately at the end of his session.

Frank Dark was ready, the show was prepared and his senior directors were waiting for him in the boardroom. As he approached the large meeting room those inside closest to the doorway saw him coming and the loud energised chatter quickly faded to an eerie hush as he walked in and heartily greeted everyone. He sat down at the head chair with his group executives closest to him in a hierarchy of seniority that diminished the further you sat down the table. At the far end, the other head chair had been pushed to the side to allow the beam of the projector sat in the middle of the table to perfectly fill the white screen on the wall.

Next to Frank sat John Dawlish and Doreen Leader, then Brett Harding and Cindy Ramar from HR with the remainder of each side filled with the regional and brand directors. Sir Kieran Sinclair was free to attend any of these meetings but usually only came in when Frank wanted him there to press a particular and contentious point home. Frank's PA Sheila sat tightly tucked into one corner behind him and would ensure the caterers kept up an adequate supply of tea, coffee, water and the ever-popular assortment of biscuits. She'd also pop out to retrieve any required managers that were asked to come in to explain or clarify something and also take the notes and minutes from the meeting, scribbling them down at an impressive speed using the antiquated Pitmen shorthand.

After Frank took the room through his latest 'thoughts' on

how the company was doing and occasionally refer directly to one of the director's performances, either a success or not, he then went through a few brief slides of his own summarising what he thought needed to be done next to push the company forward and improve its profitability. He'd rarely share these golden nuggets before such meetings and so everyone presenting were desperately trying to second guess what the boss would want and try to have some of his ideas included in their slides, a bit like corporate bingo with the boss.

After Frank, John Dawlish an older, wiser, balding man would always take a sizeable part of the agenda going through many slides covering every area of Technology across the firm, which was indeed one of the most important and integral parts of any large corporation's operations and effectiveness. He'd usually have four or five of his top team presenting their specialisms but would often interject and take over parts of their slides either through his own passion or simply his deep expertise on the subject. John Dawlish knew his stuff, and it was always his IT segment which attracted the least discussion or questions, as most people in the room simply didn't understand enough about the detail and technologies to enable them to challenge what was being said.

Next Brett Harding who was a hard-looking ex-military man would cover off his Special Operations area with only a few less well-prepared slides. He spoke it seemed off the top of his head about the projects and parts of the business his team had needed to help, or rather 'police'. He also covered the relatively small but profitable body-guarding business they had. He was chalk and cheese compared to John Dawlish and during Brett Harding's session, debate and questions deteriorated to almost nothing as everyone knew he was Frank Dark's Rottweiler, his fixer, his enforcer. Some of them round the table had been on the receiving end of getting a visit from Brett or some of his team, knowing you only got to hear from Special Operations if there was a problem. If they visited someone's backside was going to get well and truly kicked, corporately speaking, or fired. At the end of Brett's presentation, or rather brief update, they broke for a quick break before Doreen's Finance segment. Sheila slipped out to gather Doreen's direct reports including Max.

Max filed into the boardroom with his peers and quickly started to mingle and introduce himself. Whilst he'd met all the UK and some European-based executives, he'd only spoken to the others based abroad, so eagerly took a few moments of the coffee break to get around everyone else and make contact with them. Max was conscious Frank Dark was watching him work the room and hoped this was making a good impression. He was also studying John Dawlish for any signs that he'd been told about him and Sian going to the computer server's room together. Max satisfied himself with some relief that Dawlish didn't appear to be eyeing him strangely today.

Doreen Leader then took the floor and unlike the previous three presenters who had remained in their seats, she stood up front next to the screen and began a professional and impressive presentation covering all the finances, targets and her recommendations. This was the new CFO's first time in front of everyone and as Max looked up and down the line of executives sat around the table he found himself amused at the look on their faces, men and women alike including Frank sat there utterly transfixed. Maybe it was because she was the new CFO on show, maybe because she was going through those all-important numbers that needed concentrating on. Or just maybe it was because she was an unusually beautiful woman combined with the heady mix of being in such a powerful position within the company. Her presentation attracted a good amount of healthy discussion and then she formally introduced her team and to kick-off invited Max up to start with Group Procurement.

Max launched confidently into his introduction and initial findings since joining the company, playing back the current status of procurement both good and bad, safe in the knowledge that he was still in his honeymoon period and wasn't responsible for what had happened before his arrival. He then covered the scope of procurement including his staff's organisation chart and competencies with suggestions of how the structure could be improved. He then went on to a more detailed playback of the spends across the business which he and his team had been pulling together recently from all corners of the corporation. Firstly covering the expected larger spend areas such as man guarding uniforms, security van fleets, CCTV and alarm hardware, IT, marketing, HR, operational and corporate spends. His audience seemed impressed being the first time they'd ever been shown exactly how much they were spending with which suppliers. This revelation didn't go by without Frank having a lot to say about overspending and his support of Max and the procurement team getting across the immediate savings and low hanging fruit that were clearly available.

One manager ventured a challenge. "But Frank we've already reviewed some of these spends over and over."

Frank glared at the man disapprovingly. "Then it sounds like you're telling me you haven't done a good enough job? What do you think Max?"

Max was careful with his answer as he didn't want to alienate the stakeholder. "From my experience, I've never failed to find some benefits, either savings or contractual, whenever procurement has undertaken a professional review or tender of a spend. There are always improvements to be had, so I'd ask you all to allow procurement to get on and do what we're here for. You wouldn't expect a salesperson to get involved with IT, neither would I think you have the time from your day job to get involved in procurement." The stakeholder gracefully retreated as Max felt he'd been compelling but had left the man's honour intact. Frank nodded.

Towards the end of Max's spends overview he put up a slide showing a list of spends he openly claimed needed further clarification either from his team or the spend owner. He worked his way down the list with comments coming from the respective owners around the room stating what the spends were for and whether they should be reviewed. The first one to be met with silence with everyone looking up the table to Frank and John, was that of the spends against the Angel virus checker company, which was the forerunner that started this large empire. Though it was a significant contributor to the revenue of the business it had always been off-limits to everyone, leaving its founder John Dawlish to continue running it alongside Frank.

John broke the silence in the boardroom. "You don't need to get involved in any of the Angel spends thanks Max."

"But John I have a really good IT procurement manager who could go through the spends with us both and see where we can find you some improvements," countered Max. The table looked back up to John rather like the crowd at Wimbledon watching a tennis match.

John gave a slight huff. "I've been managing this company and going through its spends over and over for almost two decades, I don't need anyone looking through it for me." He realised as the sentence finished that he sounded a bit like the previous guy telling Max there was nothing more to be improved.

Max was now acutely conscious that this was a sensitive topic for John Dawlish and was about to gracefully withdraw saying, "Understood John, I will…" when Frank interjected.

"I suggest Max you take this off-line with John who I'm sure can tell you a bit more about his Angel software. I'm conscious you two haven't had a chance to spend much time together yet. Move on now," said Frank clearly.

Max quickly returned to the list and worked his way down the remaining spend queries. Another single line needing further interrogation stated simply 'Supplies' against a not insignificant spend value for the Bodyguarding firm in Beverly Hills. Max had barely finished reading out the line when Brett Harding firmly cut in.

"That's got nothing to do with you my friend, I control that area." Max was slightly taken aback by the abrupt but commanding authority of Brett Harding and the way this instruction was given. It was quite intimidating and Brett didn't care what anyone thought in the room. Max hurriedly continued down the slide.

The last items on the list referred to the unusual business owned by the corporation in India, Apex Finance, which had surprisingly obtained a licence from the government there to print rupee currency notes.

Max explained, "This is another area where my procurement manager wasn't able to shall we say get the full cooperation from the manager there on providing all their spends." Max could see John Dawlish starting to shift again in his chair looking quite put out. This time he could see the onlookers up and down the table wanting to watch John and Frank's reactions, but instead kept their heads down staring at the table in front of them.

John angrily whispered to Frank, "He's doing it again."

Frank looks at Max quizzically as if to say, 'Do you really want to go there again?'

Doreen half-heartedly tried to appease them, "Max, why don't you move on?"

Max had touched a raw nerve once more with John Dawlish but this time he was visibly fuming in his seat looking as though he was about to storm out the room. Max realised it would be far better if he quickly smoothed things over than be publicly castigated by John or Frank.

"I'll leave that one for now and pick it up with Doreen as directed by you Frank, and John." He hoped that would defuse the moment and after a few seconds could see John Dawlish's body start to relax again in his seat, whilst his angry-looking expression took a few moments to catch up and then also calmed down.

Frank, then Doreen both thanked Max for his presentation and he made his way back to his chair. Whilst Max sat there through his finance colleagues' subsequent presentations he couldn't help but steal the occasional glance over to John Dawlish to check that he had fully settled down, gauging if his dismissiveness and anger would rear themselves again when he followed up with him. Max was also now curious to find out more about these parts of the business. Less so the Angel virus checker or Brett's mysterious but relatively small bodyguarding 'Supplies' spend, however, he definitely wanted to know more about the touchy matter of the Indian currency printers. It seemed an odd fit alongside the other standard security products and services and he couldn't figure out why John Dawlish was so precious about it. The Indian currency printer wasn't even under his management and had nothing to do with him. Max wondered if maybe this untransparent part of the business could be cause for concern, or greater still, corruption. Maybe this was what caused the problems with John Lyttleton.

That evening just before Max was about to leave, Doreen came into his office and closed the door. "Good presentation today, well done Max, shame it got a bit weird at the end, but I've already had a quiet word with Frank who agrees you wouldn't be doing your job if you didn't ask about these unclear spend areas, so hopefully no damage done," she reassured him.

"Thanks Doreen. It did feel a little uncomfortable being told to stay away from those particular spends. The Indian one was a bit of an elephant in the room wasn't it," said Max.

"I'd suggest you prioritise booking some time with John Dawlish and smooth things over with him. He's got a big IT spend you need to get your guys in to work with him on. And he's helped Frank build this company. He may be fairly unassuming but let's remember he was there with Frank Dark at the very beginning of the massive corporation you and I now both work for, so cut him a bit of slack won't you," advised Doreen smiling at him understandingly.

Max agreed. He'd dealt with far worse and more grumpy stakeholders and won them over so he would get some time put into John's diary first thing in the morning.

That evening at home Max put a call into Si Lawson and told him about the drama in the boardroom. They talked through the Angel product, Brett's Special Ops and the Indian currency printing and both agreed the most likely contender for fraud or embezzlement was the Mumbai based money printer.

Si pondered out loud. "It raises concern that this John Dawlish chap got so hot under the collar when you started asking about it, especially as he doesn't even have management responsibility for that business. But something like that will be so heavily regulated and controlled by the Indian Ministry of Finance I can't imagine there could be any room for dodgy stuff going on there."

Max didn't know anything about currency printing, but he had previously had dealings with that part of the world. "It is India after all. They're not exactly beyond a bit of bribery and corruption," commented Max.

Si concluded, "See how you feel once you've spent a bit more time with John Dawlish and in the meantime, I'll get Josh here to look into him and Apex a bit further. We've already done the usual checks on the board members, but possibly they're selling it or if any money and payments are involved and they usually are, that money has to make a footprint somewhere that we can find. We'll look into that a bit more closely from here."

Max worried when Si said he'd look into things, in case any of his team somehow raised an alarm and compromised him at the firm.

"Do please be careful not to trip over anything won't you," Max said looking for some reassurance, remembering that he had fallen foul of an alert tagging system.

"Don't worry Max, we've been doing this a long time and have huge resources and access at our disposal. I can't remember the last time *we* got caught looking into these things," Si assured him.

12

John Dawlish was in his sixties, a little overweight with thinning hair and expensive Boss spectacles intersecting his round face. Like most computer-based techies he favoured smart casual wear when he could get away with it and when meetings were important, he usually fell short of being smartly dressed in anything trying to resemble a sharp suit. Ever since he was a teenager in the early days of computing he had already surpassed the Basic (beginners all-purpose instruction code) straight forward methodical programming language and was getting to grips with coding in Fortran (formula translation) and Cobol (common business orientated language).

At college, he'd written a neat program for a space invader type game where the player has a blaster gun at the bottom of the screen which fires up into space where alien UFO's peel off from their formation and fly down to attack. Once the player had dispatched the spaceships, the mothership appears and you have to keep blasting holes in it to finally kill the alien inside. Knowing nothing about copyright and protection in those days John eagerly sent his programme on a cassette tape off to Atari in California offering to sell the game in exchange for a payment and a job. He never received a reply and then a few years later when visiting a games arcade at a fairground, came across a particular game called Galaxian, which appeared to have almost entirely the same gameplay as his own earlier creation. Whilst Galaxian was made by Namco in Japan, John had always been convinced that someone had received his game at Atari and jumped ship with it to their competitor and was now sitting on a sunny beach somewhere with all his money.

The technology world was booming and while Bill Gates and Steve Jobs had led the way with their soon to be world dominating software and hardware innovations, John Dawlish was writing and perfecting programming code for software products that would protect the systems and computers everyone was now voraciously buying. After many iterations, he quietly launched his Guardian Angel protection and anti-virus software, which then came on a disc to be installed onto your computer. He and his small team had minor to medium success in getting various countries' computer retailers to list the product and gradually his company grew to a respectable size. He was never going to be a top salesman though.

Then he met Frank Dark, an engaging, successful entrepreneur who had just made millions from selling some mobile phone encryption patent and was looking for his next business venture. Attracted by John's computer security-focused product, Frank went into partnership with him and provided the much-needed funding and sales flare to properly market and promote John's 'baby', raising its profile to sit on the shelves as an alternative option to the much bigger anti-malware brands.

To keep up with encryption technologies advancing at such a rapid rate, they moved Guardian Angel's office from London to Israel, which was then one of the world's centres of excellence for cyber encryption. Within the brief space of a couple of years there, John had significantly improved the software to a level that future-proofed it for many years to come. But he disliked the ways and culture of Israel so moved the main programmer's office for Guardian Angel to a small office in Barbados, where Frank Dark had recently bought a beautiful beachfront villa. With the new improved software, Frank relaunched it to the world with the more impactful brand of Angel, dispensing with the 'Guardian' part of the label.

Frank was like John's keener, more handsome, more driven brother. Over the decades they'd formed an inseparable professional bond and though they had few other shared interests outside of work, Frank had his cars and John was an avid movie buff, they were still incredibly close and trusting of one another. As Frank's Dark Corporation grew larger he wanted his close ally to take on more control of the fast-moving technology part of the business. In no time John was the Chief Technology Officer in charge of a huge IT remit and about 500 staff worldwide. John now spent most of his time with Frank in the Guildford offices and was able to remotely manage his Angel team in Barbados whilst still popping out to see them every month, combined with a stay at Frank's villa. His Angel virus checker was now well established around the world having sold many tens of millions of copies to members of the public, with a more robust commercial version also used throughout many businesses and financial institutions.

John and Frank had been through a lot together as the Corporation grew around them, they'd rarely fallen out. John would always end up deferring to Frank even if sometimes decisions were against his principles. Despite Frank being an astute businessman, he was also extremely generous to those people who were part of his inner circle, being a wealthy man. John knew Frank would always look after him financially and even though he was a multimillionaire himself, like Frank, John wanted to hit the jackpot and with Frank's big deal looming, that day was fast approaching, but for a price!

Max arrived at John's office precisely one minute before his allotted time, he was obsessively punctual and waited for John to look up and beckon him in. Max immediately went in with his olive branch opening.

"John, thanks for taking the time to see me and let me begin by apologising for any embarrassment I may have caused you at the quarterly review meeting. I meant nothing by it other than doing what us procurement types do, we just love to poke about every spend we come across." Max hoped his smiling and charming opening gambit would put any ill-feeling to rest, and it appeared to work.

"Your presentation was very good Max and yes I've had time since the meeting to reflect on the importance of your role in examining spends across the whole business. I'm afraid I'm simply not used to anyone else being involved in my Angel business. I've always had complete control over it for several decades and am very protective of it. It's a huge recurring revenue for the business."

"I quite understand John, of course I'll only look into areas that you and Frank approve and channel any major queries through Doreen," replied Max.

"Thank you. That's good of you. A few of us had a bit of a falling out with your procurement predecessor about these sort of things and I wanted to make sure you have every opportunity of getting on board and being an important member of the team." Max was conscious to avoid mention of the firm in India, but John wanted to cover this off as well and continued. "About the Mumbai printer, even though it's not really under my management I think I was still a bit wound up over the Angel spends discussion, so apologies from me for getting a bit agitated. It's a tightly controlled slick operation down there run by a good friend of mine who I know to be a superb manager."

Max warmed to the humility John was showing but was mindful of the subtle warning dropped in regarding falling out with his predecessor. He also noted the *friend* comment that John sounded close to the person running the business in India, interesting.

Max had brought a printout of the global IT spends with him and they settled down at John's meeting table and walked through the areas they both felt would benefit from Max's procurement team reviewing. They agreed on a long list of actions for Max to take away and start engaging across John's IT empire. Max was conscious that whilst he was a brilliant procurement person, his understanding and intimate knowledge of many of the IT and communications spends they were covering was not up to the mark. John patiently took the time to explain the background and workings of several large areas. Fortunately Max's group IT Procurement Manager was really up on the latest technology products and suppliers in the market, and with the right management and doors opening he was sure would be able to spread his wings and impress.

At the end of the meeting, the discussion moved away from work and Max engaged John whilst he reminisced through his career and development of the Guardian Angel software.

"So what do you get up to Max when you're not at work, I imagine you're a sporty chap?" inquired John.

"I love sports but with work hardly ever get the chance or time to play, but if I could it would probably be tennis or golf," replied Max. "I do like messing around with sports cars and have a couple of old classics tucked away." Max was fishing with the last comment in the hope John might also have some nice cars, given his considerable wealth he could certainly afford them and have the kind of stable of cars Max could only dream of.

Unfortunately, John was not a car man so brushed over the topic. "I'm not really into sports but I have to confess I am quite a film buff. I just love the old movie eras and will always work into my schedule a studios tour and movie location visit whenever I'm over in Hollywood seeing Brett." He proudly continued, "I've also got an impressive collection of movie memorabilia props that were used in the films, you wouldn't believe what some of these items go for at auction."

Max could see that John was quite passionate when talking about his cinematic hobby and asked him lots of questions about his favourite movies and the props he owned. Among some of his possessions was the original light sabre used by Darth Vader in Star Wars, a pair of Laurel and Hardy's bowler hats and the blue-faced Tag Heuer Monaco watch that Steve McQueen wore in his film Le Mans, which John told him he'd bought at auction for over half a million pounds.

As the conversation drew to a close, Max felt he'd made good progress getting to know this clever man, who was understandably fiercely protective of what he had achieved. Max could see he'd be loyal to the end to his friend, colleague and boss Frank Dark. Max ended by asking him, "So of all the movies you love which is the one you'd take to a desert island?"

John held the back of his head in thought and ran his fingers through what little remaining hair he had left. "That's a good question, I've never been asked that one before. I'm probably drawn to my favourite duo who can always make me laugh after a hard day in the office, Laurel and Hardy. The one I'd pick isn't really a film as it's a thirty-minute short. It's probably got to be Music Box which they made in 1932 and got them an Oscar. I've even visited the long flight of steps in LA on Vendome Street and Descanso Drive. That's where they filmed it, trying to deliver the boxed piano to a house at the top. Hilarious." He reminisced with a happy smile.

At the Thames House offices of MI5, Vince had settled down at his desk with a mug of tea and for no reason other than curiosity, had started to look through Max Sargent's career and history. Having been told by Si that this unassuming office guy was an ex-Commando and Military Cross recipient, he was intrigued to have a look at the man's background. He'd already seen the top-level information from their 'Executives Pending' reports, so started to look through the other checks accessible to him beyond what is available on the internet.

Vince went through criminal records searches, registered vehicles, and noted the two expensive sports cars currently in Max's name. He looked at bank accounts, finances, any purchases on credit, properties. Everything seemed normal. He then drifted onto Max's education and schools, and then looked through his records whilst Max was in the Royal Marines. All normal apart from the accounts of his awful event in Sierra Leone. Finally, resided to not discovering anything out of the ordinary about their Max Sargent, he did a quick check on Max's family, his parents.

Vince was barely paying attention to the screen and having finished his tea was readying himself to get back to more pressing work, when something flashed in front of him as he was scrolling through birth certificates.

He sat bolt upright, staring at the monitor. "Bloody hell!" he exclaimed out loud. A few colleagues in the office momentarily looked up towards him, then returned to their work.

Vince hit the 'Print' button and hastily went to recover the sheet of paper from the nearby printer, making straight for his boss's office. He went right in.

"Si, you're not going to believe this," he offered, shaking his head in disbelief.

Si looked up calmly. "Well?"

"I was just doing some casual checks on Max Sargent, well you know, after you mentioned his military service and all that, I just wanted to know more about him."

"We got all that from his EP report didn't we?" said Si, now curious.

"You'd think so, but the EP report doesn't cover everything. Take a look at this," said Vince as he thrust the paper in front of Si.

Si gathered himself and started to scan the document. It took a few moments for him to realise what he was looking at and then he saw it, staring back at him from the copy of Max's mother's birth certificate.

"You've gotta be kidding me Vince!" He looked up at him. "His mother's maiden name is Lyttleton!"

"Yeah. The guy that died at the Dark Corporation, their CFO, John Lyttleton, was Max's Uncle!" corroborated Vince in equal measures of surprise and celebration for discovering it.

"Wow!" said Si. "Is it possible Max could have engineered getting in there through us to investigate his own uncle's death? No. That's just not possible," said Si thinking everything through quickly. "He's a very canny chap if he did!"

"There's no way boss," said Vince. "But it's one hell of a coincidence isn't it! What are we going to do, we can't have him on this assignment anymore surely?"

Si pondered. "We don't have a choice, Max is already in there and is making progress. I can't see we have a choice. Wanting to know what happened to his uncle probably helps him and us!"

"You need to have a chat with him about all this," suggested Vince carefully.

Si stared at the document for a moment longer, thinking it all through. "No. If and when the time is right I'll cover it. For now, we'll let him get on with the job. We shouldn't complicate Max's feelings by letting on we know he was the ex-CFO's nephew." Si looked up at Vince. "Well done finding this, we'll have to add it into the future EP analysis reports. For now, let's keep this to ourselves and we'll not say anything to Max about it okay."

That evening Max got a call from Si Lawson which notched things up a gear, especially as Max had had his long meeting with John Dawlish the same day.

Si imparted what he'd found. "Josh came back to me this afternoon with an interesting lead I followed up myself. We looked more closely at any hidden or shell private accounts we could find for any of the main Dark directors. We can't possibly find every account they might have without their specific account numbers and passwords, but there is one particular bank in Switzerland MI5 had done business with over the years, who have become more cooperative with discreet enquiries I make personally. I've got to know one of the directors there quite well." Max had the phone pressed to his ear and wanted to tell Si 'to get on with it and get to the point.'

Si continued. "Well Josh had mentioned the Dark director's names to him and the banker told him to get me to call him back. He thought John Dawlish's name rang a bell with him and he'd quickly look into it. When I then spoke to him myself he told me that all he could impart was that this particular name did indeed have an account with them and from time to time, no set frequency, had sizeable sums of rupees paid in via several other shell accounts."

"Oh my God, I don't believe it, he's on the take. He's getting some sort of brown envelope payments from their Indian printing company." Max's pulse was starting to race with this latest revelation.

"Now hang on again there Max. Yes, it certainly turns our suspicion into 'highly likely' that something fraudulent or criminal is going on, but let's be clear, we still don't know exactly what's happening or whether these payments are connected to the Dark company in Mumbai. Sorry Max, but before you head off to Doreen Leader's office to resign, we still need much more information and proof, so calm down and keep doing what you're doing." Si hid his excitement, the thrill of discovering a new piece of information helping a case in the right direction had never diminished for him over the years. He also knew he couldn't go in attempting to prosecute with half-cocked information that without solid evidence often tripped them up in court and let defendants walk free.

"So where exactly does that leave us now Si, what else can I do," asked Max.

Si knew what was needed and that Max wasn't going to like it. "Somehow Max you need to get over to India and check out this printing firm yourself, try to find something."

"How the hell am I going to do that, I've already told you that this weird money printing company isn't within my procurement remit. They're not going to let me anywhere near the place especially given what you've now found out. I'd have to concoct a pretty damn good reason to convince John Dawlish and Frank Dark to let me visit this place in Mumbai," argued Max, though he could guess what Si's response would be.

"Max. You're a clever, charming and persuasive guy, a top bluffer and negotiator. You'll figure out a way. Tell me when you do." And with that Si Lawson bid him farewell and put the phone down.

Max couldn't help thinking of John Dawlish's favourite comedian's famous saying, 'Here's another nice mess you've gotten me into!'

As he put the phone down he was wondering what John Dawlish was up to. He needed to see if he could find out anything else. He needed to maybe get back in to see him, have a better look round his office. An idea started to form and he went into his study and started flicking through some large books on his library shelves, eventually finding what he was looking for. He put the large book into his briefcase ready to take into the office, just in case the opportunity to use it arose.

13

Doreen Leader climbed into the front passenger seat of her driver Alan's black Range Rover to take her home after another long busy day as CFO in the Dark Corporation head office in Guildford. Frank liked to look after his key staff and as CFO she was one of only several to have an executive main board position. He usually only laid on the chauffeured Range Rover to greet senior staff for their first few days or take directors to important meetings in the city, but Doreen had enjoyed the privilege of being driven to and from the office every day so much she'd made a play to Frank asking if it could be a permanent perk. Ever willing to win over his new CFO who had such an important role to play in his future plans, Frank had been persuaded and so Alan the driver was now on permanent standby for her.

He'd always be ready to collect her just before whatever time she instructed, sometimes waiting in a nearby car park or discreetly hiding away somewhere and would then calmly roll up to the curb side or opposite the office main doors, so that Doreen had merely to exit the building she was in and step straight into the car to be whisked off to her desired location. Alan the driver would only give the shortest, politest greetings and farewells, or check on routes and timings with Doreen, other than that he was well trained to only engage in conversation if Doreen initiated it.

Today Doreen was plain exhausted and had almost lost her voice from all the speaking she'd had to do that week and glad it was Friday, quietly laid her head back on the firm black leather headrest. She was pleased with herself on how her first couple of months at the Dark Corporation had gone. She'd won over her peers across the senior management team in both the UK and the rest of the world, and more importantly, seemed to have a healthy mutually respectful professional relationship with Frank and John. She was conscious that Brett Harding got on with his own thing, only being directed by Frank, though was quite happy with that, finding Brett far too curt and cold for her liking.

She'd only met Sir Kieran Sinclair a few times mostly in a social setting organised by Frank and found him to be an endearing funny old city gent, quite happy now not to get involved in work and too much detail. Other than mentioning her sexuality to Frank during their long first dinner interview meeting, Sir Kieran being a little flirty at dinner one evening and having had too much wine, was the only other person at the company who had asked her about her marital status. When she had told them each that she lived with her partner Maureen, Frank ever the pro didn't bat an eyelid and smoothly carried on with the conversation. Sir Kieran however in his mildly intoxicated state, and this did amuse her, had raised his eyebrows with a playful smirk and then thinking better of his unintentional advances said to her, "Ahh, yes, oh, well that sort of thing is all quite acceptable these days isn't it. Sounds fun." After a short awkward pause, he'd quickly reached out to the nearest bottle of wine on the table to pour himself a top-up.

Doreen grew up on the south coast of England and went to the private girl's schools Moira House in Eastbourne which naturally served as the feeding school into the nearby main and prestigious girl's Roedean School. The grand and well-equipped premises sat behind the seafront road directly adjacent to the beach, just along from Brighton Marina and offered an impressive view across the cold, murky English Channel. The cool girls of which Doreen was included often made forays into trendy cosmopolitan Brighton on strictly approved town visit passes, but also flaunting school rules by secretly absconding to attend parties or nightclubs. Brighton had a growing gay community and the city was ahead of its time in accepting them in those early liberation days. Whilst Doreen didn't realise it at the time, it gave her and her friends their initial and fascinating insight into an alternative sexual option from what was expected of young posh girls.

After doing well in her 'O' and then 'A' levels she went to Exeter University in Devon where she spent four years studying to be an accountant, with her third year and the two years after University working with one of the top London accountancy firms as a paralegal. By the age of 24, she'd completed her qualification for the Association of Chartered Certified Accountant's (ACCA) and was hungrily sucked into one of the Big Five global accounting firms Ernst and Young.

It was University to blame or more precisely one of her male flatmates, for sewing the first seeds of her future Achilles heel. He introduced her to poker. It started with the usual harmless student card games like dirty eights, 21 or Newmarket and of course being students there was no mention of playing for any money as they had none. When a game needed stakes, they broke up matchsticks into small pieces to act as their chips. It seemed that the cool game always featured in those old movies they'd watch was poker and it was only a matter of time before Doreen's friend suggested they all tried the game.

As the months went on the matchsticks became pennies, then ten pence pieces, then fifty and then notes, as the competitive urge to win against other players gently lulled them into its embrace. They were now gambling. The games became bigger, with more students wanting to try their luck or simply join in to be cool. The number of spectators grew and the Saturday night 'big game' became quite an event with snacks and food being prepared and true to student tradition, large amounts of cheap alcohol being consumed.

Doreen started out like most people thinking it was a bit of social fun and a laugh, not bothered whether she won or lost when no real value was being put at stake. But as the money became more of an important feature when you were betting your week's wages from working behind a bar or serving tables in one of the local restaurants, then it became more serious. Players would rarely have the courage or sense to bow out gracefully perhaps when they were around the breakeven mark and put the evening down to a bit of fun that hadn't really cost them anything. No, like every form of gambling the world over players wanted to win and would keep going until they did, or lose everything whilst trying. Poker can be a cruel slave master with a fine line between success and complete failure, allowing a player to have a huge pile of winnings in front of you, only to then lose the entire evening's successes in the next single hand. To make it even more infuriating because players may or may not have good cards themselves, the winner of the hand and all that money might reveal at the end that their hand was much worse than yours. They'd simply bluffed their win.

Each player is dealt five cards then everyone places their first bet based on what they think they might be able to achieve with replacement cards. Players can then discard up to 3 of their unwanted cards in exchange for new ones, and once again bets can be added to by 'raising'. If a player doesn't want to keep up the increasing bet charge to stay in the game because they feel their cards aren't that good, they can opt-out by 'folding' losing their stake.

Doreen Leader didn't consider herself an addicted gambler as she wasn't gambling on everything she could or playing poker three times a week. It was simply a fun way of letting off steam and over the years she would frequent various London casinos from time to time for an evening out after a nice dinner. She began to gravitate towards favouring the Grosvenor Victoria Casino which was situated a little way up Edgeware Road from Marble Arch at the top of Park Lane. They had a large relaxed games room with the usual tables of roulette, craps and blackjack surrounded by numerous electronic gambling machines with spinning reels and horse racing videos to bet on. As provided in Las Vegas, fresh oxygen was gently pumped into the room to keep people awake and continue gambling into the early hours, and a never-ending supply of beverages, snacks and alcoholic drinks were served free of charge to anyone playing at a table or machine.

The restaurant was part of the same large room only separated with a low glass screen so as not to keep their diners too far away from the action on the tables they overlooked. They would quickly finish their prawn cocktail, steak and lobster so they could get back to the business of losing more money as quickly as possible. The poker rooms hung off the main games hall giving a slight air of aloofness to the rest of the gamblers outside and for beginners wanting to try their luck at poker presented a slightly intimidating prospect of venturing in without knowing exactly how things worked or what to do. You just had to hope you were walking into a room with a friendly dealer, a patient manager and that the players already sat around the table would not be too irritated at having to waste a precious few moments of gambling time for the new person to come in, sit down and sort themselves out. Often another player would have the ridiculous notion that *their* cards would now be spoiled with a new player joining *their* game or even sitting in a particular seat around the table. Emotions ran high and often come rising to the surface at the slightest interference, break of routine or gameplay, or worst of all, a major loss to another player. Especially one with a rubbish hand of cards that has just bluffed the win.

The stakes at these tables could be many hundreds of pounds rising during the course of the evening, meaning that once a number of players had put their bets into the middle of the table there could be thousands of pounds up for grabs each hand. For those regular and more well-off players they could book one of the private poker rooms upstairs to play games with invited players only for much higher stakes, all still regulated and legal being overseen by the casino. Doreen had done her time in these poker rooms and was now part of a prestigious list of London players who would from time to time be invited to a private high-stakes game being held in one of the Park Lane hotels either The Intercontinental, Hilton, Dorchester or Grosvenor.

For some years she'd wondered why they always used these particular Park Lane hotels and finally got round to asking one of the organisers who said that these bigger private games were originally offshoots of the infamous partygoers at Hugh Hefner's London Playboy Club which used to be sited at 45 Park Lane. The drunk wealthy revellers would fall out of the club wanting more serious poker action, so a group of them would get together and walk up the road to one of these big neighbouring hotels and book a room there for their game.

Earlier that week Doreen had received her invitation to the next private poker game being held on Saturday night at the tallest but less salubrious Park Lane Hilton. She'd been thinking about it all week and was now excited with the prospect of the game ahead and felt able to celebrate her new job but more importantly her much larger salary, by pushing the boat out at this game more than she'd ever done before. As a hard-working accountant, she was usually better than most at knowing when to quit. She'd had a few games where she'd won a lot of money but knowing the long-term odds are always against you, she was accepting of the many games where things didn't work out. She refrained from keeping a running tally but knew deep down over the years she'd probably lost somewhere in the region of a quarter of a million pounds.

'Well it's different this time, I have some extra money to play with and I've got a feeling tomorrow night's going to be my night,' she thought to herself as Alan the driver pulled the Range Rover alongside the curb directly opposite her Kings Road home, ignoring a brief toot of the horn from the car behind he was now holding up. Her partner Maureen opened the front door to greet her, with wine open and dinner cooking inside. 'Yes, this was going to be a great weekend.'

The five players had assembled in the designated hotel room and after a brief time of introductions, drinks and empty chitchat, set themselves round the neat table in the centre of the room. Each of them had been trying to find out what little they could of one another's characters, which just might help them make a vital judgement on their hands during the game. Equally each of them had been extremely cautious with their brief conversations so as not to give anything away about themselves. Doreen had met two of the other players before at previous games and had never seen the other two before this evening. Players hardly ever socialised or met outside of these games, caution and discretion were the keywords here.

Also in the room was 'The Organiser', two dealers, an Observer and doorman. The days of highly dubious, swindling games organised by hoodlums ending in fights and death threats had long since passed. Wealthy players who were often models of society, celebrities, bankers, popstars and politicians had to feel this was a safe and fair environment albeit the game was completely illegal and would end with hefty fines or imprisonment if they were caught. The Organiser was part of a discrete network who would arrange amongst themselves when and where to hold the games and agree who could be invited, reviewing individuals past performances, likely wealth and behaviour at previous games. They would also handle all the finances including players fees, prepayment of player's chips and settlement of money and winnings after each game.

Every game had two seasoned dealers who likely worked at major casinos and did these additional private games as a side-line extra earner. There were always two of them so that they could share the high-pressure intense dealing duties throughout the evening. The Observer was randomly selected from the pool of Organisers and would attend the evening sitting quietly in the background forbidden to speak with anyone except when adjudication was required. Otherwise, their role was simply to reinforce and ensure fair play, game rules and good behaviour. Finally, the doorman was a security guard merely for the reassurance of the players and game staff, and also just in case an altercation of some kind did break out. It was all very civil, it had to be otherwise people simply wouldn't attend these games. All the staff were paid out of the table fees each player paid to join a poker game and also the fee to remain on the coveted players invite list.

When being put forward to join this list each player would be financially vetted to ensure there was no possibility of anyone losing sums of money beyond their liquid assets. Occasionally under exceptional circumstances or for well-known players, they would advance immediate credit to a player if for example, they wanted to use a high-value personal item as collateral, for example like diamond ring or sports car. In such cases the player would be taken at their word they owned the said item and the Observer would use their judgement on what credit to extend against the item, effectively pawning it for a loan. If the player lost the game and their 'credit', they were expected to sell the item they put up as collateral and pay off the loan extended to them strictly within seven days. All most civil and polite, and no-one had ever wanted to be the first not to pay their debt and find out what might happen to them. Fear of the unknown is a huge rule motivator.

The game started with bets of hundreds of pounds and at this stage, players were quietly excited in anticipation of the build-up throughout the evening towards what they knew would be much higher stakes. Temperaments were relaxed and as they won and lost relatively small amounts of money the game continued in good humour. By the end of the first hour's play, Doreen was doing quite well being up about £20,000.

The bets now gradually increased from hundreds of pounds to thousands, with tens of thousands worth of chips now being claimed by each hand's winner. The players were gradually building up information about each other, mentally logging the hands they'd played and how often they'd bluffed or won with good hands. They'd closely study each other during the game trying to ascertain a reading of their opponents which might give some small hint or clue as to whether they were being truthful or just plain bluffing. Unless someone had an unfortunate wince, tick or mannerism which displayed itself every time they were either excited at holding a good hand or alternatively lying about a bad hand, it was very hard to genuinely gather reliable intelligence on someone else's cards. There is skill involved but with a large dose of random luck thrown in depending on what cards you're given.

Given Doreen's cool and calm demeanour she believed that her 'poker face' was one of the least easy to read. As an accountant she also had a good memory for numbers and statistics so for whatever help it might give her, she could remember the previous hands that players had used.

After several comfort breaks, they were now three hours in and players folding with dissatisfaction about their poor hands were becoming more frequent, as the bets on the table became larger, valuing between £20,000 and around £60,000. Normally around this time, Doreen would start to pull back her enthusiasm and temper her play and betting. But this was a celebration of her new significantly higher pay package and she felt if ever there was a night where she should really go for it, then this was it. She was still doing quite well overall and of the five players around the table, it was becoming apparent that she and one other were coming out on top.

As frequently happens with gamblers when either leaving the casino or coming to the end of a poker evening, that all-encompassing and uncontrollable urge 'to have just one last bet' in the hope of winning back their evening's losses, always takes hold of them. These private well organised and adjudicated poker nights were no different, they'd always crystallise down to the best two remaining players of the evening battling it out for all or nothing, not able to gracefully withdraw as equal winners, both thinking this was their night and they had to win everything.

Tensions were rising between Doreen and the other player, a gentle unassuming older businessman who'd sold several private companies for tens of millions of pounds. But neither player knew what the other was worth, nor how much a big win or a big loss would mean to them. On this occasion, the businessman was here to win at something again, like he used to win when running and selling his companies. The money bet at these poker nights didn't concern him, so he could afford to push it as far as the Organiser and Observer would allow, as long as the other players agreed.

One of the players had respectfully retired from the game and watched on from the background. The next hand was dealt and Doreen carefully lifted the edges of her five cards to view what she had. Three 10's looked back up at her, she had a good chance of getting Four of a Kind. The businessman was watching her closely. He was probably on his way to getting a Full House. They all drew replacement cards and already the money on the table had reached around £60,000. One other player folded and after a few raises, they revealed their hands and much to Doreen's excitement her four tens beat the businessman's full house. She'd won about £180,000.

Her opponent opposite her gave a large blatant frown and suggested, "Final hand, no limit?"

That moment had been reached. After four hours of play with three individuals having fallen by the wayside, they had arrived at that point. The winner had to decide whether they play just one more hand which hopefully will earn them an even larger payoff, but also give the loser the opportunity of winning their money back. Everyone in the room now looked at Doreen. The expression on the sweet old businessman's face turned into a kind of soppy pleading look. Doreen's head was firmly telling her to pick up the money, thank everyone for a lovely evening and call it a night. But her heart was already whispering to her excitedly, goading her to have one last huge win and walk out with a sizeable sum of money. She'd had a good evening and now had the chance to make it an amazing evening.

"Okay. One last hand," she announced, proudly in control of the room.

The other players, spare dealer, Observer and the doorman now all crowded round the table to closely watch the inevitable drama about to unfold.

The dealer carefully and deliberately dealt each of them their five cards. They both cautiously looked at the edges to see what they had, both completely expressionless. Unbelievably Doreen had another Three of a Kind already, with eights this time. Her mind already raced ahead as she imagined getting four eights, surely another winning hand.

However, her excitement was curtailed when the businessman led the betting with a round and intimidating £100,000. Doreen felt a little dizzy for an instant. 'What on earth am I doing, this is ridiculous, I should have finished with the last hand.' But the game had restarted and there was no turning back now. She had to hope she'd get that final elusive eight. New cards were dealt and Doreen's heart missed a beat as she saw no fourth eight appear in her hand. 'Shit!' she thought to herself, carefully trying to freeze her expression and not give anything away, but the businessman who was closely studying her face, detected just the very slightest movement around her eyes belying her disappointment. But this wasn't going to be easy for him either, he didn't have a great hand so was now going to rely on outright bluffing in the hope that Doreen's hand hadn't come to much.

Each of them now facing off like two gladiators in the Coliseum, no going back, no quitting allowed, they simply had to slug it out and find out which one of them was going to be the winner and which one of them was going to be the loser.

The businessman raised the bet looking calm and confident, so Doreen hiding her reluctance also confidently raised the number again. The quantity of high-value chips in the middle of the table was added to several times as each player raised again. Doreen was forced to ask the Observer and Organiser for another quarter of a million pounds to be added to her playing account for more chips. They agreed. She had to win this! Finally, they reached the point where the cards needed to be revealed. Both players and everyone else in the room had each estimated there to be well over £800,000 in the middle built up between the two players betting.

Doreen was the first to reveal her Three of a Kind with eights. It wasn't a great hand. Everyone immediately scrutinised the expression on the businessman's face wanting to detect any advance notice of whether he'd won or lost. He remained expressionless up to the point of turning his cards over then a crease in the corner of his mouth betrayed his calm satisfaction. He turned over his five cards and also only had Three of a kind but to Doreen's horror, his were with three Jacks.

Doreen sat there completely stunned and speechless as she stared at the businessman's cards, then back to her cards and finally focused on the large pile of chips in the middle of the table. The rest of the room broke away quickly unconcerned and started gathering things up to leave for the evening.

The Organiser closely watched the dealer manipulate and count the chips into neat piles then turning to him the dealer quietly whispered, "£880,000."

Doreen's heart sank again. The Organiser brought up a page on his iPad and input some numbers then taking a moment to look at the summary turned to Doreen.

"I'm sorry Doreen," first names were always used to protect people's identities, "but of the total pot on the table of £880,000 I'm afraid you lost your entire cash game advance of £300,000 plus you also need to pay the £250,000 credit advance you requested during the last hand within the next seven days."

Doreen had to concentrate hard not to collapse. 'Jesus Christ, I've lost £550,000 this evening!' she told herself. She felt numb and couldn't remember the advice, conversations nor making her way down to the hotel's lobby.

Doreen climbed feebly into a London black cab outside the Hilton hotel and made her way home. She started rolling through the numbers and her finances in her head desperately trying to discover some hidden investment fund or savings account she may have forgotten about, that she could now call upon to save her. Even with her huge multi-million annual salary, after tax, she'd need at least her next two months pay to cover this, and that was too long to wait, she only had a week. There was no way she could use the house even if it was mortgage-free, Maureen had also contributed to paying for it so that was definitely off-limits.

Over the last few years, she'd given Maureen free rein to completely renovate and redesign the house which she'd done beautifully but it had cost a small fortune. At the time she viewed it as a worthwhile investment on their lovely home together, but now she was thinking that the hundreds of thousands they'd spent on it could have now been used to help with what she now owed. She'd never intended to lose even a small proportion of her £300,000 game stake, but to have lost that and the additional quarter of a million she'd asked for had put her in a fix. She simply didn't have that much cash in the bank that she could just pull off.

During the short taxi journey she went round and round with the problem in her mind, she had to replace the game stake money and pay off the loan in the next seven days, so needed to find a huge sum of money from somewhere immediately. By the time she pulled up outside her home the only option she had kept rising to the surface, but it wasn't one she relished at all. Pride and humility would have to be set aside. She could only think of one person that could possibly help her out of this fix and suspected that if they could be persuaded, then she might have to pay a high price in return.

Late Monday morning Doreen tentatively went into Frank Dark's office to see him, she closed the door behind her. She had deliberately avoided the usual drama and bad timing of first thing Monday morning so that hopefully her boss had a chance to settle down into the day's routine. Frank looked up and greeted her with a smile putting his pen down to see what it was she wanted.

"Frank, I appreciate I've only been here as your CFO for a few months now but I hope you have complete confidence and trust in me to do an exceptional job here and support you," she opened with.

Frank Dark betrayed a tiny twinkle in his eye as he immediately detected from Doreen's tone and opening lines that something dramatic was about to be said. He wondered if she was about to resign or perhaps had found out something in the company untoward that she wanted to bring to his attention.

"I have been very impressed with what I've seen Doreen and yes I'm hoping you'll be a valuable member of my team here. Trust and loyalty mean everything to me, what is it you have for me?" he asked.

"I'm embarrassed to say I have a personal temporary cash-flow problem which I need some help with immediately." Frank's mind celebrated the revelation and he had to concentrate not to show his pleasure.

After a pause, Doreen continued. "I was hoping, therefore, I might be able to have some kind of advance against say part of my end of year bonus or something?" Doreen hated herself for having to ask.

Frank squirmed in his chair but in a pleasurable way. For him, this was like winning the jackpot as he realised the one person in his senior team he desperately needed to win over, indeed control and get onboard with him, had now put herself in a desperate position for him to swoop in.

He'd been aware of Doreen Leader's likely love of gambling and in particular high-stakes poker after he'd interviewed her. While talking to some friends of his he'd casually dropped in her name as one of his potential new CFO candidates and low and behold, one of them had happened to have been sat at a poker game table opposite her a couple of years previously. Not entirely conclusive evidence that his potential CFO had a gambling problem or indeed would ever put herself in the extraordinary position she was now in, but it was enough of a possibility for Frank to put it down in her favour just in case it came into play one day. And here she was two months into the job pleading for help, Frank couldn't have been happier, but wasn't going to make it easy.

"An advance on your bonus, but that doesn't get paid for ages. What kind of amount are we talking about?" he asked.

Doreen was about to give a long explanation leading up to the big number but decided it would be wasted on Frank and she should just come out with it, so she did.

"I need about half a million in the next couple of days Frank," she said more sternly, feeling even more stupid this time.

"Bloody hell Doreen, you're kidding me," exclaimed Frank so loudly that Sheila came rushing in from next door to check everything was all right. Frank held up his hand to reassure her and politely waved her back out again.

He continued. "What on earth have you done to need that

much money in the next few days, blimey, you're not in some kind of criminal trouble are you?"

"Absolutely not, I promise it's a one-off, all legit, let's just say I had a bet on something and over-extended myself. Once I pay it back it'll never happen again and you can deduct the money from my bonus or share options. Please. I'd be so grateful if you can help me out here Frank, I'm not sure what else I can do," said Doreen.

Frank took a few moments to think whilst Doreen stood there like a schoolgirl waiting for the headmaster to pronounce her punishment for a misdemeanour.

Frank made his play. "This is what I'm going to do for you Doreen, but you have to understand that you owe me big time for this, professionally I mean of course," he clarified. "If or rather when the time comes and I need to call upon you to do something exceptional for me in return, accounting wise, I must know that I can completely rely on your loyalty and discretion?"

Doreen was conscious that she had got in over her head and Frank's demand for promised loyalty sounded like it might involve some dodgy accounting practices. But she was tantalisingly close to resolving her problem and thought she'd deal with any unreasonable requests Frank had in mind for her when the time came. For now, all she could do was agree. She nodded.

"Okay. So we have a clear understanding?"

"Yes Frank," she affirmed.

"Forget the advance or paying me back," said Frank, now worrying Doreen that perhaps he'd changed his mind. But then he continued. "What I'll do for you is pay you an additional £1 million sign-on bonus, which after tax and deductions should net you well over the half-million you need to sort out your problem. I'll have Cindy personally add it to your employment contract as an addendum and ask her to make the payment through payroll within 48 hours. No need to pay anything back." Then he paused to meet her gaze more intently. "All I ask is that when the time comes and I call for you, you come sprinting."

Doreen was grateful and relieved beyond words, nodding

enthusiastically in agreement. She'd got the lifeline she needed.

Frank Dark also now had what he wanted. He had his Chief Finance Officer in the palm of his hand. Exactly what he needed to help with his big deal, when the time was right. And soon.

14

Twice a year usually summertime and Christmas, Frank Dark would have a party at his Surrey mansion for his senior staff and a few other senior managers or up-and-coming people whom their bosses had recommended for promotion potential. Most of the people that attended were from the UK and head office-based teams, but given the importance of these get-togethers, many of the global team made a point of being in the country at the time of at least one of these do's. It was prudent to be at these gatherings not only to show their support of Frank, but also because they wanted to be part of his hallowed team and present, should any interesting ideas or conversations take place they didn't want to be left out. Plus it was always kind of interesting to go to your wealthy Chief Exec's amazing Surrey mansion and just check out how the wealthy lived.

Frank was at his desk going through the invite list which just like any treasured invite list always ends up needing more thought than you think. Who might feel upset if they were left out, if so and so and they do get an invite, then which other people will expect their invites as well. There were about thirty people on the list all of whom were his employees, no partners or spouses were invited. He used to invite other halves but some years ago one of his parties descended into chaos. Apparently, after a few drinks, one of the regional sales directors let slip the usual decorum expected at such events and started getting a bit too close and flirting with one of the senior ladies in finance. Unfortunately, both of them were married and with their spouses present it soon became apparent they were having an affair. Understandably the husband of the finance woman was both emotionally destroyed and furious at this revelation and started squaring up to the sales director. At this point, the cad's wife also completely shocked by the news started having a go at him. During the ensuing tussle outside on the large patio, all three of them ended up falling into the swimming pool, where they continued somewhat comically thrashing around at one another in the water. After that incident partners never again got the invite to one of the boss's special parties. At least if it was only employees attending Frank could hopefully rely on some level of professionalism still being maintained even if they weren't all in the office setting.

As he went down the list his finger paused alongside Max Sargent's name. 'Ah yes our new CPO,' he pondered reaching for his mobile and pressing one of his speed dials.

"Brett, hi Frank here, just a quick one to confirm you'll be at the party coming up soon?" he checked.

"Sure will." Brett was a man of few words and didn't waste time fluffing up conversations or doing idle chitchat. If it was a simple question it got a simple answer.

"Great. Just one thing, I know you're not one for socialising amongst the troops but I'd quite like you to make time for a little chat with our new Max Sargent chap," said Frank.

"Anything you're concerned about?" enquired Brett.

"Not at all but as our new boy I'd just be interested to get your take on him."

"Roger Wilco," said Brett ending the call without any farewell to his boss.

Frank looked at his phone and was still slightly taken aback with his friend's efficient but curt, bordering on rude telephone and conversation manner. He knew though that was just his way and accepted that perhaps it just came with the territory given that Brett was his 'corporate policeman' heading up his feared but highly useful Special Operations department.

Frank Dark resumed his scrutiny of the invite list as he called in his PA Sheila to check on some of the finer details of the party and the caterers.

Max Sargent was dutifully getting on with his Chief Procurement Officer duties, managing his staff and chairing regular team meetings, constantly persuading, cajoling and impressing stakeholders especially those that were more reluctant to allow his buyers to get their hands on their precious spends and suppliers. All the while making sure his team were focused on handling targeted spend reviews and tender processes to deliver tangible and visible savings and benefits to the company. Such wins took the form of reduced pricing being negotiated with existing or new suppliers, transparent measurement of spends and delivered savings signed off by the stakeholder and finance, contracts with more integrity supported by legal, and finding better products and services across the marketplaces they operated in to enhance their employees and customers offerings.

Whilst ably conducting his day-to-day activities for his day job, Max was constantly aware it served as a front for the main reason he was there. He needed to find out more about any indiscretions in the company and report back to Si Lawson at MI5 so he could end all this subterfuge and get back to his normal life.

Max had to somehow wangle in a trip to the corporation's Indian currency printer outfit in Mumbai, Apex Finance, so was on his way up to talk to Doreen Leader about his proposed forthcoming travel plans. He knew this wasn't going to be easy, given everyone's reticence at the recent quarterly review meeting for him to even talk about that business. Doreen saw Max approaching her office and waved him in, grateful for the distraction away from studying a huge printout of departmental budgets.

"Hi Max, you wanted to run me through your travel itinerary for approval didn't you? Tell me what you're thinking?" greeted Doreen.

"As you know I've got the quick tour around some of the European offices to meet with my remote procurement staff and the key stakeholders, so I'll also need to do the same for Australasia and India soon. I thought to start with I'd go to Hong Kong and combine that visit with a trip to the CCTV and alarm factory in China. Then on the way backdrop in and meet my buyer based in India," explained Max.

"All sounds good to me, in fact now I'm thinking about it,

Frank mentioned he wanted me and him to travel to Hong Kong together for some important meeting. Maybe we can tie in so we all bump into one another when we cross over?" said Doreen.

"Great, will sort that out." Max checked himself before adding his final more crucial request. "I also thought that whilst I'm in Mumbai I could perhaps fit in a fleeting visit to the currency printing firm we own there, purely out of courtesy as I'm there any way to meet my local buyer?"

Doreen pursed her lips, "I'm not sure that's a good idea Max, there's nothing there for you or procurement to get involved with and after John Dawlish's slightly embarrassing reaction during the review meeting I suggest you leave it," advised Doreen.

Max tried once more, "But I'll be right by the printers when I'm in Mumbai anyway, I have to meet my buyer and it won't look good if someone visits from head office and doesn't at least introduce themselves to the manager at the printers firm. I could literally just drop in for a tea to say hello on my way to the airport?" pressed Max, conscious this was the last time he could ask otherwise it would start to sound a bit odd that he was so desperate to go to this lousy printing firm.

Doreen shrugged her shoulders and conceded, "You definitely need to go there to meet your buyer and you have a point about not upsetting our manager at the printers, so in principle, I'll approve it." Max smiled at the result. Doreen then added, "But given the sensitivities the boys down the corridor seem to have about the printers, I'll need to just run it by Frank so you're all squared off assuming he says yes." Max frowned.

'Damn,' thought Max, however it was as expected and at least Doreen seemed supportive of the visit plan. He'd just have to hope he got the okay from Frank Dark to drop in and have a look at this place otherwise that would be the end of that. He wasn't sure what else he'd be able to do if that was the case and started imagining the difficult conversation he would have to have with Si Lawson.

He left Doreen who was now concentrating deeply on a

mountain of reports and paperwork in front of her. Max walked past several of the other director's suites and could see that both Frank Dark and John Dawlish were not present and their assistants who were also absent were likely off for their regular coffee and gossip catchup. Max looked back at Doreen who was engrossed in her paperwork and realised they were the only two people on the executive floor. He looked over to John Dawlish's office to check that his adjoining wall blocked Doreen's view in and it did. His heart started to beat faster as he knew he had a unique opportunity to have a quick look round the IT guru's office, but it was very risky. If he got caught the whole game could be up. He could get fired, or worse, have to declare that he was working with MI5.

But he had an overwhelming urge to try to find out more about John and this currency printing firm and how they were connected. Max quickly went over to the top of the stairs and with no-one approaching either the stairway or the elevator, he knew he had at least a minute or so before anyone could arrive on the exec floor.

He huffed to himself as he gave in to his urge to get into that office and swiftly moved across the landing and went into John's suite. His heart raced as he urgently began looking around the office for any signs of priority or important paperwork. He avoided touching the computer knowing it would be either password protected or events trackable. Among the bookshelves, cabinets and tabletops, nothing jumped out as interesting. He moved over to a single filing cabinet and quietly slid the drawer open. His eyes darted along the file labels at the top of each partition, but nothing resembling the Indian printers appeared.

Max glanced over to the landing half expecting John and Frank to appear at the top of the stairs and come running towards him shouting in anger. But all was quiet. Knowing he might only have a few moments left he went over to John's desk, which had five different trays of papers along with various documents scattered about the desktop. He laid down his files he was carrying and his eyes frantically scanned letters, reports, email printouts and scribbled paperwork, looking for anything that alerted him to something dodgy regarding India, Mumbai, currency, printing.

Two things came to his attention. Firstly a handwritten note on a small pad of post-it notes, where John had scribbled, 'Ensure Angel software ready for Li asap'. Max dismissed it quickly as a reminder for John Dawlish to perhaps get the next upgrade for their Angel software ready for one of his programmers.

The other piece of paper that drew him in was printed with the words simply saying, 'Apex coding next month....', followed by two lines of alphanumeric gobbledygook coding language. That was it. The rest of the sheet remained blank. Perhaps fairly innocuous, but Max was intrigued due to the note including the word 'Apex', the name of the Mumbai currency printing firm.

He was just about to take out his mobile phone to photograph it when he realised someone was watching him. His heart missed a beat!

Standing in the doorway of his own office was John Dawlish, looking at Max as if he was about to murder him on the spot.

"What the hell are you doing in my private office?" John demanded as he started to stride in.

Max quickly picked up his own files that he rested on the desk, at least almost all of them, and apologetically moved away from the desk. "I'm so sorry John, I didn't mean to cause any upset, I was just…"

John cut him short. "Just what? You can't walk in here and snoop around willy nilly. What are you doing for Christ's sake? In fact, just piss off out of here, we'll see what Frank has to say about this! I can't believe you'd come into my office like this!"

Max quickly moved towards the door bowing in deference, "I'm sorry John, I just wanted to give you…"

"Get the hell out of here!"

Max retreated out of the office and quickly made his way to the stairway, as Doreen came out of her office to see what all the commotion was about. She looked at Max who held up his hand in apology but also signalling 'just a misunderstanding'. He disappeared down the stairs.

John Dawlish quickly looked around his office and satisfied himself that everything was in order, nothing missing or disrupted. His anger at catching Max dissipated slightly. But finding someone in your office seemingly by surprise was something anyone would like. He got out his mobile and sat down in his chair, pressing Frank's speed dial number. He was furious.

He sat there listening to the ring on his mobile waiting for Frank to pickup and glancing over his desktop, noticed something different. An extra item, sitting there in front of him. Something unusual, something that sparked his interest.

Frank answered, "Hi John, what's up?"

The anger drained out of John with much relief and was instantly replaced with contriteness and apology. "Ah, hang on Frank, sorry, just a mo."

John stared at the glossy book in front of him, sitting on his desk, where Max had picked up his files from.

"Well?" said Frank impatiently.

There sitting innocently on his desk, was a copy of the book, 'The Making of Star Wars, a Look Behind the Scenes'.

John felt stupid and trigger happy with his anger at Max.

"Sorry Frank, thought I had an idea but forget it. Catch you later," and before Frank could answer he cut off the call.

'Damn it, the lad was just trying to give me the book!', he thought.

Max had got back to his desk and was worrying about what would happen next and if his subterfuge had worked. His phone rang, it was John. He took a deep breath and answered.

"Max my boy," said John awkwardly but enthusiastically. "I think I may have jumped the gun a bit just now."

"I'm so sorry for going into your office John, I'd just popped up to give you a Star Wars book I'd read that I knew you'd appreciate. When you weren't there I was just leaving it for you when you came in."

John was humble. "I can see that now. What an idiot I was, I'm so sorry for flying off the handle. Let's say no more about it okay?"

"No problem, I hope you like the book, it's yours now."

"That's so nice of you Max, thank you, and sorry again," apologised John as he put the phone down.

Max hung up and smiled to himself, pleased that his simple gift had stolen the show away from him looking around John's office. Although not much to go on, he would tell Si about the Apex coding note, perhaps they'd make something of it back at MI5.

Following on from seeing Doreen, Max didn't have to wait long to find out about visiting the Mumbai printers. Later that day as Doreen finished off another of her many impromptu meetings with Frank in his office she explained Max's intended travel plans around the various companies, offices and procurement staff. At the end putting it as nonchalantly as she could, she added the visit request to the Indian printers, dressing it up as Max had based on not upsetting the local manager by ignoring him.

Frank gave her a look as if to say 'Really?'

"You're not seriously thinking that's a good idea, you saw how annoyed John Dawlish got and any way that firm has got nothing to do with procurement. Their main spends are on the special paper and ink they have to use which are both Government controlled. And don't worry about the manager getting upset about not being visited. He likes to keep himself to himself anyway. No, Max has got better things to spend his time on so no 'dropping in' as you put it on the printing company." Frank was clear and his tone denoted that that was the end of the matter. After leaving Frank's office Doreen gave Max a buzz and explained that his travel was approved but not the Indian printers visit and for him not to give it another thought, it didn't matter anyway.

Although Max feigned that this wasn't a problem on the phone to Doreen when he put the phone down he quickly made up his mind not to tell Si Lawson yet. Maybe there was some other way he could find out more about what happened at the printers, he didn't know how right now but he'd work on it.

A few days later Frank was finishing up with John Dawlish and they started talking about some of the presentations they'd had at the recent review meeting. When alone they could be a little mischievous with their criticisms of other people, it was just one of those naughty gossip things they had together.

"What the hell happened with your IT guy," joked Frank, "that was painful sitting through his mumbling and arr-ing, the poor man was mortified. One of John's managers had inadvertently deleted his Powerpoint presentation just before the meeting, then before restoring it his laptop had shut down having run out of battery. He then had to do his best when it was his turn to stand up and talk about his area without any slides, prompts or diagrams.

"It was painful," laughed John, "but I wasn't going to help the silly sod out, losing files is one of my pet hates. Shame though, he's good at his job, he just can't ad-lib presentations poor chap. Embarrassing though wasn't it."

"Talking of embarrassing, it was a bit awkward in front of the rest of the directors around the table when you got cross with Max Sargent asking about spends in India," commented Frank.

"Well honestly, the cheeky bugger, sticking his nose in where it doesn't belong," said John.

Frank reminded him, "He is our CPO and we want him to get across all spends after all, cut him a break John, he seems to be doing a bloody good job for us, saving millions. How is everything going there with your little 'arrangement'?" Frank asked raising his eyebrows at John.

"Yes, all fine, I'm getting the regular 'updates' from them and confidentiality all seems to be intact," answered John cryptically.

Frank continued his developing thoughts on the subject. "You know it would be good to put everyone's mind at rest, I mean those around the table who witnessed your rather overreaction on the topic, by maybe having someone independent visit the place after all." John looked at Frank inquisitively but was dubious. "Maybe we should let Max Sargent drop in and meet the manager, what could he possibly find out?"

John was already ahead of Frank's thinking. "I see your point Frank. Having the new CPO visit there would show nothing is off-limits to the procurement team and give the place a seal of approval for all the others to see we've nothing to hide there. Yeah, okay, I'll tell Rajit to expect Max sometime soon for a quick meet and greet. Very quick."

"I think that'll be good John," said Frank, "Sheila's sent out the draft meeting minutes but I can add into the end of Max's CPO section ref those spend queries he raised, that it's been agreed he'll include a visit to the Indian printer firm on his various travels. That way the other directors can see it's all fine when the official version of the minutes goes out."

Frank nodded to himself with the satisfaction he'd once again found a diplomatic solution to a potential problem, he was always good at doing that. "Leave it with me to tell Max and Doreen he can visit the printers," he advised John who just nodded. Frank was an expert in carefully managing the way he gave out good information, decisions or favours, always to his advantage. He'd leave this one for a few days before telling them, perhaps a good time would be to tell Max Sargent at his summer party coming up very soon. Now that he had the control he wanted over Doreen, Frank was aware that bringing his new CPO into the inner team might also serve him well.

Max had a tingle of excitement and nervousness as he pressed the remote for his garage door and stood back watching his beautiful pride and joy the Ferrari F40 slowly reveal itself. He was off to Frank Dark's party and whilst usually totally inappropriate for a member of staff to turn up in an expensive fancy car, he'd overheard a conversation his Chief Exec had had with another director about his love of supercars and some of the previous models he'd owned. He mentioned it to Doreen to get her view on whether it would be all right for him to take his own sports car as the event was on a Saturday away from the office. She had insisted he brought the best car he had, convinced their shared love of them would help build the relationship between Frank and her CPO.

Max rarely drove the car as it was so impractical to be used effectively for anything other than driving from A to B, and even then only in the dry and knowing that you had a safe parking spot waiting for you at the other end. These machines represented one million pounds driving down the road. His excitement always grew in anticipation of taking the car out as it truly was an untamed stallion, as the badges on its front, rear and sides denoted. It had a top speed of over 200 mph and a breath-taking acceleration of 0 to 60 in around four seconds depending on which car review or magazine you read. The light racing car was propelled down the road with a 2.9-litre twin-turbo V8 engine producing about 430 brake horsepower. When it was launched by Enzo Ferrari out of Modena Italy in 1987 it was briefly the fastest road car available until, with the tit-for-tat battle they'd always fought, Ferruccio Lamborghini based in neighbouring village Saint'Agata brought out his new Diablo with speed and power stats conveniently just bettering the F40's. However, the iconic brand of Ferrari and the F40's 'racing-car-on-the-road' status edged it ahead of the Diablo in the collector's popularity stakes and its longevity.

Max took a few moments before opening the door to admire this piece of automotive artwork and engineering ingenuity. The bodywork was made of moulded carbon fibre, the individual strands of which were visible through the deliberately thin layer of Rosso Corsa paint shaving fractions off the weight of the car. With pop-up lights at the front, low stance, the sweeping bodywork peppered with triangular air vents leading to the visible engine at the rear as if to be on show, framed by the huge rear wing and wide tyres, the car presented itself as a menacing, guaranteed head-turner.

Max opened the door and climbed into the left-hand side over the wide sill and carbon fibre monocot and slid clumsily into the red bucket seat, clipping in the five-point harness. For an expensive car, the interior was frankly rubbish with a coarse carpet-like covering to the dash, cables for door handles, no comforts like electric windows, stereo or even floor carpets. This was a racing car on the road. Max turned the key and the engine gunned into life. He was always nervous at this point as with all temperamental supercars, you never knew when the next mechanical problem was going to bite you and your wallet extremely hard. He listened for a moment and all seemed well, so gently pulled out of his garage and driveway checking the garage door closed securely behind him hiding the Vector safely still tucked away inside.

Max took it easy as he passed through Clapham waiting for the oils in the car to warm up and allow him smooth access to second gear, which in older Ferraris refrained from working properly until the gearbox oil was up to temperature. By the time he made his way onto the A3 dual carriageway at Wimbledon, he was able to unleash some of the power the car was wanting to give. He settled back in his seat and started to enjoy the drive down the A3. He turned off at the M25, down one junction and off at Leatherhead. From there the Surrey stockbroker belt countryside started to reveal itself as he went through Bookham and at the prestigious Effingham golf club turned left into a narrow country lane called Beech Avenue, where houses became larger and more infrequent, driveways became longer. After half a mile he slowed right down and spotted Frank Dark's house name on the large solid wooden gates, it read 'Angel Manor'.

As if by magic the gates suddenly started to open for him. Max imagined somewhere inside one of the staff must have been sat by the video monitor having to wait for each and every guest to pull in to open the gates for them. He agreed to himself that it was quite impressive though, to pull in and have the gates open by themselves. Proceeding down the driveway lined each side with small trees every 10 yards, he drove past two pristinely kept massive lawns both with perfectly straight cut lines running across them, manicured shrubs and hedges. On one side there was a magnificent walled rose garden and on the other an impressive old looking gazebo house alongside a small lake with various water features. At the end of the driveway, it opened out into a large paved frontage where cars could pull in round a central fountain and park up around the edge. A 'More Parking' sign indicated to drive around the main house where there was a large additional forecourt for parking alongside a number of garage doors.

Max parked up at the rear and walked background to the front entrance where he was greeted with a waitress offering champagne and other drinks. Another downside of driving your own sports car Max thought to himself as he opted for a glass of freshly squeezed orange juice. The house was huge, Max guessed it would probably have eight bedrooms and likely all en-suite. The building looked old but judging from its perfect finish and straight lines he assumed either a lot of work had been done to restore it or perhaps the architect had been told to give his new building that old country house feel.

Inside was modern, bright and clean with marble floor throughout, quality but comfortable furnishings, black or chrome framed pictures and paintings and all the latest electronic switches, built-in speakers and control pads dotted around each room.

As Max walked through the large hallway towards the open doors at the rear through which he could see other guests gathering on a large terrace, Frank Dark and Brett Harding came out of one of the doorways leading off the hall. Max could see from looking past them it was a large wood-panelled office with the rear wall lined with full bookshelves. Frank looked up and noticing Max broke off his conversation with Brett to come over and heartily shake Max's hand and greet him.

"Max, how wonderful to see you, it's so nice to have you here for your first 'boss's party'." Frank beckoned Brett who was hanging back to come over to them to properly introduce them. "You two have never really been in the same office for long enough to introduce you properly so let me do the formalities once and for all." Frank put his hand on Brett's wide, firm shoulder saying to Max, "This is Brett Harding our head of Special Operations across the corporation, he and I go back a long, long way and is one of my dearest friends."

Max responded with a handshake to Brett. "Pleasure to meet you properly Brett, your reputation precedes you." Brett gave him a quizzical look so Max quickly elaborated. "By that I mean the reputation your Special Ops team has in the company. I think it's good for any company to have someone keeping everyone on their toes and sorting out any problems," Max recovered himself keeping his smile engaged with Brett's cooler expression.

Frank interjected, "Now I want you two to get to know one another better today, you never know when your paths might cross and Max, Brett's a good person to have in your corner if you come across any problems or unwilling stakeholders, Brett'll sort them out for you."

"That's good to know but I've always managed to persuade even the most difficult of stakeholders that engaging with myself and procurement will only benefit them and their business," said Max hoping this didn't come across as too dismissive of Brett's services.

"Quite so, quite so, I can see your communication skills with stakeholders and indeed everyone is quite commanding and persuasive, I like that, especially when you're negotiating with suppliers on our behalf and saving lots of money," Frank laughed. He turned back to Brett. "Would you mind if Max and I have a few moments together and do make sure you catch up with Max later today and tell him some of your amusing movie star bodyguard stories. And you'll take care of those matters we talked about earlier Brett?"

"Roger Wilco," came the short reply from Brett as he made his way off to the kitchen area, favouring the options in there to having to go outside and circulate amongst the guests.

Frank took Max by the arm and led him past the kitchen towards an external side door. "Now as I was talking to Brett in the study just now I'm sure I recognised a particular engine and exhaust note driving around the side of the house, and Doreen mentioned to me you might be a fellow car enthusiast?"

Max welcomed the change in topic and the previous slightly awkward conversation with Brett Harding and detected the rise in Frank's enthusiasm when talking about cars. He felt quite pleased to steal the party host away from the other guests for a brief time to show him his F40. Before they went outside Frank grabbed a mobile phone-sized multi-button remote from the table by the door. As they rounded the house into the large courtyard Frank stopped in his tracks and with a bit of overacting held his arms up at the beautiful red Ferrari Max had backed up against the wall to show its best front-facing look. They spent ten minutes with Frank looking all around the car and asking lots of questions about it not having owned one himself. Max started to enjoy being with this charming, powerful man and sharing a moment of mutual respect for fast cars. Then his brain pinched him with the reminder that he was not here for a long-term job and that this charming man he was talking to just might be involved in something untoward. He continued with the conversation smiling, trying not to let the thought spoil the moment.

Frank dug the remote out of his pocket and pressed the large button at the bottom labelled simply 'ALL'. "Before we go and join the others, Max, I know you're one of the few people here today that will appreciate some of the cars that I have." The four garage doors opposite them simultaneously opened up, revealing a treasure trove of automobiles for Max to feast his eyes upon.

"Oh my God, that's amazing," exclaimed Max starting to walk towards the nearest one. He didn't need to feign interest for this and was genuinely excited to see such rare and sought-after cars up close, and started a return barrage of questions and compliments for each of the four cars. The first car was a monstrous classic red Ferrari 288 GTO which looked like the well-known Magnum PI TV show's 308 GTS on steroids, with larger body panels, wheels and performance. The second car was one of the latest McLaren 720's with a four-litre twin-turbo V8. Max guessed this particular car must be one of the first recently launched examples to come off the production line. The next car was a new mind-blowingly quick

Ferrari 812 Superfast 6.5 litre V12. The car sitting quietly at the end was extraordinarily out of place alongside its garage mates. It was a black 1973 Ford Falcon XB GT V8. With its black wheels and aerofoils, multi-exhaust pipes coming out the side, 'Interceptor' police-style decals and intimidating supercharger blower protruding from the centre of the bonnet. Max recognised the car as being likely a replica of the cars made famous in the Mad Max movies.

Frank couldn't wait to tell him. "I know this is a little out of the ordinary but it's just a bit of fun, I hardly ever drive it, but when it came up for auction I just had to have it. It's one of the original movie-used Interceptor cars from Mad Max driven by Mel Gibson!" he said proudly beaming at the car, then back at Max.

As Frank told him of the car's originality Max thought to himself that a collector worth hundreds of millions of pounds like Frank Dark wasn't going to bother with a replica movie car, of course they were going to own the actual one used in the film. Frank spent a few more minutes telling him about having to restore parts of the car that got damaged during filming and also confessing that the large supercharger wasn't actually functional in the movie but merely had the belt spin round with an electric motor at the flick of the switch on the gearstick, conceding that movie magic was rarely real.

"You liked what you saw?" said Frank as he closed the garage doors slowly hiding once again the hidden treasures. "Money really can buy anything you know Max, when you have enough of it." Max estimated the four vehicles in Frank's garages were probably together worth about £4 million. "I'm glad you're on board with us here at my corporation Max. I look after team players especially those whose are totally loyal and you already know I pay well over market rates."

Max knew he was being given the sales pitch and nodded agreeably, "I'll always do my best at whatever job I have Frank."

"Ah but I'm hoping you'll always have a little extra gas in the tank for me if I ever need it eh Max?" joked Frank. But Max knew he wasn't joking.

Frank put his hand on Max's shoulder, "Doreen mentioned to me about your upcoming travel plans which all sound great, it's good to get out and meet the troops in their own regions," said Frank. "I'll be travelling as well at that time and Doreen and I have a meeting in Hong Kong around the same time as you, so I'll ask Sheila to book us into the same hotel so we can have a catch-up and compare notes."

"Sounds good to me Frank," agreed Max.

Frank continued. "Oh yes, speaking to John after the review meeting thing, I think between you and me he's feeling a little bit foolish for being so sensitive about your spend questions. You have to understand Angel is his creation and he's very protective about it. I guess so am I, after all it's where the whole Dark Corporation started. But Angel Barbados really doesn't have any spend, it's just a bunch of clever programmers."

"Of course Frank I completely understand and I won't interfere without checking with you or Doreen first," coaxed Max. He could feel that Frank was positioning himself with this little speech for some kind of offer or suggestion, so thought a little humility and reassurance might help things along.

Frank went on. "Having said that though we did agree there is no harm in you popping in to say hello to the manager of the Indian currency printers when you're in Mumbai. So why don't you work that into your schedule as your first visit before you then come on to meet me and Doreen in Hong Kong. I'd like to hear what you think of the place, there's not much to it but there's always something mesmerising about watching thousands of money notes whizzing out of a large printing machine," he said with a big grin.

Frank had played his ace in the hand well making sure that Max knew John Dawlish was also happy with this suggestion in an attempt to smooth over things after he'd been so sensitive at the review meeting. Frank felt there was nothing of any interest or rather discrepancy that Max could possibly discover during a quick visit to the Indian printers and wanted Max to see there was nothing to hide there. He also deliberately suggested Max met him in Hong Kong straight after his India visit so that he could just make sure that Max was satisfied all was as it should be at the currency printers.

Max was quietly delighted at the offer, he'd now got what he needed and couldn't wait to report back to Si Lawson when he got home.

"Only if you're sure that's okay Frank, but it sounds very interesting, I'll definitely pop in there before I leave Mumbai and come on to join you two in Hong Kong," said Max.

"Wonderful, then that's all sorted, I'll tell Rajit Singh the manager there to expect you," Frank concluded as he led them through an arch in the wall to join the other culminating guests on the large terrace at the rear of the house. The patio surrounded an attractive swimming pool overlooking another huge expanse of lawn framed in the background by the peaceful Surrey countryside beyond.

Frank slipped into his charming host mode and left Max to greet and mingle with his guests. Max held back for a moment to congratulate himself on somehow getting the invite he needed to the Indian currency printers and wondered if there really was something going on there and what it could be given the strict controls they must have there. Surveying the scene in front of him reminded him of one of those posh garden parties straight out of a scene from the South Fork Ranch in 'Dallas' or the Carrington Mansion in the 'Dynasty' old TV shows.

Almost all of the people invited had arrived whilst Max and Frank had been admiring the cars and everyone was scattered around the terrace and lawns excitedly catching up, commenting on what people were wearing and admiring the impressive Manor house and grounds. He noticed Sheila busily bustling amongst the throng greeting people whilst issuing clipped instructions and observations to the catering staff, who would immediately carry out her latest wishes to ensure everything was perfect and the guests were well looked after. The servers were all looking smart in black and white uniforms carefully making their way amongst the crowd with more champagne, a choice of cocktails and soft drinks, and would also ask if there was anything else in particular guests would like brought to them from the bar. The canapés were proving very popular with a scrumptious array of combinations on toast, pancakes and pastry including beef, sushi fish, cheese, fruits, foie gras, lobster and prawns.

Max dutifully circulated around the other guests with the expected balance of work and life discussion topics, always asking lots of questions and homing in on the topics that the other person might have a passion for. He was always amazed at how few people he ever met took the time and trouble to ask questions and show an interest in the person they were talking to. As with any 'office do' he found a few people fun and fascinating to talk to, whilst unfortunately most of the conversations he attempted were quite hard work with the other person not really being able to give much or having the communication skills to avoid awkward pauses.

Cindy Ramar the HR director came over to Max looking relieved to have removed herself from the previous conversation and they had an engaging chat about holidays, some politics and Cindy was interested in hearing Max's view about the previous HR functions he'd come into contact within past companies. Max had never really been impressed with the HR departments he'd dealt with and felt it ironic that the team looking after the welfare of the company's most important assets, their staff, were often the worst at communicating, caring, showing humility, empathy and passion. He rattled through examples of tardy and underwhelming performances from his previous HR colleagues.

Fortunately, Cindy remained an interested and humble audience genuinely wanting to hear about anything that would help her be a stronger and better HR leader. Max had felt from seeing her perform around the office that she was a rarity in the world of Personnel which was reinforced from talking to her now. He concluded that Cindy Ramer was an impressive, straight down the line HR director wanting the best for her staff and with the utmost integrity. He was convinced that if there was anything funny going on in this corporation, Cindy Ramer neither knew about it nor would have anything to do with it.

Max asked her, "You must have worked with the previous CFO John Lyttleton, what was he like?"

Cindy was a little surprised by the question but thought nothing more of it. Quite understandable to ask about a departed senior director of a business you're now in. "Oh, yes, John. Very sad about what happened. He was a lovely guy, very professional, a brilliant accountant. I got the impression Frank expected a lot of him though. Doreen's got a lot to live up to, he was good."

Max gave a respectful nod in agreement. As they were finishing the staff had by now laid out the buffet outside and were starting to open up the lids of the hot and cold silver serving dishes. Judging from the quality of the canapés guests had already sampled, the lunch selection would be equally delicious and inviting, so most people began to move over to the food trying their best to look nonchalant and not rush to form a queue. Max didn't want to be part of the clamouring hungry crowd so walked down the steps of the terrace to have a quiet stroll down the lawns and wait for the rush to die down.

As Max walked along the perfect lawn towards the picturesque rolling countryside beyond the garden's perimeter, he was conscious of someone quietly approaching him from behind. He turned just as Brett Harding reached him and was slightly startled that he'd not heard him earlier coming down the steps of the terrace.

"Brett, hi, you gave me a bit of a scare just then creeping up on me," joked Max cautiously. He knew this little 'catch up' suggested by Frank was going to be a tricky one, Brett didn't seem to be one for fun or relaxed conversations with plenty of laughter.

Brett Harding was six-foot tall and filled out every inch of his powerful frame with an athletic physique, wearing a short-sleeved polo shirt and dark green slim chinos. Max could see Brett's muscly shoulders, lats, biceps and pecs outlined behind his shirt with the muscle sinews of his exposed forearms flexing in the sunlight as they shook hands. Brett's face seemed a little more engaging to Max this time who couldn't help think the man was having to put on a more friendly performance than he wanted to. His face and eyes were economical in both looks and reactions with little ability for empathy or emotion, weathered skin belying years of physical training and exposure to the elements. Brett's brown hair was cut short with a slight buzz top. Max could understand why Frank had him heading up his Special Operations and bodyguard firm, the man in front of him was intimidating enough just from looks and barely needed to speak to illicit command and attention.

Like Frank Dark, Brett Harding had also gone to Harrow and was indeed one of Frank's closest friends, including being the other boy involved in the incident where they dropped the young lad out of their study window. Brett had been Frank's enforcer and protector at school and then after a distinguished career in the military services had returned to a similar corporate role alongside Frank once again.

Brett had always been destined to become a soldier, his parents met and served in the army and their all-consuming military lives prepared him for the unquestionable career path in following them. After leaving Harrow Brett had gone straight to the Royal Marine's commando training centre in Lympstone Devon, coincidentally but unbeknown to him just as Max had done some years after, where the on-site colonel and their commanding officers oversaw the Command Wing, the Commando Training Wing and the Specialist Wing. Recruits spend a gruelling period of mental, physical and academic training, testing to destruction all parts of military prowess, stamina and skills with the majority of the initial attendees either dropping out themselves or being failed by the staff.

Brett was in his element and despite the hardships and attempts of the staff to break him, he successfully earned his coveted and prestigious green beret and became a Royal Marine Commando, the elite fighting force of the British Navy. He immediately kickstarted his career by successfully going through the Potential Officers Course and impressing the Admiralty Interview Board to become an officer.

After a decade and having comfortably attained the rank of captain in the commandos, Brett knew that any further promotions would take him away from the frontline action and move him towards a desk. So with the support of various commanding officers of influence with whom he'd done tours of duty's with, and in one case saving his senior officer's life, his unusual request to conquer a new challenge and accolade was granted as he moved across from the commandos into the Special Air Service (SAS). Despite being given a qualifying dispensation due to his already impressive service he insisted on doing most of the training again to swiftly earn his beige beret. He proudly added a second tattoo to the top of his left arm, the first being of the Royal Marines Commando dagger motif, and now the Who Dares Wins SAS winged dagger insignia. He served another decade with the SAS and was involved in numerous military and terrorist events including hostage rescues, several foreign assassinations, two wars and numerous counter-terrorism excursions.

Brett kept in touch with his friend Frank and as the Dark Corporation started to grow, Frank began courting Brett to leave the military behind and enjoy the fruits and substantial benefits he could give him in the corporate world. Finally, Frank's persistence paid off and Brett left the services to set up Frank's corporate Special Operations policing department, with a small request that he also be able to establish a top bodyguard firm in Los Angeles using ex-military colleagues and friends. He wanted to share around some of the company benefits to other long-serving men who had put their lives on the line for their country alongside himself.

As the years passed and Frank's corporation grew larger, it proved a worthy learning ground for Brett to make the transition from military enforcer to corporate enforcer. His team in Special Operations rather like their jobs in the Services, would fly to one of the corporation's companies or outposts at a moment's notice when something 'special' was required. This could involve the acquisition of a competitor and their fast education on the ways their new masters liked to work. More often than not they would drop into a poorly performing part of the business to go through the numbers and read the riot act to the management team, making it clear that if they didn't turn things around within a short space of time they would be fired. Indeed over the years Brett or one of his managers had sat in front of numerous senior directors throughout the corporation, who having had their final warnings would now be told to clear their desk and get out. Sometimes they would be given a letter summarising their severance payments, other times when they had been indiscreet, brought the company's reputation into question or plain tried to swindle money out of a Firm, then they would be summarily dismissed immediately with no pay and be escorted out of the office. The ultimate corporate walk of shame as their stunned staff looked on.

With Frank Dark's corporate connections across the business world and Brett Harding's senior network within the military, the reputation of the Dark Corporation's Special Ops team coupled with their bodyguarding firm's services built a far-reaching reputation. Before long Brett found he could occasionally dip back into his military role when he and Frank would be sought out by a country's government official or Secret Service organisation. They'd want to hire Brett and some of his boys to undertake a covert mission with the utmost discretion off the grid and away from any official and transparent channels. Brett and his ex-soldiers effectively became mercenaries, guns for hire. Such infrequent forays were tolerated by Frank as long as Brett could demonstrate nothing would come back and bite the corporation. Frank also took the view that if these quick missions kept Brett happy and prevented him from going back to the military full-time, then it was worth the risk to keep his lifelong friend alongside him.

Brett therefore went along with the corporate role with little tolerance or time for the many fools he had to deal with in the company. He didn't really want to have anything to do with this latest CPO desk jockey Max Sargent, but would always do what Frank asked and dutifully did his best to smile and start up a conversation with him.

"So Frank tells me you're a bit of a car man like him?" Brett asked awkwardly.

"Well I have to admit that is one of my weaknesses," conceded Max, thinking to himself he should change the subject of cars, it was always painful talking about them to someone you suspected didn't have any interest in them. "So how long have you and Frank known one another?" asked Max.

"Crikey, a very long time, since school, must be about 40 years on and off, but half of that I was in the military," replied Brett.

Max was thinking sarcastically to himself 'you don't say, I'd never have thought that', when it was clear that anyone with half a brain looking at Brett Harding would instantly know this was a military man. Max could by now assume Brett had no idea that he had briefly served in the Marines himself. Brett could have easily searched through the Marines records and found his name there, albeit only for a couple of years' service. If he had, he would have also seen the honourable discharge along with a Military Cross.

Clearly, the thought that their new Procurement Officer with twenty years behind a desk could possibly have served in the Commando's was furthest from his thoughts, otherwise he would have surely tackled Max about it already. Max asked him about his career. Brett was at least at home on that subject and gave him a top-level summary of his trials and tribulations in the Royal Marines and SAS, deliberately leaving out the more perturbing stories. Max feigned interest when hearing about the Commandos, pretending he knew nothing about them, but taking comfort in the fact they were the same in some small way, once.

Max asked, "Frank mentioned something about providing bodyguard services for some of the Hollywood movie stars?"

Brett allowed himself a wry smile. "Ah yes, well to be honest it's just a bit of fun for me and my guys. The Beverly Hills bunch just love to constantly try to outdo one another and my firm there has a justifiably good reputation as providing some of the hardest ex-military men for close quarter protection. They all want their bodyguard to be harder and have a more distinguished military career than the next one. It's hilarious really because it's not like we have to protect them from anything, the most dangerous it gets is stopping a bunch of crazed fans wanting to touch them or get an autograph." Brett laughed at how pathetic he felt some of the celebrities were that he'd worked with.

"I guess at least you get to go to movie premiers, nice restaurants and see their amazing Bel Air mansions," offered Max. "Any notable movie stars you can mention by name that I might know?"

Brett sucked in air through his teeth. "Ooo I can't mention names, you know client privilege and all that nonsense. But there's one story with a particular big tough action movie star, an arrogant son of a bitch, I was with him on his yacht off Malibu. Not exactly any threats to his life out there on the water, but he'd recently had some trolling on social media after making some stupid political comment so was a little bit on edge. Well, he and I were up on the top deck of the yacht and one of his family were zooming around us in the speedboat and there was what sounded like a gunshot." Max raised his eyebrows waiting to hear what had happened. "The tough-guy actor hit the deck so fast he almost knocked himself out then as he stood up I could see he'd also managed to wet himself. The noise was just the speedboat motor backfiring. What an idiot." Brett shook his head in disdain.

Max nodded his head in agreement laughing at the story more than he wanted to. "I guess you get to use all the latest gadgets in your job?"

"Yeah we have access to everything, night visions, concealed two-way radio, bugging and surveillance devices but we don't need any of that. As I say guarding celebs is not an issue. You like your gadgets do you Max?" said Brett gesturing to the iPhone in Brett's back pocket. "What model iPhone is that then, can I have a look?" Brett asked.

Max obligingly handed over his iPhone suddenly remembering this was his communication and listening device that Si Lawson's techie guy had upgraded for him. Brett asked if Max would unlock the screen so he could have a look at the functions on it, which Max again obliged in doing, feeling it was strange that

Brett was taking such an interest in his phone, but equally it would seem odd if he didn't let him have a look. Max watched closely as Brett swiped across the screens full of app icons and games. He scrolled back to the first screen which showed all the boring functionality apps that came with an iPhone as standard. Max could feel his heart rate increase as Brett seemed to stare at the screen inquisitively with his finger hovering over some of the apps including the Notes icon. 'Good God, surely he can't know about the Notes communicator!' thought Max. Brett handed the phone back to Max without suspecting anything odd, he'd only wanted to get an insight into Max by seeing what sort of apps he had on his phone like social media, news alerts or even the types of games Max played. It all formed part of getting to know someone.

Max was relieved to slot his phone back into his pocket and as they walked back up the lawn to get some lunch they talked about Frank's lovely home with Brett also describing to Max Frank's other homes in Nice and Barbados. Then right at the end just as they were about to part company out of nowhere Brett asked one final question.

"Oh I meant to ask you why you left your last company, I gather you started with us pretty quickly, didn't you have any notice period to work out?"

Just when Max thought he got to the end of their difficult 'catch up' he was quite taken aback by the intensity of Brett's throwaway question loaded with innuendo. It was a question that had the potential to blow Max's cover wide open and land him in trouble big time. He summoned a casual smile before answering.

"I'd been there a while, great company, got on well with the directors, but was already looking for the next challenge and when Frank and Doreen's CPO role came along. I'd have been crazy not to go for it. After all Frank does pay his top execs way over market rates." Max gave a playful wink to Brett.

Having given himself more time to think about it whilst answering, Max was ready for any further tricky questions, but Brett simply pondered for a moment raising his eyebrows seemingly quite accepting of Max's explanation, then disappeared off towards the food. As he turned he quietly mumbled, "Bloody Ponti!"

Max caught the insult which he remembered from his time in the military. PONTI was the army slang for Person of No Tactical Importance, basically a loser. Something in Max broke and he harshly threw out at Brett, "I heard that thanks!"

Brett stopped in his tracks and turned round to face Max. "What?" he said crossly but with some surprise.

Max regretted calling Brett out but decided to follow through with his challenge, after all, what could Brett do here at Frank's garden party. "I'm not your usual pencil pusher Brett, and there's no need to be rude to me is there."

Brett now feigned surprise. "Don't know what you mean pal? How would you know what I said?"

Max gathered himself as Brett came closer threateningly. "I ain't no-one's PONTI alright," standing his ground.

The realisation that this office exec might have actually known what a PONTI was, but even more so that he had the balls to stand up to him, quite took Brett aback. He stared at Max, searching for him to look away, or apologise. But Max calmly gazed back at him. Brett wasn't used to this kind of reaction and catching sight of Frank Dark on the terrace looking over at them questioningly, quickly snapped out of his rising anger.

Brett acquiesced. "A misunderstanding Max, sorry if you thought I said that. I can see there's more to you than meets the eye." Brett forced a smile which showed as more of a smirk and spun around on his heels to leave.

Max watched him go before allowing himself to relax and breath a sigh of relief at their encounter. He hoped that him knowing what a PONTI was wouldn't alert Brett to his military service, but it was possible a well-read civi would have known the insulting term Brett had mumbled at him.

After their little talk, Brett found he was more appreciative that their new CPO had a bit of gumption in him, unlike the usual bunch of wets he had to deal with across the company. There was certainly something about him, a hidden edge, but Brett couldn't quite put his finger on it, for now. He concluded that Max Sargent seemed like an okay desk jockey and quite harmless. Not surprisingly Max concluded the complete opposite about Brett and would be careful in trying to avoid him in the future.

Once Max had collected a choice selection of lunch from the buffet servers he noticed Doreen Leader having a conversation with a couple of leering guys from sales. She wasn't enjoying their juvenile attention and was trying to extricate herself. Max went over and politely interrupted the conversation saying that he needed to have an urgent word with his boss Doreen in private. They begrudgingly backed off, making their way back for a second helping from the buffet.

"Thanks Max. I needed rescuing. I don't know whether they were more interested in talking to me or just staring at me, couple of idiots. They're not a nice bunch in sales, how are you getting on here today, all okay?"

"Yup pretty good thanks, had a nice chat early on with Frank then did the rounds including Cindy and have just had a chat with the elusive Brett, although it felt more like I was being interviewed again," Max said summoning a forced smile and raised an eyebrow.

"Frank mentioned to me you're going to drop in on the Indian printers after all, on your way to meeting the two of us in Hong Kong. How did you manage to persuade him to change his mind?" asked Doreen.

"I didn't," replied Max, "it seems John Dawlish and he had a change of heart after the awkward moment at the review meeting and are quite happy for me to pop in and say hi to the manager when I'm in Mumbai."

"Good news then on both counts, I'll welcome the extra company when we meet up in Hong Kong," said Doreen. Max was taken aback as he thought he detected a brief glint in her eye, 'No surely not' he thought. "Anyway I need to circulate a bit more, I can see a few of my European finance directors looking over here waiting for me to be free again so I'd better go and chat. Let's just hope it's not all about work." She swept off towards the eagerly waiting French, German and Italian finance directors, as Max and the salesmen watched closely, taking in her exquisite lines.

Inside the study of the large mansion, Frank, John and Brett had congregated together purely by chance but each comfortable and safe in one another's company, especially rather than being outside making small talk with the employees. The office rear window overlooked the pool area and as they noticed certain individuals they enjoyed a cheeky gossip about some of the people, what they'd said when chatting to them, who might be sleeping with who in the office and which of the people they disliked the most. Frank then briefly touched on Max Sargent.

"I had a nice chat with our new CPO Max, quite the car enthusiast."

John added, "That'll stand him in good stead at bonus time eh Frank," laughing.

"Yes, yes, maybe it will," joked Frank. "I've told him and Doreen he can visit the Indian printers after all and I'll see him the next day in Hong Kong so I can suss out if he's the slightest bit suspicious about what's going on there. Did you find out anything else on him John?" Frank had suggested to John Dawlish to do his own vetting on their new CPO even though they knew it had already been done by the recruitment company.

"Yup I had a little look around and all seemed good, Doreen's found us quite the little Mary Poppins buyer, 'practically perfect'. Clean record, big corporate's, won awards," replied John.

Frank thought out loud, "Is it worth one of us just putting in a call to his last company as a final check?"

John replied, "Nah he's fine, don't waste your time."

"Brett, did you ask him about his last job?" asked Frank.

"I did, all boring stuff. But I'll do it anyway if you want me to," Brett quickly offered. "It'll have to wait 'til Monday, but I'll put a call into them asking to speak to one of his colleagues or staff in his old buying department." Brett chose not to mention Max's challenge of him, he simply didn't want to own up to this young executive calling him out, not good for his reputation.

"Okay thanks Brett, then that's the end of it, we'll give our Max Sargent a clean bill of health and start to bring him into the team like we are with Doreen," said Frank. "Now come on guys we need to get back out there, circulate and perform and make sure everyone has a great day. Brett, try and smile at people for heaven's sake, you're scaring some of them," he jokingly parted.

Having regretted bringing the Ferrari all day whilst watching the conveyor belt of expensive champagnes, wines and drinks passing by, Max was now glad he hadn't drunk as he was back in his F40 driving home up the A3. Having been playing cat and mouse with a little Lotus Elise for the past couple of miles, he pressed in the heavy clutch and dropped down from fourth to third gear, simultaneously letting out the clutch and pushing down the accelerator pedal hard. Even whilst already doing 75 mph the Ferrari's large rear wheels started to spin momentarily then dug themselves into the tarmac pressing him deep back into his bucket seat, as the red racing car instantaneously rocketed past the flailing little Lotus completely out accelerated and left behind for dust.

Max couldn't wait to call Si Lawson when he got home to give him the good news about visiting the suspect Indian printers. He felt his relationship was slowly building with Frank Dark and it seemed he'd managed to recover things with John Dawlish as well. However, should he mention to Si his conversations with Brett Harding who he felt was watching him closely. It certainly made Max feel uncomfortable but maybe that was just the way Brett was with everyone, he certainly had the reputation for it so perhaps Max was just being paranoid. As he slowed down coming towards the more built-up part of the A3 near Wimbledon, Max decided he would tell Si that Brett Harding could potentially be suspicious of him, maybe he knew Max was there to snoop around. He just wanted to hear some reassurance that Si had everything covered, he was sure he would.

Early Monday afternoon and Brett Harding finished a call with his guys from his Beverly Hills office who were eight hours behind, to go through the week's assignments. Crossing it off his 'to do' list the next item he'd written down for himself read 'Call MS firm'. He thought to himself, 'Oh yeah, I told the guys I'd put a call into Max Sargent's old employer'. He really couldn't be bothered but knew he had to. Brett wasn't chatty at the best of times so the thought of having to put on an act sounding all corporate and professional didn't enthral him, but it was on the list to do.

He looked up the head office telephone number for Max's old company and dialled. The receptionist answered asking who was calling and how she might help.

Brett introduced himself. "Good afternoon my name is Lee Peterson, we're one of your suppliers, and I've been dealing with Max Sargent in the procurement function. I understand he's now left the company so wondered if I could please speak to one of his colleagues in procurement?"

"Of course Mr Peterson, I can put you right through, what was the name of your company again?" asked the receptionist.

'Shit!' thought Brett, in his haste to make up a false name he'd forgotten to think of a pretend company. Banking on the receptionist not knowing the names of all suppliers he quickly made one up. "I'm with Star Stationery," he announced somewhat pathetically and held his breath waiting for this to be accepted.

"Thank you, Mr Peterson, I'll put you straight through to someone in procurement."

Moments later a new voice appeared on the line. "Good morning Mr Peterson, Jeff Simmons here, I'm one of the Senior Procurement Managers. Max Sargent used to be my boss. How can I help you, I'm not aware we had a supplier called Star Stationery?"

Brett realised this procurement guy might smell a rat with his poor choice of company name so decided to quickly cut to the chase and cover what he wanted to know.

"Well I was dealing with Max Sargent and then told he'd suddenly left your company, what did happen, he seemed to go very quick?" Brett pitched, hoping he wouldn't have to be on the line much longer.

Jeff Simmons was happy to explain. "Yes Max did seem to go quickly but he had mentioned he was looking for his next big challenge so no surprise. As is often the case with these senior directors, once they've decided to go they usually go quickly. We were all gutted when he told us he was leaving, he was a really good boss. Star Stationery you said, is it something I can help with Mr Peterson?"

Relieved he'd got what he wanted from the call, Brett made a quick exit. "Look thank you for your time, Jeff was it. I was hoping to deal with Max, so I'll find him at his new company and leave you to get on with your busy day, thank you again, goodbye." Brett put the phone down and couldn't help thinking he didn't mind being in the middle of a war zone with bullets flying around and landmines going off, but boy did he hate having to make up calls like that with corporate people. He crossed the 'Call MS firm' line off his list and moving onto the next item thought to himself 'seems our Max Sargent is clean'.

In a small, soundproofed cubicle at Thames House, the so-called Jeff Simmons put the phone down, having received a rather odd call from a Lee Peterson. He then smiled.

The man Brett Harding had spoken to supposedly at Max's old company was in fact an employee at MI5. Part of a small team who cycled through some of the more boring duties provided to various divisions of the organisation, such as long-term observation on people going in and out of buildings, trawling through long sound or CCTV recordings looking for something in particular, or masquerading as reference providers for 'Executives Pending' assignments were all part of the job for this man.

A few days earlier Vince from Si Lawson's cyber team had briefed their department on the possibility of someone calling their EP's previous employer for a reference. As part of the deal struck with the employer regarding Max Sargent's employment termination, or as it was since changed to, his resignation, the employer had been given strict instructions for their receptionist team to divert any calls with the mention of Max Sargent's name to a separate number that Vince provided. The call would then be transferred through to this team at MI5 who had received their briefing from Vince on the background to Max Sargent being one of their EP's, and what might likely be asked. All scenarios were catered for, so it was an easy call for the man to handle, simply to confirm that Max Sargent had left the company under normal circumstances and that he was a good fellow.

The man in the cubicle made a quick call up to Vince, who then immediately popped in to see Si Lawson to tell him someone had called in on Max's old firm to check there was nothing untoward about him leaving them. All had gone fine.

Si sat back in his chair pleased that the cover for one of his EP's had been protected and was still intact. After speaking with Max Saturday evening, he was quite excited to see what his pending visit to Mumbai would turn up. Maybe now they were closing in on the Dark Corporation. He was putting a lot of faith in Max Sargent though.

15

Max organised himself and settled down in the small but comparatively luxurious first-class seat pod of his British Airways flight to Mumbai, grateful for the extra space and privacy far away from the 'cattle' economy class further down the cabin behind him. He had to admit that Frank Dark really did like to look after his senior staff with all the perks like first-class travel, the best hotels, chauffeured cars for arriving in style to business meetings and generous credit card expense account limits allowing any emergency expenditures to be covered and dining at the best restaurants. He did his best to get himself comfortable in the seat for the nine-hour flight from the British Airways Terminal five at Heathrow to Mumbai.

He familiarised himself with all the extras around him such as headphones, media screen, blanket, pillow, a neat little travel bag and magazines. The cabin staff were seemingly calmly escorting people to their seats and asking what drink they would like before they'd even sat down. Mildly intoxicated and sleepy travellers were always so much easier to look after than the wide-awake ones full of energy, demands and questions. However, plying their guests with too much alcohol could have the adverse effect of keeping them calm and turn them into drunk monsters in a confined space, it was a careful balance.

Max closely studied the two female cabin staff, as almost all passengers do when there's nothing else interesting to look at in their confined cabin, each of them assigned to look after one of the two short aisles in first class. They both sported smart British Airways uniforms, medium heeled black shoes which would soon be discarded for a pair of comfy flats and carefully but overly applied makeup with pristine hair. They were both smiling, pleasant and polite. Max wondered how long they would keep up the Little Miss

Perfect act as the nine-hour flight progressed.

Frank Dark's PA Sheila had taken over all his travel arrangements and bookings and was highly efficient in sorting everything out for him. She'd booked his flights, arranged the chauffeur taking him to Heathrow, given him a mini-map of where the VIP lounge was in the airport, then an executive car to meet him at the Mumbai airport arrivals and take him to his hotel. Then after his overnight stay, his efficient itinerary whisked him briefly to Apex Finance then back to the airport on a flight to Hong Kong, where during his stay there he would crossover with Frank Dark and Doreen Leader. Everything neatly printed out on an itinerary she gave him with emergency numbers and all the details you could possibly wish for, she was good and Max thought she'd have to be to look after Frank. The only thing he'd done before the trip was a quick call to his Mumbai based buyer Abhay Khatri to invite him to dinner for a meet and catch up at his hotel. Sheila told him that Frank had alerted the Indian currency printer's manager Rajit Singh to expect him for a 'quick courtesy visit'.

As the first-class cabin filled up Max quickly surveyed his fellow passengers just on the off chance there might be some big movie star or celebrity on the same flight. There was an eclectic mix of people in the cabin, some very wealthy and showing it with their impeccable suits, suntans and gold watches. The usual few businessmen and women, Max always assumed they worked for big investment banks as not many companies now flew their staff first class what with all the cutbacks and harder times. One middle-aged guy was looking quite scruffy with jeans and T-shirt who had deliberately decided to ignore the unspoken etiquette of at least trying to dress in smart casual for first-class. Despite his rebellious appearance, Max guessed that he might indeed be the wealthiest person there, there was just something about him. Perhaps some entrepreneur with his own company or having just sold it for hundreds of millions. Finally, he recognised another man with his model-like wife or mistress as being a famous footballer, one of the world's best and highest paid, but for the life of him Max couldn't remember his name, neither frankly did he care. He settled back down again to enjoy as best he could three movies and a couple of nice meals.

The captain proudly announced that they'd managed to make up some time and would arrive 20 minutes ahead of schedule, but that there would be a short delay whilst they would have to wait for the allocated gate to be readied for them. 'Easy come easy go' thought Max.

They arrived at Chhatrapati Shivaji International Airport in Mumbai and as Max came through the Arrivals doors emerging from the air-conditioned environment, he was immediately greeted by the oven-like Indian heat hitting him unashamedly in the face. He knew he would get used to the heat but that first time you experienced it in a new hot country it always felt stifling. He met his driver who took him out to a nearby parked black Range Rover to take him to his hotel. 'Frank loves his black Range Rover's' thought Max as he climbed into the front of the car wanting to take in everything on their short forty-minute drive.

Their route took them out of the airport at Vile Parle and South onto the Western Express Highway past various Colony towns. From the vantage of the fast-moving road, Max looked out through the bright dusty haze over this truly amazing city with its incredibly busy streets, bustling with activity and people. A lot of people. The lanes amongst the low-level buildings intermingled with pockets of larger more modern structures and offices, resembled a busy ant's colony of people, cars, bikes and mopeds, taxis and Tuk-Tuk's, traders and animals casually roaming the street. At the expense of the car's air-conditioning, he put his window down a little to take in the unique mix of noises and smells, some pleasant, some not so pleasant. They passed over the Mithi River at Mahim Creek Bridge past the fish market and on through Dadar and Kamathipura towards Mumbai's southern Colaba peninsula, turning left at Nariman Point to the Taj Mahal Palace hotel in Marharashtra with its distinctive light red domed tower in the centre.

The grandiose six-floor Taj Mahal Palace hotel was built in 1903 by the prominent Indian business family Tata after they were refused entry by one of the top hotels Watson's. The Taj hotel was the first in India to have electricity and has quite a list of other firsts over its fellow Indian hotels; first to have English butlers, American fans, German elevators, a licensed bar and a disco. With the later addition of the taller Taj Mahal Tower in 1973, the hotel boasts over 600 rooms and 1,600 staff. Then in November 2008, the hotel was unfortunately in the spotlight for the wrong reasons, being one of twelve sites against which a terrorist group carried out indiscriminate shootings and bombings. Of the total number of 167 innocent people killed during the attacks lasting four days, 31 guests and staff died at The Taj hotel with over 400 other guests escaping the dreadful fate intended for them from the attack.

Max checked in and after settling into his room suite went out for a quick explore around the streets near the hotel and then went on to the waterfront behind the hotel overlooking the Colaba Reef Bay and the Gateway of India Triumphal Arch. Returning to his room he still had time for a swim in the hotel's large pool before needing to get ready to meet his local buyer.

That evening Abhay Khatri arrived at the hotel to meet Max for dinner. This was a big deal for him, he'd never met the previous Chief Procurement Officer and here was the new one coming all the way from head office in England to Mumbai especially to meet him. The importance of this meeting and dinner wasn't lost on him at all, he'd thought of nothing else since Max had called him a few days ago to make the arrangements. Even though Max had said no need for an office meeting or presentation, Abhay had still brought a printout of slides he'd prepared just in case his departmental boss had changed his mind, he wanted to do whatever it took to impress him. He was a kind-hearted and hard working young buyer eager to win over his superiors and earn more responsibility for his Buyer role in the Dark Corporation's India operations. He covered everything the regional companies and staff needed to buy for their operations whilst closely following the guidelines and corporate deals advised to him by Max and his team in Group.

As he entered the hotel Max was already waiting for him in the reception area to give him a hearty greeting, genuinely delighted to meet one of his remote team. Despite Max being aware that he may not be with the company for too long, purely out of managerial habit he knew how important it was to give a good long-lasting impression on this youngster.

"It's so nice to meet you Abhay, speaking on the phone is never as good as meeting someone face-to-face. How are you?" greeted Max.

Abhay could hardly contain himself at the warmth of the greeting. "Mister Sargent it's so nice to meet you too, I am honoured that you have come to Mumbai to meet me and at such a lovely hotel."

"I hope you like Sichuan and Cantonese food Abhay as I've booked us a table in the hotel's Golden Dragon restaurant," said Max. "Let's go and enjoy ourselves with the menu and have a good catch up over dinner."

"Oh my goodness Mister Sargent that sounds wonderful," replied Abhay dutifully following Max through the lobby.

Max tried several times to insist that Abhay called him 'Max' but gave up by the time they were ordering their food, understanding that for a first meeting with someone so important he was going to be called Mr Sargent whether he liked it or not.

Max made sure they tried lots of things on the menu and wine list pushing the boat out to treat his young buyer to a memorable dinner, all to be added to his room bill and courtesy of his company expense account. His keen protégé happily told Max all about the spends and suppliers under his remit and some of the challenges he has with local management wanting to use their favourite suppliers who were more often than not members or friends of their extended families. He was also fascinated to hear about Max's career and rise through the ranks working for large household name corporations and what it was like living and working in London.

Max managed to work into the conversation mention of the rupee currency printing operation in Mumbai hoping to get some insights into what might be going on there.

"So I'm popping in to the currency printers tomorrow, anything I should know about them to help me prepare?"

Abhay shrugged. "I don't have anything to do with them, they sort out their own buying Mister Sargent."

Max pushed. "Come on Abhay, just between us buyers, what's the real story there?"

Abhay looked a little concerned. "I'm not sure I understand you Mister Sargent. All I know is they're subject to all sorts of regulations and stipulations by the Government and Ministry of Finance I believe. I'm sure it's very tightly controlled."

"What's the manager like," asked Max, with a final attempt to get some hint of possible indiscretions going on.

Abhay seemed to feign more surprise at the questions. "Mister Singh. He is an outstanding member of the business community here in Mumbai. I would aspire to achieve half of what he has managed. An honourable man. From what I've heard anyway." Abhay switched his attention back to his food and Max felt that was enough Q and A for the humble Indian buyer, so also returned to the fabulous meal.

Max and Abhay had thoroughly enjoyed their evening together and Max felt a little sad that he would never see him again given his own likely short term stay with the company. They said their farewells in the lobby and Max retired back to his room hoping that tomorrow would somehow reveal enough information for him to hand over the whole thing to Si Lawson and his team to handle.

Abhay had also enjoyed his dinner with a seasoned Procurement Officer, learning about his career and what it was like at the top. He pressed a speed dial on his mobile as he drove away from the hotel. It answered curtly on the speaker setting, "Yes."

"Uncle, it's me, I'm leaving the Taj," said Abhay dutifully.

"Well, anything to tell me?" said the male voice.

"Not really Uncle. He did try to push me into telling him

more about the operation."

"How do you mean, what did you say?" inquired the voice.

"Don't worry Uncle, I didn't say anything," assured Abhay. "It felt like he suspected something, but there again it could have just been him wanting to get a little background on you and your firm before he meets you, I don't know."

There was a pause. "Okay. Well done Abhay, you're a good boy. Pass on my wishes to your family."

Abhay ended the call, to his Uncle Singh, who was actually his Father's Sister's husband. In Sikh his Phupher, though he'd always known him as just 'Uncle'. India was a big place, but in so many ways, especially in local communities, a very small place.

Max had arranged to drop in and meet the manager of the printers Rajit Singh on his way back to the airport before he flew onto Hong Kong. His visit to India was a fleeting one but he didn't mind as Max just wanted to do what he had to do for Si Lawson then hopefully move on with his life. It was a shame though to be in such a fascinating city for such a tantalisingly short time.

Max exited the grand hotel to be greeted once again by the familiar black chauffeured Range Rover with the same driver that had collected him from the airport. He explained to Max he was the Apex manager's driver and as they set off Max wondered how much he might know about his boss's dealings. They retraced their previous route back to the airport area then skirting around it headed into one of the many older Business Parks. Turning into an unusually named 90 Feet Road they passed a cinema, then a Police Station and turned off before reaching the Mahesh Hotel ahead of them.

As they approached a modest but secure looking building complex with surrounding fencing the driver pointing to it said, "Here we are Mr Sargent, welcome to Apex Finance, one of the securest buildings in the area." Max thought it certainly didn't look like a money printers and the boring company name would dissuade any passing thieves from bothering giving it a second look. The gates opened and two robust solid steel bollards slowly retracted beneath the tarmac to allow them to enter and the first two of many security guards were revealed in the entrance hut peering into the car before waving them through. The driver pulled up opposite a modest entrance with strong looking doors and raced around the car to open the door for Max who had already half got out the car. The manager appeared through the doorway to greet Max.

Rajit Singh had proudly been named by his parents after the famous leader of the Sikh Empire. He came from a modest Indian family whose father worked in a number of local Mumbai banks and so the dye had already been cast for him that this would also be the career he was strongly encouraged to follow. A small smartly turned out Indian man exuding more stature and importance than his size and frame offered, he was a slightly shifty person who found it hard to trust anyone before having a long and positive relationship with them. Perhaps simply as a result of a lifetime dealing with money, awarding it, loaning it, protecting it and now printing it, he had learnt it was best to start any relationship by *not* trusting the other person.

He closely eyed the smart younger executive coming towards him for a 'quick courtesy visit' and would have been quite happy and certainly not insulted to have not been asked to entertain the new CPO from head office. He wasn't used to such visits being one of the few businesses in the Dark Corporation that wasn't subject to the usual dealings with corporate or regional functions. He ran the business and only dealt with Frank Dark and John Dawlish.

He was only seeing this person because Frank had asked him to. Rajit would push himself to be welcoming and professional to this Max Sargent, give him a quick tour of the facility then have him on his way back to the airport in time for him to have his lunch there, and not with him. After the slightly stiff greetings, he led Max up to his office where his secretary promptly came in with tea and some very familiar Digestive biscuits, knowing how much this double act was so loved by the British.

"It's very good of you Mr Sargent to take time out and visit our humble enterprise," said Rajit betraying some insincerity.

"Thank you for your time Mr Singh, I couldn't pass by without at least introducing myself and I'd love to hear a little more about what you do here." Max had already picked up the 'at arms-length' vibe from his host so was just as keen to get on with the visit as he was.

"This Mr Sargent is my little Fort Knox in the middle of a Mumbai business park, quietly hidden away unassumingly, but providing a vital service to the Indian government and economy. We have around 15 security guards on the payroll all closely vetted and many long servers who we cycle through the rotas of guarding and protecting the building and what we do here 24/7, 365 days a year."

Max picked up his tea and biscuits and settled back into his chair. He was interested in hearing everything Rajit would tell him about the operation, but could see he was being delivered a well-rehearsed and used, impassionate introduction many before him had no doubt sat through. He went with it, for now.

Rajit continued. "Here at Apex Finance, we are privileged to be one of only several contingency currency printers in the country. We are effectively on standby to take up any slack in currency runs allocated to us by the Ministry of Finance where the authorised printers are unable to cover the requirements. Or perhaps have a supply problem and run out of materials or have some other disaster that prevents them from fulfilling their production orders. There are four official currency note printing presses, the central government controls two of them, one just to the north of us here at Nashik in Maharashtra and the other in Dewas in Madhya Pradesh. The Reserve Bank of India subsidiary the Bharatiya Reserve Bank Note Mudran controls the other two at Mysuru in Karnataka and Salboni in West Bengal."

Max asked, "It all sounds very tightly controlled, may I ask how here at Apex you managed to become one of the contingency printers?"

Rajit gave a slight frown at the flow of his presentation being broken, he wasn't used to being interrupted with questions and winced his eyes momentarily before answering.

"Many years back we had to go through an exhaustive vetting and tender process to win one of the honoured contingency appointments to print currency."

Given this was talking about a procurement tender sourcing exercise Max felt he could genuinely press the manager further and perhaps drive out any extra information that wasn't part of his well-worn introduction speech. "How were you measured and scored for this tender, what kind of KPIs did you have to demonstrate," he interrupted again.

Rajit's patience thinned a little more. "The usual thorough questions and investigation were put upon us to demonstrate we could ably meet all the rigorous and strict criteria they had set such as costs, security, management profile, company and holding Corporation records, IT capability and compatibility with the government's systems for encrypted transfer of communications and digital number printing. Plus secure armoured car and armed guard transportation of the currency and of course the production capability to print highly complex notes with the latest and finest digital and ink printing equipment." Rajit found that he quite enjoyed being tested for a more complete answer and being able to rise to the occasion. Max was keenly aware this man had been in charge of this business for many years and knew absolutely everything there was to know about it. He pressed once more.

"But I imagine there must be many other printers with similar capabilities all competing to be one of the governments contingency printers. Often it takes just one small edge or competency to separate the winners from the losers?" prodded Max.

Rajit was momentarily still in the frame of mind of fielding difficult questions from his visitor, showing off as he did and without the benefit of having rehearsed such answers responded willingly to Max's question.

"I think Mr Sargent that we were better than our competitors across most of the KPIs and it always helps just a little if your boss knows their boss, then you have that personal commitment to make sure you do a good job for them," said Rajit blissfully unaware that he might have given Max anything untoward. Favours, friendships and families often oiled the wheels of business in India, there was nothing unusual about that.

Max, however, was high fiving himself behind his stern look of concentration and was thinking to himself 'your boss knows their boss indeed, so that's how you get to win a tightly controlled government contract to print currency in India'. He wasn't going to press the questioning any further for risk of alerting the manager he was being a little too interested in the operation here and was relieved when Rajit continued with his rehearsed speech.

"And lastly we have to have the latest printing machines nominated by the Ministry of Finance specifically for their high definition multi-layer print and laser capabilities and extremely fast print runs with complete and uncompromising accuracy. We have to buy the ink and paper from their nominated suppliers. For example, the paper used for rupee currency notes has cotton and balsam mixed into the pulp and a tiny proportion of silk, we buy this from the Security Paper Mill in Hoshangabad, Madhya Pradesh just nearby to one of the registered currency printers."

Rajit lent forward and had a sip of his tea, annoyed that it had already gone cold gave him his cue to get on with his visitor's quick tour of the facility, so he stood up and beckoned Max to follow him to the doorway. Max obliged. They went back downstairs down a corridor passing several offices and a small lounge with a number of security guards on their break watching TV. Entering the large printing room Max could see two large printers and a smaller one to the side, only one of the large machines was operational at the time. To the side was the stores room with various roles of blank paper and containers of inks waiting to be called upon. In the corner was a small office overlooking the operation and three workers were checking on the busy printer in the middle and making adjustments on the other large machine that wasn't being used. On the side, there was a large steel roller door with a couple of the security guards standing around chatting idly.

Rajit launched into his printing room tour speech detailing

the specifications of the two large printing machines and what the staff were doing. As they walked alongside the operating machine Max could see the large sheets of rupee notes flying through the rollers and the press, past the digital and laser printing where the individual serial numbers were put on each note, ending up with the unwieldy cutting press which transformed large stacks of printed sheets into individual notes to then be bound and stacked ready for palletising manually.

"Where do you store the printed money, I haven't seen a safe anywhere large enough?" asked Max.

"We don't keep money here, that would require a far higher level of security," explained Rajit. "No, as soon as the currency is printed and packed ready, it goes straight off to its destinations in the armoured trucks. Having money just sitting around would invite potential problems wouldn't you agree?"

Max nodded politely. "What's that smaller printing machine over there for, it's quite different from these two big ones in the middle," asked Max.

Rajit was visibly uncomfortable with the question Max noticed and tried to shrug it off answering, "That's an older redundant printer, we sometimes use it for test runs, you know, to align the printing accuracy and check new ink batches." He quickly moved on to the end of the printer line.

As a buyer and negotiator Max was always highly sensitive to the body language and the subtle use of words by those people he was dealing with. He was intrigued that his question had unsettled Rajit Singh and that he'd first mentioned the printer was 'redundant' meaning surely not being used, and then immediately said they use it for test printing. Seemed a bit odd. "So it is used then for printing currency?" he asked.

Rajit looked quite put out at the challenging question. "As I said, we use it for test runs, that's all." The manager moved onto one of the larger machines signalling that was the end of that little Q and A. Max moved on to join Rajit who was watching the finished 2000-rupee notes coming out of the end of the line.

Rajit continued officiously. "We have eight different rupee note denominations from five rupees up to these ones here of two-thousand rupees. Each Mahatma Gandhi series note has an incorporated security thread, watermarks, identification mark, raised intaglio print and some fluorescent ink, and a transparent register. The individual serial numbers bottom left and top right are controlled digitally by the Ministry of Finance. We also have micro-printed texts on various locations which are only really visible with a magnifying glass, for example on the temple of Gandhi's spectacles it reads 'India' or 'RBI' with the face value of the note say 10 or 50."

Max ventured one more question. "The individual serial numbers you mentioned, how are they provided to you and used?"

"We are sent the serial number batches for particular note denominations by the Ministry of Finance via a heavily encrypted file which we don't have access to opening. We download the file into the printer's computer and activate it when we are ready to produce the notes run. The file sends the unique serial numbers to the laser printer at the end of the line and the computer also keeps a log of each number once it's been used and printed on a note so it can't be re-used or duplicated."

Max moved back down the machine to the part that looked as though it was the computer controlling it and pointing asked, "I assume this is the printer's computer?"

The screen showed a series of operating functions taking place monitoring the integrity of the printer and the notes being printed with a scrolling list of the serial numbers moving down the screen as they were used on individual notes. One of the operators was hovering beside Max wanting to access the keyboard and screen so Max apologised for getting in the way and started to move back towards Rajit. The operator brought up the home screen and then opened up another program showing the ink levels of the various colours and types being used. Satisfied with the readouts he returned the screen back to the details print run monitoring and data.

As Max turned back to Rajit he caught himself noticing the

operators home screen for the instant it had appeared and visualising the various program icons on the screen realised he was familiar with one of them that stood out to him. The Angel virus checker file. He paused for a moment but conscious the impatient manager was watching him, he decided not to mention it and then consoled himself that having the firm's own virus checker shouldn't be unusual, even if it is on a currency notes printer PC.

Rajit walked Max over to the small office which at that moment was unmanned and standing by the open doorway allowed Max to look inside. "This is the control room which oversees all production, ordering supplies, arranging the collection by the security vans and checking production-related invoices before they get passed through to the accounts office we saw earlier for payment," explained Rajit already starting to close the door.

Max wanted to visually scan as much of the office as he could with his eyes quickly darting around the shelves and desktop in a last attempt to see if there was anything unusual, knowing that his tour guide was wanting to send him on his way now. The top was untidily littered with invoices from various suppliers, printer maintenance parts and production supplies which all seemed fairly normal. Then just as Rajit started closing the door abruptly ushering Max out, one of the machinists called over to their manager, distracting him for a few seconds.

Max caught a glimpse of a small tray labelled 'Mr Singh – Confidential' with one particular small paper invoice with some bank's name on the top. It was partly covered so all he could see was '… Bank Limited'. Conscious that Rajit was gesticulating to his printer operator that he was busy with his guest, Max instinctively grabbed at the invoice and quickly thrust it into his pocket adeptly and silently. He turned to face Rajit just as the door closed. Rajit looked back round from his employee by the printer suspiciously.

"Mr Singh, thank you so much for the fascinating tour of your impressive operation here, I appreciate your time," said Max smiling and trying to end on a polite positive. He had no idea if the invoice would help but thought it strange that a bank would be providing services or products for this operation.

"Was there something in particular you were looking for Mister Sargent, in the control room?" asked Rajit, unnerving Max.

He feigned surprise at the question and shrugged it off replying, "Not at all Mr Singh. You know us buyers, we're always trying to read what's on the salesman's paperwork. Habit I guess."

Max was conscious he'd been potentially seen snooping, so having been on the defensive, decided as always to take back control. With a tinge of sarcasm he turned to Rajit and asked him, "Why do you ask me that, do you have something you don't want me to see Mr Singh?" with some sarcasm, which wasn't lost on the manager.

A couple of the staff working the printers paused what they were doing and looked round. Max's tone with their manager had pricked up their ears. They hadn't heard anyone speak to Mr Singh in quite that manner before.

Max had left just enough humour in his tone to allow Rajit to take it as a poor attempt at joking with him, so he quickly brushed it away with, "Of course not Mister Sargent. We have nothing to hide here, as you have seen." The mood relaxed again and the staff continued with their work, relieved.

Rajit had however exhausted his patience for his visitor and made a mental note to himself to suggest to Frank Dark and John Dawlish not to send him any more nosy people from head office. He escorted Max back through the building where Max excused himself to visit the gent's room before leaving for the airport.

Max shut himself in one of the cubicles and moments later flushed the toilet and emerged. When he came back into the corridor he was horrified to see the same printer operator that had distracted Rajit, now being questioned by him. Rajit Singh then turned to Max looking quite perturbed and grave.

"My operator has made an insolent accusation Mister Sargent which I have had to admonish him over. I'm so sorry," he reported.

Max's heart was thumping out of his chest. "What's the

problem?"

Rajit continued. "He claims to have seen you take something from the control room just now." He waited for Max to react but got nothing. "I've told him how ridiculous an accusation this is. But we do take security here very seriously, an example you understand to all staff."

"Of course Mister Singh, though you'll be glad to hear he's mistaken," offered Max, hoping that would be the end of it.

Rajit summoned over one of the nearby security guards. "Just so everyone can see there's been a terrible mistake, would you mind if my guard searches you quickly before you leave?" Max was stunned and about to protest when Rajit gestured to the guard to search Max.

He dutifully held his arms up as the guard, inexperienced at doing close body searches, patted and fumbled about his body. The guard backed off, to Max's relief, but then spoke to his manager. "All clean, just a pen, mobile and some paper in his pocket," pointing to one side of Max's trousers.

Rajit looked at Max and not hearing any offer to disclose what this document was, asked him, "Mister Sargent, I'm going to have to ask you to turn out your pockets please?"

Max huffed and puffed in disdainful protest, closely watched by Rajit, the guard and the print operator. He pulled the crumpled piece of paper from his pocket, then sombrely handed it over to Rajit who seemed to proudly accept it as an admission of guilt. Rajit looked to his machinist who nodded as if to verify that this was indeed what he believed he saw Max take from the control room.

Rajit slowly unfurled the paper. His face turned from satisfaction to dismay, then anger. He looked up at Max, then back to his staff, now both realising something was up.

Max waited. Rajit gathered himself, cleared his throat and awkwardly passed the piece of paper back to Max saying, "I am so sorry Mister Sargent, here is your travel itinerary back. I don't know what to say. My profound apologies, this is awful," he glared at his staff who scuttled away, "and incredibly embarrassing."

Max didn't want to let him off that easily. This man had barely hidden his contempt for his visit and had been rude from start to end. Plus Max knew something was going on here. He met Rajit's eyes, "You didn't seriously think that I, a senior Director of this company, would have any reason to take documents from your offices did you? I don't know what to say. I'll have to report this whole visit and this embarrassing incident to my boss the CFO."

Now Rajit transformed into a polite, pleading, courteous host. "Please Mister Sargent, that won't be necessary. I am so sorry about this. Let me take you out for a superb lunch before you go to the airport?"

Max milked it with more huffing and finally conceded, "Let's draw a line under this, I won't mention it as I don't want to cause you any further embarrassment. However, you might like to show a little more genuine courtesy to visiting Directors in the future."

"Yes, indeed, I'm so sorry."

Max bid him farewell at the doorway where his driver had been waiting with the Range Rover and his luggage to take Max back to the airport. Rajit shuffled apologetically behind Max and waved him off from the doorway. Max felt slightly flustered as he said farewell and was trying to order in his mind what he'd seen and what might be useful to report back to Si Lawson. He felt slightly disheartened as there wasn't much that jumped out at him but there again if something was going on there it would hardly be part of the manager's tour for him. His senses were telling him 'something at Apex stank to high heaven', and it wasn't the smell from the nearby slums.

He climbed into the front of the car and they pulled up to the exit gates and waited for them to open and the bollards to retract into the ground.

Rajit Singh was already back in his office where he picked up his mobile and started typing out a text to John Dawlish, which with the time difference he'd get in a few hours when he woke up to start his day. The text read simply 'Met and gave tour, bit nosy and annoying, but all fine. Don't send me any more head office people. RS'.

The drive back to the airport was only a short one so Max asked the driver, "Do you get many visitors from head office?"

The driver seemed pleased at the chance of having a conversation and happily replied, "Hardly any Sir, they seem to leave us pretty much alone here, apart from the IT maintenance guy, you're the only senior executive visitor I've collected for maybe three or four months."

"IT maintenance? Wouldn't that be handled by the local IT guys in our Mumbai office?" queried Max.

The driver shrugged his shoulders. "I wouldn't know anything about that Sir, I just know it's special maintenance so one of Mr Dawlish's guys has to fly in and do it every month or so."

They arrived at Chhatrapati Shivaju International Airport departures. Max thanked the driver and made his way through to the first-class check-in, through security and settled in a corner of the VIP lounge. He helped himself to a selection of the buffet food on offer then looked out over the runway wondering what he was going to tell this Si Lawson. He went through in his mind his brief visit to Apex Finance and Mr Singh's somewhat cool reception and the tour of the premises. Whilst he had nothing concrete he decided there were a few observations he could at least pass on so brought up his Notes app on his mobile, and even though it was the early hours of the morning back in the UK, called Si Lawson.

Si answered after a few rings. "Max, I've been waiting for you to call. Are you at the airport? How did you get on with your visit to the printer's?"

"Not brilliantly to be honest," said Max. "It's a pretty modest but highly secure facility, the manager there was a bit cool with me and clearly isn't used to having any visitors like me poking around, I think he was a bit suspicious of me. What I've got for you Si are more a list of observations rather than anything damning I'm afraid."

Si tried to chivvy Max along hiding his own disappointment.

"That's okay Max, tell me what you do have and I can decide if we've got something or if it's a dead end. Observations can sometimes lead to evidence so fire away."

Max went through what he had. "Firstly when I asked the manager how they managed to win their currency contingency supplier status, he said something about his boss knowing their boss, possibly referring to Frank Dark or John Dawlish knowing someone maybe in the Indian government." He shrugged his shoulders to himself.

"Okay, okay, that's something we can look at to see if there are any connections there when cross-referenced, what else?" reassured Si.

Max continued. "When I was in the main printing room there were two large printing machines and then beside them, there was this smaller obsolete machine yet when I asked about it the manager changed his mind and said it was used for test printing." Si listened carefully taking notes and deliberately kept silent to let Max continue. "The computer controlling the main printer I saw working, had John Dawlish's Angel software on it. Oh yes, and when I had a glimpse into the control room's office there was one particular invoice I saw which seemed unusual as it was from a bank.

"What was this bank's name then?" asked Si.

Back at the Apex building when Max had gone to the toilet, he couldn't wait to see what the invoice was that he'd grabbed from the control room. Pulling it out of his pocket, on quick inspection he'd noted the bank's full name which was easy to remember, and the brief description of services stating simply 'Consultancy'. He'd then flushed it down the toilet before he re-joined Rajit in the corridor.

Max replied to Si. "The bank was simply called 'PJ Bank Ltd' showing 'consulting services'. That was it. Probably nothing, maybe just one of the recipient's for a notes delivery, but I didn't have long to have a look at any of the other paperwork."

"Anything else Max?" asked Si.

"The only other thing was when talking to the driver he said they never really get any visits except for some IT guy flying in every month to fix something or other, possibly one of John Dawlish's guys, don't know." Max couldn't think of anything else to report and felt what he'd given Si Lawson had fallen flat on the call. Detecting Max was a bit down Si tried to encourage him.

"Max, that's a great job, well done. There's plenty there for us to get our teeth into here at Thames House. I'll talk it all through with Vince and the team and see what we can come up with. You're off to Hong Kong now aren't you, have a good flight and I can tell you if we've found anything when we speak again. Keep it up Max, if Dawlish is receiving payments in rupees I'm convinced it's got something to do with your Mumbai printer."

Max ended the call wondering how long this assignment of his was going to last. After waiting a couple of hours finally his flight was called and he made his way to the gate to board the Emirates plane for his 16-hour flight including a quick stop in Dubai. At least first class with Emirates was one of the best available.

16

After the long one-stop flight from Mumbai, Max's Emirates plane landed at Hong Kong International airport at Chek Lap Kok on Lantau Island, a little way outside of main Hong Kong and Kowloon. Max had been lucky enough to be sent to Hong Kong on a product sourcing trip for one of his first employer's late nineties and had been on one of the last Cathay Pacific planes to land at the famous Kai Tak airport, tucked into the corner of Kowloon with its single runway jetting out into the busy harbour. He'd always remember the amazing approach banking over Hong Kong then flying in low over the buildings to pick out the runway on a wet rainy day. Then in 1998 Kai Tak was closed and the new airport opened on Lantau Island some way out of Hong Kong, similar to other major airports like JFK New York, London Gatwick and Charles de Gaulle Paris. None of them was anywhere near the centre of the cities whose name they had.

As Max came through arrivals he spotted his driver holding up a board with his name on it underneath the words 'Peninsula Hotel'. He walked outside and climbed into the magnificent emerald green Rolls-Royce waiting for him. Ever since 1970 when the Peninsula Hotel first had seven green Silver Shadows, the hotel had operated a fleet of the prestigious cars to serve their guests with. They now had 14 Rolls-Royce Phantom VIII's. This time Max took advantage of the full experience and sat in the back. The thirty-five-minute drive would take him back to the mainland passing Hong Kong's Disneyland and across the bridges over Park Island and Tsing Yi. Max couldn't help wonder what Walt Disney would have thought of it all. He asked the driver to cut across to the top of Nathan Road rather than do down the waterfront route on the West side of Kowloon. He wanted to take in one of Hong Kong's busiest streets from the back of the Rolls, running almost the length of

Kowloon.

Nathan Road ran straight down to the harbour through a myriad of billboards, decadent shop fronts, often enclosed by fifteen storey offices or older looking residential monuments, some swathed with bamboo scaffolding. More electronics shops, fashion, lots of watch stores and the odd McDonalds filled every available space, whilst the familiar red and silver-topped Hong Kong taxis darted about the two lanes of traffic each way. Max could feel the difference from his visit in the nineties when it felt more magical with that clash of East and West, with market streets and the old Cantonese culture everywhere. Now it had that slightly dull average city feel, perhaps just how older cultures get overwhelmed with today's innovation and high-end shops, or maybe a result of Hong Kong going back to being China-owned. The Far Eastern magic had gone and been replaced with protests as the new owner China, seemed to be moving in and making changes far quicker than the locals wanted.

At the road's end, they turned right into Salisbury Road then immediately right again into the pull-in frontage of the Peninsula Hotel, also known as the Grande Dame of the Far East. Soon to be celebrating its 100th anniversary, it had quietly witnessed so many changes and events in Hong Kong during that time.

Max checked into his room and had a few hours spare before meeting up with Frank and Doreen for dinner, so took in a stroll down to the waterfront walkway behind the brown coloured Intercontinental Hotel. The view across Victoria Harbour towards Hong Kong island was spectacular, a Far Eastern Manhattan. With hundreds of skyscrapers vying for attention and skyline presence, dominated by two of the largest with the Bank of China's angular building sporting on top what looked like rugby posts and one of the tallest, Two Financial Centre alongside the Four Seasons Hotel. Above everything sat the observation building on Victoria Peak accessible by road or the old tram line up the steep hill to the top.

The concrete walkway alongside the water's edge had been commandeered for a Chinese version of Hollywood's Walk of

Fame, with plaques fixed into the floor of famous Chinese directors and movie stars. The most famous of which seemed to be the only one with a large bronze statue, that of the seventies martial arts legend Bruce Lee, striking his iconic 'poised to fight' stance. Passing away at the age of just 32 with only four completed movies over a couple of years at the Kowloon Golden Harvest studios, he'd transformed fighting action movies and had everyone the world over wanting to take up kung fu or karate.

As Max made his way back towards the hotel he looked up to see a private executive helicopter approaching the area. Along with their Rolls Royce's, another rare attribute the Peninsula could boast was its twin helicopter landing pads on top of the main tower used for hotel guests and sightseeing excursions.

As the helicopter started to hover over H pad number one, inside were Frank Dark and Doreen Leader taking in the view and smiling at one another in appreciation of the flamboyant alternative way of getting to Kowloon from the airport. Doreen thought to herself 'Frank certainly knows how to treat his senior staff'. The helicopter landed and they both disembarked running to the small staircase between the two pads, bowing down their heads as everyone does when passing under those rotor blades. Frank clutched a small briefcase and Doreen was more concerned with her light flowing skirt blowing up with the wind. The porters rushed out passing the treat of Doreen's skirt flying up around her waist, to gather up their luggage and have it in their rooms by the time they'd finished checking in.

At 8 PM that evening Frank, Doreen and Max all converged at the entrance to the Felix restaurant on the 28th floor serving modern European food and an enviable selection of wines and champagnes. The subtle dark brown décor at both ends of the restaurant served to frame its highlights which were the floor to ceiling glass on the sides giving almost a 360° view of Hong Kong mainland, harbour and the island. At night-time Hong Kong repainted itself as the colourful, vibrant and spectacular city it was, pulsing out of the dark night sky.

The three of them sat at the table Frank had booked in the middle of one of the large windows and whilst they surveyed the menu with Frank making suggestions of the fabulous selections he'd samples there previously. Frank couldn't wait to check with Max how he'd got on in India.

"So what did you think of your buyer in Mumbai Max?" Frank asked.

"I met Abhay for a long working dinner and was very impressed with him, he's doing all the right things and a worthy member of the procurement team." Max knew what the next question would be about.

"And what did you think of your visit with Rajit at Apex Finance?" Frank asked nonchalantly as if not really caring.

Max played it back as straight as he could. "Mr Singh was clearly a busy man but was good enough to show me around the printing operation. I'm sure you know it's very tightly controlled and regulated by the Ministry of Finance there. All seemed very slick."

"Good. Good. I'm glad we've sorted out that little matter. As we said there isn't anything there that procurement can help with." Frank was hopeful that was the end of the subject but before he moved back to the wine list Max followed up with a question.

"There was just one thing he mentioned which I was interested to know more about," said Max. Frank looked up at him suspiciously from behind the wine list and waited. "Being in procurement I was just keen to know what swung it all those years ago in getting the Ministry of Finance to appoint Apex as one of the contingency printers. Mr Singh said something about our boss knowing their boss?" Max tensed knowing he was pushing his luck, but he had to try to draw out any chinks in the armour of what was starting to look like a completely legitimate operation.

Frank's momentary intensity quickly changed to carefree laughter as he also noticed Doreen listening intently for what his reply might be. "Ah, you know how it is with some of these tenders and how unspoken advantages can give you the edge over the competition. It's quite simple really, one of the more influential committee members at the Ministry of Finance was with me at Harrow. Old boy's network and all that perhaps may have swayed the decision all other things being equal." He leaned forward slightly to ask Max, "You're okay with that sort of thing aren't you Max?"

Having listened to Frank's answer Max couldn't see anything so awful about Frank's schoolboy connection and was ready to play along with Frank to keep winning him over. "Not at all Frank, nothing wrong with using one's network, well done for winning the contract."

Flattery often helped when dealing with Frank who relaxed after taking Max into his confidence to see how he would react. He felt there was potential to bring him on board and into the closer top team in the future. He turned back to the food and wine menu saying, "Well I know what I'm having, the Seafood bisque, then Iberian pork. Have you both chosen yet? Let's order," as he summoned one of the waiters without waiting for Max or Doreen to reply.

They relaxed and enjoyed the rest of the meal with the fantastic views of Hong Kong outside then towards the end touched on plans for the following day.

"You're off tomorrow Max to visit our joint venture Chinese CCTV and alarm factory aren't you Max?" asked Frank.

"Yes I'm looking forward to that," replied Max, "what are you to up to if I may ask?"

"Of course you can ask Max, Doreen and I have an important meeting with a Chinese investor. I'm putting together a big deal so they wanted to see me to sort out the final details and meet Doreen who will be handling the financials with them when the deal goes through. Can't say any more at this stage what with non-disclosure agreements and suchlike but it's big, watch this space," said Frank. As they left the restaurant Frank mentioned to Max, "Probably won't see you tomorrow Max but maybe for breakfast the following morning before we all leave."

Max got back to his room and decided to check in with Si Lawson with an update and to see if maybe he'd come up with anything in the last day.

"Just wondering how it's going your end?" asked Max. "About that thing regarding Apex winning the contract from the government. I asked Frank Dark this evening at dinner and he happily offered up to me and Doreen Leader that someone in the Indian Ministry of Finance who he went to Harrow with might have swayed it for them."

Si added, "We'd reached the same conclusion here having cross-checked backgrounds of all the ministers with Frank Dark and John Dawlish. The fact that he was happy to tell you about it unfortunately means we all know there's nothing there we can follow up on and it was quite a few years ago."

Max thought to himself 'another dead end'.

Si went on. "The best lead you got us from your visit, funnily enough, was the paperwork you caught a glimpse of with the name PJ Bank Limited on it. We're checking them out and trying to find any cross-references back to Frank and John, even Brett Harding. The interesting part is that some years ago it seems this bank got into trouble with potential money laundering accusations. No prosecutions but we're trying to get more information from India's Criminal Investigation Department however, let's put it this way, they are not quite as well organised as we are here."

"So do you have enough to go in with?" suggested Max.

"I'm afraid not Max, if we could directly link this bank as laundering Indian currency printed at Apex then making onward payments to John Dawlish's Swiss account then we'd have something but I'm not going to find out any more details from the Swiss, even from my contact there. Anyhow with the apparent tight controls at the printers, I'm not sure how they could divert any of the cash they print away from the appointed destination banks."

"What about that so-called spare printer, and the regular visits from John Dawlish's IT man for 'maintenance'?" Max was desperate to hear some good news but knew he was clutching at straws hoping that something he'd seen at Apex would help Si. "And that Apex coding note I saw in John's office, what was that all about?"

"We'll keep on it Max, we still have some leads to follow through to the end. We may just have to pass it up the line to the Central Bureau of Investigation in New Delhi. Interestingly Vince here came up with a fanciful theory which we all feel is still joining too many dots that don't exist."

"What theory's that then?"

"He thinks the IT guy is one of John Dawlish's top programmers and between them they've somehow managed to find a temporary hack each month which has to be manually inputted directly into the printer's computer, allowing them to duplicate a run of currency printing and serial numbers using the spare printing machine you saw. The duplicated currency is then laundered by this PJ Bank, which let's face it would never get discovered once it's put into general circulation. They then make a payment to John Dawlish's Swiss account via several shell corporations having deducted their cut. A single 2000 rupee note is worth about £20 so they could easily print off hundreds of thousands of pounds worth an hour." Having heard himself explain it to Max, Si had to conclude that it wasn't a bad theory at all that Vince had come up with. But with no proof of any of it.

Max was stunned at the possibility this could be happening. "Oh my God, is that what they're doing, is that possible Si?" he asked.

"It's just a theory Max, settle down. Vince is known for his fanciful guesswork when we don't have enough evidence. Granted, he's been right on the odd occasion, but we simply don't have anything firm to go on here. Just let us now carry on with our job and see if we can come up with anything else. I guess we'll probably catch up when you're back in the UK."

Max turned in for the night but woke up several times as his body was trying to adjust to the different time zones he'd been through over the last couple of days. Each time he woke up he found himself fretting about all the possibilities Si Lawson had mentioned and whether they could really be what was happening at Apex, or maybe it was all complete nonsense. And even if this corruption was taking place why would it be so distressing for the ex-CFO to want to commit suicide over.

The following morning Max was up early as he had a long day ahead of him getting out to the CCTV and alarm factory in mainland China. He had a quick breakfast at the hotel's Veranda breakfast lounge then made the short walk from the hotel to the nearby Tsim Sha Tsui Star Ferry pier on the water's edge of Victoria Harbour. He boarded one of the famous and long-serving green and white Star ferries each of which had a name ending with the word 'Star'. His one was called Morning Star and had been in service for over 60 years being named after the very first ferry in service by the same name. Despite the several cross-harbour tunnels being built since 1972 to carry traffic under the harbour, the Star ferries of which there had been 25 over the years were still the best way for pedestrians to go to and from Kowloon and Hong Kong Island since 1888.

After the short crossing, Max disembarked onto the island and made the short walk along the harbour front to the Hong Kong Macau Ferry terminal building in Sheung Wan. He then caught his faster ferry and an hour later arrived at the Chinese terminal Shenzhen in Shekou. As the ferry manoeuvred itself perfectly alongside its jetty Max spotted what was now becoming the obligatory black Range Rover and driver waiting for him in the terminal collection and drop-off zone. He couldn't help but think once again 'Frank really does like all of his senior managers to have these black Range Rover's!'.

They took the short drive inland to one of the many high-tech industrial parks of Shenzhen where Frank Dark's joint venture CCTV and alarm factory was nestled amongst other similar industrial manufacturing sites and offices. Frank had some years ago consolidated all of his CCTV and alarm suppliers into just one site having done the deal with the Chinese owners to buy into shared management and partnership, given the huge amount of business the Dark Corporation would give them. All CCTV and alarm products the company sold worldwide were produced at this site. Even though the company there was partly a subsidiary of the corporation, Frank and Doreen had told Max that he should treat them as an external supplier. He should ensure they were on top of their procurement procedures for components and supplies, just like any other part of the business. How effectively they were managing their costs and suppliers had a knock-on effect on the overall profitability of this division across all the sales teams.

Max would spend the rest of the day watching and listening to various presentations, giving his presentations back to the management there, meeting the Chinese procurement manager and team. He'd have extensive tours of the factory and of course the all-important lunch and then dinner with the directors and senior management. Max was well versed in the etiquettes of dealing with Chinese businesspeople and whilst such things as giving gifts had relaxed recently, he was still mindful of the other little acts that still mattered such as presenting your business card with two hands, accepting their business cards with interest, acknowledgement and care, prioritising and respecting the hierarchy of management you are talking to, being smartly dressed, punctual and so on. Max warmed to the traditional high standards the Chinese still held dear and wished the sometimes sloppy Western world could re-adopt more professional ways of doing business. He was on show for the rest of the day and knew he was going to be exhausted by the time he caught the late ferry back to Hong Kong.

Later that morning Frank Dark and Doreen Leader started the same route to the nearby Star Ferry terminal, crossed the harbour and caught one of the ferries at Central pier 4 for the thirty-minute trip to nearby Lamma Island, just south of Hong Kong Island and Aberdeen boat city.

Frank had been rather coy with Doreen about exactly what this meeting was about other than to say it was hugely important and that he needed her there with him to meet one of their big investors. Doreen had desperately wanted to ask Frank lots of questions about this clandestine meeting but given her deference and trust of his judgement, and her subservient situation she'd managed to get herself into with him, decided to just go along with it. How bad could it be, it was just another business meeting.

During the ferry ride Doreen detected a growing nervousness about Frank's demeanour, he was starting to fidget and become a bit more restless getting up from his seat as if to admire the view from another advantage point. Then sitting back down next to her and communicating another piece of clipped advice or information about what they were doing there.

"We are meeting a very important Chinese businessman. His name is Li Xiaoping." Frank would briefly explain, admire the view again, then continue. "I've known him for many years. He is one of the corporation's biggest investors and helped me with the CCTV firm's joint venture that Max is visiting today."

"What part do you want me to play today Frank?" ventured Doreen.

"I'll do most of the talking, he might want to see me alone for a while so if that happens just bear with me. The main thing is that he wanted to meet you, so he knows who he is dealing with, after your predecessor's unfortunate demise. You know how it is with the Chinese, they like to look you in the eye and build up a bit of trust before doing any big deals," said Frank.

Doreen felt none the wiser and now quite intrigued to meet this man and find out what all this was about. She assumed that Frank was either selling part of his business or maybe buying another competitor with the help of this wealthy investor.

They arrived at the beautiful, quaint island of Lamma, with its scattered fishing villages and clusters of houses of varying age and build, pulling into the quayside at Sok Kwu Wan. Pointing towards the waterside concrete pathway Frank led them for a short stroll past other tourists and busy fishermen, with their families watching on as nets were reorganised or repaired and boats were tinkered with and cleaned after the early morning's fishing. Doreen could see that Frank had been here before and knew where he was going as they suddenly broke off the path and entered a very modest eatery on the waterfront called the Genuine Lamma Hilton Fishing Village Restaurant. Doreen thought this was certainly not the usual five-star restaurant Frank would normally choose and suspected the venue had been decided by the Chinese businessman for its quiet understated location. It consisted of the main dining area both inside and out overlooking the water with an additional long concrete quay protruding out across the water in front of them, with a domed canvas covering further tables and chairs enclosed by green painted railings.

Frank waved towards a dark-suited Chinese man waiting on one of the first few tables of the concrete wharf. As they approached him Doreen noticed another Chinese man standing a few yards on from the businessman, wearing a cheaper suit but not acknowledging Frank or engaging in the greetings. He appeared to Doreen to be more of a military-type from the way he stood, so she assumed that he must be the bodyguard.

Frank shook the businessman's hand and introduced Doreen to Li Xiaoping who noticing that Doreen had spotted his bodyguard, knowingly dismissed the matter reassuringly with excellent English. "Please Ms Leader don't mind him, he just makes sure I don't get into any trouble," he said jokingly. "I am so pleased you could join us today. I know it doesn't look like much, but the seafood is superb, caught this morning," Li enthused.

The three of them sat down at the table and focused on the menu, this time with Li making the recommendations, not Frank. The surroundings and view across the water were idyllic with some local children using the wooden jetty at the end of their dining area to jump in and out of the water from. The bodyguard started to look more relaxed and apologetically moved past them back towards the main restaurant area. He sat at a table next to the wharf's entry point as if to guard it and ordered a Coca-Cola, frequently looking over to his boss for any instructions and monitoring the goings-on in the restaurant behind him. Doreen thought she caught a glimpse of some kind of gun slung under the man's left arm, beneath his jacket and started to feel a little more nervous about this so-called business meeting.

Once they had ordered their food, a selection of scallops, prawns, chicken and dumpling dishes, Li lent forward about to get up saying to Doreen, "Ms Leader would you mind if I stole Frank away for a few moments, there are a few things I need to cover with him alone please." Without waiting for her to nod her agreement Li stood and gestured towards the far end of the wharf for Frank to follow him.

Doreen was already facing in their direction and though she couldn't hear much of what was being said between the two men, she watched them closely under the cover of contently gazing out across the Pichic Bay water. The conversation between Li and Frank began with only the Chinese man speaking with Frank listening intently. It started off in a friendly manner but soon Doreen could see that Li was becoming more angry and insistent. Frank seemed to briefly put his case back to Li then quickly backed down holding his hands up in submission when Li became even more resolute with his body language, starting to point with his finger in an accusatory way at Frank. Every now and then Li's hushed English was interjected with some Chinese word.

Doreen started to feel uncomfortable observing the two men arguing under hushed voices. It was especially surprising to see her wealthy, powerful boss Frank Dark apparently being castigated and instructed what to do. The conversation then appeared to settle down again and in no time the two men were smiling at one another, shook hands and made their way back to the table. The sudden change in candour was itself somewhat perturbing to Doreen, who was now intrigued to hear any explanation either of them might give her for their 'discussion'.

It was Frank who awkwardly ventured, "Sorry we had to leave you Doreen, just sorting out a few final bits to the agreement and business deal we've both been working on for some years now. All sorted, I'll brief you later."

Li cut in. "Come now Frank, after all, Ms Leader is going

to have to handle a sizeable payment for you."

Frank quickly clarified, "Yes, handle it in a particular way which I will need to explain to her later, not now."

At the risk of the two men starting to disagree and argue again, Doreen wanted to at least understand what kind of payment they were talking about, so asked. "How much are we talking about for this payment?"

Frank sat back in his chair not wanting to get into these kinds of details right now with Li sitting there. He knew he had a fair bit of explaining to do with Doreen to put this whole deal into context. Li however couldn't understand why Frank was being so economical with his new Chief Finance Officer. Li also relaxed back into his chair and shrugging his shoulders broke the silence by saying calmly, "Five billion US dollars."

Just as Doreen was about to repeat this sum out loud in shock, two of the waiters arrived at the table with the various plates and sides the trio had ordered, closely watched by the bodyguard who had risen from his seat in readiness. They sat there in an awkward silence looking at one another whilst the two young Chinese men finished laying the food out neatly on the table. Sensing they had interrupted something they quickly withdrew, passing the piercing glare of the minder.

Doreen was free to speak. "Five billion!"

Frank took control. "Enough. I will explain later, there's nothing you need to know that can't wait. It's a straightforward transaction," Frank concentrated his stare at Doreen, "that I *need* you to help me with." It was a clear instruction and Doreen suspected Frank was about to call in that big favour she owed him from the gambling debt payoff.

Li had had his fun but could see Frank Dark didn't want to go through all the details with his CFO now so helped defuse the situation. "I agree. Let's have no more talk of business and enjoy this fabulous lunch. The food here really is good." He gestured to the plates in front of them and started to help himself to the scallops and some noodles, expertly manipulating the chopsticks. Frank and

Doreen followed suit but were not as adept with the traditional eating implements. Li's face betrayed hiding a faint smile at his two Gweilo guests.

As the subject changed to China's views on the Hong Kong student's protests and President Trump's latest Twitter posts and clashes with the media, the atmosphere gradually relaxed and returned to a friendly luncheon in a beautiful setting. Despite the jovial conversation though, Doreen was trying to think what parts of the business Frank Dark could possibly be selling for such a huge payment. Five billion was well over double what the whole corporation was worth. It had to be something else.

The meal ended with Frank and Doreen leaving Li at the table, who'd previously told them he would stay on a little while longer as he had some calls to make. Frank and Doreen made their way back along the concrete waterside path towards the ferry pier. As they went, Li Xiaoping studied them closely.

Li was a handsome man in his late fifties, wealthy in his own right, very wealthy. Impeccably dressed with thick black hair and dark eyes, eyes that had seen a lot of amazing and also terrible things that no normal people could bear or stomach. He had been a rising star in the Chinese military, the Peoples Liberation Army, helped along by several of his family being high up members of the Communist Party of China. After a decade he was moved into the Ministry of State Security (MSS) which ran the intelligence, security and secret police agencies of the People's Republic of China. The MSS was one of the most secretive and feared intelligence organisations in the world, headquartered in Beijing. Its open remit allowed it to operate beyond any normal social or democratic laws and standards, both within China and far beyond its borders.

Li Xiaoping had taken part in and latterly masterminded many covert and violent operations and been responsible for the deaths of many criminals, protesters, terrorists, soldiers and enemies of the State. Five years ago he'd welcomed the opportunity of working in the corporate sector and had been asked to groom an impressive entrepreneur Frank Dark who had something of particular interest to the MSS. Early on in their relationship Li had helped Frank engineer the joint-venture partnership deal with his sought-after CCTV and alarm company based in China. He'd even put up the money for Frank to own half of the company as a gesture of goodwill, knowing that in due course he would expect Frank to be there for him when the time came and do the deal he wanted. Li knew that Frank likely suspected that he was more than a simple businessman, but wisely had never dared to ask him about it or press him on the subject. Like Frank, Li also subscribed to the mantra that anything can be bought as long as you have enough money. Playing to Frank's greed to be even more wealthy than he already was, Li now had him and the Dark Corporation where he needed them to be for the 'big transaction'. A transaction that would have a huge long-lasting effect on people and corporations across the world.

Li waited until Frank and Doreen disappeared from sight, then made a call to update his superior. He then looked over at his bodyguard and twirled a finger in the air gesturing to him to call the pilot and summon their helicopter, which was parked up on a deserted hill in the south of the small island waiting for them. They would walk a little way further up the Lamma Island Family Walk coastal pathway, where there was a small stony beach with clearance enough for the helicopter to land, pick them up and take them back to Beijing.

A short while later Frank and Doreen boarded their ferry to return to Central on Hong Kong Island. They'd walked back along the pathway in silence both unsure as to how to open the conversation and both waiting for the other to speak first. As they settled into their seats on the outside deck at the front of the boat, their attention along with the other passengers was drawn back behind them. They could see a black executive class helicopter negotiating itself carefully to land on a small strip of beach further round the coastline from the seafood restaurant they'd had lunch at. They both knew it must be Li's helicopter. Frank wasn't sure that even with his wealth he could organise a helicopter to freely roam around the islands of Hong Kong, landing on beaches to drop him off or collect him, and thought to himself ironically of Li, 'how the other half lives'.

Their silence continued for the first ten minutes of their ferry trip and it was Doreen who couldn't contain herself any longer. "So Frank, are you going to tell me a bit more about this massive payment you want me involved in?"

Frank drew in a large breath. "I've been putting together this deal for ages, I'm selling part of the business to Li."

"Which part," asked Doreen, "I don't know what it is we have across the corporation that's worth that much money."

"At this point in time it doesn't matter which part I'm selling, the important thing is I need your help and support handling the payment and what happens to it once it's been made," said Frank.

Doreen felt sick as a wave of realisation washed through her that this was starting to sound like something illegal. "How do you mean?"

Frank started shifting in his seat again as he became more irritated by the questions and having to explain himself. "You remember what I did for you? Getting you out of whatever fix you were in. The one million bonus." Doreen reluctantly nodded, Frank continued. "Well *now* is that time I'm calling on you. Excuse the pun but now is when I'm cashing in your chips. You owe me and you have to do this for me," insisted Frank.

"Do what?" asked Doreen.

"Once the payment is made I need you to break it up across various accounts and hide it so it's untouchable by the authorities. Put it into shell companies, ghost accounts, Swiss, offshore, figure out the best ways to protect and keep the money. It's got nothing to do with the business, this is a personal payment." Frank turned and studied Doreen's reaction closely. This was it, he'd brought her into his inner circle completely now, there was no going back.

Doreen was trying to take it all in and slowly shaking her head from side to side.

Frank pressed on. "This is great news for you Doreen. I'll pay you £20 million for simply doing some creative accountancy preparation work before the payment date, then on the day when the payment is made, you're all ready to split the money and hide it away for me. £20 million Doreen." Frank's adrenaline was pumping and he was balanced on a fine line between excited and furious.

Doreen responded like anyone else would when initially hit with the idea of committing such a massive criminal act. Her life in the UK would be over, she'd have to flee abroad to one of the 'out of bounds' countries. "I just don't know Frank, it all sounds too risky."

Frank Dark exploded. "You owe me Doreen and I'm going to collect whether you like it or not. Don't end up like John Lyttleton. It was all too much for him and look what happened to him." Frank immediately regretted the comment.

Doreen looked at him fearfully. She wasn't quite sure from the carefully chosen words Frank had just said to her through gritted teeth, whether he was implying her predecessor couldn't cope with the pressure of Frank's request of him, or whether Frank was implying that he had something to do with John Lyttleton's death. Either way the stark reminder that the person in her role before her was now dead was enough to sway her decision. Frank was glaring at her waiting.

Doreen took in a deep breath in resignation. "As long as no one gets hurt, then I can do it." Frank relaxed and started to betray a nervous smile. Doreen continued as if reassuring herself she'd made the right choice. "Yes. If it's just moving money around, that can be done. Just don't hurt me Frank, I'll do what you want."

Frank got up and strolled around the front of the boat taking in the view and letting the breeze cool him down, and calm him down. Doreen's heart was pounding, she was in shock and realised her carelessness with the gambling debacle and Frank bailing her out, was now going to cost her considerably more than the simple half a million pounds she once owed. Frank came back over and sat next to her.

Doreen tilted her head towards Frank with just one last thing to say on the matter. "Twenty million you said."

Frank nodded. "Cash into whatever account you want. Tax-free if you hide it properly."

They both settled back in their seats with their own thoughts for the rest of the ferry trip. Doreen's mind was awash with Maureen back home, severing ties in the UK, could she be caught, how she would hide portions of such a large sum, and what she'd do with her twenty million.

Frank regretted what he'd said to Doreen about John Lyttleton, he didn't mean to scare her, but he felt it had probably helped persuade her. He gazed across the water towards Aberdeen on the south of Hong Kong, passing the tiny island of Magazine with the larger Horizon island in the background. His thoughts strayed back to that awful day when John Lyttleton had died.

Frank Dark was in his office with his CFO John Lyttleton having a heated exchange. For the last few months, John had become increasingly stressed and unhappy with the expectations and demands put upon him by his boss Frank. John was a straight honest accountant, he'd been Frank's CFO for some years and they'd coexisted happily, at arm's length. But more recently John Lyttleton had become aware of what was happening at Apex Finance. Frank never even asked how he had found out, maybe he just overheard him and John Dawlish speaking about it. But the revelation to John Lyttleton, the mainboard director in charge of finance for the corporation, that there was something corrupt going on within that business, was a hard blow to this man's whiter than white integrity and professionalism.

They'd already had a bust-up months before when John Lyttleton had confronted Frank about the additional duplicated rupee currency print runs taking place secretly every month in Mumbai. Masterminded by CTO John Dawlish who was always up for a challenge, he'd found a way of temporarily hacking into the Ministry of Finances encrypted downloads to open up a window allowing reuse of the highly protected serial number sequences and instruction commands to the printer's computer. The note Max had seen on John's desk was the hack code for the following month's run at Apex. It wasn't as if John Dawlish needed the extra money being siphoned off through a clearing bank, he was already wealthy enough not to bother with this sort of scam, but Frank had let it go to keep John Dawlish happy and on-board. John Dawlish was critical to Frank's bigger plans.

After several long discussions and a meeting at Frank's Surrey home one evening, he managed to finally convince John Lyttleton to overlook the Apex Finance indiscretion. Possibly adding insult to injury by persuading him to accept an 'extremely large bonus' to help ease the burden of knowing what was happening. Even after John had accepted this, Frank knew he remained uncomfortable with the whole thing and that there would be another potentially damaging bust-up waiting to happen when Frank approached his CFO with the next big ask.

Back in Frank's office, he had thought he'd picked a good moment when John Lyttleton was appearing to be unusually receptive and had just broached him with the question of needing him to hide a significant payment. At that time it was three billion dollars, which was the original payment offered by Li Xiaoping. Frank had subsequently got him to agree to raise it to five billion by the time Doreen came along.

John Lyttleton was quite clear. "Absolutely not Frank. I'm not doing it. You've asked too much of me this time. Three billion, I dread to think what that could possibly be for. No."

Frank had pleaded with him. "John, please, it's just moving numbers around on a computer. I'll make you a very wealthy man, but I need you to do this for me."

"You always need me to do something for you Frank, my days of running around after you and looking the other way are over. I don't know what I was thinking when I agreed to keep quiet about John Dawlish's money printing in India. But now this. No, Frank, that's too much. I'm going to have to resign, you'll have my letter in a moment," John Lyttleton had said to Frank as he left his office destroyed, let down and insulted.

Frank sat there at his desk stunned, not knowing what to do or how to turn the situation back round in his favour.

Meanwhile, John Lyttleton went back to his own office and sitting in front of his computer typed out his resignation email to Frank Dark copying the other executive directors John Dawlish and Brett Harding. Finishing the email and quickly reading it through once, he went back up to the top of the page and thought it best to also add the HR director and chairman's names to the CC list. Before hitting the 'Send' button he opened up the browser on his screen, quickly searched for a telephone number and turned to his phone, unbeknown to Frank.

After explaining to the receptionist what he wanted, John Lyttleton was put through to Si Lawson, one of the team leaders at MI5 Cyber, who being in the middle of a meeting had put his call through to one of his staff called Vince.

Vince had asked what the worried CFO knew and had concerns about, but John Lyttleton had insisted on coming in for a meeting so he had time to clear his thoughts and then explain exactly what was going on at the Dark Corporation. Having agreed on a meeting date John put the phone down and glancing at the email draft he'd typed out, hit the Send button.

He'd pick up his things tomorrow but right now he just had to get out of the building and away from Frank Dark. As he came out of his office Frank Dark converged on him meeting him at the top of the staircase. John Lyttleton tried to brush him aside and pass him, so Frank grabbed John by the shoulders only to stop him leaving, so he could plead with him once more to rethink the whole thing and at least talk it all through. Unfortunately with John Lyttleton's haste and forward momentum in trying to pass by, Frank's attempt to hold him back merely deflected John towards the balustrade at the top of the stairs. John's left buttock hit the shiny rail and with the weight of his upper body moving in that direction, curved over the polished rail sending John Lyttleton over the top and into his unpreventable descent to the atrium.

Frank Dark hadn't meant for him to fall. Not really.

When Doreen and Frank got off the ferry at Central, Doreen told Frank she was going to take the rest of the day out for some shopping in Wan Chai and take the tram up to Victoria Peak. Frank headed back to the hotel to attend several conference call meetings. After the revelations of the day and their clash on the ferry, they were both glad to put some space between themselves to let things cool down a bit. No dinner meet up was arranged, they would both catch up again the next day.

Max returned late to Hong Kong on the two ferries quite exhausted having already had a long dinner earlier with his hosts in China at the factory and by the time he got back to his room was happy to go straight to bed.

He was woken from his sleep at about one AM by the soft chiming of his room doorbell. He gathered himself up out of bed wondering who on earth it could be and opened the door expecting a porter to be delivering something. He was greeted with the sight of the last person he thought he'd see. Doreen stood there somewhat apologetically, tightly clutching her Peninsula Hotel bathrobe around her front.

"Doreen?" said Max clumsily. "What the hell are you doing, it's the middle of the night?

Doreen swept through the doorway past Max brushing against him and gently put a finger to Max's lips. She pushed the door closed and went over to the end of Max's bed.

Max's internal radar was ringing alarm bells as he realised what his beautiful boss likely intended. The bells rang even louder as Doreen slowly parted the fluffy bathrobe to reveal the full splendour of her figure, invitingly adorned with black brasier, and stockings held up with tantalising suspenders. She had nothing else on around her midriff having dispensed with her knickers before she'd left her room. His eyes widened following her body down from the top, lingering in the middle, right down to her trademark black high heeled stiletto shoes. He'd never seen anyone quite so stunning. Doreen pulled her hairclip away allowing her golden blond hair to fall onto her shoulders, a rare sight for Max as she always had her hair neatly held up in the office.

By way of a final check and tiny protest, Max inquired, "But I thought you preferred women?"

Doreen shrugged cutely. "Usually I do, but there's something about being away on business in a lovely hotel in a foreign place." She paused, "And with you. I just want to escape everything for a few hours." She admired his athletic physique and was pleased to see such a body, with strong arms, rippled abdominals and almost hairless pectorals, all with a healthy tan.

Max approached her confidently, impatiently, then held her. As they kissed she removed his boxer shorts and they pressed together.

"Just remember Max," she whispered in his ear, "what happens in Hong Kong, stays in Hong Kong. Yes?"

He dropped her bathrobe to the floor around her high heels and gently pushed her onto the bed. "Fine by me!"

After the realisation by Doreen that she may soon be taking a big risk for Frank and also leaving her partner in the UK, Doreen gave herself over to Max completely.

Several hours later they both fell asleep, content and exhausted.

Max woke by seven and instinctively reached out his arm to check for Doreen, but was sorely disappointed to feel the bedding next to him was empty. He sat up looking around the room for any signs of her. Her clothing that had been discarded item by item last night, had all disappeared. Unbeknown to Max, Doreen had quietly slipped out at around five AM and gone back to her own room.

Max got up, congratulating himself on the night's activities with Doreen. It had been truly amazing and regretted it was likely a one-off. He jumped into the shower as if to wipe away his feelings for her and start the day afresh. He decided to go to the Veranda for an early breakfast.

He helped himself to a hearty selection from the buffet and watched the smart and precise chef cook his cheese and onion omelette in front of him and sat down at one of the window tables. In the distance Max could see the tops of the tallest buildings across the harbour on Hong Kong Island. However, the main and unavoidable sight in front of the lounge restaurant was that of the huge grey dome of the Hong Kong Space Museum directly opposite the Peninsula Hotel frontage. He wondered what the hotel owners must have thought when that eyesore appeared right in front of their historic building.

"Morning Max, may I join you?" Doreen appeared with a healthy-looking bowl of mixed fruits and yoghurt along with a freshly squeezed orange juice. She sat down opposite Max affording him a brief, tender smile, then it was business as usual. "How was your day at the China factory?"

Max took her lead, understanding that not a word would be said about their liaison. "Exhausting," the double entendre wasn't lost on Doreen, "as we both know these trips can be quite hard work when you're on show all day and evening with the same people, doing your best to impress everyone. That was my day," said Max.

Noticing Doreen giving him a deliberate frown he asked her, "How was yesterday for you and Frank, this big meeting of his?"

Doreen hadn't spoken to Frank since making her shopping excuses to him at the ferry terminal following their meeting with Li Xiaoping. Their discussion on the ferry had all been building inside her. She desperately wanted to tell Max everything but knew she couldn't, she was in too deep now. She pulled herself together, but her anxiety was betrayed in her voice.

"It was all quite bizarre frankly, we had this secretive meeting with a Chinese businessman, who I suspect was something much more than just an investor or business buyer. I've never seen Frank bow down and defer to anyone else before." Max put his knife and fork down to focus entirely on Doreen, this sounded interesting.

Doreen continued. "It was a little uncomfortable to be honest. I saw them having a bit of a row, or maybe it was just a negotiation, I don't know. Then when they came back to the table they explained that they'd agreed some huge deal. And as CFO I would be involved in handling the financials of course."

"What huge deal," asked Max.

"I actually don't know yet what it is Frank has agreed to sell to this man Li, but I do know it's for an awfully large sum of money." Doreen stopped herself realising that what she had already told Max was probably about the extent of what she could say.

Max could tell Doreen was upset. He decided at that moment they were perhaps kindred spirits caught up in things neither of them wanted to be involved with, so took a chance. "You don't seem entirely happy about what happened yesterday Doreen. It's okay. I came across a few odd things when I visited Apex Finance in Mumbai. Not sure what but something's going on."

Doreen looked up from pushing her fruit around the bowl. "No Max, you mustn't get involved. Don't stir things up, you saw how John Dawlish and Frank reacted at the review meeting when you started questioning some of the odd spends. It's not worth it. Did you witness anything untoward in Mumbai?"

"Not exactly but…"

"Then you didn't see anything, why would you want to stick your nose out and get on the wrong side of John and Frank," interrupted Doreen.

Max dropped the India topic and focused back on the Chinese deal sticking to questions that any interested employee might innocently ask. "So Frank's possibly selling part of the business to this Li bloke, any ideas what it is, this big deal?"

"None at all. It must be a big part of the business, maybe all of it, it was a large sum of money being talked about," said Doreen.

"Well did you hear them mention any of the corporation's brands or companies? Did you hear anything when they were talking privately or arguing?" pushed Max.

Doreen thought back to when she was sitting at the table on the wharf watching the two men having their heated exchange. She'd heard the odd clipped start or end of a sentence but not enough to piece together what they were talking about or pick up any keywords such as brands or parts of the business. Then she remembered Li using a particular Chinese word several times which had stood out amongst the whispered English.

"No companies or brands were mentioned but the Chinese man did say a word several times, presumably in Cantonese or Mandarin, I don't know," recalled Doreen.

"What word? Try to remember what word," coaxed Max.

Doreen thought hard and did her best to copy phonetically the word she thought she'd heard Li say. "Hienshi. It was something like this. Hienshi. Yes, that was it."

Max pulled out his phone and typed 'Hienshi' into his web browser's Translator, but no English translation came up for either traditional Chinese, simplified Chinese or even Japanese for that word. "No. Nothing comes up for that."

Doreen's concentration was suddenly distracted as she looked up and as Max cleared the screen on his phone he got quite a startle himself.

"Good morning you two, looks like you've beaten me to breakfast." Frank Dark walked up to them both having just come into the breakfast lounge and spotting his two colleagues at the table had come straight over to them bypassing the buffet. "What are you both up to then, you're looking very suspicious?" joked Frank who had decided today was a new day and he had to move on with Doreen and mend any broken bridges with her.

"Oh nothing much Frank, I was just telling Doreen all about CCTV's and alarms, after my visit to the factory yesterday," replied Max still recovering from the shock of Frank's surprise interruption.

Max and Doreen each felt a tingle of satisfaction at the deception and triumph of having their secret meetup the night before, with it being something their all-knowing boss Frank dark on this occasion was oblivious to.

Frank got the attention of one of the staff and asked for a new place setting to be made up on the same table as Max and Doreen. He swiped a spare chair from another table unconcerned that it would now have to be replaced or reorganised.

Doreen and Max put on a good show instantly forgetting

about their previous conversation and indeed the night they'd spent together, responding to their boss's apparent bright and cheery mood. Despite the restaurant being a self-service buffet, Frank remained seated and gave his order selection to one of the staff asking them to be a good chap and bring it over for him. They talked about Max's factory visit and Frank gave a brief summary of his and Doreen's meeting with the potential Chinese buyer, Doreen remained silent but smiled pleasantly. Conscious of bringing Doreen back into the conversation, Frank asked her if her shopping trip had been successful and agreed that the view from Victoria Peak was indeed splendid. They moved onto their onward travel plans.

"So Max you're off back home today aren't you? I'm going on to meet the regional and business teams in Australia before I come home, and I think Doreen you have some meetings in Europe don't you?" summarised Frank.

They concluded breakfast with Max and Doreen having already finished eating but patiently remaining with Frank whilst he had his. Going their separate ways outside the Veranda Max went back up to his room to pack and as he had a couple of hours before the Rolls-Royce would take him back to the airport, he ventured off to the hotel's Spa for a swim in the indoor pool overlooking Hong Kong island.

He felt weary from his Mumbai trip, from his day at the factory and from his conversation earlier with Doreen. There appeared to be lots going on in the Dark Corporation that didn't feel right, but he still couldn't put his finger on anything specific. How annoying.

For now, he would enjoy the pool, the chauffeured Rolls and the first-class flight home. 'Frank knew how to look after his staff' Max thought. He would wait until he got home and then check in with Si Lawson. Hopefully, the mighty MI5 might have found something in the meantime so he could bring this whole charade of his to a close. Max had no idea that he was far from finished, at the Dark Corporation.

17

Si Lawson was used to making steady and gratifying progress on most of the cases he worked on, as usual they would start with a healthy tipoff or piece of evidence coming their way. His team would follow up the initial lead and interview people involved, who when threatened with criminal prosecution or imprisonment, would more often than not drop someone else in it to save their own skin. If that didn't work phones would be bugged, rooms or meeting places surveyed, suspects followed and information gathered from the huge network of resources with access to most systems worldwide. Often straightforward analysis of data and plain detective work would yield the evidence they needed to then swoop in dramatically and make their arrests, sometimes easily done with no fuss such as in an office where there's been a corporate infraction. Other times with armed operatives where doors have to be broken in at 4 AM or suspects might be armed and unwilling to give themselves up without a fight.

He currently had his team working on a list of 24 different cases all at varying stages and as with many activity lists, he and his superiors would often focus on the ones at the top nearing conclusion and the ones at the bottom either just started or stalling. Si Lawson had one such case at the bottom of his list which didn't seem to be going anywhere. The Dark Corporation case. He'd taken a bit of a flyer on this one and followed a hunch that something corrupt was there to be found, but unfortunately what he didn't have was that initial piece of lead evidence or eyewitness. He'd simply gone based on John Lyttleton their CFO wanting to come in and talk to them about something and then mysteriously committing suicide. Not a huge amount to go on and perhaps this CFO had misinterpreted something or merely suspected corruption or fraud but didn't have any evidence himself.

Using an 'Executive Pending' as a mole in an organisation and then not coming up with anything quickly Si knew would be frowned on by his boss, as potentially they were putting someone at risk to hopefully drive out some evidence the team could then work with. He felt that Max Sargent had done his best engineering the visit to Apex Finance in Mumbai and although he'd managed to find several pieces of intriguing information it was all circumstantial. It didn't feel right, but without something decent, he couldn't do anything about it. He was starting to think about pulling Max out using some made-up but unequivocal excuse, sorting out his redundancy payments for him from his previous company and letting him get on with his career and life.

His mobile rang. It was Max Sargent checking in having recently got home from Hong Kong.

"Hi Max, I was just thinking about you, how was the rest of your trip?" Si asked.

"Hello Si, has anything else come up on Apex?" Max was eager to see if Si had any good news for him about the Indian printers.

"Unfortunately not, we've got nothing more on the bank or the payments into John Dawlish's private Swiss account. Vince's cockamamie theory with the programmer visits and additional printer runs sounds great but hasn't got any legs I'm afraid." Si repeated his question about the remainder of Max's trip.

"Well apart from a boring factory visit in China I do have a small piece of information but I don't think it's anything that could interest you," said Max.

"Give me anything you've got Max, we're struggling here so let's hear it, anything," said Si hopefully.

"Doreen Leader had some important meeting with Frank Dark and some suspicious Chinese businessman, possibly an investor but Doreen seemed to think there was a bit more to him than that. Anyway, it sounds like Frank is about to make a big sale to this man, possibly parts of the corporation, maybe even all of it, who knows," relayed Max.

"Yes. Is that it?" Si said, accidentally sarcastically.

Max continued. "Pretty much, maybe it's some dodgy deal going down. She wasn't party to the details at this stage and couldn't hear a private discussion Frank had with the Chinese man, Li Xiaoping I think his name was." Max then remembered the word he'd tried to look up. "Oh yes there was one Chinese word Doreen overheard Li saying during a heated exchange with Frank Dark. 'Hienshi' I think it was. Yes, that's it."

"Hienshi," repeated Si. "Is that Cantonese or something, what the hell does it mean?"

"Doesn't translate to anything," said Max shrugging at his mobile.

"Hang on a minute Max, let me just get one of my guys in here who might be able to help, I'll put him on speaker." Si put the phone down and popped his head out of his office door and called towards one of his team to pop in. The middle-aged Chinese man obliged and came in.

"Max. I've got one of my guys Lui Feng in here with me." Si turned to Lui. "We are trying to figure out what someone could have meant using the word 'Hienshi', we don't know what language it is or if it was heard accurately but have you got any ideas?"

"Hienshi?" Lui repeated. "I speak fluent Mandarin and am pretty good with some of the other dialects used but I don't know that word, Hienshi. Are you sure that's the right word?"

Max replied, "Yup sorry, that's all I've got and it was passed on to me by someone else so it's second-hand. Might it be Japanese or something?"

Lui mouthed the word a couple of times more to himself. "No, it's definitely not Japanese. Hang on a minute, I think I've got it. You're pronouncing the word phonetically as an English person would. Yes, I believe the word you're quoting is in fact 'Tiānshǐ'," which he said in perfect Mandarin, similar to but not the same as Max's rendition, "you were confusing me with the way you were saying it."

Si cut in and asked what he and Max now desperately wanted

to know. "Well Lui, what does it mean then?"

Lui shrugged his shoulders and smiling innocently gave them the translation of the word that would change everything. "Angel."

Si Lawson stood there for a moment speechless. Max didn't say anything either and after a while Lui excused himself and edged back out of his boss's office saying quietly, "Okay I'll go now then shall I". He knew the word must have been important from their reactions but had no idea what the big deal was.

"Bloody hell Si, the dodgy Chinese businessman is buying Frank Dark's Angel virus checker," exclaimed Max. Then thinking about it he couldn't quite join the dots. "So what does that mean?"

Si was thinking through his mixed emotions of excitement and concern, trying to deconstruct what this could possibly mean. He thought 'let's start with the basics'.

"Let's assume this businessman is something connected with their government, most roads lead to the top over there. The first thing that strikes me as odd is why the Chinese would be looking to buy a virus checker. China is one of those closed countries that utilise their own security and programs for things like anti-malware. 360 Safeguard and Total Security are their software I think. I've come across it before. So they definitely wouldn't want the Angel software for their use, no way." Si looked serious.

Max continued the thought thread. "So if they don't want it for themselves perhaps they're just trying to get into the virus checking business for the rest of the world?"

"Maybe, but there again given the massive distribution of the Angel software around the world..." the worst possible scenario now hit home to Si, "perhaps they want to use it as a data-gathering tool for intelligence. Or maybe as a trojan carrier program to cause some kind of virus disruption, no, surely not." Si was looking at worst cases and they didn't bode well. He would need to get his team onto this fast.

"Max, I need to have my guys get all over the Angel software products to see if we can find anything about the way they're programmed. I may be wrong, but this could be serious. Maybe we've been looking too hard at the India operation and have missed the real problem. Max, just carry on at the business, stand down now and keep a low profile, just get on with your job there okay. Call in soon or if anything else turns up." Si's thoughts and instructions were racing as he could barely contain himself. Max signed off.

Si Lawson immediately summoned Vince and a couple of other managers into his office and briefed them about the possibilities of China taking control of the Dark Corporation's Angel software business. He asked Vince to get the Technology team to buy and download the latest version of the Angel software and thoroughly examine the program files for hidden software, back doors, sleeping 'execute' files, encrypted programs, everything. He wanted them to go through it and report back with anything suspicious.

Si also asked Vince to do a search on a certain Li Xiaoping across their known persons, military and operatives of the Chinese government, businesses, armed forces and Ministry of State Security. Si knew it was very unlikely the name would yield any information unless this man had been involved in a joint Chinese-CIA-MI5 operation. Detailed information on Chinese operatives was still scarce even in these modern times of technology and data, plus the name could also be a false one so he didn't hold up any hope of finding anything, but it had to be investigated as part of the expected due diligence.

Si Lawson hoped he was wrong about all this but he was painfully aware that the espionage or cyber destruction capabilities of any commercial program that had been sold to tens of millions of households, businesses and government networks and infrastructures, could be devastating if manipulated in the wrong way or fell into the wrong hands. He left his office heading off to see his superior, he needed to speak to him now, the written report could follow later today. This matter would now have to be given an orange flag and be included in the MI5 Director General's daily briefing for the British Prime Minister, albeit as an IO 'Information

Only' item. This then allowed the Prime Minister to ask for more details if they chose to, which Si hoped would not be the case because he didn't have any details at this stage. It was a potential threat but still at this stage based on a lot of supposition. He would ask the Technology geeks to work through the night on this one.

Max returned to his office and job following his India China trip and set about continuing with his normal activities in the CPO role. He had a number of meetings with John Dawlish the CTO where not a word was spoken between them about Max's visit to the suspect Apex Finance printers in Mumbai, which Max found very strange. He imagined that Frank would have been straight on the phone to John from Hong Kong immediately following his satisfaction that everything was fine and reporting that he hadn't stumbled across anything they needed to worry about.

Indeed John Dawlish had been nicer than usual to him and several times at the meetings when one of John's IT managers was challenging Max and procurement on a particular spend review or supplier contract, John had come down on Max's side and shut his staff member down even when Max felt he hadn't needed to. Max wondered if now that the threat of him sticking his nose into the India operation had they believed gone away, they were now more relaxed and were back to grooming him to be part of the inner team so he'd look the other way in other areas as well.

Max bumped into Sian Reeves who insisted they went for a coffee as she wanted to hear all about his travels to India and Hong Kong. Apart from the usual party destinations in Spain she'd never gone far abroad and was planning to ask for a two-month sabbatical from work to travel around Asia with a friend. During their coffee, Max thought there was no harm in asking her about the Angel anti-malware product.

"We've got a project in procurement supporting some of our software developers," Max concocted, "and I'm trying to find out a little more about how these programs like for instance Angel get written. I don't want to look stupid by asking John Dawlish. Do you have anything to do with the Angel virus checker?" asked Max.

"Crikey no, that's way above my pay grade, there's only a couple of guys here at head office who John Dawlish would let anywhere near that kind of sensitive stuff. That's his baby. The top programmers for Angel are all based in Barbados. Lucky sods." Sian gazed upwards for a moment imagining going into work every day in sunny Barbados.

"So how do these guys have access to writing and developing the program for these software products, like Angel?" said Max casually.

"Hmm, firstly they'll have various logins and security to access each part of any programming system, kinda basic stuff like passwords to view, passwords to make amendments and heavier passwords to access different parts of the program. That way the control of the program is fully auditable and can be set up to be accessed remotely from anywhere online or from specific computer locations and IP addresses," explained Sian.

Max listened feigning interest but didn't know enough about programming to ask the right questions. Noticing Sian was starting to look a little puzzled on why he was wanting to talk about programming rather than travelling abroad, he switched the topic back to asking her where she was planning on going for her trip. He happily listened while she ran through her two-month itinerary.

The day Doreen Leader came back into the office following her meetings in Berlin and Paris, Max was booked in to see her for their weekly catch up and was keen to see if Doreen was now okay after their breakfast conversation in Hong Kong. As he walked into her office and she greeted him with her usual charming, calm smile, he felt perhaps things were back to normal and maybe he and Si Lawson were making a lot of fuss about nothing. They briefly chatted about Hong Kong, neither of them mentioning Max's stated concerns about the India printers, then got into their normal catch-up meeting covering everything that Max and procurement were doing across the business.

At the end, Max wanted to just check that Doreen was okay

and asked, "So do you know any more about this potential sale, that you're allowed to tell me of course?"

"No, but that's fine Max, I'm okay with that. Once Frank's ready to conclude any sale he's got to get me involved, after all, I'm his CFO. He can't do anything without me." She leant forward and briefly touched his hand knowing that he was concerned. "It's okay Max, everything's fine, I appreciate you looking out for me."

Max change the subject as he got up to leave. "So have you got any more business trips planned or do we have the pleasure of your company back here at head office for a while now?"

Doreen replied, "No more long trips in the diary like last week, but I am going to Frank's villa in Barbados soon which I'm looking forward to. I gather he's got an amazing house on the beach there and if that's where he wants to hold an executive board meeting, then I'm in," she laughed.

"Wow, sounds amazing, so who's going, can I come too?" joked Max.

"You know I'd love it if you were there as well but I'm afraid not, it's just the executive directors Frank, John, Brett and myself. I don't think Sir Kieran is coming though. Apparently Frank has us all out there a couple of times a year, sounds great doesn't it."

That evening Max decided to check in with Si Lawson even though he didn't have anything to report. He was hoping that Si's techie guys might have had a chance to look at the Angel program. A part of him was excited to see if this whole corrupt mess was a real thing and part of him hoped there was nothing to be found. Maybe then this whole charade he was going through could come to an end.

Si Lawson quickly picked up Max's call. "Max, glad you called. I've literally just had the techie chaps in here taking me through what they found within the Angel program."

"Oh yes," said Max almost sounding like he'd forgotten about the matter, but he was all ears.

Si continued. "It's all a bit complicated and nerdy but the top line is that they've found a number of compartments or lockers within the program, some easily visible and a few that have been blocked off. All with varying degrees of encryption, randomly generated key codes and basic to highly complex passwords. Nothing I hasten to add that the guys wouldn't have expected from any commercial software programs. Are you with me so far Max?"

Max shrugged at the phone, "I guess so but keep it simple."

"Okay. The guys think they've found a couple of these hidden lockers that might give them access to viewing other hidden lockers we don't even know about yet. That's where we're stuck at the moment. Even though access would only be 'view only', if we can get into some of these compartment's we might actually be able to see any sleeping programs, data miners or Trojans. The good news is that they've already worked out one of the passwords to a locker is a 20 string of alphanumerics, a bit like your basic password such as 'max123'." Si was getting more excited as he relayed the update to Max.

"Sounds complicated," observed Max. "How the hell did your guys work all this out anyway?"

"Max, this is MI5 Cyber. Do you think we sit here playing Xbox games all day? We've got some of the best programmers and encryption crackers in the UK working here." Si was proud of his guys, he'd seen what they could do on other operations and knew that for every person creating the next best encryption, there would be a hundred people having fun trying to hack it.

Si continued. "You know this John Dawlish guy. You've mentioned that he keeps his Angel product very close to him. It's what started up Frank Dark's corporation. So it's a long shot, but it could be that the password for this locker was set by him. We can set programs onto it which might crack it in a few weeks, but if we can tune our password decipher targeting into known topics and subjects that might be used within the password, then we can prioritise the program to use those subjects first. It's an amazing piece of software with built-in artificial intelligence, so if you tell me John Dawlish has a cat called Tom, we can search and try thousands of Tom cat-related password attempts every few seconds, including random numerics as well."

"So how can I help," asked Max.

"I need you to tell me everything you've learned about John Dawlish. We'll go back through his childhood, schools, friends, holidays, homes and all the easily available stuff, but what we don't know is about him, his personality, hobbies?"

Max thought for a moment. He'd only had a couple of conversations with John Dawlish that weren't all about the business. "He's a clever guy John Dawlish but to be honest he's pretty dull. He never talks about anything other than work, at least not to me."

"Come on Max. There must be something he's mentioned to you that he is interested in other than computers?" insisted Si.

Max then remembered. "You know what, there is something. He's a big movies fan. He loves his old movies."

"Brilliant. That's the kind of thing we need that could cut down the permutations to crack one of these passwords. Tell me more about the movies he likes?" pushed Si.

"I don't know, he just loves old movies."

"What old movies Max? Any in particular? Which movie stars? Think Max."

"He mentioned he likes Laurel and Hardy," said Max remembering their conversation now about going to a desert island. "His favourite film was of them in the Music Box or something, where they have to lug it up some steps."

"Great Max, that at least gives us something to go on, we'll get the programs running and maybe we can get a bit more access to look behind the scenes of the Angel software," parted Si.

The following evening Max had gone to bed around 11 PM and was fast asleep when his mobile beside the bed rang. Surprised that anyone would possibly be calling him at 2:30 AM in the middle of the night, he picked up.

It was Si who wouldn't normally call Max unless it was urgent and he knew that Max could not possibly be with anyone at work. "Max, I'm sorry to call you in the middle of the night, but the guys have just had some luck with the password cracker on one of the hidden compartments of Angel. It's bad news."

"What is? Tell me?" demanded Max.

"Thanks to your information on John Dawlish they gained access to part of the program that allowed them to at least view hidden coding," said Si.

"What did the password end up being then?"

"Funnily enough it was 'halroachpresents1932'," said Si. Max was silent, it meant nothing to him. "Laurel and Hardy films all start with 'Hal Roach Presents' at the top of the screen. He was their producer and studio boss, and the '1932' numeric was the year they made their short movie Music Box."

Si went on. "This hidden coding included part of a dormant execute program bundle. It's basically a sleeping Trojan," said Si.

"Why would he put a Trojan in his own software, I don't understand?" asked Max.

"The guys can't see all of the coding but they are pretty sure it's a wipe-kill Trojan which has the ability to delete everything across the system it's in, all files and all other software. It could then permanently damage the operating system of the device it's in, so for example that computer can't be turned on again!" Si's voice had a tinge of panic in it not lost on Max.

Max played it back in simpler terms. "You mean it can wipe everything off your computer and then knacker the actual PC itself."

"Yes. If it's a botnet this is disastrous. With the widespread use of Angel across most of the globe in homes, businesses and governments, it could have the potential of bringing the world to its knees. Every network and system, database and server linked to a device with the Angel software on it could be compromised. It's the cyber equivalent of that awful Coronavirus the world had to endure with job losses, businesses collapsing and economic stagnation."

"So why don't you just tell everyone to delete their Angel software?" said Max.

"It's not that simple Max. Tens of millions of these programs sold worldwide over the last several decades. We don't know how the sleeping wipe-kill Trojan gets activated and we absolutely cannot risk doing anything to alert whoever can bring this program to life. Somehow we have to stop it at the source. Find out where the keyholder might be. Or how to access the master program and delete the Trojan through the botnet."

As Si thought through it out loud Max chipped in. "I was talking recently to this girl I know in head office IT, she's been helpful in the past. She seemed to think the programming for Angel was now all done and accessed by probably only John Dawlish and his team of programmers at the Barbados Angel office."

"Good point Max. But we can't just send our guys bundling in there, if they could set off the Trojan from there or even somewhere else the game would be up. We've got to someway get full access to these hidden compartments in the program and delete them," outlined Si.

Max then trumped up. "Blimey. Doreen told me they're all off to Barbados shortly for some board meeting, just the directors Frank, her, John Dawlish and Brett Harding. You don't think that's got anything to do with the deal with the Chinese businessman Li. The big payment Frank's expecting and activating the Angel Trojan do you?"

Both men on the call froze as they realised the likelihood that Max's simple conjecture could actually be about to happen.

Following the brief silence, Si spoke. "I do. Shit. This is bloody huge. Max, I need to get my team in and think this through carefully, brief the Director General personally and come up with a plan. Just one thing though, this meeting in Barbados. Where the Angel office is. Any chance you can get yourself invited Max?"

"No chance Si, it's executive directors only," Max stated emphatically.

Si Lawson's reply was predictable just before he rang off. "You're a clever, persuasive chap, you'll figure out a way. But do it quickly. You've got to get an invite to Barbados."

18

The relationship between Max and his boss Doreen Leader had gone from strength-to-strength Max felt. They shared high standards of professionalism and work ethic, but also had that unseen chemical match where two people just click together with their characters and chemistry. Max had been wondering how to engineer himself to somehow getting invited to the Barbados get-together. He'd thought about some big plan to save the company a lot of money but felt they'd simply ask him to present it here at the head office. Perhaps pretend he'd be out there on holiday, but he hadn't mentioned this previously or put in a holiday request. His first and most straightforward line of attack had to be to try to use his relationship with Doreen and just ask her outright, plead if necessary, to be included in the upcoming trip.

At the end of a quick catch up with Doreen in her office, he played his hand. "Doreen, we've got on really well, shared a few moments together like in Hong Kong, and I don't think I've ever asked anything of you." Doreen looked intrigued and wondered what favour was about to be requested. Max continued. "I know how much being part of the 'team' means to Frank, and want to prove myself to you all. My CPO role here gives me access to all parts of the business and I was hoping you'd get me the opportunity of attending your trip to Barbados with you? You did say it would be great if I could go."

"Oh Max, I'd love you to be there but it's only just Frank's Exec team." Doreen thought for a moment searching for any consolation she could give Max. "Frank does place a lot on loyalty, so you'd need to come up with something really impressive to show him you're worthy of his trust and 'inner circle'. Believe me, I know." Doreen pondered on her own circumstances getting into this inner circle and how she'd give anything to get out of it now. She feared that once you're in, you can't ever get out again.

Max nodded at her advice as he left. What Doreen had said had prompted an idea which he spent the next few hours moulding into something else he could try out, to demonstrate to Frank he was a worthy ally. A big demonstration of trust and loyalty was required. An idea formed, but it was risky.

It was an ace card he'd have to play though. One that could go horribly wrong and mess up everything and was unfortunately going to be based on pure gut instinct, but it was the only idea he could come up with. He made up a reason to go and see John Dawlish and nervously proceeded upstairs to the fourth-floor executive suites.

He was sat opposite John Dawlish and having finished covering his fabricated topic regarding one of their upcoming supplier contract renewals, Max composed himself and carefully confronted his CTO.

"John." Max allowed the pause to linger making the brief silence turn awkward, grabbing John's full attention with the building seriousness of what he was about to say. Max took the gamble. "I know what you're doing at Apex Finance."

The silence was deafening as the two of them stared into one another's eyes trying to read thoughts and reactions. The awkwardness was killing him, but Max held out determined not to be the first person to speak.

John Dawlish gathered himself through his seething fury. "I have no idea what you're talking about," he pronounced. It was then him who sat back in his chair glaring at Max in silence. Another uncomfortable standoff.

Max lent forward and spoke quietly, carefully measuring how much information he gave away. He couldn't have John suspect that he had the backing of a higher authority such as MI5 involved. "You've got something going on in Mumbai with the money printing there."

John Dawlish had been quietly and successfully running his petty cash operation at Apex for some years. He didn't need the money, but he saw it as his reward, his prize for hacking the Ministry of Finance's encrypted serial number files they sent in with every month's printing order. He couldn't be greedy about running off too much duplicated currency, if it got too big more people would get involved wanting larger cuts. Also, there'd be a higher chance of the notes being detected when re-introduced into general circulation. John Dawlish looked at Max thinking, 'And after all this time, here comes Max bloody Sargent ruining it all. No.'

John reiterated, "What are you talking about. How dare you." Then mistakenly goaded Max with, "What's your proof?" implying there might be evidence to be found.

"I don't need any proof, I saw enough to know what's going on there," said Max hoping more than ever his bluffing had hit home. Now Max could play his trump card, just in time before John looked as though he was about to explode with rage and hit him.

Max was conciliatory. "But look here John, I know how these things work and I like it here at the Dark Corporation working for you, Doreen and Frank. I want to be a part of it all. Frank keeps on telling me how important his 'team' is to him and loyalty. So I'm not going to tell anyone about it." His latest announcement to John was first viewed with suspicion. Then Max felt the atmosphere in the room relax a little.

Eventually, John broke the silence again. "Well it's good of you Max not to discuss this with anyone, not that I'm saying anything is going on, but I think it's wise of you not to make any trouble. As you say, we need people at the top who are loyal."

Max left John Dawlish's office and as he started down the stairs, glanced behind himself to see John coming out of his office and striding along the large open landing towards Frank Dark's office. 'Bloody hell' he thought to himself, 'now what's going to happen next'.

For the rest of that day, Max had a knot in his stomach and on one occasion had to disappear to the men's toilets as he thought he was going to be sick. He had a few calls and conversations with his staff in the office and was conscious that nothing was going in.

He couldn't think about anything else other than what Frank and John would be up to and how they would react to his robust conversation with the CTO.

Max didn't need to wait too long to find out. Just as he was gathering up his things to leave for home that evening, Sheila called down asking him if he had a few moments spare could he please pop up as Frank wanted to see him. 'Showtime' he thought as he went up, taking in a couple of deep breaths to compose himself in readiness.

He went into Frank's office and quietly sat at the chair on the other side of the desk to him, feeling rather like a naughty schoolboy about to be told how many swipes of the cane he would get by the headmaster. To his surprise, Frank greeted him warmly and seemed to be in a good mood. 'Surely John would have told him word for word about their conversation earlier?'.

Frank calmly opened up. "John's told me about your chat with him earlier and your ridiculous notion that something's going on at Apex." Max thought to himself he was about to get kicked out. "I can't say I'm delighted about you confronting him like that. However, having talked it through with John, I am impressed that you have decided not to mention this matter to anyone and have deferred to us."

Max pitched in. "I don't want to cause any trouble Frank and as I said to John I like working for you. I like being here at the corporation and hope I've got a long-term career here. I do want to be part of the team and hope I've gone some way to demonstrating that by overlooking whatever may or may not be going on in Mumbai," said Max, now starting to wonder how to broach the topic of Barbados with Frank.

As if reading his mind Frank continued. "You've certainly demonstrated your loyalty and I have been impressed with everything you're doing anyway in your CPO role." Frank stopped to check himself on whether to continue with his intended suggestion. "I'll tell you what Max, me and the other exec directors are having a little retreat at my Barbados villa next week and I'd like you to come along as well. We can all get to know you a bit better, spend a bit of downtime. You'll love the Villa it's amazing and there's a couple of really nice cars I have out there I know you'll like."

'Bingo' thought Max who was so excited he had to make sure in his own mind that he hadn't just gone and said it out loud. His idea to win them over with his offer of silence about the Mumbai money printing had worked, along with the whole inner team, loyalty and trust thing he knew Frank Dark treasured more than his fancy sports cars.

"I'd be honoured to attend Frank, thank you, I appreciate it, I won't let you down," thanked Max almost bowing to Frank with deference as he left the office.

Frank added as Max left, "I'll ask Sheila to sort out all the details for you."

Frank's eyes followed Max as he crossed over to the staircase and descended. He still wasn't quite sure what to make of Max Sargent but was at least starting to believe he could be a worthy asset in his team. John Dawlish didn't like the idea of bringing Max to Barbados, but Frank's view to John was that he was doing it not just to get to know Max better. More importantly, he wanted to keep Max close until they could decide whether he would be helpful to them, or trouble. Either way, if he was in Barbados they could keep a close eye on him when the final transaction was due to be completed with their Chinese businessman. Nothing could be allowed to interfere with that. It's what he and John had been working towards for years.

Frank dialled Brett Harding's number. "Hi Brett, you're in South Africa this weekend on a job aren't you, before then coming out to Barbados for our get together?"

"I am Frank, why what's up?" asked Brett.

"Nothing. I'll fill you in later. I'm going to ask Sheila to put you on a certain flight to Barbados from London, hopefully that will tie in with your plans. Me, Doreen and John will fly out the day before," said Frank.

"Roger Wilco. I think I have to fly from Johannesburg to Barbados via London anyway so that will work out fine." Brett hung up sensing that was all Frank required of him.

Frank Dark sat back in his chair and slowly looked around his office. Various pictures, awards and artefacts hung on the walls and sat on the shelves, each reminding him of a prestigious event or meeting with notoriety. He'd spent his life building up this massive corporation. He was worth many hundreds of millions of pounds, his entire company had a valuation of around one and a half billion and he could easily retire and live happily ever after. But that just wasn't the way he was made. One of the blessings but also a curse that many successful entrepreneurs often have, is that they are never happy, always striving for perfection, always wanting more and better. Perhaps thought Frank, the deal he was about to do with Mr Xiaoping would finally put his restless spirits at ease and he would be satisfied with the staggeringly large amount of money he would soon have. Sure, where there were winners there were even more losers, but he always believed in the mantra of 'survival of the fittest'. If among the sacrifices he'd have to make was potentially not coming back here to the UK, his home and this office he was sat in and worked in for decades, then so be it.

Max got home that evening and sat down to enjoy his dinner and savour his latest masterminded accomplishment a little longer before calling Si Lawson. When he did he started the call by briefly and proudly stating, "I did it."

"Did what?" asked Si.

"Barbados of course. I've managed to get them to include me in their Barbados trip next week. Just don't ask me how I did it. It was pretty touch and go," said Max congratulating himself.

"Well done Max, that's brilliant, you see what you can achieve when you put your mind to it. While you've been booking yourself on Caribbean holidays we've been pretty busy here as well," joked Si quickly realising that none of this was a joking matter. "The team here have been going through the options and the only one that keeps coming to the surface is that we need to introduce our own 'seek and destroy' kill-ware into the master Angel software program. It's got to be via an authorised programmer's terminal that's already logged into the system. We can then in theory instruct via their botnet all the embedded sleeping Trojans everywhere to immediately delete themselves the moment they're online." Si knew this was going to be a long shot and would inevitably require timing and luck if someone like Max was going to pull it off.

"What does all that mean for me?" asked Max.

Si explained. "The guys here are working on a kill-ware program which will be self-executing once it's plugged into a computer's USB port. The hard bit though is that you are going to have to figure out a way of introducing it probably at either Frank's villa or more than likely it will be in the Angel offices, wherever there is a PC terminal that allows access to the master program. But given we won't know the encryption and passcodes to get into that system, you can only do it once someone else has logged into the system using that computer."

"You mean like jump up behind someone that's working on their PC and shove some bit of hardware into the USB port. Really?" Max wasn't enthralled with the idea at all.

Si shifted in his seat, he was just as uneasy about all of this is as Max was. "Something like that yes, we'll keep working on the final details. One other thing we are not entirely sure about is that there might be a failsafe protection mechanism built into the program, alerting a keyholder or asking for authorisation when someone is trying to make a major change to the master program. One assumes if this is the case the programmers at the Barbados office will have that authority or know where to get it from. Unfortunately, there's nothing we can do to prepare for that, if it happens at all, we'll just have to figure that out at the time. When are you leaving for Barbados? Will aim to get you the kill-ware file well before you leave to take with you."

"I'm off in three days," said Max completely overwhelmed

by what he was trying to take in and everything he seemed to be committing himself to do. He felt as though he should have lots more questions about this somewhat sketchy scheme, but right now he couldn't think of anything else to ask.

"Okay, we'll make sure we've got a file ready for you in time. Don't worry it's not a big piece of hardware, the self-executing file can be put on a small USB memory stick. I'll get back to you as soon as possible with anything else we can think of to help you."

"That's reassuring of you Si. I can't say I'm feeling great about all this, but it seems like the only way of doing it," said Max regretfully.

"Believe me, Max, we've gone round and round trying to think how we can do this without involving you, as you say this is the only option we have that has a chance of succeeding. By the way, MI5 will have a few guys in Barbados on standby for me to call upon, just in case anything gets a bit silly or we need to pull you out quickly."

Max fantasised these 'guys' to be SAS type operatives, hopefully armed. Then realising it wouldn't be great to be in the middle of a situation where Si felt he needed armed support. He quickly checked with him. "Not armed I assume," said Max.

Si said flatly, "All our field operatives have access to whatever ordnance, arms or equipment they require. Don't worry Max, we'll be right there for you."

But Max *was* worried. Very worried. Somehow he'd gone from being asked to snoop around an office and collect a bit of information, to now being expected to single-handedly avert a global cyber catastrophe. How the hell had he got himself into this!

19

Over the next few days Max kept on going through everything in his mind, what might happen, different settings, what the Angel offices were like, what might go wrong, it was an endless conveyor belt of scenarios. He also called Si Lawson every night asking when he'd get this USB kill-ware dongle. Each time Si told him the techies were still working on a program file that had the best chance of success and that it was a highly complex program with intricate coding. Max was now due to leave for the airport in the morning, unless Si got him this stick before then they would miss their window to do anything.

Max was starting to fret, he was packed and waiting for a driver to collect him in a couple of hours, so called Si again.

"Si have you got this file for me yet, I need to leave in an hour also?" asked Max.

"Sorry Max I've been pushing the guys and they're just putting in some finishing touches, looks like they'll have something for us but I'm not going to be able to get it over to you in Clapham in the next hour. I'll bring it to Heathrow and meet you myself at the BA first class check-in area before you go through security. That will give me a little bit more time. I'll be there," Si promised him.

Max soon after climbed into the chauffeured black Range Rover and as they pulled out of his driveway looked back at his precious home wishing he could just stay there and lock the doors, rather than have to be embarking on this trip. What worried him as much as the uncertainty of how things would unfold, was the inevitability that at some point there was going to be a conflict crossroads. Whatever he had to do he knew there would be people there trying to stop him and if Si was right about the Chinese wanting to use the Angel software for a Trojan, he was frightened about the repercussions whether he succeeded or not. The uncompromising massive foreign power involved, the huge sum of money that Doreen mentioned, MI5 in the thick of it and so much at stake, with him stuck in the middle of it all, provided a weighty cocktail of responsibility and danger.

The driver took them up through Battersea and over the bridge onwards to Earls Court where they joined the A4 coming out of London. This then became the M4, they briefly joined the M25 and pulled into Terminal five Departures.

Max found a spot in the middle of the concourse near to his check-in desks and waited for Si Lawson to appear through one of the entrance doors. He looked forward to seeing Si again and his face-to-face reassurance that he so desperately needed from him at this point. He looked at his watch and thought that he needed to check-in in the next half an hour. Looking up and scanning the various faces across the terminal and people outside approaching the doorways, he finally spotted Si entering the building at the far end furthest away from him. What a relief, 'about time' he thought to himself.

Max fixed his gaze on Si walking towards him, waiting for him to notice him, then just as Si recognised him and Max was about to raise his hand to wave, to his shock and horror Max instantly noticed another familiar but unwelcome face coming through one of the entrance doorways nearer to him. His heart missed a beat. It was Brett Harding!

Max had to think quickly. Si Lawson was ambling towards him from a distance smiling and ready to greet him. Brett had now also just spotted Max and adjusted his direction and was coming directly over to him, but in front of Si. Max couldn't let them converge on him at the same time let alone actually meet. He quickly closed the distance between himself and Brett enthusiastically meeting him halfway and shaking his hand in greeting. Max hoped that this would signal to Si that they had company and he shouldn't come over and make contact.

As Max escorted Brett over to the check-in desks he noticed Si breakaway from his pathway towards them and as he came level with them started to ask one of the check-in staff about a flight. Many years of covert missions, tailing people and interpretation of changing situations prepared Si well, as he saw Max deliberately go to greet someone else in front of him. 'Thank heavens' thought Max as he told Brett how surprised he was to see him here. Brett was slightly bemused by Max's enthusiastic greeting but thought no more of it as they bypassed the queueing travellers for business and economy classes and went straight to the front of the red carpet laid out at the first-class check-in desks.

Max and Brett made their way off to passport control and security, after which Brett suggested they waited for their gate to be called in the BA Concorde first-class lounge.

Si Lawson had watched them check-in and walk over to the departure's security control area. Waiting until the pair passed through and were out of sight he looked around for the nearest policeman. He needed to bypass security quickly without having to go through lengthy explanations to airport or check-in staff who would no doubt not recognise his identity badge. So as not to startle them he walked up to a pair of police officers sporting their body armour vests and Heckler and Koch MP5's. He held up his MI5 identity card immediately introducing himself and explaining that he needed one of them to take him round the security controls and into the flight-side concourse. Both police officers recognised the MI5 badge and one of them hurriedly led Si off to a side door marked 'Private' to take him through a couple of corridors. Following another quick badge check from a security guard, the policeman pointed to the exit door for Si to quietly slip into the passenger holding concourse.

Max and Brett settled down in the corner of the Concorde lounge to amuse themselves with the Buffet, magazines and television for the next hour or so until their flight would be announced over the speakers. Max was quietly fuming at Brett's surprise appearance and spoiling his critical reunion with Si. He felt isolated and exposed for without this anti-Trojan file he was now left helpless, with the prospect of having to continue his acting charade with the directors of the Dark Corporation, knowing that they were up to no good. He knew Si was an exceptional operator and wondered if maybe he was right now booking himself onto the same flight to perhaps give him the USB stick during the trip or once they got to Barbados. Unlikely. He resigned himself to not being able to do anything more for MI5, they'd let him down.

Si Lawson bought a cabin bag from one of the shops and made his way to the BA lounges. After flashing his card and asking at reception, he spotted Max and his colleague whom he recognised from his photo as Brett Harding, both sitting at the far end of the lounge in the corner. Si slipped into the lounge and sat at the opposite end behind shelving holding newspapers and magazines. He positioned himself in a seat where if he just moved his head slightly he could see Brett and Max, who had his back to him. Si then waited, and hoped. He had an idea.

Max looked up at the boarding times screen and figured they'd need to leave in the next twenty minutes, so headed off to the toilets which he knew would be relatively luxurious compared to the cramped facilities on a plane. After relieving himself he stood in front of the mirror and started to wash his hands. At that moment another man came in, but Max didn't look up and continued at his basin.

Instantaneously a hurried and hushed voice started talking to him. It was Si Lawson who'd seen Max going towards the toilets and got up to adeptly follow him. "Max, it's me, don't say anything just listen, we've got maybe fifteen seconds." Si leaned towards the two toilet cubicles checking more closely they were both empty and continued with the concise speech he'd been rehearsing in his mind, pulling a watch out of his pocket as he spoke. "Give me your Rolex Submariner quickly and put this one on instead. It's the same model but the guys removed its guts and your supermini USB stick with the kill program is inside. Just unscrew the back when you need it." Max was mesmerised and quickly did what he was told with bewilderment, checking the new watch. "It still works fine with a tiny cheap electronic movement. Remember, just plug in the stick, but only once a computer has been logged into the Angel master program."

With that Si quickly wet his hands under the tap and turned to the air blade hand dryer. Max finished clipping on the replacement Rolex watch and was just about to speak to Si when the door opened and in came Brett who seeing someone else in the room, paused for a second before then saying to Max, "We need to get going to the gate now Max." He then came in to go to the toilet himself as Si nonchalantly passed him in the doorway and exited. Max smiled at Brett then went out. He looked around the lounge and noticed Si taking his seat down the far end and yearned to go over to him but returned to his corner to gather up his things, by which time Brett re-joined him and they made their way to their flight.

As they waited at the gate to board, Brett got onto his phone. Max took the opportunity to gather himself after the rushed, clandestine meeting with Si and nervously fingering his surprise new Rolex, went over in his mind everything Si had hurriedly said to him just to make sure he'd got it all. He wanted to have a look now at this mini-USB stick inside the watch and decided he could do that during the flight in the toilet. Listening to Brett, Max deduced that he was just checking in with Frank Dark who was already in Barbados, merely to tell him they were on their way and about to board the eight-and-a-half-hour flight. At the end of the call, Brett signed off with his usual "Roger Wilco."

On the flight, Max and Brett's first-class seat pods were on different sides of the plane which Max was grateful for, so they barely interacted during the trip. Apart from on one occasion when Max had gone up to the self-service snacks and drinks counter behind the bulkhead. He was rummaging through the dried fruit and chocolate bars when Brett appeared round the partition looking for another bottle of water.

"You know Max, I wasn't sure about you to start with, but I think you're okay. You'll do well at the Dark Corporation," said Brett.

"Why thank you Brett, I appreciate your candour," replied

Max.

"I've known Frank since we were at school together and I can tell you he values loyalty above anything else, maybe even as much as money," Brett said with an awkward laugh, "and once you're on board with him and he's accepted you, I guarantee he'll look after you. Impress him and you'll soon be wealthy."

"I certainly don't want to miss out on that opportunity Brett."

Then bizarrely Brett abruptly finished the conversation with a much harsher tone. "No, what you *don't* want to do is get on the wrong side of him. Or me." Brett forced a wry smile as he went back to his seat leaving Max confused and perturbed at how quickly Brett had turned what he thought was a reassuring 'onboarding' chat, into what felt like an intimidating and threatening warning. Max made a point of avoiding any more chance encounters with Brett up at the snacks bar.

They arrived in Barbados and were met at the bottom of the steps from the plane by a smartly dressed VIP escort who led them through the private fast track security lounge of Grantley Adams airport. They were then offered more champagne and drinks in a small waiting room, whilst their 'first-class priority' labelled luggage was extracted from the plane's underbelly and brought through. It was then scanned through an x-ray machine in the lounge.

They walked through the airport which was named after the first Barbados Premier in 1976, beneath the large arching bare concrete structures and white canopies, to be greeted by a suited driver and stunning black Rolls-Royce Ghost with blacked-out windows. Max was impressed, finally a change from the black Range Rovers.

The driver took them up the Tom Adams Highway into the Errol Barrow Highway. Impromptu traders peddled their fruits, drinks and freshly cut open coconuts to drink from on the side of the road. The weather was perfect with a few wispy white clouds scattered in the otherwise clear blue sky. Barbados was a beautiful place, no wonder so many tourists and wealthy celebrities made the long trip here with its stunning beaches and friendly locals.

They passed the Emancipation statue in the middle of the JTC Ramsay roundabout, symbolising the breaking of the chains of slavery. At the busy Warrens roundabout surrounded by car dealerships, tractors, offices and takeaway's, Brett lent over and pointed to a small building with dark glass saying, "That's one of ours. Angel software."

Max's interest was alerted by Brett's mention of the word Angel. It didn't look like a very secure building he thought, so asked Brett, "Quite modest looking isn't it, I thought it would be more secure?"

Brett shrugged one shoulder. "Why would it need any security, it's right by the highway for everyone to see and there's nothing inside worth stealing, just a few computers and a bunch of John's techie nerds."

They veered off left from the roundabout towards Stanmore where they turned right joining the H1 beach road along the beautiful West Coast. The climate was mostly hot, warm and sunny but also allowed for enough rain on this tropical island for lush vegetation to grow, strong grassy lawns, palm trees and foliage lined the roadside and beyond. Progressing north along H1 Max could catch glimpses of the stunning blue and turquoise clear waters to his left, in between the interspersed single and double story homes lining the soft sandy public beaches. The backs of the waterfront houses looked plain and modest and betrayed the beautiful million-dollar views the front of the houses had across the beach and water. It was very similar to the fabulous beach houses in Malibu most of which abruptly back onto the Pacific Coast Highway 1.

Smiling, content locals were going about their business, waiting for the next bus and chatting to friends and neighbours, while perfectly turned-out children in their matching school uniforms walked home laughing and fooling around. Barbados also played host to numerous wealthy businessman and celebrities, many British, some of whom had impressive $20 million beachfront villas mainly from around Sandy Lane up to Port St Charles. Others preferring seclusion and security were further inland away from the public beaches, from which anybody could walk up to their properties if they so wished.

After passing by the entrance to the Sandy Lane Hotel and Club complex and then just after the Colony Beach Club in Porters, the driver turned the Rolls into a long narrow private driveway. At the end, it opened out into a picture-postcard beachfront estate with private grounds surrounding a contemporary villa.

"Here we are Sirs," announced the driver proudly as if the Villa were his.

Max climbed out of the car's rear-hinged 'suicide door', so-called because of the likely damage it would cause an exiting passenger if hit by a passing car. He looked around the impressive two-story clean, modern property with well-kept lawns all around the house and several garages. He could see down the side of the house, the edge of a large patio terrace with an infinity swimming pool beckoning, leading down through some large rocks to the sandy beach and the clear waters of Heron Bay beyond.

Frank Dark came out of the front door to greet them wearing chinos and a lightweight, colourful shirt. "Brett, Max, hope you had a good trip, lovely to see you both here." Brett busied himself at the back of the Rolls-Royce organising their baggage. He'd been here many times before so didn't expect or want the big greeting or tour he knew Frank would want to give Max. "Welcome to my humble abode in Barbados Max, come with me and I'll show you around. Doreen and John are already here out the back."

Frank took Max straight to the garages knowing their shared love of cars and proudly showed him one of the latest Ferrari F8 Spider cabriolet's in yellow, only just launched to restricted list regular customers as demand for every new Ferrari always outstripped the sparse production runs. Alongside this sat a new menacing-looking Pagani Huayra Roadster in metallic blue and black carbon fibre. Frank told Max, "In such a beautiful sunny setting one has to go for the open-top versions of these rare supercars."

He then took Max inside and around the cool air-conditioned house, where they found John Dawlish in the study sitting at one of the computers on a call with his IT team in America. The kitchen and lounge slide-away doors opened up fully onto the rear terrace which had various fountains, palm trees, a large Jacuzzi and thatched gazebo surrounding the crystal-clear blue infinity pool. Doreen was sitting at one of the tables enjoying a cup of tea, wearing a bright red one-piece bikini teasingly masked with a floral-patterned cover-up over the top.

In addition to the driver who when not in his suit would also act as security, maintenance and pool man, there were two other local lady staff who would share the housekeeping, shopping and cooking. Frank explained to Max, "The husband-and-wife staff live in the self-contained annexe above the garages and look after the house when I'm not here and look after me and my guests when I am. Their meals and cocktails are to die for, you'll see later at dinner. Once they've served us I've let them have a couple of days off, so we'll have the place to ourselves."

Looking across the pool and down the short garden, Max could now see a large low shed to the far side near the beach, carefully covered in ivy and honeysuckle to attempt hiding it from view. Frank noticed him looking at it and said, "Oh that's the water sports shed, you'll love it. I've got a couple of jet skis, a small speedboat, some kayaks and paddleboards, and just yesterday took delivery of one of those electric hydrofoil surfboards, haven't tried it out yet."

Max was truly impressed with everything, all this hidden away just off the main beach road, all so private and secluded. He estimated the place had to be worth getting on towards $30 million.

Max sorted things out in his room and for the remainder of the afternoon came down to join the others by the pool, everyone content to get on with their own thing, some paddle-boarding, helping themselves to snacks and drinks, before getting together for dinner by the pool later.

Late evening they assembled by the pool all looking a little smarter and sat down for a scrumptious three-course meal cooked and served by all three staff before they left. The conversation was natural and relaxed switching from talking about people in the business to reminiscing about previous management get-togethers. Though whilst the others were making an effort to include Max and make him feel at home, he couldn't help but feel he was the odd man out, the outsider. The wine flowed. That helped everyone.

Frank and John Dawlish even started joking about how uptight Rajit Singh was, their manager at Apex Finance in Mumbai. Frank smiled over at Max and commented, "Well we don't need to worry any more about what's going on at Apex, eh Max, now that your on-board with us and part of the team." Max nodded and smiled.

At one point John Dawlish brought up when they were celebrating the successful acquisition of a large security man-guarding company. The next day he'd gone and bought Frank his gold Rolex Daytona and that he couldn't believe he'd actually managed to choose something that Frank liked and was still wearing.

"One of your better choices John," complimented Frank, "I'd had so many Rolex's before, but this is my favourite one."

"I see you're a bit of a Rolex fan yourself Max, nice watch, may I have a look?" said Brett.

Max froze inside then hoped he hadn't given away the sharp bolt of anxiety that had shot through him. "Of course," he said holding his arm out towards Brett.

"Lovely those Submariners, the original classic divers Rolex," commented John, as Brett admired the robust steel watch with its black face and numbered bezel.

When Si Lawson and his MI5 team had been discussing the kill-ware program they needed a way for Max to get it through security, keep it from being found, but also ideally be on him permanently ready to use if the opportunity arose. Ideas of some kind of bracelet or neck chain were rejected in favour of Alan's suggestion, the MI5 techie who had sorted out Max's iPhone for him. His idea was to hide the mini USB stick inside a similar watch to the one Max wore. Alan was very excited to have the opportunity of trying out for real his Roger Moore inspired watch. He requisitioned one of the Rolex Submariner non-date watches they had in stores, along with another of the many replica watches they had, both confiscated from criminal activity. Then working with a colleague who specialised in hardware gadgets at Thames House, they managed to replace the bulky genuine Rolex mechanism with a miniature battery-operated one complete with the genuine looking Rolex sweeping second hand. The small dongle fitted neatly in the empty space within the casing and the back lid was screwed on only finger tight.

Max was practically holding his breath waiting to see if his replacement watch would pass muster under Brett's inspection. After a few moments which felt like minutes to Max, Brett said, "Very nice watch. But I think I'll stick with my Breitling." He gave Max his arm back.

They finished the meal late and once the conversation felt as though it had come to a natural tail off, Frank said, "Big day tomorrow," then looking to Max, "I mean for our review meeting. What we like to do Max is have an open brainstorming discussion about how we can improve anything and everything across the whole corporation. If it's alright with you Max I'd like to have a walk down the beach and steal away these three, there's a couple of things I need to cover with them you'd find very boring." Frank stood and gestured for Doreen, Brett and John to accompany him down to the beach.

"Of course," said Max getting up and making his way back into the villa, "I'm whacked after the trip so I'm going to turn in. See you all in the morning." He gave them an awkward wave which was returned by Doreen.

The villa was empty as the staff had long since left, one of them lived locally and the live-in couple had gone to stay with nearby family for a few days. As Max climbed the staircase, he was painfully aware that he had absolutely no idea what he was going to do, or what opportunity might arise for him to get anywhere near an Angel programmer's terminal. Tomorrow was the weekend, so he assumed there'd be no visit to the Angel offices he'd passed earlier, as there'd be no one there until Monday morning. By the time Max had got up to his room, he had figured out to himself that he had to do something. The only thing he could come up with was to go back down to the study and see if the main computer in there might look as though it had access. He appeared out of his balcony window just in time to see Frank, Doreen, Brett and John round one of the large boulders at the bottom of the garden onto the beach.

With his heart racing again, he quickly went downstairs and confidently straight into the study and up to the main computer which was in sleep mode. He touched the mouse button bringing it to life with a picture of a black Bugatti Veyron for a screen saver wallpaper. In the middle of the screen however the empty 'User Password' field box stared back at him, it's blinking cursor mocking him. Max swore to himself thinking 'Jees, I can't even get through the damn screen unlock password, this is useless!'

His thoughts turned back to the quartet walking on the beach and without thinking any more about it he made his way down the short garden to the large boulders. As he went, he was already thinking ahead as to what he would say if he bumped into them, he could just say he wondered if he could join them or something. As he approached the large rock, he could make out Frank's voice a little way down the dark beach amidst the rippling water peacefully washing up onto the sand. He slowly and carefully appeared around the side of the stone and looking through a piece of foliage growing from one of the crevices of the rocks, Max could now see the four people continuing to walk away from him down the deserted beach. He realised there was no way he could get any closer and he still couldn't hear what was being said.

As he started to turn away from the rock thoroughly despondent, a light bulb went off in the back of his brain. 'My phone. The listening device!' remembering when he tested it out in the MI5 offices and listened to the couple agreeing what time to go to lunch. He pulled his phone out and opening 'Notes' readied himself as he typed in 'listen22'. He then held the phone up through the foliage and pointed the mic as carefully and accurately as he could directly at Frank and his directors still walking away from him on the beach.

Max held the phone still, desperately hoping it was doing what it was meant to do and was quietly listening to and recording whatever they were talking about. His arms started to ache, it felt as though he'd been pointing the phone at them for about four or five minutes when they stopped walking away from him, whilst Frank appeared to be concluding what he was saying to them. They all nodded in agreement and Frank then gestured for them to turn round and head back. That was Max's cue to withdraw from the rock and quickly make his way across the small lawn, past the pool and back up to his room. He stripped down to his boxers and climbed into bed. They'd only been gone no more than ten minutes, but Max didn't want to have to talk to any of them again so decided to settle down and keep quiet hoping they'd assume he was already asleep.

As he lay there in silence with his pulse throbbing, the only thing on his mind was wanting to listen to the recording he hoped his mobile had gathered and what they'd been talking about. He grabbed the phone next to him and set the alarm to 'vibrate' at 3 AM. He would wake up when everyone else was sure to be fast asleep, especially with the amount they'd all drunk at dinner, and listen to the recording then.

Max heard the others coming back into the villa and quietly say their 'goodnights' to one another before each of them turned in for the night. He then heard Frank and Brett whispering including his name being mentioned. Moments later he heard the door to his room being carefully and quietly opened. Max was in bed and covered over facing away from the door. He froze. Waiting to see if anyone said anything, at least a 'good night' maybe. The silence remained and to his relief, he then heard the door quietly close again. Max looked over his shoulder to make sure the door had indeed been shut again and was quite freaked out about someone 'quietly looking in on him', or perhaps checking that he was tucked up in his room and hadn't tried to overhear the conversation on the beach.

Unbeknown to Max it was Brett who had felt it necessary to check that Max was indeed in his room. Tomorrow was going to be a big day. A day that would be remembered across the world for a long time. Finally, the deal they'd been working on with Mr Xiaoping would be concluded. Payday. Frank and Brett wanted Max close to them, right where they could keep an eye on him, just in case their trust in him had been misplaced. Nothing could go wrong tomorrow.

20

The mobile phone started to gently vibrate on the bed next to Max who woke with a start. Rubbing his eyes, he peered at the screen. It was 3 AM, and he felt as though he'd only just gone to bed wishing he could just go back to sleep. Then his brain got the jumpstart it needed as he remembered the recording. He found the sound file duly stored and waiting to be summoned by him, looking up at him beckoningly from the screen. As he didn't have any earphones, he reduced the volume right down and held the phone tight against his ear to listen to the recording.

Max was immediately rewarded with a fairly clear recording of the conversation on the beach and was surprised how good the quality was. Alan the techie had surpassed himself. Every now and then the recording had momentary fades in it, which Max realised was due to his inability to maintain the mic consistently pointing in the right direction accurately. He listened intently to the voices, mainly Frank's, resisting the temptation to fast forward over anything sounding inconsequential. He needed to hear everything. After some preamble, Max could hear he was starting to listen in on his and Si Lawson's worst fears.

Frank Dark was speaking. "Brett will go into the offices tomorrow morning to activate John's 'ghost code', which John and I can check it's worked from here on the computer that has the Angel software loaded onto it. We'll watch it wipe the files off the computer then permanently shut it down."

Max heard Doreen cut in. "Frank are you sure about all this. It's going to cause complete chaos around the world. It's not just all the poor people at home who'll lose all their files and the use of their computers, I'm still worried about the effect it will have on all those financial businesses, authorities, investments and things like stock markets."

John then spoke. "That's the whole point of it I'm afraid Doreen. That's what Xiaoping is paying so much money for. The Chinese want to cause massive disruption and chaos across the world outside their borders, get some economic advantage and all that. Anyway, that's not our concern."

Frank continued. "Doreen, you've got to get past this. I know this is a big deal and yes it is a bit scary, but it's not as if anyone's going to get hurt or die. Look, let's cover the matter of the payment. You've prepared all the hidden accounts ready haven't you, so as soon as Li transfers us the five billion dollars once he sees we've activated the program, you've got it all covered using the other computer here which won't be affected?"

Max couldn't hear Doreen replying so imagined she was nodding her agreement back to Frank, by the sounds of her tone earlier, probably reluctantly.

Frank spoke again. "Great. Well done Doreen. I've agreed the final amounts you'll each get that Doreen will transfer into your various nominated hidden accounts. One billion to John, eight hundred million for Brett and three hundred million for you Doreen, a hell of a lot more I might add than the original number we talked about eh. Our lives will completely change from tomorrow. We'll meet up again once things have calmed down. Brett, you're all clear about our final loyalty test for Max?"

Max juddered at hearing his name mentioned and was breathing heavily as he waited to see what would be said next.

Brett replied. "Sure am. I'll take Max with me to the Angel offices and explain to him what we are doing here, then tell him he's got fifty million coming his way." There was a pause before Brett continued. "He's either in, and we're good. Or if not, then he can take the rap at the office."

Max's heartfelt as though it jumped right out of his chest. The implication at the end of Brett's comment was unmistakable, given he would never willingly agree to take responsibility for this horrendous plan. The only other inevitable option hit him hard. 'Effing hell. He's going to kill me at the computer there so everyone will think I've done all this then committed suicide. Oh my God, I've got to do something!' Max thought to himself, churning inside.

The last voice Max heard was that of Doreen saying she hadn't signed up for anyone getting hurt, first John Lyttleton and now this, starting to protest about Max's involvement before the sound recording abruptly finished. Max checked the sound file to see if it had finished and assumed that was the point where they had turned to come back to the villa and he had stopped the recording.

His thoughts were tumbling over themselves, 'Five billion, Doreen had said it was a huge sum, she wasn't kidding' he thought. 'Cyber apocalypse, every computer, system and network that had the Angel software in it or attached to it was going to get wiped and shut down. All this happening tomorrow. And me Max, right here in the bloody middle of it with Brett about to bump me off. I've got to get out of here and now'.

Max quietly put on jeans, T-shirt and a fleece and slipped into his trainers and grabbed his phone wallet. He wanted to call Si Lawson immediately but that would have to wait until he'd got clear of the villa. He silently slipped out of the bedroom door. He'd never been more frightened in his life as he meticulously crept down the stairs listening out for the slightest of movements in the bedrooms around him. Fortunately, the polished marble flooring allowed him to make his exit without a sound. Unsure quite what he was doing or where he was going, he instinctively crept up the driveway towards the deserted road. Then heading back the way he'd been driven previously, he ran.

After running for about a thousand yards to get clear of the villa he came to a junction with a left turn labelled Highway C which he followed. Max instinctively felt he needed to get off the beach road and head inland towards the main highway running down the island. Everywhere was quiet with only the occasional car passing him on the road. As he continued walking he pulled out his phone and called Si Lawson.

Max started speaking as soon as he heard Si's voice pick up and he barely paused to draw for breath until he'd relayed everything he'd heard them talk about on the beach. Whilst talking on the phone Max also attached the sound file and sent it over to Si who patiently listened, allowing Max to say whatever he wanted to first. He could tell from his tone Max was highly agitated and concerned. Max got to the end of his tirade gasping for breath.

Si Lawson spoke calmly and reassuringly, but also very carefully as he knew Max wouldn't like what he was going to have to tell him to do.

"Max, you've been incredibly brave so far and done more than I can ever ask of you, but you're still the only person that can prevent this whole mess happening tomorrow. Have you still got the dongle in the watch?" Si asked.

"Come on Si you've got to be kidding me. You're not going to ask me to do anything more are you?" pleaded Max.

Si assumed Max still had the dongle and continued his efforts to try to explain things to Max. "That small memory stick you've got is now the key to everything, we've got to get it into one of those terminals to kill this awful program before it's activated tomorrow by Brett. This is now of national, no, global importance. I will send a couple of our MI5 field operatives to meet you at the Angel offices. You've got to go there Max and wait for Brett to log into the system. They'll protect you Max and can detain Brett while you plug in the USB stick."

Max didn't say anything for a while. He felt he was in so deep now that he was almost compelled to see this through to the end and reluctantly acquiesced. "Okay, so I go to the offices. But now that I've run away from the villa if Brett sees me or your men he's hardly going to calmly sit down and log in to the system for us."

Si realised Max's reticence to continue cooperating had turned the corner back in his favour. "Good point Max, I'll tell the guys to be close by, observe and be ready to move instantly on your signal once you feel Brett's logged in."

"And how am I going to do that?" asked Max regretting immediately he'd opened his mouth.

"You'll need to be close by so I'm afraid you have to try and work out a way of getting into the offices, hiding, then at the right moment signal the guys to come in. I promise they'll be watching closely from outside, so as long as they can see you through the windows they'll act," insisted Si.

"What about Frank, John and Doreen back at the villa? I'm pretty sure Doreen is a very unwilling participant in all this."

"Forget them for now Max, we need to concentrate on the goal here and that's at the offices. I've only got two field operatives in situ available for this kind of job and I want them both with you at the Angel office. Once it's all sorted we can easily pick up the others. I'll contact Barbados border control and put a 'code red and detain' alert on all their passports," said Si. Max was warmed by his confidence that this would all be 'sorted' and remembered that in his haste to get out of the villa he'd left his passport back in his room. "Get yourself off to Angel, get in and hide." They ended the call.

Max began half-heartedly turning behind him each time he heard a car approaching, holding his thumb out to see if he could hitch a ride in the right direction. Despite the absence of drivers on the road at just after 3 AM in the middle of the night, Barbados yielded him a merry, friendly driver within five minutes. The young Caribbean local man was driving an old Datsun and on his way home after attending a very late party in Lascelles just down the road. He seemed pleased to see someone else out and about at such an ungodly hour and was very happy for the company, not the slightest bit interested in asking Max what he was doing walking down the road at such a time.

Max asked him if he might be going anywhere near the big roundabout on the main highway where the car dealers, tractors and takeaways were. The local thought for a moment through the haze of his considerable number of rum punches he'd had earlier. Then proudly announced to Max that he must be meaning the roundabout at Warren's and that he was indeed going back that way down the highway to his home just beyond at Waterford.

The driver was content to continue listening to his reggae

music blaring out of the speakers in the car and Max was quite happy to sit there quietly, gathering his thoughts and starting to wonder how he was going to gain entry into the offices.

The relatively small ground floor building that served as the registered office for Angel Software Ltd was both modest in look with its dark wall panels and smoked glass windows and also modest in build. Many years ago it hosted one of the numerous fast food establishments, many of which favoured the large intersection roundabout traffic flow. With increasing rent, the takeaway moved to cheaper premises and Frank Dark bought the building, having seen it for sale on one of his many trips to the villa. He and John Dawlish then refurbished it to house John's top programmers along with a few back-office staff, when they moved the operation from Israel, wanting it somewhere more easily accessible.

The work ethos of the team there began at a very high standard with a mixture of employees from Israel, London and even Barbados, but over the years the lax and casual local Caribbean attitudes had taken their toll on the team, who despite still being highly effective coders and programmers, were now far more chilled about the small things in life that might keep others awake at night.

Late on during the previous evening's rushed departures by the staff to get home to their family, friends, parties and beaches, the last one out the door was already running late for her best friend's engagement party. She had pulled the main entrance door closed which then self-locked behind her until the next key holder wanted access. It was only then that she remembered that the last one out should set the somewhat basic alarm system which included door beams and a couple of motion detectors inside the open-plan office, but she was not a keyholder. Faced with the prospect of now having to call one of the managers to come out, open up, set the alarm and then shut the place up again, and her friend's party awaiting her, she huffed and went on her way, thinking to herself 'I'm not messing about with all that, I need to get off to the party. No one ever sets the alarm anyway, and who would want to break-in to this place'.

As she walked past the side of the building towards her car, she noticed one window still open. Huffing and complaining to herself again she went over to it and slid the pane of glass down, ignoring the fact that it still needed locking into place from the inside.

Max and his reggae driver soon arrived at the Warren's roundabout where the local man pulled into the side of the road briefly to let Max out, giving him a gleaming smile accompanied by a "Stay cool man." Max looked around the entire roundabout area and surrounding businesses and except for one of the fast-food huts and the odd passing car the place was pretty much deserted. He made his way over to the dark building of the Angel offices and to hide himself from any passing traffic on the highway, went round to the rear of the building. He immediately spotted an old dilapidated looking alarm bell box on the sidewall and thought to himself that was the end of any chances of getting in undetected. Before completely giving up he walked alongside the windows and peering in could see that inside it was one single medium-sized open office with what appeared to be a meeting room, toilets and a row of filing cabinets and cupboards at one end.

He strained his eyes to look around the entrance area and spotted what he was looking for. On the wall right next to the main exit door was the alarm control box with LED display, key slots and various coloured light covers, but there was no sign from the panel that it was activated in any way. No lights were on nor was there anything showing on the LED. 'That's a miracle' he thought to himself, but now he still had to get in somehow without alerting Brett in the morning that he could be inside.

Still not wanting to go round to the more exposed front of the building Max stood back and closely scrutinised for any potential access point. He tried getting his fingers into the slits around the fire escape door to no avail, then worked his way from one end of the building to the other putting his hands on the glass windows and trying to push them open to see if any might not be secured. With only a couple of windows left to try he had pretty much given up all hope and was thinking of calling Si again, perhaps for some assistance from one of the field operatives, they'd know how to get him inside. And then as he pushed up on the last window expecting it to be immovable, it slid up.

Once inside, relieved that no alarms appeared to have been set off, Max congratulated himself and for a moment stood there in the dim light thinking to himself, that this was where the Angel software virus checker product was controlled from, worldwide. He looked around at the fifteen or so computer terminals in the office wondering which might have access to the master program, but they all looked pretty much the same to him. He then remembered he needed to find some sort of hiding place to wait for Brett to appear any time from four or five hours onwards, but after turning 360 degrees realised that with such an empty open-plan office his only options were the toilets or the large cupboards against the wall.

He went over to the units and found that one was full of folders, however, the other one was a half-empty stationery cupboard and with a little reorganising, he was able to free up the lower half of the space so that he could fit inside. He climbed in to test it out and by peering through the tiny crack between the two doors when they were pulled shut, he had a good view of the open-plan office.

He couldn't stay in the cramped cupboard for the next four hours so decided to take a bit of risk and catch some sleep on the floor right next to the cupboard for a few hours. He set the vibration alarm on his phone to 8 AM thinking it was unlikely Brett would arrive any time before that and as he settled down on the hard floor, he also unscrewed the back of the Rolex and took out the small USB stick. Examining it closely he was poignantly appreciative of how incredibly important this tiny thing was that he was holding. He put it in his pocket so it was immediately available for use later. Max put his watch back on then settled down to catch up on his desperately needed sleep for a few hours, wondering when Si Lawson's backup would arrive outside and where they'd position themselves, and would they be armed. He started to doze off, but the darkness of the room and anticipation of the inevitable confrontation with Brett, started to wander his thoughts back twenty years to that first and last fateful mission he'd had as a young Commando in May 2000. He began drifting off to sleep.

The UK's Prime Minister Tony Blair had begun a military intervention in Sierra Leone West Africa, codenamed 'Operation Palliser'. Max and his friend Pete's Four-Two Commando unit had been ordered to take over from One Para and were flown out on transport aircraft along with several long-distance travelling Chinook helicopters. The Sierra Leone RUF, Revolutionary United Front, were rebelling and had advanced on the country's capital Freetown, prompting the British operational reconnaissance and liaison team to prepare evacuation of notable officials, peacekeepers and civilians. The RUF blocked the main road leading from Freetown to the city's airport in Lungi. British forces were forced to engage with the RUF to secure passage to the airport for the evacuations and assist the United Nations staff and the local Sierra Leone Army.

A splinter faction militia of the Armed Forces Revolutionary Council known as the West Side Boys, had stumbled across a British patrol team near Lungi airport, which Max and Pete were part of. A close-quarters firefight ensued around tightly packed buildings and the two Commando boys had successfully taken out eight of the rebels before they were overwhelmed and surrounded. In the chaos just before having to give themselves up, five of their Marines colleagues were gunned down by the rebels leaving just the two Corporals Max and Pete, and their Colour Sergeant nicknamed 'Fifty' due to his uncanny ability to hit the bullseye on a dartboard.

The three of them were roughly bundled off to a nearby building away from the possibility of coming across other British troops. They knew they were in deep trouble having killed so many of the rebels' fighters and from what the angry men were saying, mainly in English with some local Krio mixed in. There were six of them, shouting and waving their AK47 Kalashnikov's threateningly at them. Having taken away their weapons they did not attempt to bind their hands, another sign they had little intention of keeping them alive, let alone holding them hostage. Max quickly conceded the furious men just wanted revenge for their lost comrades and as they were shoved against the wall inside a deserted house, he didn't need to wait long before his fears unfolded.

Despite the three of them not engaging with eye-to-eye contact with any of their captors, trying to avoid being singled out, the gang started to set upon Fifty having realised he was the higher ranking of them. Fifty was punched and smashed with rifle butts until instinctively Pete called out for them to stop, pleading with them to trade the three of them for arms or money. But the rebels were beyond trades, they wanted the British soldiers to suffer. Spurred on by the vicious leader they now singled out Pete, dragging him unceremoniously across the room, boots and butts flying at him.

Max and Fifty had to stay silent as they watched the rebels break him, not mentally, but physically, again and again. Pete screamed out as the blows inflicted their damage, organs being compressed and punctured, bones broken. Max watched the brutality and with each and every blow, forgot his own predicament and channelled all his being into avenging his friend and killing these unmerciful sadists, at whatever cost to himself. He could see the life draining from Pete and knew he had to act, or he and Fifty would be given the same treatment next, for the amusement of these killers.

Five of them were gathered around Pete dealing out the blows, some with clenched teeth, some laughing and jeering. Just one man was guarding him and Fifty who was already the worse for wear, semi-conscious. Pete was fading now, the excruciating pain from his injuries dragging him into black unconsciousness. Max watched as the leader raised his handgun to Pete's head. This was it for his friend, but he instinctively knew this final execution act would be intently watched by his guard as well. He only needed a second of lapsed concentration by the man in front of him and Fifty.

The instant the handgun fired, ending Pete's life, Max went

straight for the guard's AK47 rifle and in one lunge grabbed it from his loose grip and shoved him back onto the floor. By the time the closely huddled group of five rebels standing over Pete's body had time to turn round to see what had happened, Max was unloading upon them what remained in the magazine. At about ten rounds a second it was plenty and created carnage as their bodies shattered across the room behind them.

Fifty was shouting at Max to take out the last man on the floor, now recovering from the shock of being jumped and seeing his friends killed in front of him. He pulled out a curved knife but before he could stand, Max was already on him. Having emptied the gun Max was now using it as a club. The rebel slashed out with his blade but fell back after the second strike to his head, another blow rendering him senseless.

Max was out of breath, pumped up from the huge adrenalin rush he'd conjured up to tackle the last few moments of horror. He looked at Fifty, though a big and seasoned Commando, he was still dazed and lethargic from his initial beating. Max turned to look at his friend Pete, lying there discarded on the floor. Gathering himself, he grabbed Pete's blood-stained dog tag from around his neck, then went back to help Fifty up to his feet.

Max was numb from the shocking events which felt like had lasted ages, but it had only been about twenty minutes since the whole patrol were together before coming across the West Side Boys rebel's gang. Retracing their route back to the British Commando camp at the airport took fifteen minutes. As they approached the perimeter amidst relief and huge consternation at their surprise battle, losses and return, Max knew this would change everything.

Sunrise began at around 5:30 AM and within an hour also, back at the villa, the occupants were starting to rise and make their way down to the kitchen for breakfast. Despite the planned events and repercussions of the day, Frank Dark and Brett Harding had both had a good night's sleep. Brett always slept well as nothing really worried him and years of disturbed nights in the battlefield had made him appreciate a safe night's sleep in a nice bed. John Dawlish was momentarily stirred from his sleep when he thought he heard something outside his room at around 3 AM but had immediately put it down to one of those many noises of the night, creeks in the house or drapes blowing in the breeze. Doreen, however, had a restless night fighting with the morality and danger of what she was involved with and the finality of when it happened, her life would instantly change. Would she ever see Maureen again. She hoped the hundreds of millions she'd got Frank to promise her would help.

By 7:30 AM the three of them were well into their breakfasts and by now Max's absence was quite apparent.

"Looks like we've got a tired chap upstairs. Brett, why don't you look in on him and tell him to join us for breakfast," said Frank.

Brett obligingly went upstairs and after knocking on Max's door slowly entered. He immediately saw no one in the bed which alerted him, but then relaxed slightly when he noticed Max's baggage and clothes still in the room along with his passport sitting on the table. He called out Max's name as he approached the closed bathroom door and when there was no answer, he went in. Now Brett was worried. He came bounding down the stairs saying to Frank, "His room's empty, he's gone. Baggage and passport still there though."

Doreen added feebly, "He's probably just gone for a walk on the beach." But none of the three men in the room believed that for a moment."

"He must have overheard us talking on the beach last night, he's gone to the police," fretted John standing up.

"Don't be ridiculous, that's impossible, there's no way he could have heard us, we were way too far down the beach last night and completely alone. Apart from the India currency printers, he can't possibly know anything about what we're doing today," said Frank.

Brett added, "We've got his passport here so he's not getting off the island, he'll probably reappear back here shortly. Even if he doesn't turn up we don't care anyway do we, there's nothing to prevent the deal going through and then we're home dry."

Frank pulled a face. He didn't like that Max had mysteriously disappeared but remained convinced that he couldn't possibly know what they were doing today. "Let's not worry about Max, if he does come back here then me, Doreen and John are here anyway to check the ghost code has been activated and sort out the money. I can speak to him about the fifty million we have for him."

"And if he doesn't want the money, what then?" asked Doreen.

Frank shrugged his shoulders and gave her a grave look. "Brett, you get off to the offices as soon as you're ready, take the Rolls and let's get this thing done. I'll call Li Xiaoping to confirm everything's on and we'll be activating the code in about an hour and a half's time."

"Roger Wilco," parted Brett.

Max was already awake staring at his phone in a trance waiting for the clock to show 8 AM and start buzzing. Eventually, when it did it made him jump, jolting him back to reality and also giving him his prompt to climb into the cupboard and settle himself down. He felt his pocket for reassurance the memory stick was still there, then with one last look around the office area, he pulled the doors to. Sitting there in the dark cupboard he found himself concentrating hard to listen out for the door or any noises signalling when Brett was arriving and entering the office. He wondered which computer Brett would choose to sit at and whether it would be near to him and what he was going to do. He also thought to himself 'those MI5 blokes better bloody be waiting out there somewhere right now'.

Max didn't have to wait too long, about forty minutes later he heard the unmistakable purr of the Rolls Royce Ghost pulling up in the small car park. He froze and his eyes widened. He could feel his hands tingling with anxiety and quickly rubbed them together to settle himself. Moving his head so that he could see through the crack in the doors he watched and waited.

Brett sat in the Rolls for a few moments to survey the area. Old habits die hard. The usually busy Warren's roundabout area hadn't yet sprung to life on this early Saturday morning. The takeaways were quiet with a few people grabbing breakfast, the offices were deserted and the large car dealership had a few salespeople inside preparing themselves for the tough selling day ahead with their first coffee's. There were a few large dense bushes dotted around and a small electricity station metal hut nearby. All seemed very quiet.

Brett approached the Angel office main door and unlocked it using the key John Dawlish had given him. As he came into the office he looked at the alarm panel, ready with a second key and the memorised code, but was greeted with a blank LED and alarm box sitting quietly inoperative. John Dawlish had mentioned to him the guys in the office were not the best at setting the alarm every night.

Brett was familiar with the simple open office layout and quickly looked around the room to locate one of the several desks and computers that John had told him to use. Only the two most senior managers had the deep program access he needed. He had the choice of the desk in the middle of the office or the one at the back near the filing cabinets and stationery cupboards. He chose the latter preferring to have his back against the wall, again old habits.

Max was watching Brett's every move. He was barely breathing and was convinced even his pounding heartbeat was loud enough to give away his hiding place. Brett walked across the office towards him and for a moment Max readied himself for Brett opening the cupboard doors and calling him out. But instead Brett then casually sat at the desk in front of him and slightly to one side of the stationery cupboard. Max could move his head minutely, allowing the eye he was using to look through the crack in the doors to view the screen Brett was now looking at. He watched closely knowing that any moment now he was going to have to do something. Max's hand silently felt for the large heavy metal hole punch in the bottom of the cupboard.

Brett took a small piece of paper out of his pocket and placed it on the desk between the keyboard and the screen. There were four password gates he had to go through before bringing up the ultimate screen ready for authorisation to execute the ghost code in the master program. This would in turn set off the worldwide signal to every single installed Angel anti-malware program, instructing it to delete that system's files and render its computer operating system useless. Brett carefully typed in the computers screen lock password followed by the employee's network username and password. Max continued to watch closely, his muscles tense with anxiety and adrenaline.

Next Brett focused on the longer scrambled password for a manager to begin accessing the main coding and program of the Angel product, from which any upgrades were sent out. Max was straining hard to focus on the screen, trying to decide if Brett had reached the point of final access to edit the master program's software. He was about to spring up when he read the warning box that appeared in the middle of the screen and immediately stopped himself.

The text in the pop-up read, 'WARNING; You have accessed the master program of Angel Software Ltd®, owned by the Dark Corporation. All amendments must have authorisation from John Dawlish and will be tracked and auditable. Please insert your encrypted passcode fob for access to the control program'.

Max was starting to feel faint with the incredible stress levels he now had.

Brett took a memory stick out of his pocket and carefully pushed it into one of the several USB ports on the front of the PC tower on top of the desk. The hard drive and components inside the tin box wurred for a moment, as it examined the contents of the stick and checked the built-in encryption pass, before then executing its command to bring up the final access menu on the screen.

Max immediately focused on the displayed text and read down the menu. As he saw the third item which read 'RUN GHOST PROGRAM', the explosion of adrenaline and pent-up anxiety propelled him up and bursting through the cupboards doors towards

Brett, whose finger was already descending on the number '3' button of the keyboard. Simultaneously Brett heard the cupboard doors behind him open and could see a reflection in the computer screen of a figure lunging at him. He instinctively started to dodge and was just fast enough to avoid Max bringing the heavy hole puncher squarely down into the back of his head. But it still struck him hard between his cheek and jawbone, sending him flying sideways away from the desk and onto the floor.

Max now stood in front of the desk and looked at the screen. The message had now changed to something else. It read, 'GHOST PROGRAM EXECUTED, AWAITING REMOTE AUTHORISATION'.

He'd been fractionally too slow. Just before the hole punch had made contact with the side of Brett's face, he had depressed the number '3' key instructing the program to run. But it seemed it was now waiting for yet further authorisation before sending out its destructive commands to the millions of user systems out there.

Brett gathered himself on the floor. He could take the hit and even the fractured jawbone, but he was more shocked that Max Sargent had completely taken him by surprise and managed to get off a swipe at him.

"You little bastard," Brett sneered through the discomfort of his fractured jaw. "I can't believe you're here, and you just hit me. And to think we were going to cut you in for fifty million. You're too late anyway. There's nothing you can do to stop the final activation going ahead."

To Max's horror Brett slowly stood up and produced a black Glock 17 handgun, his SAS's preference, which he slowly and gratifyingly raised up to point at Max's head. Max had a flashback to what he'd been through in Sierra Leone all those years ago, what he'd evaded, got through and escaped from. Surely after all that he wasn't going to die here, in an office in Barbados, with Brett shooting him over a stupid computer program!

"Adios kid."

Max was desperate to stall him. "You wouldn't kill a fellow

green beret?"

It had the desired effect. Brett was momentarily perplexed. "What the hell you talking about?"

"I served in the Marines. Twenty years ago." Max could see some bewilderment sinking into Brett's expression. "I went to Sierra Leone. Operation Palliser."

Brett's mind was working overtime as he tried to make sense of everything. Loyalty in the forces was drummed into you every day, to look out for your own, whatever. But rage grabbed him back. "Bollocks! No way were you a Commando!"

Max could see Brett's trigger finger slowly starting to squeeze in.

'Bang!'

Max stepped back hearing the gunshot with the instantaneous thought, 'That's it then, I'm dead'. But his movement backwards was actually his involuntary response to the assumption of being shot.

The noise Max heard was the impact of a sniper's high-velocity bullet thudding into Brett and passing through his upper body, instantly collapsing him to the ground dead.

The two MI5 field operatives had been watching everything unfold. One of them was nearest to the office entrance inside the metal substation hut with a small view hole. The other with the sniper's rifle was positioned inside the large dense shrubbery and had a clear unobstructed view of the whole office through the branches and foliage.

Max looked down at Brett's body lying on the floor in front of him. He could see a tiny hole in the back of his jacket and a slightly larger bloodied exit area on Brett's chest. After piercing the office window, the bullet had hit and passed through Brett's shoulder blade, heart and chest plate so fast, that its trajectory had remained concise and clean. After exiting his body, the bullet had smashed into the bottom of the breezeblock wall on the other side of the office.

One of the MI5 men came bursting through the main doors

holding an automatic weapon up to his eye line, while at the same time the other man smashed through the fire exit at the other end of the office with a handgun held out in front of him. Both dressed in black military-style fatigues with the obligatory body armour and carrying various other weapons and devices. Whilst Max was yet further shocked at their robust entrance, he was also relieved to see that they were there with him. Seeing the rifle slung on the back of one of the men, Max knew they had shot Brett as soon as he'd raised his gun to him.

"Did you prevent the activation?" asked one of the MI5 guys.

"I was just too late," said Max pragmatically.

Max moved back to the computer feeling that having come this far, whether it was too late or not, he was damn well going to get Si Lawson's mini USB stick plugged into this computer. He took it from his pocket and quickly shoved it into one of the free USB ports. He turned to the two MI5 men. "Let's just see."

The screen worryingly flickered as the computer worked to analyse and adjust itself to the new set of automatically executed coding it had just received.

Frank Dark, Doreen Leader and John Dawlish were all anxiously gathered in the study back at the villa waiting to hear how Brett was getting on. Frank had instructed John to build in one last authorisation for the ultimate failsafe check for the activation of the ghost program. John had set up the system to send Frank's mobile a simple 'Accept' or 'Decline' message, that way Frank alone had the final word on whether or when the destructive virus went live. The moment Brett had selected '3' from the menu, that final authorisation request had been triggered and now needed to be agreed to by Frank.

The Accept and Decline choices now flashed on the screen of Frank's mobile. They had reached the critical point and Frank wanted to check in with Brett to make sure that everything was okay before he pressed on 'Accept'. He grabbed John Dawlish's mobile and called Brett.

Back at the Angel office, Brett's mobile phone started to ring in his pocket. One of the MI5 men instinctively pointed his gun towards the sound and quickly looked at Max to check what they should do.

Max noticed a new message appearing on the computer screen beside him. It now read, 'MI5 KILLWARE PROGRAM EXECUTED, AWAITING REMOTE AUTHORISATION'!

"Oh my God. Si's programme has been accepted. It's in the system. It's replaced the Ghost program waiting to be authorised," gasped Max, "but authorised how?" Brett's phone continued ringing.

Max edged over to Brett's body and bent down to retrieve the mobile phone. As he picked it up he could see the caller ID on the screen said, 'John Dawlish calling'.

"What the hell do I do guys. It's John Dawlish," said Max.

The man holding the handgun now relaxing his grip on the weapon suggested, "You've got to answer it one way or the other."

Max slid the 'answer' bar sideways and held the phone up to his ear, preparing himself to explain why he was there and make up a story about Brett popping outside or something. Expecting John's voice, he was immediately surprised and dismayed to hear Frank Dark speaking.

"Hi Brett, well done activating the ghost program, just a quick call before accepting the authorisation to check all is well, okay to go ahead?" said Frank.

Max's mind raced as he realised Frank assumed it was Brett that had answered, of course he would, but now he was faced with having to speak to Frank knowing he'd recognise it wasn't Brett but actually him. He needed to say as little as possible and was about to simply say 'Yes' when he remembered Brett's frequently used sign off.

Max cupped his hand over his mouth hoping this would provide some muffling, then replied. "Roger Wilco." He waited for a second but with no immediate reply from Frank, Max ended the call, hoping he'd done enough. The two MI5 agents gathered around the screen with him and they waited.

Frank Dark listened to Brett's confirmation all was good at the Angel office, then the call ended. He contemplated for a moment that something wasn't quite right about the call, the voice maybe, it was a little muffled. But that was definitely Brett's classic phrase, and he often put the phone down when he thought calls were done.

"All okay?" asked John Dawlish, now eagerly awaiting his master creation to be unleashed on the world. He'd spent years developing it and years patiently waiting for Frank to sort out a huge deal for someone to buy it, and use it. He wanted to see it in action for himself.

"Brett gave us his 'Roger Wilco'." Frank Dark stared down at his mobile screen, "Here we go!" and carefully touched the 'Accept' button. He and John then closely watched the computer screen in the study that was a standard home PC with the Angel software loaded onto it, just like millions of other computers had around the world. Doreen sat at the other computer which had no Angel software on it and was monitoring the balance screen of their secret Swiss bank account, ready to tell Frank when Xiaoping's five billion-dollar payment was in.

They waited a few minutes then the home screen flickered once. 'This was it' they thought focusing even more closely on the screen.

A message box appeared in the centre and immediately John Dawlish knew something wasn't right. His program should simply delete all the computer's files then permanently shut down, he hadn't incorporated any warnings or messages. Frank looked at John for reassurance, but as the text appeared on the screen he also knew it had gone wrong somehow.

It read, 'IMPORTANT NOTICE; YOUR ANGEL SOFTWARE HAS BEEN IDENTIFIED AS HAVING IRREVOCABLY CORRUPTED MALWARE AND HAS THEREFORE BEEN DELETED FROM YOUR SYSTEM. WE

APOLOGISE FOR ANY INCONVENIENCE. FROM ANGEL SOFTWARE LTD.'

They stared at the screen disbelievingly. Totally stunned.

"Angel software deleted, from *us*. What the hell's going on here John. Talk to me," demanded Frank. Doreen left her station and came over to them with a frightened look on her face.

John moved the screen message box to the side to check the small icons showing the major programs installed on the computer and searching for his Angel icon said to Frank, "Crikey, the Angel programme's been completely wiped off the system. It's gone." He continued searching through the backend protocols not accepting it had been deleted, hoping to find it somewhere. "No, no, no, this can't be happening. How could anyone else have known about this let alone get into my system? I thought Brett had done everything correctly, it's not possible for this to have happened."

"I don't believe it. *We've* been hacked!" said Frank.

Max and the two MI5 men watched the screen back at the Angel office until a new message appeared. All three of them read out the words together in chorus.

'MI5 KILLWARE PROGRAM EXECUTED, LIVE TRANSMISSION AUTHORISED AND COMPLETED'.

They looked at one another in shock. "We've done it. It looks like we've done it," said Max. "I think it must have sent Si's programme out to every device around the world that has the Angel software on it, and hopefully it'll have been completely deleted."

One of the black-suited men's mobiles went off and after answering a few questions being asked of him and telling the caller that Brett Harding was dead, he handed it straight to Max saying, "It's Si Lawson for you."

Max took the phone to hear Si's voice. "Max. You've done it. I'll let the MI5 guys fill me in with what on earth happened there, but you've done it. It's about 4 AM here at Thames House but we can see that all Angel products on computers and systems have just self-deleted!"

"No way!" exclaimed Max.

"You've averted a world-wide cyber apocalypse. I can't believe it myself." Si said jubilantly.

Max composed himself and quickly had a burning question rising to the surface. "What about Frank Dark, Doreen Leader and John Dawlish?"

Si spoke clearly with purpose. "As soon as Alan, one of the MI5 guys with you, told me Brett Harding had entered the offices, I instructed the Royal Barbados Police Force Special Branch to go and surround Frank Dark's villa. They should be there very soon and will wait out of sight. For political reasons I can't have them taking over and sending in their lead arresting officer. I need that to be done by one of our MI5 operatives with you now, Alan Reid. This is way above the local's pay grade. Frank Dark and the other two aren't going anywhere."

"You sure about that. I hope so," said Max.

"Hand me back to my guy Alan," said Si, "the other chap will stay at the Angel office. You and Alan go now directly to Frank's villa where they'll all be arrested by him. Have you got transport there?"

Max looked through the windows out to the beautiful Rolls-Royce Ghost that Brett had left outside.

21

The arguing and panic amongst Frank, Doreen and John at the villa was abruptly hushed as Frank's mobile started ringing. Cautiously looking at the screen his worst fears were now staring back at him from the mobile. This was the call he dreaded. The caller ID showed 'Li Xiaoping calling'.

Frank looked over to Doreen's screen where their Swiss bank account balance was being displayed. Somehow he hoped that Li might have already wired the five billion dollars but that was wishful thinking. The balance still read zero. Frank answered his phone nervously.

"Li, we're just sorting out a few minor problems here. Have you transferred the money yet?" Frank knew that neither of these were happening now and regretted his pretence with his potentially dangerous Chinese 'businessman'.

Li exploded. "You insult me. Of course I haven't transferred the money yet and won't be at all it seems. My people tell me your clever Angel software is deleting itself from all systems it's on! That's not what we agreed on Mr Dark. Is it?" Frank was taken aback at Li's anger on the call. They'd had hard conversations and tough negotiations over the years, but he'd always taken Li to be courteous and professional. This was a side to him he didn't enjoy dealing with. He'd kind of suspected Li had something to do with their Secret Service.

"Mr Xiaoping, please give us a little longer to correct this. Right now I honestly don't know what just happened," replied Frank pleading for more time.

Li continued shouting. "What's happened you idiot, is that someone has presumably sabotaged your program and software. You clearly have a traitor in your corporation, but that's your problem now not mine. I've got to explain this mess to my superiors now. Don't call me again, I'll be deleting this number."

"But Mr Xiaoping, John Dawlish and I can sort this out. We can work with you," begged Frank.

"You're on your own now. Goodbye." Frank sensed the stern finality in Xiaoping's tone.

"Shit! Damn it!" Frank's thoughts turned back to how this could have happened and Li's comment about a traitor. John Dawlish and Doreen Leader were both staring at him waiting to hear how the call went, but they already knew from Frank's responses and body language they were all in big trouble.

In Beijing, Li Xiaoping swiped alphabetically through the hundreds of contacts in his phone and located the sleeper agent he needed to call again. Li had hundreds of such agents around the world who had each infiltrated their local communities, government services and businesses. All patiently on standby until such time as their People's Republic of China MSS required them to provide intel or act on something, or someone. He touched the screen which read 'Zhang Wei - Bābāduōsī' *(Chinese for Barbados)*.

During the next twenty minutes Frank, Doreen and John busied themselves with arguing pointlessly, discussing how this could have happened and who could have deceived them, with accusations flying around and repeatedly coming from Frank and John suspecting and questioning Doreen. They also intermittently spent time looking over John's shoulder while he tried to figure out what had happened, by remotely logging into the program system at the office, but to no avail. Concerns were also now turning towards what they would do, where they would go and how they could talk their way out of this. It was only at the end of all this shouting and screaming that Frank started to try to hold Doreen to calm her.

"Just settle down Doreen, we've got to think this through, the three of us together," said Frank through slightly gritted teeth. He was getting increasingly fed up with Doreen's behaviour and still had a suspicion that she was the one that had somehow compromised the whole operation.

"Take your hands off me Frank. This whole scheme of yours was stupid from the beginning. Did you two really think you could get away with setting off this cyber catastrophe for some dodgy Chinese secret agent man," screamed Doreen at the two men.

John Dawlish cut in. "What are we going to do Frank?"

Doreen replied. "I don't know or care about you to, I'm going upstairs to pack and then I'm getting out of here. We can all explain our part in this to the authorities. You need to face it now, this is finished."

They had a bit of a tussle and Doreen started hitting Frank's arms for him to release his painful grip on her. She rushed upstairs leaving Frank and John looking at one another not knowing what to do next.

As Doreen was standing by her bedroom window gathering up her clothes, she was conscious of unusual movement in her peripheral vision. She turned to look out the window which was on the side of the villa and had a clear view along the narrow driveway. At the end of the driveway, beyond the tops of the shrubbery and hedges, she could see several men in light suits. More alarmingly she saw a policeman with several cars parked up along the roadside in the distance, including a marked police car.

Doreen called out, "Frank. Frank, you'd better come up here and take a look at this." Frank begrudgingly came upstairs and into Doreen's room. "Look out there. Police."

"Shit. They're here already. This is getting crazy." Frank rushed across the landing to the bedroom on the other side of the villa and standing on tiptoe peered out the window and over the hedges. Sure enough, there were more men standing around waiting, including a couple in police uniforms. He went back into Doreen's room. "They've surrounded the villa and seem to be just waiting out there."

Doreen had had enough and throwing down her clothes giving up with the packing, she stormed towards the door. "That's it Frank. It's finished. I'm going straight out there to hand myself over and explain what's been going on."

Frank darted after her determined to prevent her from going outside and handing herself over to the police. He hadn't yet thrown in the towel and certainly didn't want anyone else forcing him into any course of action just yet.

He caught up with Doreen at the top of the staircase and grabbed at her arm. Doreen then violently wrenched herself away from Frank's grip, but as she did so was already on the edge of the top stairway. She attempted to balance herself by stepping back with her spare foot but there was no landing floor, only thin air as she was now across the threshold of the step. She fell awkwardly and violently down the full length of the unyielding marble staircase. Her body initially fell onto the edge of the steps with her back taking the first impact, she then rolled over backwards and as her head came back over and down, it was the side of her skull that impacted on the edge of one of the steps near the bottom of the staircase. Doreen died instantly. Her distorted body crumpled to a standstill at the bottom of the stairs.

Frank Dark stood at the top of the stairs in horror and disbelief. With everything else going on, now this. He'd tried to stop Doreen's impulsiveness to give herself up. Give them up. Frank had a feeling of déjà vu as he looked down at Doreen and remembered the similar fate of his previous CFO John Lyttleton.

He hadn't meant for Doreen Leader to get hurt, and certainly not have this fatal accident. Not really.

Max and his accompanying MI5 agent Alan had retrieved the Rolls-Royce keys from Brett Harding's body, left the other agent at the Angel office and raced back to the villa. It had taken them about twenty minutes. As they approached Max could see a cluster of plain-clothed and uniformed Barbados police at the driveway entrance and another group further down the road on the far side of the villa's property boundary. The uniformed police looked smart in their light blue shirts and dark blue trousers with a red stripe down the sides. Heads turned attentively at the arrival of the Rolls-Royce and when the black-suited and armed MI5 man stepped out, several of the police officers appeared to stand to attention in deference.

Alan the MI5 operative immediately asked the group, "Who's the lead officer here?"

One of the plain clothed men immediately stepped forward. He was a smartly dressed, fit Asian-Barbadian stemming from his local mother marrying his Chinese father.

"I am," he said, "Zhang Wei, Superintendent with the Royal Barbados Police." He continued efficiently. "I spoke to your Mr Lawson of MI5 London. We've been here about ten minutes. I have the perimeters of the property surrounded and we've seen several people inside, so believe all three suspects are still in the villa. We don't know if they're armed."

Zhang briefly studied the MI5 man up and down, noting his automatic weapon slung to his side and a holstered handgun, then gave a cursory nod to Max who gave his name.

Alan spoke authoritatively. "Let's be on alert for weapons, but from talking to Max here it's more likely they're unarmed, these are businesspeople we're dealing with not hardened gangsters. You've got the land borders of the villa covered, what about the beach side?"

Zhang thought to himself 'what do you think they're going to do, swim for it', but didn't want to admit he hadn't thought of that so styled it out saying, "Yes, the guys either side of the boundaries will have sight of the beach."

Alan gestured towards one of the other police officers to pass him the megaphone he had ready in anticipation. Alan started walking down the driveway accompanied by Zhang and another police officer. Max followed them as well but kept his distance.

Alan said to the superintendent, "First things first, let's see if we can get this sorted easily by talking to them."

Once in full view of the villa, he then held up the megaphone and clicked the trigger. "I am agent Alan Reid of British Intelligence MI5 and I am addressing Frank Dark, Doreen Leader and John Dawlish. The property is surrounded by police officers and I would ask you to cooperate by walking out of the front door with your hands on your heads. We would like to talk to you about the recent attempted cyber attack. You will be taken into British custody. I will wait here for three minutes for you to respond."

Alan Reid was content with his flawless opening address and put the megaphone down on the floor to rest his right hand on top of his holstered Glock handgun. Just in case. Zhang and the accompanying police officer both gave a slight nod at the MI5 agents slick, commanding professionalism. The police officer looked down at his watch. They began waiting and hoping for a response.

Inside the villa, John Dawlish had come out of the study and almost tripped over the body of Doreen Leader at the bottom of the stairs. Noticing Frank standing at the top of the stairs he cried out, "What the hell happened Frank? Is she dead?"

"It was an accident John, I swear, she tripped and fell," said Frank.

"You mean a bit like John Lyttleton tripped and fell eh?" John's cutting comment was made in anger and frustration. He was fed up covering for Frank. A bit of messing about with creative accountancy or Indian currency printers were fine, no one was getting hurt. But this, on top of John Lyttleton's supposed suicide, it had all gone too far now.

Frank countered. "That's a bit harsh John, they were both accidents. Pull yourself together, we've got to work out how we can get to our escape plan now. I've only got to make a call and we can both be…"

John interrupted. "No Frank. Doreen was right. We need to give ourselves up now, you can pay the best lawyers to somehow get us off. You heard the guy outside, it's bloody MI5 for Christ's sake. Police everywhere." John started to make his way across the hall to the front door.

Frank rushed down the stairs and asked one last thing of his old friend and business partner. "John, I'm afraid I just can't do it, give myself up. You go and let's hope the lawyers can sort out something for you. All I ask is that you give me a couple of minutes before you go out that door?"

John gave a deep sigh, then nodded his agreement. For old time's sake.

Frank disappeared off to grab his wallet, phone and passport then moments later exited the villa out the back.

As the police officer at the front said to his boss and Alan, "Two and a half minutes," the three of them were startled by the harsh opening of the front door. They waited for two men and a woman to come out and were perplexed that only one man came out through the doorway, his hands placed on top of his head. It was John Dawlish.

"Don't shoot, I'm giving myself up willingly and will cooperate," offered John shouting urgently.

Alan asked, "Who else is in the house and is anyone armed?"

"Doreen Leader accidentally fell down the stairs and is dead. I don't know about Frank Dark. No one is armed." John Dawlish was remorseful and wanted to cooperate fully, but out of blind loyalty pretended not to know that his partner was likely trying to make a run for it hoping to utilise their backup plan.

Max heard what John said and ran up to Alan and Zhang saying, "Doreen dead! We need to get in there now," and ignoring John Dawlish made his way towards the villa.

Alan shook his head at Zhang, who went to stop Max, saying, "It's fine, just go with him. Alan Reid had a lot of respect for Max Sargent after what he'd been through, he was a hero really, averting this massive cyber attack. The pair of them had already been through a lot together in the last hour, so was happy to cut him some slack here.

Zhang gestured a couple of his officers behind them to retrieve John Dawlish saying, "Hold him in the car for now." Several more policemen followed Alan and Zhang to the house.

Max was the first to enter the open door and straight away saw Doreen lying at the bottom of the staircase. He could see some blood coming from her nose and ear. He thought to himself that whatever had happened here this morning, she would have been an unwilling participant and wondered for a moment how Frank Dark had persuaded her to join his inner circle with John and Brett. Alan came in with Zhang and the other policeman and immediately started giving instructions to the officers regarding this now being a crime scene requiring the photographer and forensics. Zhang fetched a towel and respectfully placed it over Doreen's upper body and head. Several of the other officers were going from room to room throughout the villa to see if anyone else was present.

Max wandered out onto the terrace and as he looked down the garden and out to sea, quite by chance his gaze focused on the unusual sight of a clothed man preparing to start up a jet ski. As the penny dropped he gasped as he realised the man climbing onto the seat now was Frank Dark. Without taking a moment to alert Alan and the others he instinctively started to run down the lawn, past the boulders and out onto the sandy beach. But he was too late, Frank Dark had started up the jet ski motor and looking over his shoulder briefly catching sight of Max, he pulled in the throttle lever and accelerated away from the shore. Once across the surf he briefly slowed to make a call.

Max could see the trolley device Frank had used to transport the jet ski across the sand and down to the water and remembered Frank had told him he had two jet skis in the water sports shed. He ran back to the hut and there inside the open doors was another jet ski on its trolley. Surveying the inside of the hut he soon found a small key locker and grabbed the key marked 'JS1' and testing it in the key slot of the jet ski found it fitted. He grabbed the handle of the trolley the jet ski sat on and aided by the large diameter wheels was easily able to pull it across the silky sand beach towards the water. He saw Frank Dark beyond the surf finishing a call, then power off again across the water.

As Max climbed onto the jet ski he noticed Alan Reid running towards him across the lawn with both hands in the air as if to say, 'what are you doing?'.

Max turned the key and the 1.6-litre Sea-Doo RXT 300 horsepower jet ski engine willingly started up. He turned and shouted to Alan. "Frank Dark's on that jet ski," as he pointed to the jet ski disappearing away from him. "I'll follow him. I've got my phone."

Alan beckoned for Max to wait and let him pursue Frank instead of Max doing it.

Max shouted, "I'm going after him. It's personal now!" With that Max tightly grasped the throttle lever and as the intense jet of water was thrust through and out the back of the machine, the jet ski dug into the sea and accelerated off fast.

Zhang Wei had seen Max then Alan disappear down the garden to the beach and coming out to the terrace had heard what Max had shouted to Alan. He promptly left his team fussing around the villa and trotted back up the driveway to the police car where John Dawlish was now sat in the back with handcuffs on. He got into the front passenger seat and told the policeman in the driver's and rear seats to get out. They obliged at once.

"Who are you?" asked John Dawlish nervously.

"I am Zhang Wei the Superintendent and officer in charge here. You're John Dawlish CTO of the Dark Corporation aren't you?" Zhang was straight to the point as John nodded deferentially. "I'm guessing you and Frank Dark had some sort of escape plan to get clear of the island?" John nodded again. "I'm only going to make this offer once. If you want any chance of leniency I want to know where Frank Dark is going? He's headed off out to sea on a jet ski. Do you have a boat waiting for you?" Zhang turned round in his front seat to look straight at John Dawlish and repeated, "This is your one chance."

John Dawlish was now firmly looking out for himself and the offer of any sway against the anticipated heavy fines and imprisonment was welcome. He told Zhang exactly what their escape plan was. Zhang got out of the car waving his two officers to get back in to guard the suspect and climbed into his unmarked police car.

Frank Dark powered his sleek black and red new Sea-Doo jet ski through the light swell of the sea, keeping up a consistent and steady thirty to forty miles an hour, well below its top speed. He was fully clothed and couldn't afford to fall in. He just needed to get to one of the sandy beaches further up the coastline to be well clear of the police around his property and as near as possible to his ultimate destination. He glanced behind him and could see Max Sargent setting off in pursuit, but he was quite a way back. He'd figured that Max must have gone to the police but still didn't know how their planned activation of Angel's ghost code had been thwarted. He hugged the beaches for almost a mile until he spotted the open beach he was looking for, with an adjacent public car park and open grassy area opposite Crick Hill Road.

Max followed Frank on his jet ski skimming across the turquoise clear water past families and couples on the beaches and playing in the shallows. Despite the shock of seeing Doreen dead at the villa, and Brett being shot in front of him, and everything that had happened to him, Max was revelling in the challenge of catching Frank. He'd always liked a challenge since his mother would often set him little tasks by saying, "I dare you Max, let's see if you can do it." Having been quite reticent about working with the famous MI5 organisation, effectively being a corporate spy for them, he realised that he was starting to relish the excitement of it all, racing along on this jet ski in Barbados chasing Frank Dark.

Frank beached the jet ski up on the sand past the water's edge and jumped off. He looked back again to see where Max was and estimated he was no more than a minute behind him. Frank ran towards the local Bajuns milling around the car park and grass area having picnics and barbeques and shouted to them, "I need to borrow a car. Whoever lends me their car can have the fifteen-thousand-dollar jet ski right there," pointing back at the Sea-Doo. There was some consternation and much joviality as the beach revellers guffawed at the idea someone would just hand over their new jet ski. But a couple of young locals thought they'd call the man's bluff, eyeing up the handsome looking Sea-Doo sitting on the sand ahead of them. One of them came forward first and approached Frank, who hurriedly reaffirmed his offer of handing over the key to his jet ski to immediately borrow the lad's car. By the time the deal was agreed and Frank was running towards a small Suzuki car, Max was approaching the beach on his jet ski.

Max could see that Frank had persuaded one of the lads to lend him his car and as he beached his jet ski next to Frank's, he was greeted with some surprise but also jubilation from the two young men, upon seeing yet another brand new black and red Sea-Doo turn up on the same beach.

"Sweet Lord, here comes another one," said one of the boys high-fiving the other. He then said sarcastically to his friend, "Maybe you can get yourself your own Sea-Doo brother and we can start our own jet ski business." He jumped on his new toy as both boys were cracking up with laughter.

Max turned to the other lad. "You got a car I can use right now? And you can keep this." Max's tone was dead serious as he watched Frank drive across the car park towards the road.

The boys couldn't believe their luck this beautiful sunny day and the lad Max had directed his offer to spoke, fighting back the hilarity of the whole situation. "Really? You're gonna give me your jet ski as well?" Looking at his friend, "We've got ourselves a couple of rich tourists here that might have had a bit too much rum," he joked.

Max pressed him. "Well? Do you want it or shall I find someone else?"

"Okay, okay, it's a deal my man," as he handed over a rusty key, "I don't have a car but there's my moped. It's all yours."

Moped! Max didn't argue and ran over to the small motorbike leaving the two boys on the beach high fiving again, closely inspecting their newly gained jet skis in disbelief. As Max scooted across the car park he thought of calling the MI5 man Alan Reid, but then realised with all the commotion he'd never taken his number. It seemed he was on his own, again.

22

Max had seen Frank's Suzuki crossover the main beach highway road and followed the direction he'd gone taking him up Crick Hill in Weston. As he rounded the first bend the relatively straight road rewarded him with a quick glimpse of Frank way ahead of him. He continued to follow him up this road for another minute, most of which was lined with large neatly placed boulders and thick trees either side, as the small but agile moped managed to maintain the same gap between them. A little way on he saw Frank take a right and a brief while later Max took the same right turn himself in into Westmoreland Road. Max wondered where on earth Frank Dark was heading, purposefully driving inland wasn't going to help him evade the authorities.

The Suzuki soon took a left turn into a large decorated, walled entrance and as Max approached and turned in he could see boldly displayed on the walls either side 'Royal Westmoreland'. 'What's Frank doing at a golf club?' thought Max. Ahead of him, Frank had just pulled away after being stopped and checked at the barrier by security. Max kept his eye on the Suzuki as he pulled up at the barrier and said authoritatively to the bewildered security man looking at his old moped, "Max Sargent. I'm late for an important meeting at the golf club, would you let me through immediately please." The look and confident tone of Max seemed enough for the security man not to want to be responsible for this visitor's lateness, especially if he had a meeting at the club.

At that moment, the attention of both of them was drawn skyward as they heard the buzzing from a single prop engine of a small light aeroplane. The sleek executive four-seater Cessna 400 TTx was one of the best premium private aircraft available at almost $1 million. It came towards them and seemed very low as it flew over their heads and descended out of sight across the Westmoreland estate. Max could hear that the plane was throttling down and assuming it was tourists sight-seeing, didn't think any more of it at the time.

The security man begrudgingly pushed down on the counterweight of the barrier to raise the long bar, then as Max pulled away, retreated into his air-conditioned hut to note down the names of the three visitors he'd just let through in succession. He wrote, 'Zhang Wei – Police' who had arrived a minute before the other two. Then he filled in 'Frank Dark – member' and 'Max Sargent – visitor'.

Frank drove past the main car park and skirted around the small island in front of the main clubhouse, skidding to a halt by the entrance. He climbed out of the Suzuki and ran around the side of the main building so as not to alarm members inside, heading for the small courtyard where the golf buggies were kept. Max arrived at the clubhouse moments later and throwing his moped down on the grass alongside the building, appeared at the rear overlooking the golf course just in time to see Frank driving off along one of the pathways for the player's buggies. He ran over to the buggy car park jumping into the first one available, where each buggy already had its key inserted waiting for its next prestigious member or guest player.

The Cessna 400 small aircraft's operational guide stated that the minimum take-off and landing distance required was 1200 feet. The pilot of this particular aeroplane was highly experienced and had been one of the original members of the Red Bull aerobatics team many years ago. It would be tight, but he was confident he could land and take-off on a narrow, relatively flat runway of well under 1000 feet.

The par-five fifth hole was furthest away from the clubhouse and sported the longest and flattest fairway of the course. It was uninterrupted by meddlesome sand bunkers and allowing for the continued flat rough grass at both ends of the fairway, could offer about 300 yards of 'golf course runway', so 900 feet.

The pilot had flown Frank Dark in his Cessna many times,

got paid well by him and was also allowed to use the plane for his own excursions business. When Frank had explained to him that he and a couple of colleagues would need to be collected from the fifth hole fairway of the Royal Westmoreland he'd been intrigued, but also relished the excitement of the challenge. His curiosity was quickly put to rest when Frank had offered him $100,000 upfront and he could keep the Cessna afterwards.

The landing on the fairway had certainly been very tight, both in the width and length available, but he'd successfully negotiated the landing with the help of the highly able and well-specified little aircraft. Fortunately, no one had been playing the fifth hole at the time, though the players on one of the neighbouring fairways seemed quite perturbed at the small aircraft landing in the middle of their course. Grabbing their phones they'd no doubt complained profusely to the club secretary.

The plane had turned around at the end of its landing, almost on a dime, and the pilot now sat waiting for Frank Dark and he believed his colleagues. The aircraft had a range of around 2000 kilometres so could reach any of the Caribbean islands, the Dominican Republic or Venezuela. He kept the engine running as instructed by Frank Dark.

Max had his right foot flat on the floor of the buggy, but it refused to go any faster than its limiter had been set at. Always frustrating thought Max having played many rounds of golf with buggies that never seemed fast enough. He continued to follow Frank down the endless path passing the length of three very long holes. As he approached the fairway furthest from the club, to his astonishment he could see the small aircraft sitting on the grass near the green. It was facing back down the long fairway, engine running.

Frank had by now veered off the path and was heading straight to the plane. Max was still some 200 yards away but could now clearly see Frank as he stopped his buggy just short of the aircraft and jumping out, walked hurriedly towards the open cockpit gullwing door.

Zhang Wei had also arrived at the fifth hole moments before

the Cessna had made its astonishing landing on the fairway. John Dawlish had indeed been accurate with his description of their getaway plan. Zhang was now ensconced within the shrubbery and trees adjacent to the middle of the fairway and could also see Frank Dark's arrival at the small aeroplane. Before commandeering his buggy outside the clubhouse, he'd removed a black bag from the boot of his car. He now held in his hands the neat, lightweight Chinese made JS 7.62mm sniper rifle. Smuggled in for him many years ago it was modest but precise, with a bolt action operation, telescopic sights and a small five-round magazine. Its effective range in the right hands was almost 1000 metres, so Zhang could comfortably hit a golf ball anywhere on the fifth hole had he wanted to, with effort to spare.

Zhang raised the rifle and resting it on a small branch, put his eye up to the rubber eyepiece of the scope.

Frank Dark had now climbed up into the cockpit and was gesticulating to the pilot to get going, as Max arrived alongside the plane. He remained seated in the buggy as the cockpit door was still open, not wanting to get too close in case Frank produced a gun.

Max wanted to say so much to Frank. He was angry at him. His scheme of cyber chaos. The corruption in India. His resentment of this wealthy man abusing his power out of greed to have even more. But first, he wanted to ask something else. Something far more important. He shouted above the engine and propeller noise. "Frank. What happened to Doreen, Frank? The same as your previous CFO John Lyttleton? Did you kill them?"

Frank glared at Max through the open door.

"It's over Frank. Give yourself up. You've done too much to get away with it," shouted out Max.

"I will get away with it Max, watch me!" taunted Frank.

Max exploded with anger. He wanted to delay him and now also play all his ace cards for his own unbridled satisfaction of beating Frank. He wanted him to know. "Brett's dead. Shot by MI5 Frank. I've been working for MI5, yes, me! I stopped you and your Chinese computer virus. Angel's finished!"

Frank was furious and had to stop himself from getting back out of the plane to go at Max. He wished he had a gun for he would surely have used it on Max. This young man had scuppered his huge deal for his five billion and killed his friend Brett. Frank grasped the door handle ready to leave.

Max yelled again calling Frank's bluff. "You'll never get away with murdering Doreen and John. MI5 will hunt you down wherever you go."

"What are they to you anyway?" said Frank angrily.

Max squinted his eyes against the buffeting air from the revving propeller blades and stared at Frank. "John Lyttleton was my uncle!"

Frank froze, shocked at the revelation. Still in disbelief that Max had upset his plans, whilst all along being his ex-CFO's nephew. "Revenge, really. Is that what this is about Max?"

"You'll never get away with it Frank, give yourself up."

Frank tightened his grip on the door handle and gave Max a half-hearted smile saying, "Remember, money buys you anything, as long as you've got enough of it." He pulled down the cockpit door holding his look at Max through the smoked window for a moment. The plane throttled up increasing the engine's noise and lurched forward accelerating quickly back down the perfectly maintained fairway.

As Max watched Frank Dark's aircraft gather speed, he heard a muffled crack mixed in amongst the burbling engine noise, but then realised the unique sound had come from the tree line down the fairway.

The Cessna's momentum dropped off, then uncharacteristically it veered from side to side a couple of times, lifting one of the wheels off the ground. Something was clearly up. The small gleaming aircraft then clumsily lumbered off to one side over the rough and dramatically careered into some trees on the far side of the fairway.

Zhang had homed in on Frank Dark the moment he'd sat in his cockpit seat. He'd calmly taken a few moments to steady his target in the centre of the sight's crosshairs, through the windshield. He was ready to fire but he wanted to do the job perfectly, this was his one chance to really impress his superiors and hopefully finally be recalled to Beijing. After many years of waiting quietly and doing his police job in Barbados, that crucial call had suddenly come through earlier from a very high-ranking MSS officer Li Xiaoping. Zhang had decided on one definitive shot when the plane was passing closest to him on the adjacent fairway, just to be certain. As the plane came level Zhang squeezed the trigger and the bullet had passed straight through the side of Frank Dark's head, entering his right temple and exiting his left temple. Frank Dark was killed instantly.

Zhang hadn't intended to hit the pilot nor given him a thought, he'd been so focused on his priority target. But because they were directly level when he'd fired, the bullet had unfortunately gone on to also hit the pilot shattering the top of his skull.

After the plane crashed Max couldn't believe what had just happened and ran over to the smouldering wreck hunched into several trees.

Zhang could now clearly see the young man Max Sargent in front of him, whom he'd met earlier at the villa, had managed to follow Frank Dark all the way here, impressive. He instinctively repositioned his rifle towards him. Max was peering into the cockpit area and could see both men were dead, so was reticent to climb in for fear of the plane catching on fire.

The crosshairs settled over Max. Zhang lingered for a moment, studying him, his finger on the trigger.

Si Lawson deeply regretted involving Max Sargent in such a dangerous operation. It had started with an innocuous request for him to simply gather more intel on the Dark Corporation's activities. They wanted to see if they could flush out any corruption potentially flagged to them by the stressed CFO who had then mysteriously committed suicide. But as discoveries and indiscretions quickly snow-balled, Si had been driven into a position where only his young 'corporate spy' was in a position to delve deeper, and in the end, avert a global cyber disaster. Si had felt partially helpless having to rely so much on Max and not being able to be there for him, nor just send in his teams to sweep things up.

Three days had passed since that fateful Saturday in Barbados and with the help of John Dawlish, their key sole surviving Dark Corporation executive director, things were becoming much clearer and starting to get wrapped up.

Vince entered the main MI5 Cyber team's office at Thames House, followed by the person Si Lawson was waiting for. His boss the Deputy Director General had just asked Si for another update on the Dark Corporation Cyber case, but on this one occasion had agreed to put their meeting back ten minutes, once Si explained who was on their way up to see him.

Max came into the office and as people started to notice him gradually the whole team started clapping him and stood up. Si came out of his office clapping as well. They all knew how brilliantly Max had done to pull off this operation with no counter-espionage training. Max awkwardly bathed in the appreciation then walked over to Si, nodding at other members of the team who'd helped him.

Si Lawson greeted Max with a hug and led him into his office followed by Vince. They sat and Vince handed Max's Rolex Submariner watch back to him.

"It's so good to see you again Max after briefly meeting you at the airport yesterday. I know you wanted a quick catchup today before we get into the detailed de-briefings, interviews and statements over the next few days I'm afraid. How are you?" said Si.

"It's all been quite surreal to be honest," said Max, "I still can't believe what I went through. Everything keeps churning round and round in my head, what I could've done, what I should've done."

"Well, I can't tell you enough how appreciative we and MI5 are for what you did on this operation. I'm sure there'll be more senior people than me wanting to thank you during the coming weeks," congratulated Si again.

"So, I've got a lot of questions, but can I start with the big ones today Si?" said Max.

"Of course, fire away."

Max took in a breath. "Firstly, what did happen to Doreen? And John Lyttleton?"

"Yes of course, your uncle," said Si. Max had long since figured they must have made the connection and was appreciative that they still let him continue with the assignment. "I can't believe we originally missed that your mother's maiden name was Lyttleton!" said Si briefly looking at Vince. "But we did work it out about halfway through the case and decided not to bother you with it. Let's just say I trusted that you wouldn't do anything stupid. Regarding how they died, the jury will be out on that forever. Unfortunately, we'll never know for sure if anyone was involved in their deaths, the only witness to both was Frank Dark, and he's dead himself now. I know what I think, but it'll never be proven. We're so sorry about your uncle's death Max," said Si regretfully.

"And the Mumbai operation. And the Dark Corporation as a whole?" Max asked.

"We handed over everything we had, including Dawlish's statements, to the Indian Central Bureau of Investigation. I gather they've raided the Apex Finance printers site and arrested anyone involved in the currency printing scam, including the manager of course." Vince nodded in agreement. "Seems likely Dawlish had found a way to hack into the Finance Ministry's monthly serial number coding file and using that spare printer you saw, run off a load of notes for himself. They were shipped straight to that dodgy bank who laundered the currency back into general circulation, then made a payment to John's Swiss account."

Si went on. "As for the Dark Corporation, we'll have to see what happens to Frank Dark's shares and what other shareholders and the new board decide to do. Apart from Angel and Apex the rest of the group seems legit. And before you ask, Angel Software is completely shut down, we'll find out which of their staff were involved, I suspect only a few." Si glanced at his watch. "I'm going to have to go and see the Deputy Director General in a minute if that's okay Max.

"What'll happen to John Dawlish?" said Max.

"I can only guess at this early stage," said Si, "but I gather the Crown Prosecution Service will charge him with a long list of offences under the 1990 Computer Misuse Act for starters, which covers offences, attempts or attacks against computer systems, including hacking and denial of service. Most of the various sections of the Act have either been breached or were intended to be breached, each carrying from two up to fourteen years imprisonment and hefty fines. But that's just England and Wales. He could get the same charges in other countries."

"Wow, that could be pretty harsh then?" added Max.

"Well he's cooperating fully telling us everything, so if he's lucky he'll probably pay a huge fine, serve some time and then go into our 'confined to home' plan, maybe even work for us for the rest of his sentence."

Si stood up signalling that he needed to go. Max stood as well and slipped in one final question. "What happened to Frank Dark and the pilot?"

"Zhang Wei the Superintendent you briefly met, shot them with a sniper's rifle as they took off. We never caught up with him after that, he's probably back in Beijing by now. Sleeper agent for the Chinese Ministry of State Security who wanted to use Dark's Angel software as the Trojan carrier for the cyber attack. It would have put communications and economies outside of China back to the dark ages. We can't prove it was China though."

"But killing him?" asked Max.

Si frowned. "From what John Dawlish told us it seems only Frank and latterly Doreen met Li Xiaoping, who was the Chinese MSS officer masquerading as the 'businessman'. Unfortunately at the time, there was no way we could make any connection to Li when you saw that note on Dawlish's desk a while back, likely reminding himself to put the finishing touches to the virus program into his Angel software ready for the sale. Anyway, back to Barbados, Zhang had already seen that Doreen was dead at the villa, so only had to go after Frank, having got Dawlish to tell him about the plane at the golf course." Si shook his head. "There's no way China or Xiaoping would let anyone they'd dealt with directly, on something as big as this, live to tell the tale. Whether it had been successful or failed as it did, I'm afraid Frank and Doreen's cards were marked the moment they each met him. You were lucky Zhang didn't take a pop at you as well."

"What about Li Xiaoping?" asked Max hoping for some justice.

"Forget it Max," frowned Si, "he's pretty much untouchable being MSS, but we've marked his card now, next time he tries an Op away from his homeland we can knab him, maybe!"

Si ushered Max to the door saying, "I won't ask you if you somehow deliberately engineered a way onto our EP list to get into Dark." Max contemplated the potential question as if ready to say something. Si didn't really want to hear the answer so quickly continued, letting him off having to reply. "Anyhow, we should work together again. Any immediate plans?"

Max stepped out of the office then paused and smiling, turned back to Si. "As you've told me before, I'm a clever, persuasive chap. I'll think of something."

THE END

Max Sargent Corporate Espionage Mystery Thrillers

currently available in the series by the author BEN COLT

ABOUT THE AUTHOR BEN COLT

A senior executive of three decades in the corporate world, having been a management consultant and Chief Procurement Officer for many big brand companies in various industries.

Most of his roles had a global remit, which took him around the world on business to many different countries and cities.

Procurement has a privileged role in firms, with unquestioned business-wide access and control of large spends, suppliers and intellectual property.

His extensive procurement and management experience, gives him first-hand insight of the potential for corporate corruption and espionage, to quickly become dangerous.

Printed in Great Britain
by Amazon

67640020R00169